After Her

ALSO BY JOYCE MAYNARD

Fiction

The Good Daughters

Labor Day

The Usual Rules

The Cloud Chamber

Where Love Goes

To Die For

Baby Love

Nonfiction

Looking Back

Domestic Affairs

At Home in the World

Internal Combustion

After Her

Joyce Maynard

HARPER LUXE
An Imprint of HarperCollinsPublishers

"My Sharona." Words and music by Douglas Fieger and Berton Averre. Published by Small Hill Music (ASCAP)/Eighties Music (ASCAP), administered by Reach Music Publishing, Inc. (ASCAP)/Wise Brothers Music LLC. Copyright © 1979. International copyright secured. All rights reserved. Used by permission.

HarperCollins books may be purchased for educational, business, or sales promotional use. For information, please e-mail the Special Markets Department at SPsales@harpercollins.com.

FIRST HARPERLUXE EDITION

HarperLuxe™ is a trademark of HarperCollins Publishers

Library of Congress Cataloging-in-Publication Data is available upon request.

ISBN: 978-0-06-225742-0

13 14 ID/RRD 10 9 8 7 6 5 4 3 2 1

For Laura Gaddini Xerogeanes and
Janet Gaddini Cubley,
also for Martha, and for Dana.
This is not their story, but their story inspired this one.

And in memory of Detective Robert Gaddini,
Marin County Homicide

Come a little closer huh . . .
Close enough to look in my eyes Sharona

—from "My Sharona" by Douglas Fieger and
Berton Averre,
#1 single by the Knack, 1979

After Her

Prologue

A little over thirty years ago, on a June day just before sunset—alone on a mountain in Marin County, California—a man came toward me with a length of piano wire stretched between his hands, and the intention of ending my days. I was fourteen years old, and many others had already died at his hands. I carry the knowledge of what it is to look into a man's eyes and believe his face is the last thing I will ever see.

I have my sister to thank that I am here to tell what happened that day. Two times, it was my sister who saved me, though I was not able to do the same for my sister.

This is our story.

Nothing much ever happened on the mountain where we lived, growing up, and we didn't get cable. We were always hoping for a little excitement. So my sister and I made up situations. All we had was time.

One day we decided to see what it felt like to be dead.

If a person's dead, they don't feel anything, Patty said. This was Patty for you.

I had a red sweatshirt, the kind with a zipper up the front and a hood and pockets to keep gum. I spread it on a patch of grass on the hillside behind our house, with the sleeves stretched out as if they were a person who'd been run over by a truck—the hood off in a different direction, so as much of the red part showed as possible, like a pool of blood.

Lie there, I told my sister, pointing to a spot in the middle, over the zipper part.

She might disagree, but Patty nearly always did what I told her. If she had questions, she kept them to herself.

I lay down next to her. Close enough so plenty of the red part showed on either side of our bodies.

Now what?

Don't move. Don't let your chest go up and down when you breathe.

Some people would have asked for an explanation, but not Patty. Letting her find out in her own time was part of my idea, and she understood this.

For a long time nothing happened. It was hot that day, but we just lay there.

My nose itches, she said.

Never mind, I told her. Just think about something else. Something interesting.

For me at the time, that would mean Peter Frampton, or the jeans I'd seen at the mall a couple of weeks earlier, that were perfect in every way except the price. And the notebooks I wrote in, where I made up stories I'd read to my sister, that she said were better than Nancy Drew.

For Patty it would be Larry Bird executing a hook shot. Or some dog she liked. Which would be any dog that ever lived.

Did you notice that cloud? she said. It's shaped like a dachshund.

Quiet.

Who knew how much time passed. Ten minutes? An hour, possibly. Then I spotted it: a vulture, circling above our heads. First one, then two more. They were high up still, but it was plain from where they'd positioned themselves that we were the target. The place they were circling was directly over the spot where we lay.

What now? Patty asked me.

Shush. Be still.

Two more birds joined the others. The circle was getting tighter, as if they were zeroing in. They were coming lower too, closer to our bodies.

What if they try to peck our eyes out?

No answer from me. Getting the vultures to spot us was the whole point. My sister should know this, and basically did.

The vultures were swooping lower now, dive-bombing, making this terrible shrieking sound. They were closing in around us. Shrieking not so much at Patty and me, from the sound of it, as at one another. They were fighting over who would get to eat our eye-balls, probably.

Then came one final shriek, not from one of the nearest birds, but one we hadn't noticed until now, a little farther off but zeroing in. He sailed down toward us, body like an arrow, beak and talons aimed at our faces.

I didn't have to tell my sister what to do. We jumped up screaming, running down the mountain toward our house. No time to claim my sweatshirt even—though later, when the birds were gone, we'd return for it, out of breath and holding each other, screaming. A person could scream as loud as she wanted on the mountain, and it felt good. We were always looking for excuses to scream.

Later again, when we could catch our breath, we lay in our yard going over it all.

I could feel the feathers brush against my arm, I said.

I could feel the wind their wings made when they flapped, blowing over my face, she told me. Like hot breath.

Now you know what it's like being dead, I told her.

Or not dead yet, just about to be.

This is how I remember it. I could be wrong. I had a big imagination when I was young. I was good at making up stories, and my stories were so good, I even believed them myself sometimes.

And I was always looking for excitement, until I found some.

My little pretty one, pretty one

The town where my sister and I grew up lay in the shadow of Mount Tamalpais, not far north of San Francisco. The aging housing development where we lived, on Morning Glory Court, sat just off an exit of Highway 101, eight miles north of the Golden Gate Bridge. Buses ran from where we lived to San Francisco—the bridge marking the entrance to that other world, though we also knew people came there to jump. But for us, the city might as well have been the moon.

Our father had grown up in the city—North Beach, home of the real red sauce, he told us. This was where the hippies had come for the Summer of Love and where Janis Joplin had once walked the streets of the Haight, and cable cars ran, and that crazy Lombard Street snaked past rows of pretty pastel Victorian houses, and where another Patty—Hearst—had walked into a Hibernia Bank one day, a few years back, carrying an M1 carbine as one of the Symbionese Liberation Army.

Later, rock stars started buying houses on the other side of the highway from where our house sat, but back in those days, it wasn't a fashionable place yet. The day would come when people built high walls around their property and posted signs alerting would-be burglars to the existence of their security systems. But those were still trusting times. Our yards flowed into one another, free of hedges or fences, so girls like us could run from one end of the street to the other without the soles of their Keds once touching asphalt. People moved easily among their neighbors, and few locked their doors.

Our house, number 17, was the smallest on the street—two dark little bedrooms, a low-ceilinged living room, and a kitchen the previous owners had decorated with green Formica and matching avocado-green appliances, none of which could be counted on to function reliably. The living room was covered in wood paneling, an effect meant to make the place seem cozy, perhaps, though one that hadn't succeeded.

Our parents had bought the house in 1968, when I was two years old, shortly after my sister's birth—the best they could manage on a policeman's salary. My mother said Marin County was a good place for raising children, though our father worked in the city at the time—meaning San Francisco. He was a beat cop then, not yet a detective, and knowing him, he would have liked it that his work took him a ways from home, over that red bridge he loved. It was probably better that way, for a man like him at least, to be off on his own, with the three of us tucked away in that little bungalow while he was off saving people.

These days, nobody could think of building low-income housing in a spot like the one where our house was situated. The land that made up our development would be reserved for six-thousand-square-foot mansions with swimming pools and yards with outdoor kitchens and expensive patio furniture. There would be three-car garages, and the cars in them would be of European design.

But whenever it was (the 1940s probably, after the war) that the houses were constructed on Morning Glory Court and the neighboring streets (Bluebell, Honeysuckle, Daffodil, and my favorite—named for a contractor's wife probably—Muriel Lane), a premium had not yet been placed on proximity to open land and views. It was possible back then to have as little money as our family did and still find yourself in a house that backed up on a few thousand acres of open space. So that whole mountain was our playground. Mine and my sister's.

For the first five years of her life, Patty barely spoke, except to me. Not that she couldn't talk. She knew words. She had no speech impediment. She had strong opinions about a lot of things, in fact—not only dogs, and basketball, but also (speaking now of her dislikes) foods that were red, other than marinara sauce, clothes whose labels rubbed her neck, all dresses. She developed, early on, a hearty sense of humor, particularly concerning anything to do with body parts or bathroom activities. Burping never ceased to amuse her. A fart—particularly coming from a well-dressed woman or a man in a suit—sent her right over the top.

But if someone asked her a question—and this included other children besides me, her kindergarten teacher, and our own parents—she said nothing, unless I was there, in which case she'd whisper her response in my ear, leaving it to me to convey to the outside world—the world beyond the unit that consisted of the two of us—what her answer might be. Young as I was, I didn't know for a long time that other five-year-old girls had a lot to say. I didn't know this wasn't how things went with everybody's little sister.

When we'd go to the bank with our mother, and the teller would ask what flavor of lollipop she'd like, Patty whispered her choice in my ear and I would speak it for her. *Green.* She ignored it when kids called her Bucktooth, because of her overbite, and on our street, if a boy came up and wanted her toy, she'd hand it to him rather than protest, though if any of these boys had teased me (about my outgrown clothes, my inability to hit a ball in our occasional neighborhood games), she would confront the offender (but silently) with one of our jujitsu moves, learned from our father. Once, when a boy took the seat she'd saved for me at a puppet show our mother had taken us to at the library, she jammed her elbow in his stomach and kicked him for good measure before magnificently sweeping me into the place next to her. All without words.

A person could have thought she was shy, but when we were in our room, Patty's true nature revealed itself, a secret entrusted only to me. This was when she'd break into her panty dance, or imitations of her teacher, Mrs. Eggert, preparing the class for inspection of their bottoms by the school nurse during an outbreak of ringworm, or her particular favorite game of pretending to be a puppy, down on her hands and knees, with her tongue out and her butt wagging an imaginary tail.

My sister could be wild, leaping from the top bunk onto a pile of pillows she'd built for herself that proved to offer insufficient cushion for her landing. I saw the look on her face when she hit the floor, and I knew it had to hurt, but she was never one for crying.

Sometimes speaking for Patty might require nothing more from me than explaining she wanted mustard on her sandwich, or what flavor of ice cream she preferred. She'd let me know in a surprisingly husky voice, so low only I could hear. I'd give voice to her words.

"Patty isn't that interested in dolls," I told our mother when Patty opened her Christmas present of a Tiny Tears with a layette. "She says this one is really cute and she thinks I'd probably like it. But actually, what Patty would like is a basketball or a baby pig."

What she really wanted was a dog, of course. Our mother had ruled that one out.

But here was an interesting thing: as little as Patty said in those days, and as quiet as she remained even later, she had the biggest voice. Not high and shrill either, like some girls', but surprisingly low and resonant, and it carried, to the point where sometimes our mother said—times we'd be out riding bikes and having one of our discussions—she'd know Patty was coming home five minutes before she got there. According to our parents, she had been famous for this even as a baby.

"Rachel sounds like a normal kid," our father said, referring to me. "But when Patty lets out a yell, they can probably hear it all the way to Eureka. It's a miracle I still have my eardrums."

A picture of my childhood does not exist for me (I'm speaking of my memory here, not photograph albums, which our mother never got around to making) that doesn't feature Patty in it. Nearly always when an image comes to me of the two of us, we have our arms around each other, or her head is on my shoulder, or (because she grew tall, young) mine on hers. If the picture was taken after she was six or seven, it's a safe bet Patty's mouth will be closed over her teeth. But where I am likely to look worried in the picture, my sister will be smiling.

The term *depression* wasn't much used then, but I think we both sensed, even early on, that our mother was fragile—that no space or energy existed to deal with more than she already had on her plate. This was the period when our father had gone to night school, working on getting the master's degree that was his ticket to the rank of detective. From the beginning, when he first joined the police force, his goal had been to work in homicide. He had no interest in parking tickets or petty crimes and robberies. Maybe he'd seen some character of a detective in the movies—William Holden, Humphrey Bogart, Robert Mitchum—and the image appealed to him. That would be like him: to model himself on a movie hero, only he'd be one in real life.

So he was working double time at that point—days on the job in San Francisco, nights at school—while our mother stayed home with Patty and me. No doubt the hours were tough for him, but it was glamorous too, learning about psychology and forensics, while our mother stayed home with the babies. And knowing our father, he wouldn't have come running home to her after class was over either. There were probably a few female students at the police academy. There would certainly have been waitresses at the clubs he went to after.

"Your father always liked making women happy," my mother told me once. No particular harshness in her voice when she said this, just weary resignation, a statement of fact, and I knew it anyway. Maybe, in his odd way, I could see him feeling a responsibility to spread the happiness around. Many women. Made very happy. (For a while, anyway.)

The problem between our parents, maybe, was that of all the women, our mother may have been the only one who appeared immune to our father's romantic tactics, and for a man accustomed to charming the female population of the entire San Francisco Bay Area, this must have taken the wind right out of his sails. Our mother was smarter than almost anyone, for starters. She was also coolly resistant to the seduction of flattery. Honesty she liked. Sweet talk got you no place once you'd committed the offense of betrayal. Lie once and you lost her.

A scene comes to me from when we were very young: my father walking in the house, home from work, and twirling our mother around the kitchen, untying her apron and wrapping his hands around her waist to kiss her hard on the mouth. (Do I remember this? Or have I made up the picture, wanting it to have been this way once?) He pressed her close against his chest.

"Nice cologne there," she said, pulling away. "New scent?"

She hardly looked up, just tied her apron back again with this weary look that seemed to say, *Don't waste your time.*

After a while he didn't.

Our father had earned a few medals in his days as a police officer, but it was being a detective that he loved. It was all about psychology, he told us. Reading a person's character. This was what his own father had done, back in North Beach cutting hair and listening to his customers' stories. Not so different from what my father did, when he'd bring a criminal into the interrogation room with the goal of getting him to confess.

First you had to understand what made the person tick. Then you got inside, like a watchmaker.

Among the detectives in the Marin Homicide Division—and beyond that, the greater San Francisco Bay Area, and probably beyond that too—it was known that nobody was better at breaking down a perpetrator than Anthony Torricelli. "His own mother could have had this secret she swore she was taking to her grave," his friend Sal told me once. "Ten minutes in the room with Tony, she'd be crying into her hanky that she had sex with the milkman. That's how good he was."

Not just good. The best.

One of the skills required of a person if he or she is to be a first-class detective, our father told us (*he or she*, he said; that was like him), was the ability to pay close attention. You had to know the questions to ask, and how to listen well when the answers came. You had to recognize when the person you were talking to was handing you a line, and spot all the things he wasn't saying too.

But as much as anything else, you had to pick up on all the things besides the words he handed you (*he or she*; women could be criminals too after all, as well as objects of worship).

You had to pick up on a person's body language. Can they look you in the eye when they say where they were last night? What does it mean that their hand is on their hip, that they keep crossing and uncrossing their legs? Are they picking at their sleeve when they tell you they never heard of some guy named Joe Palooka that sold crack down in Hunters Point? Why is it their nails are chewed down to the quick, or past it? Widow Jones might be wearing black, but why is it that three days after the funeral she's got a hickey on her neck?

(That last observation of our father's was nothing he ever shared with my sister and me, actually. I overheard that one when he was cutting Sal's hair, and he was explaining to his friend how he broke a case in which the wife of some banker type got her lover to do him in for the insurance money. What our father forgot sometimes, when we were around, was that at least one of his daughters had inherited the attributes of a good detective herself. The apple doesn't fall far from the tree: I pay attention.)

My father didn't stop paying attention when he went off duty either, if he ever went off duty, and I doubt he ever did. Most of all, he paid attention to women, but not in that way some men have, of turning their gaze to the breasts, or sizing up a woman's rear end and grinning. He listened to what every woman he talked with had to say and seemed to take it seriously. He might like to see her naked, but he would also like to massage her feet or touch the skin on the inside of her wrist. He would ask about her children, if she had them, but he also made it plain that in his eyes, a woman was never simply a mother. She could be eighty, and he would still manage to locate the girl in her. I am not sure he ever met a woman he didn't look at without picturing how it would be in bed with her.

We were at a convenience store one time. Buying cigarettes, his usual Lucky Strikes.

"Don't move," he said to the woman behind the counter, with a sudden urgency that may have left her thinking this was a stickup.

He reached over the counter toward the side of her face, and for a moment his hand seemed almost to disappear in her hair. When it emerged, he was holding an earring. So small you had to wonder how he had ever spotted it.

"The back must have fallen off," he said. "I didn't want you to lose it."

She just stood there then, with the small gold cross in one hand, the other reaching for her naked lobe.

"Don't expect to find a guy like him when you start dating," one of the waitresses told me one night when he had taken us out to Marin Joe's—our regular tradition. "Because there aren't many like that."

Our mother would have said this was good news.

He had a gift for hair, inherited from his father, and he loved brushing ours. He cut hair like a professional—using his dead father's scissors.

"Sometimes I think I should have been a hair-dresser," he said—though in fact he could never have settled for that. "A man could do a lot worse than spend his days with his fingers running through women's hair. Instead of chasing down a bunch of low-life mutts."

First came the shampoo in our sink. He'd test the water with his wrist before he poured it over us, and when he lathered our heads, it was more like a massage. He used a special brand, with peppermint, that made the skin on your scalp tingle. All my life I've looked for that shampoo.

He put a record on. Dino, probably, but it might be Tony Bennett or Sinatra, and he might sing along, though never when he got to the cutting part, where all his concentration was required. That and a steady hand.

He set a chair in the yard. When we were little, he carried out whichever one of us he was working on that day, with a towel around our shoulders. The way he stepped back to study us was as if he was an artist, and we were his artwork. Then he began to cut.

He could sing like Dean Martin, to my ears at least, and he knew all the words to the songs, including the Italian ones.

There was a thing he did for us, a trick he could perform, that no other human being I ever met has known how to re-create. Something so strange and amazing, just describing it is difficult.

You'd be sitting on the couch next to him. The person sitting there would be me, or my sister. Maybe he'd done this once for our mother, but if so, that day was long past.

Then he'd pull a hair from the top of your head, so swiftly it never hurt. My sister and I kept our hair long from when we were little. So he had plenty to work with. And black, like his.

You never knew when he might do this. You'd be sitting there watching TV next to him, or reading, and there'd be this sharp little tug at your scalp, no more than a pinprick. Then you'd look over at him, sitting next to you, and he'd be twirling this hair between his fingers. They moved so fast I never understood how he could do this. But after a few minutes, he'd hold your arm out in front of you and on your skin—olive colored like his—he'd set this creation he'd made that looked exactly like a spider. Made out of your hair.

It never worked to ask for a spider. Months might pass that he didn't come up with one for you, and then he did. They were so tiny and delicate, it was impossible to hold on to one. Just breathing could make it blow away. Or when he exhaled his cigarette smoke.

The first time he made a spider and I lost it, I cried. "Don't worry, baby," he said. "There's plenty more of those in your future." For a surprisingly long time, that's how I thought my life would be—men would perform magic for me—and for a longer time, that's how I thought it should be, even when it wasn't.

Years later—in my twenties, when I met a man I thought, briefly, that I'd marry, I asked him if he knew how to make spiders.

"Spiders?" he said. He had no idea what I was talking about.

"You know, out of my hair." I actually thought for a long time that this must be something all men did for the women they loved. Their daughters or their girlfriends or their wives.

But it was only my father who did that. The only person ever who did that, in the history of the world, possibly.

Patty and I adored our father, simple as that. Young as we were back then, he taught us to wrestle and instructed us in self-defense moves to protect against the unwelcome advances of the boyfriends he told us would pursue us tirelessly all our lives. But he also ran us bubble baths and lit candles for us when we got in the tub. He put on Sinatra and taught us to slow dance, with our toes resting on his shiny black shoes.

If she had the right dance partner, he said, a woman should be able to close her eyes and let him take her anywhere. But steer clear of a man with a limp hand. You want to feel strong pressure on your back, and his hand pressing against yours, as he led. It's fine if he smells your hair—you want a sensual man—but not his hand on your rear end. And if he doesn't walk you back to your table after the dance, he's danced his last with you. Then again, how could a man ever stop dancing with either of the Torricelli girls?

Never let a man disrespect you, he said. You deserve a man who treats you like the queen of the world.

We were not yet six and eight when he told us these things. What did we know of love and romance then, or cruelty and rejection? We took his words in anyway, to file for later.

He never yelled at us. He never had to. If one of us had done something we weren't supposed to, it only took one look from him to stop what we were doing.

Often he worked late, but if he came home early enough, he was the one who'd cook for us. Garlic was always involved—those large, beautiful hands of his finely chopping and sautéing it in good olive oil. He prepared his sauce from scratch, and pasta too, hung up all over the kitchen like laundry, with meatballs made following his father's recipe. He claimed to speak Italian, and sometimes spewed out foreign-sounding words while he cooked, but at some point we figured out they were made up.

After the meal, if he had to yawn, he'd stretch his arms as wide as possible, open his mouth all the way, and let out a roar. We'd curl up on the couch with him to watch TV—*The Rockford Files,* his favorite—and he'd rub our feet. When we got tired, he'd carry us to bed, one in each strong arm, then sit in the dark and sing to us.

Our mother stayed home mostly, but on his days off, we'd pile in his car (bench seats, before he got the Alfa Romeo) so Patty and I could both snuggle up in the front—and take off on the most winding roads. He drove stick and took the curves like a race car driver, which made me want to be one.

"Don't tell your mother," he said—his regular refrain—as the speedometer reached seventy-five. Of course we never did.

One time he took us to Candlestick Park for a Giants game. "That guy on first?" he said. "Number forty-four? Take a good look at him. For the rest of your life you can tell people you saw Willie McCovey play."

Once, standing in line with our father at the supermarket, a man just ahead of us started giving his wife a hard time, or maybe she was just his girlfriend. "Shut your trap if you know what's good for you," the man told her.

Our father stepped out of the line then to face him. "Does it make you feel like a big guy, bullying a woman like that?" he said.

"Listen hard to what I tell you here, girls," he said after, in the parking lot. "I wouldn't normally use this language, but you need to hear this plainly: Never let any man give you shit. One stunt like that and you're out the door."

He took us on the cable cars and out to dinner at some grown-up restaurant, not McDonald's or Chuck E Cheese. He brought us gardenias, or a 45 rpm single he thought we'd like, a ring with our birthstone. One time he took us to a double feature of his two favorite James Bond movies—*Thunderball* and *Goldfinger*. That was supposed to be a secret except that when Patty came home, she told our mother she wanted to get a cat and name her Pussy Galore.

Our mother had been, briefly, the object of our father's adoration, but he moved on early, while she stayed in the same place. Hard to say which one of them gave up on the other first, but it happened, and once it did, there seemed no way back for either of them. Our mother must have seen him slipping away—like a piece of an iceberg that breaks off and drifts out to sea to form a whole new continent—and there was nothing to do about it but stand there and watch him go.

He moved out when I was eight, Patty six. After that he lived in an apartment back in the city, with a hideaway bed for Patty and me when we came to visit, which we hardly ever got to do. We stayed at old number 17, with its small dark rooms and thin walls through which the sound could be heard of cars on the highway, and keeping a secret would have been impossible. It was through those too-thin walls I learned the reason for my father's departure. A woman of course. Margaret Ann.

In the early years, when our father still lived with us, there was a set time when we ate dinner. Our father's cooking filled our house with wonderful smells: onions and oregano simmering in the tomato sauce, and garlic of course. Red wine on the table, and candles, even on weeknights. Music, always.

Our mother tried cooking for a while after he moved out, but she gave up on that early on. Then we were left to heat up frozen dinners or soup. The good nights were the times our father came to take us out to the restaurant we favored, Marin Joe's, where we had our special booth and the waitresses all knew what to bring us: a plate of spaghetti with marinara sauce, garlic bread, tiramisu.

Back on Morning Glory Court, there never seemed to be enough money. We got used to the fact that we didn't get TV at our house anymore. We owned an old Zenith, but its sole function was to hold a plant, and the piles of books our mother brought home from the library, the bills that came and sat, mostly unopened, until their replacements showed up, with even bigger print on the front, in red: *Last Chance.*

In those first days after they disconnected the cable, my sister had drawn a picture exactly the size of the TV screen, which she taped on the front where the pictures used to be, featuring a person who looked like a news anchorman with a bubble coming out of his mouth and the words "Traggic News!" (The spelling is Patty's.) "The Torricelli Girls cant watch their favorite shows any more! Mean mother says USE IMAGINASHUN." Now even Patty's drawing was barely visible, since the philodendron leaves had wound their way over the front of the set, curling clear to the floor.

The notion of a life without TV had felt harsh, briefly, though in truth, we replaced it with better. We invented a ritual called Drive-In Movie for watching our shows. When darkness fell—earlier in fall and spring; later in summer—we cruised the backyards of the houses along Morning Glory Court until we found a spot in the backyard of one of them where the TV set was on. This part was never difficult. Every house on Morning Glory Court featured an identical picture window, and at nearly every one the TV set had been placed directly in front of it, facing that hillside. All we had to do was find a set tuned to a channel we liked and hunker down low to look inside and watch.

Mostly we'd position ourselves in the yard of our elderly neighbors, Helen and Tubby. Their viewing habits weren't always to our taste, but they had the biggest TV, which made it easier to make out the faces on the screen.

We'd lay out a blanket—the one we'd used for picnics, in the old days when our parents were together, and we used to spend Sundays with our parents at Golden Gate Park. (Maybe we only did that once, but we remembered it.) If the evening was cool, as evenings tended to be by that hour, we'd huddle close to each other and wrap the blanket around ourselves. If there were saltines at our house or those little packets of oyster crackers people buy to scatter into their soup (though for our mother, those sometimes amounted to breakfast), we'd have brought those along to munch on while we watched.

Charlie's Angels was a favorite, but Tubby and Helen seldom watched that one. After Tubby died, Helen's personal preference appeared to be *Little House on the Prairie*—a show that got on our nerves. But she also tuned in to *Brady Bunch* reruns. Eight o'clock every

night, the show came on, and we'd be there on the hillside out back, waiting.

You had to squint to see the faces on the screen,
from the outside, but we knew well enough what all
the characters looked like that it didn't matter. There
they'd be, the nine happy-looking faces of Mike and
Carol Brady and their six children and housekeeper,
each one occupying a separate box on the checkerboard
displayed across Helen's TV screen. We couldn't hear
the sound, of course, but we could get the basic idea
and make up the rest.

"I think Cindy's in some kind of trouble," I told
Patty during one scene. Not very big trouble. We always
knew it would work out. In our version of the show, in
which we supplied the dialogue to accompany the silent
images flickering on the screen in Helen's living room,
Mike could turn to Carol and tell her he was leaving
her and running off with the housekeeper, Alice (this
was so implausible as to be funny), or one of the kids
needed a kidney transplant, and they had to figure out
which of the others was a match. (Lots to choose from,
luckily.) I made up a story where Marcia got pregnant,
and one of Mike's sons was the father. Not a blood rela-
tive, so at least their baby wouldn't be retarded.

In some ways watching the show this way, without
the virtually needless element of dialogue, allowed

for a level of entertainment that the real show—the one Helen was watching from the comfort of her blue Barcalounger—failed to deliver. Outside, Patty and I would be practically wetting our pants from laughing so hard, while in her living room, there sat Helen, knitting some sweater and taking a sip from her cup now and then.

What was in that cup anyway?

"I bet she's a wino," I told Patty. "She just pours her whiskey in a coffee cup so people won't suspect."

"She wouldn't need to hide it in her own house," Patty pointed out. "She's not expecting that we're looking in the window at her."

"So what do you think is going on?"

"Maybe the Bradys got a dog," Patty offered. She was always working hard to keep up with her own interesting contributions to our conversations, but sometimes it was hard for her thinking up ideas. One topic that held abiding interest for her, however, was dogs.

"Then what?" I said.

"They named him Skipper."

Other times, the story lines I thought up concerned the people whose living rooms we looked into, rather than the shows on their television screens.

"Maybe Helen sneaks into people's houses when they're away at work and steals their jewelry and money," I suggested. "Maybe Tubby figured it out, and she killed him, and now she keeps his body in the basement. That's why she's always burning those vanilla candles. To cover the smell.

"She got fed up with him asking her to cook him dinner all the time, so she did him in," I went on. "He was always wanting to have sex."

In fact, Helen's husband, Tubby, had been suffering from what my sister referred to as old-timer's disease for years before he died, and he had mostly just sat in his chair for as long as either of us could remember. But the idea of anybody wanting to have sex with Helen was pretty funny. The idea of sex was funny, period—funny and terrible and thrilling.

After our father left, we liked it better outside of our house than in. Inside, things kept breaking, options narrowed. Every month we seemed to have less of everything but unopened bills and the smell of cigarettes. Inside, we could feel the sadness and disappointment of our mother, and as much as we loved her, we had to get away or we'd be swallowed up in it too. But beyond the four walls of our falling-down house, anything was possible.

We had a game called Ding Dong Ditch that required one of us—always Patty—to ring the doorbell of a house on our street. More often than not the door we'd choose was the one belonging to our next-door neighbor Helen.

Once she rang the bell, Patty would hightail it to a ditch, or some spot behind a hedge, where I'd be waiting already, watching for the great moment when Helen (or Mr. Evans down the street, or the Pollacks, or Mrs. Gunnerson and her retarded daughter, Clara, if it had been their doorbells my sister rang) would open the door and look out at the empty doorstep with a baffled expression. (Not so baffled after a while, no doubt. Helen in particular had to know it was us, we rang her bell so frequently.)

Sometimes we picked up rocks in the neighborhood— possibly decorative white rocks originally laid out as part of the edging for a flower bed—and painted them with poster paints, if we had some, or melted crayon wax if we didn't. Then we sold them door-to-door, very possibly to the people whose houses they'd come from in the first place. We might get a nickel or just a penny. The idea was to save up the necessary funds to buy a Slurpee. Once we'd raised enough (probably just for one) we walked the mile and a half to the mall to buy it. Taking our time, as usual. There was nothing to rush home for.

But our main diversions lay beyond the neighborhood, to the wilder places beyond it. Morning Glory

Court backed up on the outer reaches of the Golden Gate National Recreation Area, which included a network of hiking trails so vast it stretched from the park's southernmost borders in San Francisco to a spot almost fifty miles north of that known as Point Reyes. Beyond that lay the entire Pacific Ocean. More than anywhere else—the bedroom we shared, our messy kitchen with its frequently malfunctioning refrigerator and broken oven, or the houses we didn't go to of the friends we didn't have—the mountain was where my sister and I spent our days.

For most children in our neighborhood, the vast expanse of open land abutting our houses had been off-limits, for fear of snakes or coyote attacks or, more likely, poison oak. But Patty and I rambled where we chose. Our only limits: how far our legs could carry us.

Sometimes we'd make ourselves a picnic—those saltines again, and peanut butter, or possibly just sugar. We'd take it, along with whatever book I was reading or the notebooks I took everywhere to write stories in (and, for Patty, a stack of *Betty and Veronicas*), and then spend the day out on the mountain. We might make our way to the Mountain Home Inn, at the base of a major trailhead to the mountain, where (at my direction) Patty would race in, bearing no possible resemblance to the kind of person who'd be a registered guest, and fill her pockets with peanuts from the bar, then race out again before anyone could tell her not to.

After, we might just sit there on the mountain, alongside the trail, or on a rock, splitting grass in two or imagining scenarios of things we'd do if one of us got on a game show and won ten thousand dollars, or (though this was my interest, not my sister's) analyzing photographs of haircuts we liked, or John Travolta's crotch in teen magazines.

"You'd think someone as famous as him would be embarrassed to have his picture taken in pants that tight," Patty said. "He has enough money to buy a new pair if he's outgrown his old ones."

Some things I explained to her. Some not. At times we'd just lie there together not speaking at all, just breathing in the faint breeze carrying the smell of wild fennel, or we spit seeds to see whose went the farthest. We took our shirts off and lay in the grass, sun on our skin, checking for breast development. Mine negligible. Hers nonexistent.

Other times we hung out in an old rusted-out truck body abandoned on the hillside, with weeds growing up through the middle, whose presence in this spot formed the basis for endless speculation. We liked to believe we were the only ones who knew about the truck body, though once, when we settled into our spot there, we found a couple of old condom wrappers that suggested this was not so.

The truck body sat about a mile up the hillside from our house, tucked away off the trail. A little way beyond lay an outdoor amphitheater where, every summer, a local semiprofessional theater company staged a lavish production of some popular musical (*The Sound of Music* one year, *Brigadoon* the next), accessible only on foot. The cost of tickets for the Mountain Play exceeded anything our mother could have come up with, but during the period of weeks every summer when performances took place, we sometimes hiked up to the amphitheater. We had located a spot close enough to the actual performance site where we could spread out a blanket, listening to the music and observing the actors hanging around during rehearsals—changing costumes, smoking pot, necking, possibly—which was more interesting than the actual show.

Guys and Dolls had been our favorite. Patty and I had never actually gotten to see the show, but over the course of the weeks they'd performed it a few summers back, we'd gotten so familiar with the songs that from our post a little ways off, we sang along with them: "I Got the Horse Right Here," "Luck Be a Lady Tonight," "Take Back Your Mink."

Even better were the times when no rehearsal was going on, and the two of us could occupy the performance space ourselves, putting on our own shows. Shy as she was out in the world, up on the mountain with nobody seeing her but me and the occasional red-tailed hawk or deer, my sister was fearless. One time when she was seven or eight, out there in the amphitheater—against a backdrop meant to be the main street for *The Music Man*—she performed a complete and glorious striptease.

"We're like the kids in Charlie Brown," Patty said. Had anybody, reading that strip, ever seen those children's parents getting in the way of their adventures? From how it seemed in the comics, they carried on their lives without the least evidence of adult intervention.

I had read a book once about a boy who got lost in the forest, and some wolves found him and took care of him. (It would be a boy, of course, who got to have an adventure like that.) Still, I loved that story. I saw us running free over the hillside, unencumbered by parental rules or concern for danger. We were a couple of wolf girls—but with fashionable jeans, though really what we wore were just Levi's.

We rode our bikes a lot. No destination in mind. But you never knew what you might find. Once, riding

around, we'd passed a Dumpster with a bunch of records stacked up next to it—someone's entire record
collection from the looks of it, and not things like
Mitch Miller or Mantovani either, or Herb Alpert and
the Tijuana Brass, which was the kind of music our
neighbor Helen favored, or Jennifer Pollack's favorite,
which we could hear out the Pollacks' window all day
long, the Carpenters.

For some unfathomable reason (though, as a girl
who liked to make up stories, I invented a few scenarios concerning what had brought this about) someone out there had chosen to throw out his or her entire
album collection. The Beatles and the Rolling Stones,
of course. Also Black Sabbath and the Moody Blues,
Procol Harum and Led Zeppelin, along with folkier
types of music too—Cat Stevens and Linda Ronstadt,
Leonard Cohen, Arlo Guthrie and Judy Collins, Crosby,
Stills and Nash, and Simon and Garfunkel. There was
one unlikely component in the mix that Patty in particular loved: an album by Dolly Parton and Porter
Wagoner called *Burning the Midnight Oil.* It had
two side-by-side images on the cover: one of Dolly,
sitting by a fireplace, bursting out of an amazing red
gown, with a heartbroken look on her face; the other of
Porter, in a rhinestone shirt, raking his fingers through
his yellow hair, looking equally devastated. My sister

loved Led Zeppelin and Cream, but after finding that album, Dolly Parton became Patty's favorite singer of all time.

There were way too many records to fit in our bike baskets. We hid part of the stash, in case someone else came along and took them before we could get back for the next load. It took us three trips getting the whole collection home, and for the rest of that summer, our main activity was playing music on my tinny little monaural record player from when I was little, decorated with old Disney characters.

We memorized the whole of *Alice's Restaurant* and sang "City of New Orleans" and "American Pie" now as we rode our bikes. *"This'll be the day that I die, this'll be the day that I die."*

We loved how Leonard Cohen sang "Suzanne," and though the words made no sense, we could tell it was a sexy song. We loved Donovan. We actually wore out the Crosby, Stills and Nash album with "Suite for Judy Blue Eyes." We turned the volume up to the loudest it could go for "Whole Lotta Love," but we liked more gentle music too. We knew Jim Croce had died young, tragically, which seemed to make it even sadder listening to the song about trying to call up his old girlfriend but he can't read her telephone number on the matchbook where he wrote it down. If there was one thing we loved about a piece of music, it was the presence of heartbreak, or better yet, tragedy.

"Every time I hear that song, I keep hoping he'll finally figure out the number and get another dime," said Patty. "You know if he did, they'd be together."

One time, after we first brought home those records, I had asked our mother what kind of music she'd loved when she was young, and for a second, a look came over her I'd never seen before. "There was never anyone to equal Elvis," she said. "But I'm over him."

It wasn't only Elvis she'd gotten over, but every man. After our father left, it was as if she'd drawn the curtains, and all she wanted was to be left alone, with as little opportunity for loss or sorrow as possible.

We were wandering on the mountain one time—a little higher up, farther from home than usual—when we saw an amazing sight: a man and a woman running through the grass, totally naked.

We hung back, not wanting to embarrass them, but the woman waved in our direction. The two of them walked over to us, laughing—still without their clothes on, but acting as if there was nothing unusual about this. We tried hard not to look down, at the man in particular. Though neither of these people seemed even close to shy.

"Beautiful day," the woman said. "Can you believe these wildflowers?"

It was the season for California poppies. They were everywhere, like something you'd see on a postcard, though if this was a postcard, the naked people wouldn't have been part of it.

They held hands and walked off. Patty and I didn't say anything, even to each other. We knew each other so well that even when something amazing happened, there was no need to speak. We just burst out laughing and held hands, running back down the hillside so fast we almost fell over ourselves.

One time we met a man playing a guitar and singing, with a long-haired woman with a baby on the grass beside him.

"I think that was Jerry Garcia," I told my sister. I had to tell her who that was, before she got impressed, and even then, not all that much.

We were in the middle of some game one time— Charlie's Angels, maybe, or just drifting along, as we often did, snapping the heads of timothy grass while reciting "Momma had a baby and her head popped off"—when we came upon The Thing. Patty spotted it first: the weird, hairless body of a small unborn animal—a deer fetus probably, still in the sac, with its spindle legs folded into itself and shut eyes with their translucent lids that were never going to open, ears flat against the skull, a map of blue veins threading just beneath the skin. Somewhere not far from this spot, we imagined a deer mother wandering, bloody and dazed. Within hours, you knew, the vultures or coyotes would have found the body of the doe. Tomorrow it would be gone without a trace.

Sometimes we pretended we were a couple of Indian maidens, the lone survivors of a slaughtered tribe, who roamed the foothills of some vast mountain range by day, trapping our food and hunting game, returning to our teepee only at night to eat our cornmeal mush and gnaw on a little pemmican, wrap our threadbare blankets around our rawhide shifts before another sunrise sent us back out onto the range. I wanted to light a campfire and throw popcorn kernels in to watch them pop, but Patty wouldn't go along with it. Fire made my sister nervous. The only thing that did.

There were a couple of horses on the hillside. They must have belonged to someone, but they just grazed there, so we could pretend they were ours. Sometimes we brought them carrots, if we had enough at home. We gave them names—Crystal and Pamela, because those were the names we wished we were called. They seemed to know us after a while, letting us come up alongside them, stroking their backs. With Crystal, especially, you could almost imagine riding her bareback, if there had been a way to get up on her, which there was not.

We played we were blind people, with our eyes shut, turning in circles five times, then walking fifty steps to see where we'd end up. We'd open to a random page of *My Secret Garden* (a book I'd seen in the bedroom at the house of our neighbors, the Pollacks, one night when I was babysitting, full of wild stories women had made up about sex, that I'd snuck home in my book bag) and read it out loud to each other. We pretended we were boys and peed standing up.

For us, back then, it was exciting enough, just speaking certain words out loud. Each of us assembled a pile of pulled-up grass or dandelions in front of ourselves and when it was our turn, we'd have to think up some forbidden word—tossing some of our grass in the air as we uttered it, though for us the list was frustratingly short because our vocabulary concerning the language of sex was limited: *Intercourse*, naturally. *Butt. Nipple. Vagina. Penis.* And the one that had become, for me that year, the scariest. *Period.*

Twice, in our rambles on the mountain, we came upon a couple making love in the grass—though on neither occasion did they see us. From years of playing detective, we'd gotten good at being stealthy, though later—safely home—we couldn't stop laughing.

You might have thought some of our experiences would have discouraged further exploration, but it was just the opposite. The mountain opened up for us the picture of a bigger world than what we ever could have known in the safe confines of our tiny house and yard, and the fact that this other world had dead animals in it, and naked people, and predators, just made us want to discover more.

The days stretched out, one after another, vast and unbroken as the grassy landscape of that hillside and the darkening sky overhead. Other kids had to go inside at dinnertime. We'd hear their mothers calling to them, though often they knew, without being called, when it was time to head in. For us, there was never anyone calling, and no worry or guilt that our mother had worked all afternoon to make a steaming family dinner now left to cool on the table. Dinner was whatever cold cuts we located in the refrigerator, whenever we got home to eat them.

Going back outside after we ate, we might stay out until ten o'clock, just making up stories or prowling behind the houses, looking in windows to see if anything interesting was happening, which it never was. When we let ourselves back in, we'd hear our mother's radio in her bedroom and smell her cigarette smoke, call out "Good night, Mom," and head into our own room, where we'd set a stack of records on the record player. We'd lie on our beds and read out loud to each other—from a joke book, possibly, or one of the biographies I got from Scholastic Book Club, or another one of the wild stories from *My Secret Garden* (though these mostly baffled my sister)—and whisper to each other until one of us fell asleep. Usually Patty.

With the window open, you could hear the sound of crickets, or an owl, or a coyote howling, and on rare occasions, a mountain lion. You could look out to the mountain and see stars, and when the light came in the morning, there were the horses grazing—horses mating even—and hawks circling overhead.

It was the place we found out about everything, that mountain. Animal bones and deer scat. Birds, flowers, condoms. The bodies of dead animals, the bodies of men. Rocks and lizards. Sex and death.

S ome years before—when I was around ten, Patty
eight—an old woman who lived in a house on the
cul-de-sac at the far end of our street died following a
long illness, and her husband moved to a nursing home.
Their house sat vacant for close to a year while their
children worked out what to do about the place. Then
sometime in the spring the house had been sold. All
we knew about the new residents was the name on the
mailbox, Armitage.

They had no children. Over the months we'd become
vaguely aware of Mr. Armitage—a man of stocky
build and thinning hair, who evidently worked (this
much we learned from Mrs. Gunnerson) as a teacher
at a ballroom dancing studio in San Rafael. We saw
him walking to the bus stop a few blocks away most

afternoons and returning home around nine o'clock at night. Later, when hardly anyone was out but us, he'd walk their small dog.

On rare occasions—only at night, if we were out later than normal—we'd see the woman we determined to be Mrs. Armitage carrying a large pocketbook and wearing some unbecoming dress over her shapeless body, and (a little strangely) a hat, regardless of the weather. She always wore high heels, as if she was headed someplace special, though from the looks of things, her walks around the neighborhood with their little dog—a mutt who seemed to have some Jack Russell terrier in him—took her to no particular destination. Other than those times—no more than three of them—we never saw her, and because the hat featured an odd little veil in the front, we never got to see her very closely either.

Somewhat surprisingly, Mr. Armitage appeared to be an outdoorsman. Sitting on our back steps, eating our Pop-Tarts or granola bars, Patty and I often observed him heading up the mountain, carrying a walking stick, with his little dog trotting alongside and a pair of binoculars around his neck. Mrs. Armitage was never part of these expeditions, we noted.

"Maybe he's meeting a girlfriend up there," I said. "Maybe he's a spy."

"He doesn't look like the type," Patty offered. As much as I would have liked to think otherwise, I had to agree, this was so. And anyway, Mr. Armitage's hikes seldom lasted more than half an hour: a quick jaunt up the trail, then down again. My sister and I decided this was probably his fitness routine, though if so, it did not appear to be having much effect, so far. Like his wife, Mr. Armitage remained on the chubby side.

One noteworthy fact about our new neighbors had to do with their landscaping efforts. Early on in their time on Morning Glory Court, Mr. Armitage had hired a man with a small tractorlike machine to come in and tear up the lawn, and we briefly imagined that the Armitages might be doing something exciting like putting in a pool or constructing an elaborate garden at least. But when the job was finished, it turned out all the Armitages had elected to do was rip out the grass of the lawn and replace it with concrete blocks. Karl Pollack, who'd spoken to Mr. Armitage around this time, as none of the rest of us on the street seemed to have done, reported that our neighbor had done this as a way of avoiding the inconvenience of yard maintenance and reducing his water bill.

The other big disappointment where the Armitages were concerned had to do with their television set. At this point, our neighbor Helen's husband, Tubby, was still alive, and he had taken to watching the shopping channel during the very time slot when we liked to catch our episodes of *The Brady Bunch* through their window. Viewing our show through the Pollacks' window had also become an iffy proposition. (Their newborn son evidently suffered from colic, and they had recently acquired a VCR—a new invention—on which they tended, maddeningly, to play episodes of Mr. Rogers they'd taped for the purpose of getting Karl Jr. to sleep.) This had left Patty and me searching for a new viewing location for Drive-In Movie. Briefly, we'd thought of the Armitages.

But unlike every other house on our side of the street that backed up against the mountain—whose TV sets we could see, glowing blue through their picture windows—it appeared the Armitages didn't own a TV. Not one they kept in the living room anyway—the spot necessary for us to look in through the picture windows at night to catch our shows. This left us wondering how they spent their time.

There was the dog, of course. Maybe they liked doing jigsaw puzzles, Patty suggested. Or Scrabble.

But suppose the Armitages were living a secret life, as international jewel thieves, or spies? Maybe Mr. Armitage was one of those people who provide information about the mob to the FBI, and he and his wife had to go into hiding with a whole new identity. Maybe Mrs. Armitage had suffered a terrible accident that left her face horribly scarred, which accounted for her staying inside all the time, except for those rare walks in the night. As the Charlie's Angels of Morning Glory Court, we would get to the bottom of their story.

We started a scrapbook, devoted to Mr. Armitage. More accurately, I started the scrapbook. Patty just went along with it, as she did with most things I suggested.

Years before, our mother had begun a scrapbook documenting my babyhood, but she'd stopped keeping it up after a couple of months, which had left many blank pages. I saw no harm in ripping out the pictures devoted to me: my newborn footprint, a photograph showing our mother, with an expression I barely recognized, of eagerness and hope, and our young and lanky father— skinnier than we'd ever known him, with a cowlick— wrapping his arms around the two of us in a gesture that would have made you think no harm could ever befall this family. The entries—daily at first—had slacked off dramatically around the point of my six-month birthday. Mention was made of my first tooth, and a time when—hearing Andy Williams singing "Moon River" on the radio—I'd reputedly run to get our copy of *Goodnight Moon* and started dancing. My mother had stopped writing in the book not long after this.

I made a new title page now: "The Mysterious Life of Albert Armitage," and wrote the date, along with our stated mission—to learn everything we could about our inscrutable neighbor (*inscrutable:* a word from my fifth-grade extra-credit vocab list), though what the purpose might be for our project we never said.

For Christmas that year, our father had given me a Polaroid camera and five rolls of film that I'd been saving ever since. I decided to dedicate these to the project of documenting the life and habits of Albert Armitage.

We wanted to include Mrs. Armitage in our project too, but sightings of her were so rare, we would have nothing to put in our scrapbook if we relied on documenting her brief forays into the neighborhood. The hope was that once we understood more of the husband's story, we'd get an idea of what was going on with his wife.

We began our scrapbook with the more mundane aspects of our neighbor's existence: Mr. Armitage carrying out his daily routines of heading up the mountain for his morning hike with his dog, walking to the bus stop, and picking up the Sunday paper on the curb. With no lawn to mow, he spent little time on yard work, though we had spotted him once or twice standing on the edge of his cement-covered plot of ground, pulling up the occasional dandelion that made its way through the cracks. Another time we saw him lining up the rocks that edged the cement blocks. Patty and I exchanged a meaningful look when we saw him doing this—both of us concluding that it would be a poor idea to try stealing rocks from this house anytime in the future. He kept close tabs, evidently.

Recognizing what Mr. Armitage's attitude was likely to be concerning the idea of our taking pictures of him, we had cooked up a method for concealing our actions. This called for Patty to stand in front of whatever location it was where we spotted our subject, but slightly off to one side or the other. She'd strike an elaborate pose (hand on hip, waving to the camera) while I aimed the camera in such a way as to capture an image not of my sister at all, but of Mr. Armitage and, on occasion, the dog. To complete the ruse, I'd announce in a loud voice, "Great shot, Patty," or "You really looked cute in that one."

On our way up the street toward home we'd peel back the paper on our latest Polaroid and watch the image develop before our eyes: Mr. Armitage checking his watch. Mr. Armitage hosing down his rocks. Mr. Armitage getting his mail. The most exciting page of our scrapbook featured photographs we'd taken (while pretending to be fixing my bicycle chain) of Mr. Armitage giving his dog a bath.

Patty participated in our investigation, but unenthusiastically. From the first time we encountered Mr. Armitage, my sister maintained a protective attitude where he was concerned. He was a dog lover. That's all she cared about.

"He's just a person," she said. "He isn't hurting anybody. I bet he's just sad because of his wife's accident."

My sister was referring here to an idea I'd proposed as an explanation for why we only laid eyes on Mrs. Armitage at night, and hardly ever, even then. "Someone threw acid on her face," I had suggested. "She used to be incredibly beautiful, but now she doesn't want anyone to see her." Of all the scenarios I'd suggested to explain the Armitages' odd behavior, my sister chose to subscribe to the theory that Mrs. Armitage was a tragically disfigured burn victim, and she felt sorry for them.

But for me, there remained something troubling about the activities of the couple at the end of the street. Keeping our scrapbook was, for me, a way of addressing, in a tangible way, an intangible feeling of uneasiness about our neighbors.

Or maybe it was this: so many questions remained unanswered in our lives at the time. We were looking for hard data to explain the inexplicable. Maybe I hoped that if we assembled enough simple data concerning an individual whose behavior confused us—investigating the contents of his trash can, tracking the times of his departure for work and subsequent arrival home, and whatever else we might record through the viewfinder of my camera—we might come to understand the things that struck us as odd. We were too young then to recognize that the discovery of hard facts seldom yields true enlightenment.

After a few weeks of working on our scrapbook—and finding no additional data of significance—our interest in documenting the comings and goings of Mr. Armitage tapered off, to the point where one day, finding the scrapbook, I realized that nearly a whole year had gone by since we'd made any entries.

I put the scrapbook on our shelf. Now, except for his walks with the dog, and his regular morning hike up the mountain, we hardly ever saw our neighbor, and we thought about him even less. Him or his wife.

Sometime later it occurred to us that months had passed since either my sister or I had laid eyes on Mrs. Armitage, which led to our conclusion that they might be getting a divorce. That was one story we felt no need to investigate further.

Once, when she was seven or eight, Patty was walking home—just wandering around the neighborhood, looking for dogs probably. It was one of those rare afternoons when, for some reason, I wasn't around. For Patty, spending an afternoon without me was like the sky doing without the sun.

As she told me later, she noticed a basketball lying on the ground near the playground. It had rolled into some bushes, but she could still make out the faded orange surface and the last few letters of the word *Wilson*. She walked over to investigate.

The ball was a little flat, but usable. She picked it up. Checked to see if the ball could still bounce. It did.

That was the beginning for my sister. I doubt Patty had ever even held a basketball before that day. Now, for the first time, she had, and once she did, she liked the feeling.

There was a patch of blacktop nearby. At one end was a pole with a hoop attached. No net, and the backboard was a little off-kilter. Patty started dribbling and aimed the ball at the hoop. It didn't go in on the first try, she told me. But after that, yes. Many times. Later, she dribbled the ball all the way home.

The next day we went over to Helen and Tubby's. Tubby had been a school custodian before he retired— meaning he owned every tool known to man, including an air pump and the needle you need for inflating a basketball. Once the ball was filled with air, Patty's dribbling got even better.

Later she mastered dribbling behind her back and through her legs. She mastered crossovers and balls-against-the-wall. Other kids noticed and asked her to play with them. On the court my sister was nimble and fearless, and surprisingly aggressive for a girl who, off the court, seldom spoke up or made waves. When she was shoved to the ground, which sometimes happened, she never betrayed any sign that it hurt, though it must have.

But Patty's greatest gift with a basketball was her shooting. Right before she made a shot she would freeze dead in her tracks. Just seconds earlier, her body had been tearing up and down the court so fast it was hard to keep track of her; now, about to take a shot, she stood stock-still, spring-loaded. Then she would look up, lock her eyes on the back of the rim, and with a brief glance to the right or left, she would release the ball, keeping her gaze on that rim until the moment the ball swished through the hoop and scored her points. Then she was off again.

Kids wanted my sister on their team when they saw her. Even boys did, if they were smart. And one more thing about Patty: Even though she was such a star on the court, she never hogged the ball. She appeared to feel no requirement that the points her team scored be hers. She was a true team player. But she was probably never happier than when she was alone on a court, as she was that first day, when it was just her and the ball, dribbling and shooting. That was the sound that let me know my sister was coming—the sound of a basketball hitting the pavement. Steady as a heartbeat.

I spent all of seventh grade waiting for the blood to come. Other things must have been going on that year, but that's how I remember it. Waking up and sliding my hand under my pajama bottoms to check if anything had happened in the night, moving it over

my belly, my two new breasts—hard little mounds—
and the soft place where a small tuft of pubic hair had
sprouted, but there was nothing more.

As far as I knew I was the only girl in my class who
hadn't gotten her period yet. Nobody said this. I'd figured it out by process of elimination, based on all the
girls who talked about their cramps, or stood around
the Tampax dispenser, exchanging stories about acci-
dents or pool parties they had to navigate, wearing a
cover-up. I alone had none to tell.

The fact that I, alone of the girls I knew, had not
begun to menstruate obliterated all else as summer
approached and I passed my thirteenth birthday. Ever
since school started the fall before, I'd been carrying
a sanitary napkin in my book bag. I lived in fear of
being one of those girls we'd all known, who stands
up to go to the blackboard to write out a theorem, and
they've got this red spot on the back of their skirt.
Maybe, if she's got a good friend, someone says something to her later. More likely people just whisper and
stare.

My sister said she hoped it wouldn't ever happen
to her—meaning getting her period, not the accident
part. Good luck with that, I told her. But I had started
to worry that it never would happen to me. I'd be the
one girl in the history of our school who got all the way

to graduation without ever seeing that gash of red in her underpants.

It was an odd thing to hope for. Who would want blood dripping out of them? Gushing out possibly, I wasn't even clear.

Only I did want it. Because everyone else had that happen to them, and it gave you something to share with the other girls. I was different enough as it was, without this. I figured if I could stand around the Tampax dispenser holding my stomach, complaining about cramps, I might fit in with the rest of them. Instead, all I did was carry around that same unopened sanitary napkin that had been lying in the bottom of my book bag so long now it had sandwich crumbs and bits of melted chocolate bar stuck to the wrapper, ballpoint pen marks, and lint. Checking my underpants every time I went to the bathroom. Finding nothing. Feeling like a freak, though hardly for the first time.

Our mother was not the sort of person you discussed these things with, but she had to know. She did our laundry.

Our father, when he touched down to see us, had started treating me differently, as if I was breakable. With Patty, he'd roughhouse—pat her on the butt, toss her a basketball, never mind if it hit her in the stomach, because she'd just laugh if it did, pick her up (tall as she was) and twirl her. With me he displayed a new and unfamiliar distance that sometimes made me feel as if he didn't even know me anymore.

It must have unnerved my father to think of me entering into the territory of sex. He knew how to act with little girls, and I knew—Patty and I both did, from all those times at Marin Joe's, and every other place we ever went with him—that he definitely knew how to act with a woman. How to be with a daughter who was no longer a child might have left him at a loss—a rare state for our father to find himself in, but it seemed this was so.

The only person I talked with about this was my sister. She was the only one I talked with about anything real, same as I was the only one for her.

Nights in bed (Patty top bunk, me bottom) we listened to music on our transistor radio and our tinny portable record player (Peter Frampton, Cat Stevens, Linda Ronstadt; the wilder stuff like Led Zeppelin and Lynyrd Skynyrd reserved for daytime).

We whispered to each other for hours, and it seemed there was no topic we couldn't discuss: What would Patty choose if our mother suddenly allowed us to have a dog: an adorable puppy or an old rescue dog that really needed a home? What happened to your body when you died? And—after seeing *Jaws*—whether we'd want to go on living if a shark bit off our legs and arms. (Or where we'd draw the line. Two legs, one arm? Both legs? One arm, one leg? We considered every possible variation.)

We discussed God (I didn't believe in him; Patty did) and our parents' divorce—though that was long ago now. Knowing he wasn't with us, and he lived alone, we speculated about what our father did those times he wasn't at the Civic Center working on one of his cases. Though he never talked about this, even when we asked, he definitely seemed like the type to have a girlfriend, and if he did, we knew she must be beautiful. One name stuck in my head, but I didn't ask about her. If our father wanted to say something, he would, and meanwhile it felt disloyal to our mother to speak it out loud.

Our mother's story contained little mystery. Since the divorce she had inhabited a deep, irretrievable place of cold, gray sadness, as if our father's departure from her life had banished all that remained of sunlight. We never questioned that she loved us, but her behavior suggested that of a person suffering from some contagious disease, who knows she might contaminate the people she loves if she gets too close to them. She brought home groceries after work from her job as a typist (the term *secretary* implying more status than she afforded herself) and took us shopping for school clothes when she could, but more than any children we knew, we were left to our own devices much of the time, with a mostly empty refrigerator and too-tight sneakers, saltines and cheese slices or canned soup for dinner, and a faint smell of smoke coming from the crack under her door to let us know she was in there with one of her library books.

But our father's story was more complicated. There was the mysterious Margaret Ann (whose name our mother cried out on the last night our father ever lived at our house; then never again).

Then there were all the others. Patty and I would be out with him, and some woman we'd never met would call out to him or come over to us, and there'd be this look between them that made us feel she knew all kinds of things we didn't.

After, I might ask who that was, and he'd say, "Someone I met one time." He might mention that she worked at a flower shop he stopped at (buying flowers for someone else, more than likely), or at the dealership where he got the Alfa serviced, or she sold him a pair of boots a few months back. One time it was the judge in a case in which he'd testified. But the way she'd looked at him in the parking lot outside the gas station where we'd seen her—rearranging her hair, or that thing they all seemed to do, touching their neck—made her seem like a woman more than a judge.

"I don't see what's the big deal about sex," Patty said one time. The teenage daughter of a family down the street, on Patty's paper route, had made the comment to my sister that our father was sexy. This led to a discussion of what made a person sexy, and from there, to things people did in bed together, as I understood it. Not our mother, but other people. Our father, definitely.

Why would anybody think that was fun? she said. It sounded dumb to her. She'd rather play basketball.

I couldn't say exactly why, but I definitely knew people cared a lot about sex. Supposedly, it made them feel very good, though it made them do crazy things too. This was how I saw it at the time. I figured I might understand better once I got my period. Only the months passed and it never came, and things reached the point where the sanitary napkin I'd been holding on to got so ratty I threw it out, and I didn't even bother putting another one in my book bag to replace it.

Our father had many secrets. The recipe for his special marinara sauce that he promised to divulge when I turned twenty-one. The places he'd take us on our weekend afternoons with him. ("You'll see," he said, as he buckled us in the front. "You just can't tell your mother.") His famous talent for getting criminals to confess their crimes, and how he knew if we were sad or scared, or that some boy at school made fun of my sister's teeth, before we ever told him. There was his gift for making spiders out of our hair of course. All this contributed to our belief that our father was magic.

We lived for those afternoons when the Alfa pulled up in front of our house—or possibly, if he was on a job, his unmarked car from the sheriff's department, which meant he'd have a gun strapped to his ankle, and a radio on his belt—and for the next hour and a half, if he took us out to eat, or maybe just ten minutes, if that's all he had time for, it was as if the whole sky lit up, and I was so happy my chest could have burst, and we laughed so much our faces hurt.

In the car, he always had an eight-track on. If it was Sinatra, he just listened. (Who'd sing along with Frank?) But when it was Dean Martin, our father would join in, English or Italian, it didn't matter. "Mambo Italiano" . . . "Ritorna-Me" . . . "Send Me the Pillow You Dream On" . . . And our favorite: "That's Amore."

Our father knew all the lyrics, of course, and probably Patty and I did too, we'd heard them so many times, but we let him be the one to sing them.

When the moon hits your eye like a big pizza pie . . .

"That's amore!" Patty yelled, in that big voice of hers.

When the stars make you drool like a pasta fazool . . .

"That's amore!"

After a while, we'd make up our own lyrics:

When your pants start to itch, like a bug's in your crotch . . .

That's amore!

When you're sore in your heart, and you think you might fart . . .

That's amore!

We sang all the way home, and we'd still be singing when his car pulled in the driveway.

"You girls," he said, scooping us up. "Loves of my life."

Then he was gone, the last notes from the eight-track fading away as he turned the corner toward the highway, and there we were, just sitting on the curb again, watching his car disappear down the street like a flash of heat lightning.

We never knew when he'd be back. You couldn't even be mad at him for this—though later, Patty would be. The times we had him made up for all the times we didn't, I used to tell her.

To me, it just seemed too much to expect that a person like our father would hang around a couple of girls like us in a normal way, that we could hold on to him like a regular dad, any more than you'd expect to hold on to a sunset or a breaking wave.

Nobody else had a father like ours. He was like a movie star or an astronaut, like someone you'd expect to see on television, sitting on the couch talking to Johnny Carson, only we were his daughters and he came to our house, just to see us—and as many women as there were who might love him, we knew he loved us more than anyone.

We were his all-time favorites, and we had no doubt we would remain so forever.

Summer 1979. I was thirteen years and two months old, and I had just graduated from seventh grade. I didn't have a best friend, but I loved my sister more than anything, though our father came close. I was also in love with Peter Frampton and John Travolta, and when I grew up I planned to be a writer. Possibly an international spy also, or the first female race car driver. I had read *The Diary of a Young Girl* four times, folding over the page on the parts where Anne Frank talked about sex and being angry at her mother, and I was keeping a diary of my own, except that instead of writing about things that really happened, I made stories up, in which the two main themes were tragic love affairs and wild adventures in places I read about in *National Geographic*.

From the one marriage I'd observed closely—my parents' brief, sad union—I had acquired a low opinion of that institution. Marriage opened up the possibility of divorce, and divorce had broken our mother's heart. Divorce took our father away—not only from our mother but from my sister and me too. Now he was always running someplace, swooping down to take us to Marin Joe's, gliding up in front of our house in his blue Alfa Romeo, leaving us breathless.

Then gone again, on one of his cases. Or someplace else, anyway.

Marriage caused divorce, which caused the current situation, which in our mother's case meant she was never happy anymore. If that was where marriage took a person, who needed marriage? I'd rather be the one driving away someplace exciting than the one getting left at home. And anyway, I was going to be a writer. I'd be too busy to get married.

I didn't ever want to have a baby either. (Observing Jennifer Pollack's body after giving birth to Karl Pollack Jr. got me thinking, and changing the diapers of Karl Jr. sealed the deal.) But I counted the years till

I'd be old enough to move out of our house and get a better job than babysitting, and buy a convertible, which would be black, not red like everybody else who wanted a convertible. It had also occurred to me to get a tattoo, which was not as common an idea in those days as it became later. And I would travel around the world, having adventures and doing research for my books, and sometimes I'd fly off to some city to meet my fans, and they would stand in a long line to get a copy of my latest bestseller, and when it was their turn to talk with me, they'd say it was the best thing they ever read, besides the diary of Anne Frank, or *To Kill a Mockingbird.*

How do you think up all those stories? someone would ask me.

When I was young, I'd say, that's what I did to make life interesting. My sister and I were always looking for a little drama, and if the world didn't provide some, we'd invent it. We could make up stories so real we believed them ourselves.

And then something really did happen, of course. And all we wished for then was that it never did.

It was June 21, the summer solstice. We'd been out of school exactly one week. The number one song was "My Sharona," by the Knack. On the radio station Patty and I listened to, the DJs played it about a hundred times a day. We mouthed the words and danced to it in our room and later, out on the mountain, naked— not entirely clear what the lyrics meant, but recognizing that they were bad.

Sometime around my thirteenth birthday that spring, I had discovered that I liked to feel my heart beating fast. Not owning my convertible yet, I did the best I could to replicate the state of being a person might experience driving very fast on a road with sharp curves and extreme drop-offs. It was like being on drugs, without actually using them.

For me, the wild parts happened mostly in my head, but my sister would try anything. If she saw a sign on a fence that said NO TRESPASSING—STAY OFF, she climbed over it. If a boy said she'd be too chicken to take his skateboard down a hill, she hopped on. My job was watching, and thinking up the ideas.

It was closing in on eight o'clock. We'd spent most of that morning scrounging up change in the house—looking under pillows on the couch, and in the dryer, where we'd managed to come up with a grand total of a dollar eighty-five in quarters, nickels, and dimes. Most of the afternoon had been taken up with walking to the mall and back for the purpose of looking at clothes (not trying any on; that would have seemed beyond our scope) and sharing a Slurpee. Home again, we lay on my bottom bunk for a while, listening to our Rolling Stones record *Sticky Fingers*, eating radishes, and zipping and unzipping the fly on Mick Jagger's crotch that decorated the album cover.

Dinner that night had been SpaghettiOs. No relationship between that food and any meal our father ever created for us, back when he did.

Now we were settling in on our blanket for Drive-In Movie, the *Brady Bunch* hour. We were a little old for the show by this point, or at least I was—and we knew every episode by heart—but watching had become our tradition.

It was a hot evening, the longest day, meaning the sun had not yet fully set, which made it harder to see the images on the television set at Helen's house, and from the looks of things, Helen was opting for *Lawrence Welk* over the exploits of the Bradys that night, which was not good news. (She kept switching back and forth. Watching for when the accordion player she liked came on, most likely.)

So we decided to move our blanket farther along on the hill, to an alternate spot, behind the house of Karl and Jennifer Pollack, who had recently purchased a set even larger than Helen's. Moving our blanket was our version of changing channels.

The show was just starting—those old familiar faces smiling out at us, of all the Bradys smiling either up or down or sideways at each other from inside the grid framing their faces—when the screen went black for a second and a new image replaced the opening of our show. We couldn't actually make out the words on the screen but I knew from past experience this meant they were interrupting the broadcast to announce some kind of emergency, a report of breaking news.

"Maybe there's a wildfire," I said—always a fear in those days. "Either that or the president got assassinated."

The next image took us by surprise: it was the face of our father filling the television screen. He was wearing his sport jacket and a tie and standing at a podium in a room that appeared to be filled with reporters.

Our father. *On television.* We didn't even get to see him that much in real life, and now there he was, up on the screen.

We had no idea what he was saying, naturally. His face looked serious, the way it had when Patty broke her arm trying to ride a borrowed skateboard down a hill—first time she'd ever ridden one. Though even now, seeing him this way, I was aware of how handsome our father was. It seemed appropriate that he would be on television, like he belonged there.

"Something bad must have happened," Patty said. Maybe a bank robbery or a high-speed chase and a crash somewhere out on 101. Only those were more the kind of crimes the ordinary police took care of. Not the detectives.

I had never wished harder that we had cable, so we could watch TV like normal people and know what our father was talking about. This was one time when making up pretend things for a person to be saying on the screen was completely unsatisfactory.

"We could knock on the Pollacks' door and ask if we could watch," Patty said. Only then they'd know we'd been looking in the window, and anyway, by the time we got through all that, our father would probably be done saying whatever it was he was saying now, and they'd be back to *Brady Bunch.*

We could ask our mother what was going on. Only we wouldn't. Long ago we'd learned, whenever possible, to keep her out of things.

So we just sat there, taking it in the best we could: the sight of our tall, strong, handsome father speaking to the reporters. Whatever he was talking about, you could tell it wasn't good news.

Right at this point we heard a low noise overhead, but growing louder, till it was a roar almost directly overhead: a helicopter. The helicopter was hovering over the mountain.

When the special report was over, we gathered up our blanket. But we didn't head back to the house the way we ordinarily would at that hour. Though it was mostly dark by this point, we trudged up the hillside that led to the outer reaches of the open space and the trail—one of dozens—that led to the peak of Mount Tamalpais, and the sound of the helicopter.

Somewhere off in the distance I could make out the static from a two-way radio—police, from the sound of it—and still that roaring engine, and blades spinning, low enough that they actually blew our hair around. A couple of police officers were standing near a trailhead, talking with a group of people carrying flashlights. We walked over to them.

"What's going on?" I asked. Patty, holding the blanket, was pressed up next to me. In situations like this it was up to me to do the talking.

"You two shouldn't be out here," one of the men said. "A girl went missing on the trail yesterday. At first they were treating it as a runaway, but someone found a bloody sock. They've asked for volunteers to carry out a search."

"Like maybe a coyote got her?" Patty could only whisper. At least once a year, someone's cat or dog would go missing, and for a few days the neighborhood would be papered with flyers showing her picture and advertising a five-dollar reward. Then the news: another mauled animal body had been found on the mountain. Could be a coyote. Could be a mountain lion or a cougar.

"Dad doesn't investigate when it's animals," I told my sister. "When they call Dad in, it's because there's been a murder."

The next day they found the body of Charlene Gray lying in a thicket of young madrone just below the Steep Ravine Trail, near where it intersected with Little Salmon Creek. She was twenty-one, newly graduated from San Francisco State, and breaking in a new pair of hiking boots, her boyfriend said, in preparation for a trip the two of them were planning on making down the Pacific Coast Trail.

The details we picked up—that she was naked, except for one sock, with tape over her eyes, and in a position that suggested she'd been on her knees, as if begging— were not the kinds of things our father would ever have shared with us, or our mother either. This information we learned the next day from a girl from my class named Alison Kerwin, who had never shown any interest in being friends, before, but called me up shortly after the press conference—his second in a twenty-four-hour period—in which our father announced that the victim's death had been ruled a homicide.

She was the coolest girl in our class and had been even before the Elvis Costello song. Someone had spread a rumor at school that it was written about her, and a few kids actually believed that.

"I saw your dad on television," Alison said. "It must be cool having a real detective for a dad."

When I didn't say anything, she went on.

"The killer raped her too. Sometimes these types of sickos have sex with a person when they're already dead, but my mom said she was probably still alive when he did it. I guess there's some kind of test they do where they can tell the difference, but you probably already know that."

Again, I said nothing. Mainly because I had nothing to say.

"If anybody ever tries to do that to you," she said, "you should close your eyes. That way you won't know what they look like and they might not think they had to kill you.

"But your father probably already told you that too," she added. "And a whole bunch of other tips, I bet. I'd feel really safe having him around right now, with that killer on the loose."

I didn't mention that my father wasn't around, exactly. Not now, or before the murder either. The difference was that now we could see him on television.

He called us the next day. It always felt like a big deal, getting a phone call from our father.

"I guess you heard there's been some trouble up on the mountain," he said. "I don't want you and your sister to be scared, but I know you two like to spend time up there. You need to steer clear of there for a while."

"We always go on the mountain," I told him. "That's where we play."

Only to my father would I admit to playing. At school, most girls spoke of hanging out, but the truth was, I didn't have friends at school, and neither did my sister. Who we had was each other, and we still played together all the time. Mostly on the mountain.

"Just until we get this guy locked up, I need you to keep away from there," he said. "You need to promise me you'll stay around the yard."

I said we would, but with my fingers crossed. There was no way Patty and I were going to remain inside all day on our long-awaited summer vacation. Some kids—Alison Kerwin, for instance, and most of the girls in my class at school—hung out at the mall, or the rec center pool, unless they were off at camp or taking trips with their families to Disneyland, or Lake Tahoe, but in Patty's and my case, it was up to us to make up ways to pass the time. The mountain was our favorite place.

"What are we supposed to do, Dad?" I said. Maybe I was hoping he'd suggest we spend a little time with him at his apartment in the city, though I knew this was unlikely.

"Bake cookies. Go to the library. Play Monopoly," he said. "You're smart girls, you'll think of something. Help your mother. Learn Morse code."

"What did that guy do to the girl on the mountain?" I asked him. "Was it someone that used to be in love with her, and then she dumped him?"

"You don't need to be thinking about those things, Farrah," he told me.

He called me that a lot in those days, not that I resembled the actress in any way. But Patty and I liked to pretend we were Charlie's Angels. Sometimes, if we had made up a scenario where we pretended one of our neighbors was really a bank robber, or an international spy, I'd tell her, "Go get him, Bree," and she'd take off like a shot, though of course she never actually used her jujitsu moves on anybody but our father or me.

"Do you have some good clues?" I said. Our father didn't talk about his cases, but asking was a way of feeling close to him, and special.

"Don't fill your head up with this mess, baby," he said. "Take it from a guy who does. It's not good for you."

"I know you'll get him," I said. "You always do."

"Just stay off that mountain," he told me.

The spot where they'd found the body of Charlene Gray lay on the side of the mountain close to where we lived—a part frequented by hikers, though there were fewer of them in those days than later, when the idea of suiting up with special poles and shoes and shirts made out of interesting materials that didn't absorb sweat got really fashionable. You might see half a dozen people heading up the trail on a Saturday. Or only two.

There was a parking area a half mile down our street, and a second parking area with a ranger station partway up the mountain, but it was also possible to access the trails—miles of them, going out in all directions— from behind our house. The day after they'd found the body, two officers appeared in the neighborhood, canvassing the residents of our development to ask if anyone had seen a suspicious character two days earlier, heading toward the trails, or away from them. Nobody had anything to offer from the looks of things.

After that one call he made, following the discovery of the body, in which he'd told us to stay away from the mountain, Patty and I did not hear from our father for many days—and knowing how busy he'd be with the case, and how seldom he called even when he wasn't busy, we didn't expect to. From our neighbor Jennifer Pollack, whom we'd run into when she was pushing Karl Jr.'s stroller shortly after the police had questioned her, we learned they appeared to have no description to go on. But a man wandering down from the mountain alone would have stood out, so it was worth asking around.

It was not lost on Patty and me—in fact, we dwelled on this realization—that we spent more time on the mountain than just about anybody. Maybe the murderer was someone who knew Charlene Gray and had a particular reason to want to harm her, but if this had been a random killing, I pointed out to Patty, we could have been the victims.

Suppose we'd chosen that day to hike up to the ranger station, or venture into the eucalyptus grove on the mountain not far from our house for a game of

Truth or Dare or spies, or to sled down the hillside on a piece of cardboard as we liked to this time of year when the grass got brown and dry enough to slide on. The picture came to me of the two of us, holding hands and running as fast as we could down the steepest part, until one of us tripped and we fell down on top of each other, rolling and laughing. Looking up then, into the face of a man, staring down at us.

What would we have done if he'd nabbed us? From the jujitsu moves our father had taught us, we knew that a kick in the balls was one sure way to throw off a male attacker, at least momentarily, but very likely he'd recover well enough to carry on with his assault after a few seconds. Unless she could deliver a hard blow to her attacker's Adam's apple—not likely in our case—a person would need more than one good kick to stop a murderer.

We were fast runners—and there were two of us. But suppose he caught up with one. Me, probably, since Patty ran faster?

"I'd throw poison oak leaves on him?" she offered. Patty was fearless about physical challenges, but not always the best problem solver.

"When he had me in a headlock, I'd bite him," I said—a tactic I'd learned from *Charlie's Angels*. "You'd come up from behind with a rock and bash him."

"Then once we had him unconscious we'd run home and call Dad."

"Too risky. The guy might come to and get away while we were off making the call."

"I'd keep an eye on him while you were gone," Patty said. It was like her to disregard any thought of danger in a situation like that.

"We'd take his clothes first, so he'd be too embarrassed to go anyplace," I told her, not that being naked ever stopped my sister. "Then we'd tie him up with vines."

"I wouldn't want to look at his bare butt," Patty said. The rest—those even more alarming or more likely comical body parts—was more than she could speak of, though on other occasions (when the object of our curiosity seemed sexy enough) we had been known to contemplate them. Tying up someone like Peter Frampton with his clothes off, for instance, or (after we saw *Grease*, John Travolta)—and making him our slave—could have interested me.

"Sometimes you have to do this kind of thing, in the line of duty," I told her. "You think Dad hasn't ever had to do something gross like that?" The Angels didn't, but real life was different.

"He could get here pretty fast, once I told him what was going on," I said. "He'd turn on the siren in his glove compartment and bring backup."

We imagined the scene then: Our father in his black leather jacket, gold watch glinting in the sun, snapping handcuffs on the killer. The other officers leading the offender away as he shuffled down the hill, drool coming out of his mouth. As he passed Patty and me, he'd spit out some curse words, but we'd just laugh.

After, our father would lift us up and whirl us around—both at once, knowing how strong he was. "If something ever happened to you two . . ." he'd start, but he couldn't even finish the sentence. "What do you say the three of us go out for spaghetti and meatballs at Marin Joe's?"

We would get our favorite booth in the back, with the picture of Tony Bennett hanging on the wall behind us, and Gina Lollobrigida and Anthony Franciosa. The waitress would know our father, naturally. "A couple of beautiful daughters you got there, Anthony," she'd say. "You better keep your eye on those two."

"Any guy tries to get his hands on my girls," our father said, lighting his cigarette, "he's going to have to deal with me first."

In the interest of protecting the investigation, according to the *Marin Independent Journal*, Detective Torricelli was saying almost nothing about the particulars concerning the murder—what leads the police had uncovered, or if the killer had left clues. But in those first days after they located the body, there were a couple of articles about Charlene Gray, with a photograph of her at her senior prom and another of her and her brother at a Giants game, wearing their baseball caps backward and holding hot dogs. There was an interview with her boyfriend—initially a Person of Interest but swiftly eliminated as a suspect—in which he talked about Charlene's love of hiking, as well as the students in the church youth group she led, the music she listened to (the Carpenters), and her collection of stuffed koala bears.

Except for the one sock, she had been naked when they found her. No mention in the article of whether her clothes had been left at the scene of the crime. My father was quoted in the article, explaining that for reasons of pursuing the investigation effectively, the sheriff's department was not at liberty to divulge information about the crime scene.

For three full days after the murder, police swarmed the mountain near our house. It wasn't something either of our parents shared with us, but we knew why they were there. Our father had told us stories in the past about how he approached a crime scene—if it happened in a house, the importance of not disturbing a single piece of furniture, or even the position of a coffee cup on a table, a cigarette butt in an ashtray, or even the ash. The breakthrough that led a detective to his suspect might be nothing more than a hair. Nothing more than an eyelash.

"First thing I do when I arrive at the scene," he told us, "is nothing. Just stand there a long time, taking it in. You only get one chance for that. Once the homicide team gets to work, everything changes. I need to lock in the picture of how it was the moment it happened."

Now the crime scene was our own backyard, practically. As good a job as we knew our father would do, collecting evidence, it seemed obvious we should try to locate something ourselves. This was our Charlie's Angels moment at last.

There was no point attempting to survey the precise spot where the murder occurred. The homicide squad would have combed over that patch of ground and the surrounding area a million times and no doubt were still going over every inch of it. We needed to adopt a different strategy for our investigation.

As always, I was the one in charge, with Patty my loyal follower. "I have to be quiet for a while," I told her. "I need to work on this."

My sister understood what I meant. I was going into my zone—a very different one from our father's. Less focused on the physical. More about feelings. My father looked at the outside world to provide clues. I looked inside myself.

There was a thing I could do sometimes, though up to that point only on certain unforeseen occasions. I saw things before they happened. Or after they happened, even if I wasn't present at the time. I had powers. Or believed I did. Others might be skeptical, but Patty never doubted that this was so.

All my life—as long as I could remember it at least—pictures had come to me. *The visions,* Patty and I called them. They might be images of people I knew, or people I'd never met. Sometimes a scene that took place in the past would play out for me like an old movie, but only in my head. Other times I'd glimpse some moment in the future. I'd hear a voice talking, telling me something, or possibly speaking to a whole other person, a little like how it was back when there were party lines and you'd pick up the phone and listen in on someone else's conversation. Only these conversations didn't come through the phone lines. They entered directly into my brain.

On other occasions it might be no more than a feeling. *Trust this person.* Or *This one is bad news.*

Our mother recognized and accepted this gift of mine. She understood that on occasion I'd come out with observations or remarks that seemed to suggest I had access to some other sense beyond the usual five.

"Even as a baby, you'd know when the telephone was going to ring," our mother had told me. "Sometimes you'd run to the door at some odd hour and stand there. A minute later, your father would show up. Even though it wasn't his usual time to come home."

There had been an earthquake once, when I was in third grade or maybe fourth—nothing major, but enough to knock some dishes off a shelf. The morning of the day it happened, I told our mother we should take them down.

"Your blue mug's going to break if you don't," I told her.

Now every time she used that cup, with the glue showing from where she repaired the handle, I knew she thought about it.

Once, on an errand with my mother, dropping off a pair of loafers at the shoe repair shop, I had started crying. I told her I was worried about Pete, the shoemaker who used to give me a candy when we stopped in.

Two weeks later when we went back to pick up the shoes, there was a sign on the door to say the business was closed. DEATH IN THE FAMILY.

My visions didn't pop up all the time—or even often—but on certain rare occasions a feeling would come over me, as if I'd floated into another time zone ahead of the one we were located in, and all of a sudden

I'd see something as clear as a photograph in *Life* magazine.

No discernible pattern existed to the kinds of pictures that came to me: Helen's husband, Tubby, getting that heart attack. My mother bringing home a gallon of chocolate ice cream. A Volkswagen bus pulling up in front of the Gunnersons' house and their hippie son who hadn't paid a visit in two years getting out. (One day later, there he was, though his car turned out to be a Datsun.)

I imagined myself walking past the principal's office at school and seeing my math teacher crying, a week before we found out they were firing her for stealing someone's wallet. I had a vision of Patty bringing home a bird she'd found on the mountain, and then she did. That night, a second vision came to me: we found the bird dead in the shoe box she'd placed it in. And there he was the next morning, lying still in the bed of grass she'd made for him.

More likely, an image would present itself that didn't come from anything in front of my own eyes at the time. I could be out on my bike with Patty, or in gym class, and all of a sudden I'd know what some other person was seeing—not simply know, but see through that person's eyes. The most disturbing moments occurred when I'd seem to enter the brain of a person I barely knew, or didn't know at all, except that now I understood what she was thinking about.

This could be nothing more than worrying about a pimple that was developing on her forehead. But it could be major too: I'd look at an ordinary-looking man in the supermarket, running his hand through his hair, and recognize that he was heading over to the house of some woman that wasn't his wife, whose husband was out of town, to go to bed with her, but that her husband would come home early and find them there. (Sex hung over everything now. I saw it wherever I looked.)

I'd observe a teenage girl, one aisle over at the mall where I was hanging out with my sister, and know there was a bottle of nail polish in the pocket of her jeans that she hadn't paid for. Purple. I'd see a woman standing at the bus stop and know: She had a miscarriage the week before. The baby her husband had wanted badly. The boy.

My father never liked to hear about my visions. In some ways this was out of character, because my father was, himself, a man who operated a lot on instinct—someone who followed leads that came from no discernible place but a gut sense he was onto something, which very often he was. Maybe part of his attitude concerning what I experienced came from not wanting to saddle me with the weight of some kind of otherworldly abilities that might in the end create sorrow or trouble for me, as perhaps they had for him. (He never said this, but I felt my father saw things too, though he just chalked it up to a detective's instincts.) Suppose I saw into the future, and what I saw was frightening? Better to believe it wasn't real.

So he offered alternative explanations. There had been minor tremors for days leading up to that quake, he said. Pete the shoemaker had been so old he was bound to die before too long. If a person predicts the phone's about to ring often enough, she's bound to get it right now and then.

"What you observe in Rachel," he said to our mother, back when they were still together, "is how perceptive she is. She's tuned in to her gut, and she's a great observer. These are traits of a good detective, incidentally. She's watched my comings and goings so well she's gotten a feel for when I'm likely to come home. Even if it's not the same time every day."

I had not mentioned, then, the other time I saw an event happening before it did. The night our mother found the key in our father's pocket and knew who it belonged to. The crying I heard through the thin walls of our house, and our father's low voice, saying little, denying nothing. Then gone, that same night. My vision had not revealed the woman's face, but I knew she'd have black hair.

Of all the people acquainted with my abilities to tune in to some other place besides the one we inhabited, Patty was the most fervent and steadfast in her conviction that they were real. In the past, my sister and I had considered the possibility that my gifts might be put to use in the purchase of winning lottery tickets or (if we could only get someone to take us there) at the racetrack. But I'd explained to her that this was not a gift I could call on at will. I wasn't a fortune-teller. I was more like some CB operator, tuning the dial of his radio, picking up random frequencies. The moments when my powers presented themselves occurred spontaneously and seemed up to this point beyond my control. They could show up at any moment. They could also fail to do so.

Now, though, I sought to call on this gift of mine for the purpose of locating the killer of Charlene Gray and seeing to it that he was put behind bars—though more so, probably, out of a desire to demonstrate to our father what wonderful and helpful daughters he had, what great members of his team we were. I knew he'd love me—love us both—whether or not we helped him solve his case. But we wanted to be more than his precious little girls. We wanted to be his helpers and sidekicks, his secret weapon. We might not get to live with him anymore. But we'd be irreplaceable.

Where we lived, the only crimes you generally heard about—the kind they had laws against anyway—were things like driving under the influence or shoplifting. In his career in the city, my father had handled many murders—and once, back in his days as a beat cop, he had taken a bullet in a domestic dispute in which a husband had put a gun to his wife's head while she held their screaming baby.

But mostly—as with that one—these crimes occurred among people who knew each other already, where things got out of hand. Because murder interested me—and someday in the future, as a writer, I felt it would be important to understand the workings of the criminal mind—I'd followed the story, the summer before, of a series of killings of women in New York City by a man who called himself "Son of Sam." For a period of many weeks, it seemed as if people all over that city had been so terrified they hardly left their apartments at night.

"If you were on that homicide squad, you would have gotten him," I'd told our father. Patty and I believed he must be the smartest detective in America. The world probably.

"It's not always about the detective," he told us. "Sometimes you've got a killer on your hands who just doesn't give you much to work with. David Berkowitz was like that. You know how they got him in the end? A parking ticket."

"You would have figured something out," I said. "You always do."

"I'll tell you one thing," he said, lighting up a cigarette. "It must have been driving those New York homicide guys crazy, having that animal at large. Women showing up dead, and them not finding anything to go on. For a copper, there's nothing worse."

Once when we were little, our father took us to the neighborhood where he grew up, in North Beach. He showed us the corner where his father's barbershop used to be, and his family's apartment, the place where his mother used to hang the laundry out. That was in the early years, before she ran away. After that it was just him and his pop.

He seemed different in his old neighborhood. Walking down Columbus Street, he had a kind of nervous energy to his step. People knew him in this neighborhood, and not just the women. A couple of old-timers greeted him in Italian.

"God, I love this place," he said. "People that knew me when I was young would never believe it, that I'd end up living in a town where you can't buy a decent cannoli."

We didn't know what that was, so we kept quiet.

On our way home, we pulled into an observation area just south of the Golden Gate Bridge. Holding his hand—one of us on each side—we walked across it. "Who would ever think of painting a bridge red?" our father said. "That's the great thing about this city. That and a few million other things.

"I should bring you here more often," he said. But except for the handful of nights we spent on the hideaway bed at his apartment after the divorce, he hardly ever did.

Back in his days as a San Francisco cop, our father had handled some scary situations, but after the divorce from our mother, he'd taken the Marin County job. Patty and I both knew he'd missed the excitement of the city.

So I knew it was good news for him, in an odd way, that he had a real murder to work on for a change.

It made him angry, knowing someone got killed—especially a woman, most of all a young one. But I could also tell from his voice on the phone when he told us there'd been a killing that he was charged up. This was the kind of moment our father lived for—what he did best—and he'd waited a long time for a case that would call on his best abilities. If there was ever a moment for my father to be a hero, this was it.

Somewhere just beyond our house, no more than a mile away, a man had lurked in the brush, waiting for a girl not that much older than my sister and me—to have sex with her. He was willing to kill her to get that. Maybe he was out there still. Or safe at home someplace, believing he'd got away with what he'd done. Maybe he was even stretched out in some Barcalounger like Helen's, watching the latest news reports about the murder, thinking how smart he was.

Only now the killer had Detective Anthony Torricelli on his tail—olive skinned, smart as a fox, and lithe as a jaguar—in that black leather jacket that he always wore, even when the weather turned hot. I could see him now, cigarette in hand, poring over clues and possible leads, tracking license plates and makes of cars, interviewing the boyfriend probably, or the ex-boyfriends, interviewing gas station attendants and hitchhikers who might have been passing through the area at the time of the murder, studying plaster casts of shoe imprints found near the crime scene. But mostly, though he was never the hiking type, he'd be endlessly making his way along the trails himself, back and forth, back and forth, in search of anything—a broken twig, the fiber from a pants leg—that might lead him to the killer.

There was no doubt in my mind my father would find him.

Two days after Charlene Gray's murder, Patty and I tromped up to a place we knew, a rock outcropping a little ways up the mountain, in the hopes of my communing with the dead girl's spirit, and thereby uncovering information concerning her murder. Patty carried a tin can from which we'd removed both the top and the bottom. Uneasy though my sister was around fire, but ready as always to follow my instructions, she stuck it in the ground and piled dry grass inside, while I struck the match. Not having many other options to choose from, she sang a verse of "Kumbaya."

I folded myself into the lotus position and closed my eyes, with my fingers in a position I'd seen on a TV show Jennifer Pollack watched sometimes, *Lilias, Yoga and You*. I took a deep breath and held it. Slow exhale. Another breath.

I could smell the smoke of the burning grass and hear my sister's own more shallow breath beside me. Farther off, the sound of birds overhead, and the faint murmur of male voices higher up on the trail. (Police officers, probably. Not so far off, though beyond sight. In search of the same thing we were.)

I sat there for a long time, waiting. In times past, pictures had sometimes come to me with a stunning clarity—pictures of things that happened or were going to happen—but this time none did. I could almost feel my brain hurting, I was trying that hard to locate anything that might offer up some clue.

Girl ties shoelaces, fills water bottle, sets out on hike. Girl stops to apply insect repellent, adjusts strap on canteen. Man approaches. Asks the time maybe? Asks if she has bug spray he can borrow. She reaches in her pack.

Girl sits on rock. Takes out granola bar. Takes swig from canteen. Realizes need to pee. Heads to the ranger station. Sees man.

Maybe he was chewing gum that day. The whole time it was going on, his jaw kept working it. Maybe it took his mind off things, having that gum in his mouth.

"You want a stick of gum?" he says. "Cinnamon. My favorite."

Once, long ago, in our parents' bedroom, I'd found a book called *The Joy of Sex,* with drawings in it of men and women naked together. After our father moved out, the book disappeared, but now, to get my vision started, I tried to conjure images. Without the joy part. Nothing.

That gum again. After, he'd want to get rid of it. A wad of gum always ended up tasting bad once you'd chewed it for a while. Once he was finished with the girl, he wouldn't need it anymore. He'd have that taste in his mouth you get when you've had a wad in there for too long. Never mind the particular associations on this occasion.

"We need to go to the ranger station," I told Patty.

It was a half hour's hike up, and the sun was high by now, but my sister didn't complain, though she did ask once if I had M&M's or saltines in my pocket, which I had neglected to bring along.

Normally we would have passed at least a few hikers on the trail, but that day, none. When we reached the ranger station, we spotted one police officer talking on a radio, but no apparent investigative activity under way.

"When you're finished with your gum, and you're in a place like this where you don't want to be a litter-bug, what do you do with it?" I asked Patty.

"Throw it down the toilet?"

"Possibly," I told her. "Me, I might stick it under the water fountain."

I bent over the spigot then, slid my fingers over the metal housing beneath. With the first one, nothing, but my sister pointed out a second fountain, next to the men's room. (The men's room. Of course. He would have stopped there too.)

I watched her reach her fingers underneath the stainless steel bowl of the fountain, feeling around. I could see from her face that she'd located something. Now she handed me a wad of gum, grayish in color, which made sense. Only girls chose strawberry, or grape.

I hadn't thought to bring a Baggie, but I had a gum wrapper of my own in my pocket to wrap it in.

"Good work," I told her. Not that we knew what we'd do with our evidence. "Now wash your hands."

After, we started back down the mountain. The sun was getting lower in the sky now, making a golden glow on the hillside, and the California poppies were out. Partway down the trail, my sister stopped still and got down to her knees, in a way I recognized from a hundred other times with her on the mountain. She was studying an owl pellet.

She cupped the small, dry brownish-gray lump in her palm, then held it out to me, breaking it apart to reveal the evidence of fur and tiny, twiglike fragments of bone. With two fingers, she picked out a single hair, smaller than an eyelash.

"Mouse," she said, her face a combination of interest and regret.

"He waited till she was dead to have sex with her," I told my sister.

"He's afraid of girls. That's why he had to kill her first."

This time I hadn't tried; the picture just appeared, as clear as the bits of mouse skeleton in my sister's palm. *A man's hands—thick, chubby fingers—working her shirt over her floppy head, unzipping her pants. Burrowing in her pubic hair.* I didn't want to, but I saw the next part too.

I could hear him breathing, in that labored way some people have, if they're very old, or overweight, or they suffer from emphysema or asthma. Or maybe just from being out of breath.

His fingernails were well tended, almost as if he'd had a manicure. Smooth skin, like a person unaccustomed to manual labor or spending time outdoors. Though he'd ventured here, out on the mountain. He'd passed this very spot.

We walked home in silence—my hand in my pocket, around the wad of gum, my sister with her own treasure: those tiny precious fragments of mouse skeleton, encased in fur.

For weeks we'd been planning to spend Fourth of July weekend with our father in the city: see *Alien*, go out to dinner. The Thursday before the long weekend he called to tell us that it wasn't going to work out for our visit. Some problems had come up at work, he said. He didn't talk about the murder, but we knew that was it.

We kept seeing him on television, and some statement by him appeared almost every day in the pages of the *Marin IJ* that Patty delivered on her paper route. Every day now, she'd bring home an extra copy of the paper, where we were likely to see his name, if not his photograph.

Our father had always been like a movie star to my sister and me, but now he was a celebrity in the whole county and the Bay Area beyond it. He always looked so brave and reassuring, standing at the podium at those press conferences, fielding questions. He and his team were doing everything they could, he said, to locate the killer. If anyone had any information that could help (maybe they'd been on the mountain that day and seen someone suspicious, remembered a make of vehicle parked alongside the road?), they should call the Homicide Division hotline. He would personally see to it that every single possible lead was investigated. No stone unturned.

Whenever he appeared in the paper, we cut out his picture and stuck it on the bulletin board in our room, alongside all the others of movie stars and rock musicians. On the transistor radio in our room—in between the endless replays of "My Sharona" and "Summer Love"—we could turn on the news and know the announcer would have some comment by Detective Torricelli concerning the murder on the mountain. Our father had become the hero of the county. Our name was famous.

There was an outdoor pool we sometimes went to at the rec center a couple of miles from our house. We didn't own passes like most kids in our neighborhood, but you could usually sneak in if you waited for a bunch of people to come in a clump. We didn't go often, knowing it was a hangout for the popular kids, and neither of us qualified. But the temperature had stayed in the nineties all that week, and they'd taped off access to the mountain behind our house, making it impossible to hang out there.

So we rode our bikes over to the pool. We figured we'd splash around there, or more likely, work on our tans. Hot as it was, I kept a shirt on over my swimsuit, to cover up my lack of a bustline.

We didn't expect it that as soon as we laid out our towels Alison Kerwin would come over to our spot. She sat on the ground next to me, peeling the paper off her Creamsicle.

"I saw your dad on TV again last night," she said. "He's so cool."

I told her thanks, though it seemed strange to me, thanking a person for something nice they said about a member of your family. As if you had anything to do with it.

"He probably tells you all the grisly details they don't put in the paper," she said. She was sitting there in her sunglasses on her towel, wearing a string bikini. I hated it that all I had was a one-piece from a box of hand-me-downs given to our mother by a coworker at the insurance agency where she worked. From where I sat on the grass, I could see Alison's toes, with their pearly silver polish. A professional job, from the looks of it. This was the second occasion she had spoken to me since the murder. Before that, the only time she'd acknowledged my existence had been to check my hall pass when she was Hall Monitor of the Week.

"There were bite marks on her neck," I said. "And he cut off one of her fingers." No special psychic vision this time, just words that came out of my mouth from someplace I barely recognized. A pure invention, though it was the song with her name in it that gave me the idea. That part my sister and I never understood, where Elvis Costello sang about the fingers in the wedding cake.

Now Patty looked at me but said nothing. I knew she would never betray me, which made me feel guilty about how I felt at the time, myself: Embarrassed to be seen with her. Wishing she was someplace else.

"But don't tell anyone," I said. "They don't want that part in the papers. It could create a panic."

Alison nodded. "You want to come over to my house later?" she said. "Or do you have to look after her?" She gestured in the direction of Patty, who was listening hard though she wouldn't let on.

The development where Alison lived was out by the golf course, in an area called Peacock Gap. To get home from the pool, Patty would need to cross the highway on her own. She was eleven, and tall for her age, but I knew getting to the other side of that highway was scary for her. Always in the past, I'd held her hand when we crossed. We pretended there were bad guys after us, and gunfire. It was one of our Angels moments. "I'll cover you, Bree," I'd say, and then we'd run for it.

Alison was getting up to go now. "There could be some boys coming over," she said. "Teddy Bascom probably. You know where I live, right?"

"My sister's okay on her own," I said, though in all the years, I'd hardly ever left her. Patty, hearing this, said nothing.

Of all the boys in our grade, Teddy Bascom was the coolest. He was one of the best basketball players—one of the showiest anyway—but his particular claim to fame was karate, where he'd competed at the state level and brought home a trophy that we heard about on the announcements at school. He had a deep voice before any of the other boys did, and when he raised his arms executing a jump shot, you could see the hair in his armpits.

He'd been my lab partner one time, in sixth grade, for a fruit fly experiment. I still remembered the comments he'd made about fruit flies having sex, and the strangely stirring effect this had on me.

"I could kill him with one kick if I wanted," he said, speaking of our biology teacher, Mr. Long. This was during that brief period when the two of us worked on the fruit fly project together—my work mostly—and Mr. Long had accused Teddy of doing nothing but putting his name on the report, which was true, not that I'd minded.

Apart from this, I'd never breathed the same air as he did.

That afternoon at the rec center, I didn't get my hair wet, knowing I'd be headed over to Alison Kerwin's house and that Teddy Bascom would be there. Patty had wanted to play Marco Polo with me, but I said I wasn't in the mood. I lay on my towel for a while, after Alison and the others left, with my copy of *A Tree Grows in Brooklyn* open to the same page, not wanting to look obvious about following them.

"I guess I'll stop by Alison's," I told my sister.

"I thought we were going to go back on the mountain to look for clues," Patty said. We had placed the wad of gum from our information-gathering expedition in a jewelry box, along with a notebook we'd started, labeled "Murder Investigation." When we got something really good, we'd turn the whole thing over to our father.

"Can't you ever do anything by yourself?" I told her. Even as I said this, I knew I was being mean.

Patty hardly ever complained about anything I did. She was like the most loyal dog, the kind who follows her master in a snowstorm even if it means she'll freeze to death, or goes into a burning building to lead her to safety or die at her side, whichever. Now, though, her mouth was tight in that way she had that was about more than simply concealing her overbite. "You'll be fine," I told her. "Mom should be home in a couple of hours." As if this meant anything. I could see from Patty's face she wasn't happy, but she left.

The Kerwins had one of those refrigerators with an ice dispenser on the front that gives you crushed ice, and a whole pantry filled with sodas. Alison's bed had a canopy, and there was a vanity table next to it with all kinds of makeup and a little metal tree holding earrings. But the place we hung out that afternoon was the rec room, where there were beanbag chairs and a Ping-Pong table and a real jukebox filled with 45s. The boys mostly leaned on the jukebox, punching in songs, while the girls lay on the couch.

"It must be so exciting having a detective for a dad," one of them said—a girl named Sage whose father owned a company that manufactured corrugated boxes. "Like your life's a TV show."

"Does he wear his gun under his clothes?" Alison said. "Even around you?"

"Shoulder holsters are just for characters on TV shows," I told her. "Real police officers wear their gun strapped to their ankle."

"At least you know you're safe," the girl named Soleil—Alison's best friend—offered. "The killer's never going to try anything with the daughter of the detective in charge of the whole thing."

"Not necessarily," Alison pointed out. "He could take her hostage, to make a statement. Like, 'I dare you to come after me. I've got your kid.'"

I said I didn't really worry about that. The other girls seemed focused on the killer. I was more focused on them and worried I'd do something uncool, which was pretty much inevitable.

"Does your dad think the murderer's still in the area?" Soleil asked. Once, back in fourth grade, when she'd first come to our school, I pronounced her name wrong, though everybody now knew it was French for sun.

"It's just a matter of time before he strikes again," I told them. "Once they get a taste of blood, they always come back for more."

Three weeks after the disappearance of Charlene Gray, a twenty-three-year-old named Vivian Cole set out late one afternoon on a hiking trail on the far side of Mount Tamalpais in search of wildflowers to press for handmade notecards. She was reported missing. Her body turned up on Mount Tamalpais next to a stream on the Matt Davis Trail. We found out about that one when Patty ran into our neighbor Helen taking out her trash.

"Your dad must be one busy fellow these days," she said. "Everybody's counting on him to put this terrible person behind bars."

The county was still taking in the news of Vivian when Daniella Carville and Sammi Raynor, best friends since grade school, and about to enter their senior year in high school, disappeared somewhere between the parking lot where they'd left their bicycles and the East Peak of the Bolinas Ridge, where the brother of one of the girls had sprinted up ahead, waiting to meet them for a picnic they would never share. It was the second week of August, and brutally hot.

Their bodies turned up a few hours later, just after sundown—strangled (and raped, no doubt) with that same electrical tape over their eyes, arranged in the same begging position as the one in which Charlene Gray and Vivian Cole had been found. That last information we learned when a reporter at the press conference led, once again, by our father, had called out, "Why do you think he makes them get down on their knees?" As if there could be any good reason.

This time, I actually managed to see our father's press conference on television. I had gotten a job babysitting for the Pollacks, who were headed to the city for the afternoon and left us in charge of Karl Jr. I had figured out from evidence in the Pollack home—the fact that Karl Pollack no longer kept a stash of condoms in his bedside table the way I'd observed in the past, and a chart on the refrigerator listing her temperature every day for the last seven weeks, and an appointment reminder card on the counter for a medical office, with a picture of a smiling baby on it—that Jennifer Pollack must be trying to have another baby.

I was fixing Karl Jr.'s lunch when the phone rang: it was Jennifer's mother, calling to tell her daughter to turn on the television set. When I told her my name, she seemed to know who I was.

"What do you know? Your father's on TV right now, talking about the most recent murders. Two more girls dead, out on the trails, can you believe it?" she said. "I sure hope your dad's got some good clues to catch this maniac before he strikes again."

The first murder had been terrible enough. But not surprisingly, the news of three more killings within the space of less than six weeks seemed to have left the entire population of the county in a state of panic. Mothers drove their children to the pool now (all mothers but ours) rather than letting them ride their bikes, and practically overnight the trails behind our house, where we used to see hikers setting out on weekends, were mostly empty.

Back when the first murder took place, a person might have held out hope that the killing of Charlene Gray was some isolated event, but with the discovery of Vivian's body, and Daniella's and Sammi's, it had become clear that we had a serial killer on the mountain (the mountain and the extensive trail system that wove beyond it, over a stretch of nearly fifty miles). If he had killed four young women, there was no reason to suppose he would not kill more.

The media were all over the story, of course. One of the papers, demonstrating its penchant for alliteration, dubbed the killer "the Sunset Strangler," referring to the general time of day the four bodies had been found. The girls might have been killed at any time during the day, but somehow the image of the sinking sun lent an extra note of poignancy to the growing scandal.

I could see, from my father's face at the press conference, and even more so from his voice, the pressure he was under now. There he was again, up on the screen—looking grave and purposeful, so handsome in his sport coat, with his sideburns and his jet-black hair, his big hands gripping the sides of the podium. I hated what was happening, but I loved being his daughter—and this would have been so even if it hadn't resulted in my sudden and unexpected rise in social status with the likes of Alison Kerwin and her friends.

In art class the year before, when we did ceramics, I had made a medallion with the words *World's Best Dad* inscribed and a hole that I threaded with a silk cord and gave him for Father's Day. Maybe, in certain ways, he wasn't the world's best dad, but he had promised he'd wear my gift every day. Watching my father now on the television screen, I thought I could detect the shadow of the medallion under his shirt. I liked thinking that every day, when he stood in front of the mirror getting ready for work, he fastened that cord around his neck.

Hearing him as he made his statement to the press, I had no doubt that my father would find the killer very soon—my magic father, stronger than anyone else's. Whenever I heard his voice, it seemed to carry the promise that everything would be okay.

"I stand before the people of Marin County today," he said, "to assure you that, along with every member of our dedicated force, I will not rest until the perpetrator is brought to justice. We will find him, and once we do, we'll see to it they lock him up forever, so the women of this county and everyone who cares about them—which is everyone—can sleep soundly again."

There were a million questions. What weapon had been used to commit the murders? Had anybody spotted a suspicious character on the mountain that day? Did the killer leave any evidence—footprints, an item of clothing? Was there any relationship between these most recent victims and the first one?

Only that they were young and female and—from the photographs displayed on the screen—all of them dark haired and good-looking.

A reporter asked how anyone could feel safe in Marin County with a serial killer at large. My father said they were posting police officers on all the hiking trails now, as a safety measure. "If you want to enjoy the trails," he said, "do so in a larger group, preferably in the company of a male. We're speaking of a ruthless individual, single-handedly capable of murdering two women at the same time, from the looks of it."

"Given that four girls have now been murdered within a matter of weeks," a woman asked, "we have to ask: Is the police force taking these crimes with sufficient seriousness?"

"I have two daughters of my own," my father said. "Nobody needs to remind me of the urgency here to find this man and make the mountain safe again."

This was us he was talking about, on television—Patty and me. I felt a glow of pride, hearing our father speak of us this way. He was thinking about us, looking out for us. Of all the fathers, all the police officers—all the detectives, even—they had chosen our father as the one to stand up in this place and reassure everyone, because he was the strongest and the best. And he belonged to us alone.

They put up signs at all the trailheads. CLOSED, BY ORDER OF THE MARIN COUNTY HOMICIDE DIVISION. HIKER ADVISORY: PROCEED AT YOUR OWN RISK.

But Morning Glory Court was not connected by trail to the mountain. The mountain was just there, in our backyard. There was no way we were staying off it. Least of all now, when something exciting was finally happening there.

Looking now at pictures of our mother's young self, I can see she was a pretty woman, with a trim figure, slim ankles, and bouncing brunette curls. Knowing my father—a man incorrigibly drawn to beauty, with the endearing ability to locate what was beautiful in nearly every woman he met—it's not that surprising he would have struck up a conversation with her that first day they met. He was working on the city road crew, fixing a pothole just as she approached it on her old one-speed bicycle. Her glasses fell off and he picked them up. Picked them up and polished them.

She had been on her way home from her favorite place, then as now—the library. She was twenty-one years old—had never kissed a boy before—and she loved to read. For three years she'd been saving up money for college. Our dad was twenty-five, working two jobs while attending the police academy at night. Standing there on the sidewalk, holding out her glasses, he had actually started singing to her.

When he found out she was called Lillian, he made a song out of her name.

The affair would have lasted no more than a few weeks if my mother hadn't gotten pregnant. In fact, it may have been over already by the time she found out. I know she rode the bus to his house then, knocked at the door, was met by his Italian father, and introduced herself. Shy as she was, my mother had always possessed a strict sense of fairness and an unblinking eye when it came to seeing that a person did the right thing, or failed to do so.

Our father would have honored his responsibility and did. Their wedding—in church for the parents' sake, but a small ceremony, pulled off on a low budget—was set for the end of November 1963. The day after the Kennedy assassination, as it turned out. My father's mother had been gone for years by this point; his father would die of a heart attack the following spring. My grandmother on my mother's side, who'd kept JFK's photograph on her nightstand, wore black and wept through the ceremony.

"I don't know which fact about the day made her cry," my mother told us. "Everything, most likely."

Our mother had remained dry eyed. "I never trusted that man," she said, referring to Kennedy, I assume, though the remark could have been construed other ways. Even before all the stories about JFK's cheating came out later, she'd known. She maintained a strong affinity for Jackie, a woman she claimed to identify with, though the two could hardly have had less in common.

With a baby on the way, the college plan was scrapped. Three months later she suffered a miscarriage.

Our parents could have split up then, but something had changed. Where before my mother dreamed of college, and my father had his eye on a big career as a city homicide detective, in their grief and shock all they could think of was another baby.

My mother enrolled in secretarial school and got a job as a typist. Our father graduated from the police academy, joining the force around the time my mother finally got pregnant again, with me. From the photographs she had of that time—one of her and my father on a cable car, and another of her in a maternity dress and him with his hand on her stomach, grinning—I figured this must have been a period my parents were actually happy together.

One of my earliest memories concerns how handsome my father looked in his uniform—the sparkling
badge, shiny shoes, the hat he'd put on my head or
twirl with his finger or toss in the air and retrieve
without even seeming to try. Good as he looked in that
uniform, though, what he always wanted was to be a
plainclothes detective.

Plainclothes: hardly the word for how my father
dressed. Even in those days, when his salary was very
low, he paid regular visits to a tailor to make sure everything fit just right: a black leather jacket that showed
off his broad shoulders and narrow waist and hips;
shoes of the softest leather; a shirt of some very good
cotton, or sometimes silk. His pants were perfectly
pressed (ironing, the one domestic chore he performed,
other than cooking). His hair was black and shiny as
my tap shoes and he cut it himself, perfectly—a gift
he'd learned from his barber father.

I have no memory of my sister's birth, given that I
was not yet two years old when she was born. That's
when we moved to Marin County, the house on
Morning Glory Court. And all the other places that
made up the landscape of our childhood: Marin Joe's,
where our father took us for tiramisu. That wonderful
bridge—the Golden Gate—its implausibly red beams
spanning the dark and churning water of San Francisco

Bay. On one side, the glittering city. And on the other side, the mountain.

Always, before, it had been the city that conjured images of danger, while our side of the bridge remained a safe and sleepy haven. That summer, 1979, everything changed.

The fact that he was married to our mother—back when he still was—never got in the way of our father's expressing interest in other women. More than that. He didn't try that hard to conceal this, even from us. He never saw his appreciation for the opposite sex as anything to be ashamed of. That's how he was, and the rest of us should just accept it. Love him for it, even.

When we were out with our father, we were always bumping into women we'd never met before, who seemed to know our father well, or think they did.

Once, when I was walking down a street with him— heading to his office at the Civic Center—a woman had mistaken my father for Dean Martin (or claimed to anyway; that might have been her way of striking up a conversation). Oblivious to the presence of a little girl in a Brownie uniform holding his hand (or if she noticed, this didn't stop her), she'd told a long story about seeing him—meaning Dean—with Sammy and Frank one time in Las Vegas on an anniversary trip with her husband. They were divorced now, she told my father—that look in her eye I knew so well. That look in his.

He let her tell every detail of her trip to the Sands, not simply taking it in but conveying, as he always did, the impression that nobody, ever, had told him a more compelling story than this one. My father was not one to cut a woman's story short, and when it was over he asked if she was in show business herself.

"I was thinking you must be a dancer," he said. "It's something about how you hold yourself. There's nothing more attractive in a woman than good posture."

You had to believe him. Even when he said something that would probably sound like a line if delivered by anybody else; he had this unimpeachable sincerity about him. Our father could walk into any bar and find someone he knew, or if he didn't know them before, he would in five minutes. Men bought my father drinks and offered him cigarettes. Women flat-out adored him. Partly because he was handsome, but it was more than that. He was so unmistakably a man who loved women, which is a rarer kind of man to find than a person might think.

But there was one who occupied a different place for him than all the others, though neither Patty nor I could identify exactly what it was.

The first time I heard her name—a wail that pierced the night like the cry of a wounded animal and made my sister and me tremble in our beds—was the night our mother told our father to leave.

"Don't come back," she called out, into the night.

He didn't.

Margaret Ann. A year might have passed, after that night, in which her name was never spoken. And then it was.

It was one of our Saturdays. He'd picked us up in the Alfa he'd bought after moving out. He got the car used, from a buddy on the police force whose wife had a baby; all of a sudden a car with only two seats just wasn't practical. Not that having a couple of daughters stopped our father from taking us out in that car: he just buckled my sister and me in together in one bucket seat. We were skinny enough.

He'd taken us to the beach that day and set out bocce balls. (What other father did a thing like that? Only ours.) Now we were headed back up the highway. "Volare" had just come on the eight-track player. I was on the side next to the shift column, close enough to my father that I could smell his aftershave and play with the thick dark hair on his arms.

"I thought we'd stop by Margaret Ann's on our way home," he said. He said her name as if she'd been around forever. No explanation needed. *Margaret Ann.*

I felt something then, like what a field mouse might sense on the mountain in the moments just before a hawk dives down for him. I didn't ask "Who's Margaret Ann?" It seemed I should know.

She lived in an apartment complex on a lagoon somewhere in Corte Madera. There was a pool and a tennis court, which made me think she must be rich. She was wearing a dress that day we met her—and high-heeled shoes though it was the middle of the day, and she smelled like night-blooming jasmine.

When we got there, she had cookies on a plate, and Kool-Aid, already poured, with colored plastic bendy straws of the sort I'd always wanted us to buy, but that our mother said were a waste of money.

She was very pretty—slim, with dark hair that hung down her back in a way that the hair of our friends' mothers never did. In the car on the way over, my father had instructed us not to ask Margaret Ann if she had kids.

"It's a sore spot for her, girls," he told us. "Margaret Ann doesn't have any children."

She had a doll collection though, arranged in a glass case in her living room, and a music box that played the song from *Dr. Zhivago,* she told us, and a lemon tree with real lemons on it, and a little dog that looked like a combination of two breeds that never should have gotten together, with patchy fur that probably clogged up her vacuum cleaner. Patty kept that dog on her lap the whole time we were over at Margaret Ann's, naturally.

"This one's got your eyes, Tone," Margaret Ann said, as we seated ourselves around the table, nodding in my direction. She knew without asking that our father liked three scoops of sugar in his coffee.

We played cards, and I won, though it seemed to me that Margaret Ann might not be trying. She wanted to give us manicures and brought out a little silver tray with four different colors of nail polish. I would have liked to have her put some on me, but I didn't think it would go over well with our mother.

"No nail polish," I told Patty. She looked disappointed but did not argue.

"You girls can each pick out a doll," she told us. We'd been studying them closely already, in the cabinet. Close enough that Patty's breath had fogged up the glass.

This time the offer was too good to resist—even for Patty, though she was not generally a doll lover. "You take your time deciding," Margaret Ann said. "Choose whichever one you want."

She and our father went into some other room for a while then, and I could hear music playing there, a smoky-voiced woman, singing slow. The choosing was hard and took a while. I couldn't decide between a Spanish dancer with gold shoes that came off and a shepherd girl who came with a tiny miniature sheep. Patty liked the baby, even though I tried to talk her into a different one, so we could trade doll clothes. After, we got to turn on the television and watch cartoons. We sat on a mauve-colored love seat with needlepoint pillows and watched two whole shows before they came out and my father told us it was time to go. When we left, Margaret Ann hugged us for a surprisingly long time.

In the car on the way home, our father took a deep, slow drag on his Lucky.

"What did you think of Margaret Ann?" he said.

"She's okay."

"Not as pretty as Mom," Patty said, though we all knew this was untrue.

"She likes you two a lot," he said. "It probably made her a little sad seeing two great girls like you and not having her own little girl. But happy too, that you came over."

"She's nice," I said. The fact that this was so confused me and made me feel disloyal to our mother, who never made Kool-Aid.

"We might start seeing a lot more of her soon," my father said. "If that sounds okay with you two."

Patty had taken the diaper off the doll she'd picked out—taken it off, put it on, taken it off again about a hundred times in the car. This was the early days of Velcro, I think. She'd never seen it before. I was wondering what our mother was going to say about the dolls.

"Next time, maybe she can get us ice-cream sandwiches," Patty said. "We never get those at home."

I was right of course. Our mother spotted the dolls right off when we came in the door from our visit, even though I'd been planning to stuff them under the bed, quick. Uncharacteristically, she had been waiting on the steps for us.

"Go to your room," she said. "I need to talk with your father."

We weren't supposed to hear them, but we did.

"I draw the line at this, Anthony," our mother said. "Do what you want but keep my children out of your shenanigans."

"I need to move on with my life," he said. "You need to do that too. I want to marry Margaret Ann."

Scarier than words were our mother's silences.

"Make that choice and your daughters will never get over it," she said.

Our father had never seemed afraid of anything before. But he was afraid of our mother. Even more so, afraid of losing my sister and me.

———————

I called him up the next morning, at the number of his apartment in the city, but he wasn't there, and I knew now why he never was. He was at Margaret Ann's. I understood now: he was with her when we were not, which would mean he was with her most of the time.

I got my father's answering machine, but I was ready with my message.

"If you ever have any kids, besides Patty and me," I told him, "I will never speak to you again."

The Sunset Strangler had done wonders for my social standing. When the invitations to Alison's started that June, they were sporadic, but pretty soon it was an unspoken understanding that I'd meet the other girls at the pool most afternoons—and often, after, we'd go over to one of their houses. We'd play the radio (still "My Sharona," every twenty minutes, in rotation with Donna Summer's "Bad Girls" and Rod Stewart's "Do You Think I'm Sexy"). We read one another's horoscopes and tried on makeup, but we always ended up talking about the murders. When we did, I now felt the obligation—burdensome, at times, but also an interesting challenge for a girl like me, who planned to be a writer when she grew up—to come up with some new and chilling scrap of inside information about the crimes, known only to a handful of homicide detectives, and myself. (And the assembled group of girls, all of them sworn to secrecy.)

"He put lipstick on her mouth," I said. "After he killed her."

"He left a dead kitten next to her. Also a live snake."

"He said he'd turn himself in if Olivia Newton-John came to San Francisco and went to bed with him."

I was going to the pool almost every day now, and nearly always, after that, I'd head over to Alison's house with the other girls. Not always, but sometimes, Teddy Bascom stopped by, and though he paid little attention to me, just being in the same room with him was enough.

"I think he likes you," Alison told me. I couldn't get those words out of my head, not that I wanted to.

My sister stopped going to the pool with me. "What's the point?" she said. "You don't talk to me when I'm there."

"I just thought it would be good, making some friends," I told her. "You could do that too."

But we both knew she wouldn't. Patty spent her afternoons without me practicing basketball shots or cutting out pictures to paste in her scrapbook of

"Favorite Dogs." Our neighbor Mrs. Gunnerson had hired Patty to play Candy Land with her retarded daughter, Clara. She let Clara win.

Patty had sharp words about the type of person she believed Alison Kerwin to be, and—though she said nothing on this score—I knew she had a low opinion of Teddy Bascom too. She had watched him on the basketball court and said he was a dirty player. Always elbowing kids on the court, and hogging the ball when he should have passed, to make the glory shot, or talking about his karate dojo and some tournament he went to, where, according to him, a talent scout had said he should come down to Hollywood and get some head shots made. He could be the next Bruce Lee.

Still, my sister did not give up on me. When I came home now, from Alison's house or hanging out with Teddy, Patty was always out there on the curb waiting for me.

"I can't believe you want to spend all that time with those dumb kids," she said. "Can't you tell they're just a bunch of jerks?"

Patty had asked if I thought any reason existed for Alison being interested in being my friend, besides our father's sudden visibility on television as the head of the homicide investigation. I had conceded there probably was not. As for Teddy Bascom, thoughts of him now occupied a significant portion of my waking hours, though when Patty asked me if I thought he was a nice person, I had similarly conceded that no, he probably was not.

Still, that summer I lived for my visits to Alison's house. To ensure that my invitations there would continue, I was now regularly making up things to tell her and the others who came over to the Kerwins'— purportedly inside information about the murder investigation gleaned from my detective father, though in fact I barely ever heard from him these days.

"The guy left a Care Bear at the scene of the crime," I told them. "With all the stuffing pulled out."

"Before he left the crime scene, he peed."

"He drank her blood."

I spent my afternoons that summer pretending to be a cool and popular thirteen-year-old, but when I returned home and got back with Patty, we were weird, crazy girls again the way we used to be, and even at the time I recognized that the ideas my sister came up with, of things for us to do, and the adventures we cooked up together were invariably more interesting than the activities of Alison and her friends.

Point-blank my sister put the question to me: if being a popular girl meant sitting waiting for nail polish to dry, or listening to Teddy Bascom describe every move he'd made at some karate tournament in Vallejo, and being unpopular left your days open for swinging by a vine off the branch of a madrone or doing cartwheels down a mountain, or hanging out with your sister in the old truck body with a bag of Fritos, writing stories in your notebook and then reading them out loud to her—and making her laugh so loud they could probably hear her all the way down the mountain—then what was so great about being popular? Or so terrible, if you weren't?

But I chose Alison—a girl who shoplifted nail polish and drew mean cartoons of the boy in our class with forceps dents on the sides of his head, a girl who could be depended on to make fun of my sister. Almost every day now, I went over to her house. Usually one of the mothers drove me home from these afternoon get-togethers—those pretty, normal-seeming mothers, who didn't go to the library all the time or smoke in their bedrooms, or hang out in their bedrooms at all (because they were in the kitchen, making dinner, like normal mothers).

When I got home, my sister would be waiting on the steps for me. "I thought you'd never come home," she said, as I came up the walk. She never acted mad. Just happy to see me.

"Suppose we took the bus to the Golden Gate Bridge on Saturday and dropped bottles off the side with messages in them?" she suggested. Or we could put up signs around the neighborhood, offering our services as clowns to entertain children at birthday parties. We could buy a couple of helium balloons and let the helium out in our mouths and make phone calls to people. (What we'd say was a minor detail, still to be worked out.) We could send in an application to *Supermarket Sweepstakes*—a TV show in which teams of contestants raced around a store, throwing food items in their cart, with the goal of racking up the highest total at the cash register. If we got picked, we'd get enough groceries that our mother wouldn't have to worry about food bills for a year, not to mention the prize money.

And of course, there was always the mountain— off-limits according to our parents since the murders began, but that kind of thing never stopped us before. Every few days, we took our tin can up there and lit our little fire, and my sister sang her song, and we closed our eyes and chanted. I kept hoping for a vision. But we never stopped looking for hard evidence too.

"Suppose we snuck out with flashlights this week-end after Mom goes to sleep and camped out someplace near where he got the girls last time," Patty said.

"And then what?"

"We could bring your camera and take pictures."

"What if the murderer was there? What if he saw us?"

"We'd be quiet."

"Mom would kill us."

"So?"

"That would be ironic," I said. But the real reason I couldn't do a stakeout with my sister was because I'd been invited to a sleepover at Alison's. I wasn't just friends with the popular girls now. I was one of them.

"You never used to be this way before," my sister said. "What's happened to you?"

"You don't understand what it's like," I told her. "You just aren't a teenager yet."

"If you're this big teenager all of a sudden," she said—with a tone in her voice I could not remember hearing from her before, that could only have come from how deeply abandoned she must have felt that summer, by the person she loved most in the world—"why don't you even have your period yet?"

There it was. My big, shameful secret and the question I asked myself daily. I could have said something back, about her teeth, but I didn't.

"I didn't mean that," she said. She looked stunned and horrified. In all our lives, I could not remember my sister saying a mean thing to me, though I'd said many to her.

But that was the question all right, as burning to me as the identity of the Sunset Strangler: The fear that I would never become a woman. The terror that I would.

In late August, we had another heat wave. Karl Pollack had come home from work early and was sitting on the grass with his shirt off, watching Karl Jr. running through their sprinkler. The Gunnersons were barbecuing, and farther down the street, Mr. Marcello was washing his car.

I was sitting on the front step flipping through the back-to-school issue of *Seventeen*—filled with all the clothes Alison would be wearing this fall, and that I would not. Patty was dribbling her basketball in the driveway. That's when we spotted Mr. Armitage's dog, tearing down the street from the cul-de-sac with something in her mouth that looked like a chicken leg, or maybe a shoe.

A second later, there came Mr. Armitage, in pursuit. He wasn't much of a runner, so he was out of breath—the distance ever widening between the little dog and his own panting figure.

Somewhere around Helen's house, the dog disappeared, leaving Mr. Armitage standing there clutching his chest. For a moment, I thought he might burst into tears.

Two years had passed by now, since Patty and I had made our last entry in our scrapbook, and since then neither of us had paid much attention to the comings and goings at his house, except for my sister's occasional observations about his dog, and our mutual agreement that for whatever reason, Mrs. Armitage appeared to have moved out.

"I need your help," he said, still panting hard. Because he'd kept to himself so much, it was the first time I'd ever heard him speak.

"I just opened the door for a moment to carry out the trash and Petra got out," Mr. Armitage said, still panting. "I have to watch her like a hawk. She doesn't know her way back home.

"It's those coyotes I worry about," he said. No need to explain.

Patty didn't have to think about what to do then. She was off. She shot across the street, headed in the direction of the trail, the direction of the dog. Too fast for anyone to remind her we weren't supposed to go up there. Now Mr. Pollack jumped up, as well as Mrs. Gunnerson. But Patty was gone.

Even without the motivation of catching a fugitive dog, my sister was a fast runner, but that day she flew. Five minutes later—less, probably—she was back, holding Petra in her arms.

"I don't know how to thank you," Mr. Armitage told Patty.

"I could feel her heart beating against my chest while I carried her," Patty said, handing the dog back to Mr. Armitage, though I could tell she wanted to keep holding her.

"I knew she was scared," my sister said. "She wanted to get home, she just didn't know how."

"I want to show my gratitude," he said. He had taken out his wallet, and was extending a ten-dollar bill. Not what Patty would ever want, for rescuing an animal.

"Maybe I can take her for a walk sometime?" she said.

"Nobody has ever walked Petra but myself," Mr. Armitage said, with no mention of his absent wife. "But why don't you come over to my house tomorrow, and I'll fix root beer floats and peanut butter cookies. Then we can talk about it, and Petra can get to know you better. It might be good for another person to spend time with Petra, now and then, and maybe she could get a walk in while I'm off at work, if you were interested."

My sister was, of course.

"We'll need to discuss this carefully," he said. "This little pup means everything to me."

Next day, Patty went over to the Armitages' house, to get to know Petra better. And Mr. Armitage.

Although our original enthusiasm for compiling information about our neighbor had long since waned, the prospect of my sister actually gaining access to his house (and to Mr. Armitage himself)—combined with the growing mystery concerning the whereabouts of Mrs. Armitage—inspired me to revive our investigation into "The Mysterious Life of Albert Armitage." As occupied as I'd been lately thinking about the Sunset Strangler, and Teddy Bascom, the Armitage case appeared to offer a greater prospect for resolution. Unlike the Sunset Strangler investigation—where police tape and barricades had made it impossible to get close to the scene of the crimes—this one was unfolding, or had already, right on Morning Glory Court.

The Polaroid photographs I'd taken of Mr. Armitage, before losing interest in our project, had failed to enlighten us about his inner character. Beyond the photographs, the fact that he preferred white stones to grass, and owned a dog, the only hard information we'd gleaned about our neighbor had come from the refrigerator magnet of the ballroom dancing school where he taught, that he'd given to my babysitting clients, the Pollacks. But now, with my sister having made direct contact, it seemed as if we might finally get to the bottom of things in the most direct manner—by simply putting some questions to him.

Patty was the perfect person for the job, and not only because she'd been invited into the Armitage home. People trusted her, and with good reason. There was something in Patty's manner that made it impossible to think of her ever doing something that wasn't exactly what it appeared to be.

As usual, I laid out the plan for my sister. Once Mr. Armitage came to the door, she'd explain that she was doing a report and was hoping to interview him. Here came another dicey aspect to our detective work: school was out, and anyway, what could her report be about (for *summer school*, I suggested) that might require her to talk with Mr. Armitage? We knew so little about him it was hard to create a topic for Patty's interview. A report on people who pull up the grass in their gardens and replace it with stone? A report on people who take the bus to work?

It was Patty who came up with this one. She would say she was doing a paper on dogs. Just to narrow it down, small dogs.

Once he invited her in, she'd ask the necessary questions, while taking in as many details as possible. Full name, for instance. Date of birth, and where did he come from? What were his parents' names, where did he work, what were his hobbies? Where had he met his wife, and what was her birthday? And her name, of course.

The question about Mrs. Armitage was bringing us around to our real mission, naturally, but by mixing it in with a bunch of other questions that were less loaded, I felt it wouldn't set off alarm bells for Mr. Armitage as it might if asked on its own. (This was not unlike my method of purchasing sanitary napkins at the drugstore—something I'd done, even though I hadn't had a single period, so I'd be prepared, rather than having to ask our mother about it. Along with the sanitary napkins, I included at least three other items in my cart—bobby pins, thumbtacks, a pencil—cheap items, since money was always an issue, but enough different things that the cashier, who might be a boy, would not pay so much attention to that one single, incriminating purchase.)

"I need to ask about Petra," Patty reminded me. "That's the whole point of my paper."

Since Patty was the dog lover, I asked for her suggestions here. What would a person want to know about a dog?

Where to begin? There was so much to discover. You wanted to know about a dog's food preferences, if she had a particular favorite toy; how did she feel about getting bathed? Had she been fixed, and if not, might she have puppies sometime? It was hard to imagine a dog as small as Mr. Armitage's having puppies, but if she did, they would definitely be adorable. Patty could ask our mother again if she could have one. Though we both knew the answer to that one.

"You're getting off track," I said. "You aren't getting a puppy. You need to keep your focus here.

"You can ask him what he likes about small dogs over large dogs," I said. "You could ask if it's a lot cheaper having a small dog, since they probably eat a lot less food. But the main thing is to bring the conversation around to Mr. Armitage's wife. Without getting him upset."

Here was another tip for Patty to keep in mind while conducting her interview. Although it was important to take notes, she should not write down any observations that directly related to the aspect of Mr. Armitage's life that inspired our greatest curiosity: the mysterious absence of his wife. On the chance that he was suspicious of my sister, I wanted to be sure that all he saw on her notepad, if he looked at it, were things like his birth date and his job that wouldn't make him uneasy. Anything he said about his wife, my sister would have to remember and write down later, once she was home.

She wasn't wild about the idea of this interview. "It feels like I'm snooping," she said.

"Of course you're snooping," I told her. "That's what detectives do."

Reluctantly, she went ahead with her assignment. Knocked at the door—same as she'd done all those times in the past when we'd played Ding Dong Ditch, except this time she didn't run away when Mr. Armitage came to the door. She stepped into the house.

He fixed her a root beer float, evidently, to go with a plateful of homemade cookies, oatmeal raisin. He showed her a collection of china dogs he had— not simply small dogs, but all different breeds. He explained that actually, he'd love a large dog but given that he traveled home to Ohio twice a year to see his parents, and he'd never want to leave a dog of his in a kennel, it was important for him to have a dog small enough to take on an airplane.

One amazing fact did emerge over the course of Patty's interview. In the living room, there had been a framed poster of a dancer, a handsome young man, bare chested and wearing tights, holding a woman over his head. When Patty had asked if Mr. Armitage was a ballet fan, he'd offered the surprising information that in fact this was a photograph of himself in his younger days. Back in Ohio, he'd been a member of a dance company in Cincinnati for several years.

"As you can tell, I don't do much dancing anymore," he told my sister, patting his stomach. "But I still love to attend the ballet in San Francisco."

The afternoon she conducted her interview with Mr. Armitage, Patty was in his house so long I started to get worried. Finally, after close to an hour, she emerged. She got down low to the ground to hug the dog good-bye. Mr. Armitage had told her how rare it was for Petra to lick a person's face this way and wag her tail as she did for Patty.

"See you soon," he called out as she was leaving. "Glad I could help."

Later, at home—transcribing my sister's findings into the scrapbook and taping a few strands of dog hair that had stuck to her pants onto a page labeled "Sample Hair from Subject's Dog"—she expressed her hope that she might get to know our neighbor better.

"I think he's my kind of person," Patty said. "Shy with people but not with dogs."

"What about his wife?" I said. "Didn't you ask him anything about her?"

"We didn't get around to it," she told me.

"He showed me this trick he taught Petra," she added. "When he puts on this one record of an opera singer, she sings along. Not really singing but she gets up on her hind legs and makes noises."

"You were supposed to ask about the wife—"

"It seemed like that might be a sore subject," she said. "But other than that, he seems like a pretty regular person. Friendly and cheerful."

"Some people have a secret dark side," I told her. "They wouldn't call it a dark side if there wasn't a bright side too. That's the part he showed you."

"Maybe *your* dark side is criticizing Mr. Armitage," Patty said, "when he never did a single mean thing to you."

It was one of those afternoons when I'd gone over to Alison's to hang out. She and her mother had gone into the city the previous weekend—the city meaning San Francisco—to stay in a hotel and do school shopping, and now she was going to show us all her new clothes and maybe let us try on some of them. This meant that I'd left Patty on her own again as I'd been doing more and more.

I felt bad about this, not because my sister complained but more because she didn't. "You could get some new friends too," I told her. "I bet there's lots of kids in the fifth grade who'd like to have you over."

I wasn't actually so sure of this. When it was just the two of us, my sister could be the funniest person, but her shyness around everyone else made it hard for her to make friends. On the basketball court, going after the ball, she was a wild woman, but the rest of the time, with other people, she hardly opened her mouth.

But this one afternoon, when I got home from Alison's—carrying a shopping bag she'd given me from Bloomingdale's with some hand-me-down clothes she didn't want anymore—Patty was not in her usual spot on the steps waiting for me, or over at the Marcellos' shooting hoops. Not out in back either, though it had seemed unlikely she'd go up on the hillside by herself. Not in our room. Her bike was in the driveway. So was her basketball.

I was starting to worry when I saw her coming up the street from the far end, the cul-de-sac. Except for a time when our father came to her game the year before, just at the moment she'd made a perfect hook shot, I could not remember a moment my sister had a more euphoric look on her face.

Tall as she was, Patty had a tendency to slump her shoulders and bow her head forward—something our father, with his belief in the importance of good posture, used to get after her for. But that day she walked like a fashion model down the runway, except what she was showing off was not an outfit; it was Mr. Armitage's dog, Petra.

Mr. Armitage was paying Patty fifty cents a day, but that wasn't the point for her. She would have paid him for the chance, if she had the money.

"You need to be very careful," he had told her. "My dog is my life."

Petra was six years old. She had a brown spot in the shape of a heart on her face and her tail was mostly missing, due to a mistake at the puppy kennel when they'd clipped it. Because of this, Mr. Armitage had gotten her at a discount, but to him she was priceless beyond measure.

This was my sister's first day on the job, a tryout. The trial didn't last long. It was apparent to everyone (Mr. Armitage, Patty, and Petra) that this was a perfect arrangement. Patty would have come home at lunch to walk Petra too, if this were possible.

After a few days, I reminded Patty about our scrapbook project, accumulating data on the Mysterious Life of Albert Armitage. But her focus had shifted, so that now, if she made an entry in the book, it concerned something particularly cute Petra had done or some little-known fact about Jack Russell terriers.

Though her great love was the dog, she was becoming fond of Mr. Armitage too. He was still mysterious. But where I remained fixated on the fact that his wife no longer seemed to live with him—and that no mention was made of her ever having done so—my sister seemed to have largely forgotten about that, or put it aside anyway, in favor of a friendship forged over a mutual passion for Petra.

On one occasion, she even raised, briefly, the idea that we could introduce Mr. Armitage to our mother as a possible romantic interest, but even Patty recognized the impossibility of this connection. Really, all she wanted was to ensure that Petra could be in our lives forever.

If she couldn't have her own dog, walking Petra was the next best thing.

After that one time, the year after he left us, I never again heard our father speak of marrying Margaret Ann, but the fact of her, and who she'd been to him, was always there, off in the background somewhere. In my mind I could still hear the quickness of my father's boots on the step, climbing the stairs to

Margaret Ann's apartment that day he introduced us to her, where we let Patty ring the doorbell. Running a comb through his black hair as he stood there waiting for her to open the door, though as soon as she did the first thing she did was muss it up.

He took us to her apartment only a few other times. "Don't tell your mother," he said, as we pulled into the parking space in front of her apartment. Sky blue, with a window box of petunias, and beyond it, the glittering pool where I pictured the four of us—Patty and me, our father and Margaret Ann—jumping off the diving board and sipping drinks with paper umbrellas in them. And then felt instantly guilty, for having dreamed up such a scene.

She had sewn us matching dresses. That was the reason for the visit. She had chosen just the kind of fabric we loved: a slightly shiny turquoise cotton with yellow kittens on it, unraveling balls of yarn. There were big pockets, and wide sashes long enough to tie into a giant bow at the back that made us look like presents.

"What are they supposed to do with these, Maggie?" my father said, when we put them on. But he was smiling when he said it. His face, when he was around her, took on a different look from the rest of the time, and even Patty, though she normally hated wearing a dress, looked happy.

"I couldn't help it," Margaret Ann said. "I saw the pattern and it just seemed like so much fun."

After we took them off, we hung the dresses in the closet at her apartment, next to Margaret Ann's own beautiful dresses—so different from anything our mother had. We wore them only twice, when my father and Margaret Ann took us to miniature golf in Santa Rosa one Saturday, and another time, to brunch at the Hotel Flamingo, where we swam in the pool with them—Margaret Ann in a white bikini, our father looking like Rock Hudson, she said—and after, we loaded our plates high with so many rolls Patty got sick in the car driving home, all over her dress and Margaret Ann's too. The dress was white like the bikini.

"You think I care, honey?" she said, when Patty apologized. "Dresses don't matter. Just people."

"Don't tell your mother about this," our father said. But we knew that already.

The end of August brought another murder. This time it was a park ranger, clearing brush on the trail, who came upon the body: Sally Jansen, age twenty-nine. She was a freelance journalist who'd driven from Sacramento to take pictures of the mountain in the hopes of selling a story about the Sunset Strangler to some magazine. They found her camera next to her, with a full roll of film inside, with shots of her own dead body. Taken by the killer, evidently, though as before, he'd been careful to leave no fingerprints.

Five murders. No evidence. (I knew this from a call our father made to us to explain why, once again, he'd have to cancel our weekend visit.)

"Are you getting closer to catching the killer?" I asked.

On the other end of the line, I heard him let out a long breath. Exhaling the smoke from his Lucky, probably.

"This guy's smart," my father said.

"When this mess is over," he said, "I'm taking you and your sister to Italy."

"Just the three of us?" I asked him.

"Yes."

After that fifth murder, we saw our father even less, except on television, and in the paper. He stopped by just before that Labor Day weekend—one of those brief drop-ins our mother spoke of as his cameo appearances. He had a present for each of us—an Adidas jacket for Patty, a necklace for me.

"It's been a little stressful lately at work," he told us—the closest he came to mentioning the Sunset Strangler investigation since his original call to tell us to stay off the mountain. "But I want you to know that even when I don't come by, I'm always thinking about you two."

"This is so you'll look sharp on the basketball court, Patty Cakes," he said, zipping the jacket up for my sister.

"As for you, Farrah," he said, handing me the box with the necklace, "this is the year you figure out how beautiful you are. You've got one of those faces that take a little time to grow into. But you're getting there.

"Any boy wants to get near you, he'll have to talk with me first," my father said. "They'll all be wanting to soon. Just don't waste your time on someone who doesn't deserve you."

My father had never even heard the name of Teddy Bascom. So how did he know?

School started. We wore our new back-to-school outfits—of which we had two, purchased on sale at JCPenney. Our mother had insisted on cutting Patty's bangs, and they'd turned out so short they were like the fringe on a placemat, nothing more—leaving a broad, pink expanse of forehead. When she saw herself in the mirror, Patty cried. Our mother had none of our father's talent for hair.

"It's not so bad," I told my sister. "It'll grow." But I wouldn't let our mother go near me with the scissors after that, so Patty knew my real opinion.

Even with Patty's bad haircut and my bargain jeans, we were in big demand with our classmates that first day back. I was, anyway. Alison Kerwin had been away with her family at Lake Tahoe, so she hadn't checked in since the most recent murder. Now she came up to me in first period to say I should sit with her at lunch.

This was a definite step up from my old spot in the cafeteria.

She wanted to know if my father had any new leads. "Even if it's top secret, none of us would breathe a word," she said. "Pinkie promise."

"Like that thing about the bite marks," Soleil said—though I'd only told Alison that one, back in the summer, with the reminder that it was for her ears only. "And the panty hose."

So much for her pinkie promises.

"I don't know," I told Soleil. "Our father made us swear we'd never discuss this part with anyone. Certain information is classified."

"I bet it has to do with sex, right?" Alison said. "Some really disgusting thing he made his victim do before he strangled her?"

"Let's just say, by the time he killed this one, she must have wished she was already dead," I told them. Sometimes the details you withheld could be more terrifying than the ones you shared. Also, as active as my imagination was, I'd found myself running low on ideas lately.

We talked a lot about boys. Whatever minuscule piece of information any of us had gleaned that day about a boy one of the others considered cute, we shared with the group. This data would be along the lines of a particular boy looking in the direction of one of us, or a different one appearing to have shaved and cut himself. Somebody else would have an opinion about the socks Vincent was wearing that day. One of us would observe that during history class when Mrs. Brennan called on a boy named Larry Odegard, a boy about as unpopular as I used to be, his voice had cracked—starting out in one octave, slipping or more likely rising into another, the old one. To hear me laugh you would not have known that only a few months earlier, these girls might well have been laughing at me.

Our own mortifications we did not discuss, though some attention was given to outbreaks of skin problems—Alison's one beauty flaw—and attempts to cover them up with concealer. She owned a vast range of products for this.

"Teddy Bascom decided he wants to go out with you," she told me. "He said Heather's butt is too big, and you're hotter."

"You know someone else that's hot?" Soleil said, mouth full of tuna fish, gesturing in my direction. "Her father. When he came on the news last night, my mom said if he ever gave up being a detective he could have his own TV show. She said he's as sexy as Paul Michael Glaser."

When she said this, I was still taking in the news concerning Teddy. The part about my father inspired an odd combination of emotions. Partly pride. Partly discomfort. You didn't really want your friends to view your father as sexy. On the other hand I recognized I'd never have been invited to sit at this table or find myself lying on Alison's big canopy bed with these girls after school—and never would have attracted the attention of Teddy Bascom either—if it hadn't been for my father and the Sunset Strangler case.

Patty was never around for any of these discussions. Now that I was in eighth grade I ate in a whole different cafeteria in another building. But when we saw each other after school, waiting for the bus, my sister looked at me in a way that I recognized meant she was onto me. Not mad, just disappointed looking, and sad. She was like a dog that, even if you hit it, still brings you the paper.

On the bus now, I sat with Alison and Soleil. We might go over to Alison's house, or to Soleil's or Heather's. When we did, there would usually be other kids there too. We'd lie on Alison's bed and play records or try on clothes or watch the little portable television she had on her dresser, her own personal set. We ate peanut butter crackers or nachos—though the girls were always on diets—and sometimes we'd order pizza and have it delivered, without even needing to pay, because her parents had an account.

I'd get a ride home from one of the mothers around dinnertime. (Their dinnertime, anyway—mine and Patty's still being flexible to nonexistent.) When this happened, the mothers were as likely as their daughters to want to hear about my father and what he was doing on the case.

"Tell your dad we're all thinking of him," Mrs. Kerwin said to me one time. "I sleep better knowing he's out there tracking this monster."

I always asked the mothers to drop me off at our corner so they wouldn't see our yard, with its dead grass and broken garage door. "I can walk from here," I said. "That way I can pick up the mail."

Patty would be waiting for me at the house. Our mother might or might not be home, but either way, more than likely Patty would be out in the driveway dribbling a basketball, in her old shoes with the soles falling apart.

It would have been easier in some ways if Patty had blamed me or said mean things, but she never did. Apart from asking what kind of pet Alison had, we didn't discuss what it was like over there or what we did.

"I would have thought her family would have a dog," she said when I told her about the giant aquarium

Alison's family had in their living room. "Something like a poodle or an Irish setter. A purebred."

My sister was more of a mutt person, but the least the Kerwins could have done was have a poodle.

Never mind. The main thing in my universe that day was the news concerning Teddy Bascom. According to Alison, I had earned his approval. At the time, the question of whether he'd earned mine never occurred to me.

B y that fall, with those five unsolved murders in the
paper every day, and those warning signs posted
at the trailheads, hardly anyone went hiking on the
mountain anymore. But there was no way to seal off
the entire outdoors. Like a mutating virus, the killer
seemed to be adapting his M.O. as his potential victims,
and the homicide force trying to protect them, altered
their approach in response to the most recent murders.
Hikers seldom ventured onto our part of the mountain
now. But the Sunset Strangler had expanded his range.

The body of the sixth woman, Willa DePaul, was
found at Phoenix Lake the third week of September.
She was older than the others—thirty-six—but like
them she had long dark hair, she was pretty, and her
corpse was discovered at the end of the day.

"I told her not to go there," her husband said in the interview they played a few days later on the radio. "She said Buster needed some exercise."

The dog had shown up back at home, whimpering. That's how the police knew to look for her.

The newspaper did not offer many particulars concerning what the killer might have done to Willa DePaul, but the reporter did say that her body was found "in a position similar to that of his previous victims" and that "electrical tape had been employed"—a phrase my sister and I understood to mean that Willa's eyes, like those of the women he'd killed before her, had been covered in tape, in the Sunset Strangler's trademark style. Mention was made of "certain other details about the manner in which the victims were found." Our father had explained to the reporter that because an ongoing investigation was under way, he could not elaborate on those. One source in the Homicide Division was quoted—anonymously—as saying that the killer appeared to take a certain item of clothing from the bodies of his victims, as some sort of souvenir. What that might be, he could not say, for reasons of protecting the investigation.

Once again I tried to summon a vision, but the pictures that came to me were too vague to offer any clues, and I wasn't even sure myself if they were real, or just something I made up, like the stories I told Alison and her friends. I pictured a man standing over the motionless body of a woman. Imagined I could hear his slow and labored breathing. Tried to summon a picture of the item of clothing—blouse? panties? bra?—the killer might have chosen to keep for his collection. But no picture came to me—nothing to offer to my father to help him break the case.

Knowing how busy he was now, I didn't call my father on the phone at work anymore—and I didn't like to call his apartment now, in case Margaret Ann might answer, but even more so, knowing that most likely no one would. I didn't like to think of my father at the apartment of a beautiful woman who smelled like jasmine. I hated it, that there was this other person out there who knew our father as well as Patty and I did.

I saw him mostly on television now, times I'd be at Alison's, or babysitting for the Pollacks. But from a couple of quick visits he made to our house, I could see that the case was getting to him.

The vision that came to me then was of my father, not the killer. I saw him sitting on the mountain, next to the motionless body of Willa DePaul. Raking his fingers through his hair. Out of respect for the victim, he did not light a cigarette. But later he would. Many.

I saw him in his black leather jacket, out on the mountain, pacing over the crime scene for clues. Back and forth, back and forth. As he paced, it seemed to me that I knew what he was thinking.

All his life, he'd seen himself as a protector of women, but women kept getting killed on his watch. (*Four . . . five . . . six . . .*) As hard as he tried, he was no closer now to finding the killer than he'd been in June, when he'd stood over the body of that first victim. This was eating him up. I saw it on his face now, and more than that, I could feel it. Of all the visions I'd experienced so far, this one seemed clearest, but it wasn't going to help me assist my father in capturing the Sunset Strangler. For that, I had to see the killer's face.

Nights in my bed, staring up at the slats of my sister's bed above me, I tried to summon him. I tried to picture where he was right now, where he was going next. But all my brain revealed was a blank screen, like our disconnected television set. Nothing there when you turned it on but snow.

At home, at night, the urgency of locating the killer occupied all my thoughts. I saw my father's face on the television set, strained and anxious. His shirt (that would have been perfectly pressed before) looked rumpled.

At school, it was Teddy Bascom I thought about. I could look across the room in geometry and see him there, sitting in that boy way, with his legs apart—crotch to the world. I'd study the hair on the back of his neck, and as much as I studied him, I also knew: He barely looked at me. And saw me not at all.

I still hadn't gotten my period, and I was flat as ever, or close to it. But sex seemed to be all around me now—in the locker room at the pool, where the other girls and I put on our suits, and in Alison's rec room, and in the bedroom of Karl and Jennifer Pollack, whose bed I sat on sometimes, babysitting nights, imagining the two of them there, trying to conceive a baby.

The images blended then: the cheerful, wholesome animated egg and sperm drawings from our health class movie gave way to those scary but fascinating drawings in the *Joy of Sex* book from my parents' long-ago bedroom. (The man with his beard. The woman, with hair in her armpits. The penis that I didn't want to look at but did.)

Sex was as much a part of the world as air, or air pollution. No longer as the health class movie portrayed it—as something precious and beautiful, and private. But to me, that summer, sex had become something ugly and toxic, displayed across the front page of the papers my sister delivered every afternoon. Sex was dangerous—possibly fatal. And in a terrible and twisted way, it was out there on the place I'd always loved the most—the mountain.

An odd thing had happened over the years after my parents' marriage ended. I couldn't call them friends exactly, but now and then, late at night—on his way home from work, or who knows, maybe heading back there—he'd stop by our house and they'd have a cigarette together in the kitchen and talk. Despite whatever old wounds surely existed—the unspoken name of Margaret Ann still hovering over the two of them—they seemed to have arrived at some form of friendship. Maybe they were like a couple of weary soldiers who went through a war together, side by side in the trenches, and having no inclination to relive the old battles found a certain comfort in the simple knowledge that they'd been young together and present at the same terrible moments of bloodshed. Even though, in my parents' case, the injury sustained there was my mother's, at the hands of my father.

There had been a time when she could barely look at him, but maybe enough other hard things had happened by this point, or enough time had passed, that this was no longer so. She didn't have a lot of other people to talk to for one thing—or any. And maybe specifically because she, alone among those who knew him, did not view him as a hero, there must have been a certain relief for my father—when he was with her in our old living room, and no place else—that he could speak freely for once about the terrible inadequacy he felt at not having located the killer who was terrorizing the county.

By that fall, he was coming over more. Not in the afternoons so much, but at night, when Patty and I were in bed, for no apparent reason other than to unburden himself about the case. It might be past midnight, but this was no problem for our mother. She never went anywhere except work, and she always seemed to be up. The light was always on.

They thought we were asleep on these occasions— and Patty was, usually, but the sound of our father's heavy sigh would wake me. Then came the familiar ritual of the cigarettes, the drink. Ice in the glasses. Click of the lighter.

"You look tired," she said. She sounded like a wife when she said this. For a moment, then, I let myself pretend they were still married to each other, and that the voices I heard now came from my mother's bedroom, where the two of them lay side by side, instead of leaning on our green Formica counter, with a couple of juice glasses of whiskey.

"This case is getting to me," he told her. As if any of us didn't know.

I'd be huddled on the floor by our door now, listening in. I'd been hoping he'd tell her more about what was going on, not so much to share with Alison and her crowd in the cafeteria the next day—because I could make those parts up. Just for myself, to know.

"After he takes off all their clothes," my father said, "this guy actually folds them up next to the bodies."

The lighter again. Another Lucky.

"All they have on when we find them are their shoes," he said. "Damn tape over their eyes. I shouldn't be talking about this, but sometimes I just have to."

"It's okay telling me these things," my mother said. "I just don't want it around the girls."

"We're keeping this part quiet at the department," he said. "But you know the one thing he takes away with him, when he's finished?"

He hesitated for a moment. I held my breath.

"Their shoelaces."

No sound from my mother. She would know he didn't need her to say anything. Just listen.

"It's like he wants a souvenir," my father said. "A little something to remember them by. And here I am like an idiot, out looking for the one guy in the county with a goddamned shoelace collection."

October came. We'd turned the clocks back, so it got dark early now. Through the windows of the houses on Morning Glory Court—all but the one belonging to Mr. Armitage—we could see the blue glow of the television sets now, as up and down the block families tuned in to hear the latest news about the Sunset Strangler.

Patty was off doing her paper route. Normally I'd be over at Alison's, but the girls had set out after school with somebody's mother to get pedicures in the city and go out for dinner after at Pier 41. I'd told them I was busy, though the real reason I didn't go was the money.

I was lying on my bed flipping the pages of my Amelia Earhart biography that I'd read twice before when I heard the familiar sound of my father's car and looked up to see the blue Alfa pulling up to the curb in front of our house. My father stepped out, looking like a guest star on *Fantasy Island*.

As always on these rare occasions when our father came to see us, I felt my heart expand just at the sight of him. Nothing—not attracting the interest of Teddy Bascom, or an invitation to a sleepover at Alison's, or having Patty say she loved one of the stories I wrote—could feel as exciting as a visit from my father, however fleeting.

I watched as he swung the car door open, his easy, natural gait as he strode up the path to our house, the way he ran his hand through his hair.

"Your sister home?" he said.

"Paper route."

"I only have a minute," he said. "I just thought it would be good to see you. My spirits could use a lift."

He sat down next to me. "You know I'll always love you," he said. "Nothing would ever change that. No matter what, that part's nailed down."

I looked at him. For a moment I thought that maybe he was going to tell me something. He might have thought so too.

"Whatever happens, I want to be sure you know that. You'll always be my girls."

"I know," I told him.

"Sometimes, I mess up."

"Not really," I said. "Not much."

"I'm never leaving you," he said.

Then he was gone again.

A couple of weeks before Halloween, Alison had a party. In the rec room, on the yellow vinyl bean-bag chair—"My Sharona" on the radio, as usual—Teddy Bascom kissed me.

I had expected this to be a bigger deal than it turned out to be. As little as I knew of kissing, I got the impression there were better styles of doing it than Teddy's, which featured his tongue a lot, jammed up against my gums in a way that reminded me of being at the dentist, just you didn't spit anything out after. Sometimes it felt as if the kissing part was only something Teddy did to keep me occupied while his hand crept up under my shirt. But the truth was, what occupied me then was the simple embarrassment over how little he'd find there. I went along with what was happening, but I was looking at the wall the whole time. A poster for *Grease.*

Soon I was making out with Teddy Bascom on a daily basis, mostly in Alison's rec room, but also in back of the school when classes got out, and out by the basketball court, and pretty much anywhere else I was likely to run into him.

At the time I made no particular differentiation between the concept of a boy being genuinely interested in me and the simple desire of that boy to get his hands on my breast, or any breast. At least three afternoons a week now I went over to Alison's house after school, and on other occasions I would head over to the rec center and watch Teddy play basketball. Sometimes my sister accompanied me then. What she really wanted was to play, herself, but even though she could have held her own against some of those boys—tricking her defender with a pump fake, then diving past him with her amazing feet to bank it in—they would never have invited her to join them.

Least of all Teddy. More than any of the other boys his age, Teddy possessed a kind of confidence and assurance, and obliviousness to the needs of anyone but himself. But I loved how cool he was, and even more, the way his choice of me as his girlfriend—as the girl with whom he hung out at least—conferred a certain coolness on me.

He carried himself like a person who knew that whatever came up, he'd be able to handle it. The only other person I knew like that was our father. Though where our father's sense of command seemed rooted in the desire to protect, Teddy's appeared to emanate from the desire to vanquish.

And Teddy Bascom was nothing like my father. Teddy seemed to possess no interest in making me feel special or beautiful. Or making me feel anything, actually. With Teddy you were always left with the uneasy sense that something was going on you didn't really understand. There were secrets, and it made you want to be the one who discovered them. The fact that Teddy didn't answer when you asked him a question made you think he must have something really important on his mind, though perhaps all it meant was that he couldn't be bothered.

Or maybe the fact that you wanted to hear an answer from him was sufficient reason for Teddy to withhold it. It had occurred to me that Teddy Bascom derived satisfaction out of maintaining control. The more offhandedly he treated a person (me, for instance), the more clearly he established his own power. Teddy Bascom's calling in life, if he had one, was to please himself.

We shared this goal, Teddy and I: the goal of making Teddy happy.

Back before the murders, my seventh-grade English teacher gave us an assignment one time that actually inspired me to deliver something good for a change. We were supposed to choose a person we admired and interview that person (him or her) about the work the individual did. In part no doubt as a way of ensuring that I'd get to spend some time with him, I chose my father.

I had told him I wanted to discuss the field of homicide investigation. The topic being so broad, it was my father's idea that we narrow this down to the subject of conducting an interrogation of a suspect. As the head of the Homicide Division in our county, our father had the reputation of being better than anyone at getting a suspect to admit to his crimes.

My father took me to Marin Joe's that day to conduct the interview. I brought a portable tape recorder with me.

"So, Detective Torricelli," I began. I was trying hard to sound like someone on television. Barbara Walters, maybe. "I understand you are an expert in the field of police interrogation. Can you tell me a few things about why this is such an important aspect of police work?"

"I would be happy to do this, Miss . . . Miss . . . What did you say your name was, miss?"

"Torricelli," I told him. My father always made me laugh.

"Amazing coincidence! That's my name too. Maybe we have relatives in common, back in the old country."

"Very possible," I told him. "Now, about those interrogations . . ."

"Right, right. I know you're a busy person, Miss Torricelli. I don't want to take up too much of your time."

"Why they matter . . ."

"Here's the thing," my father said. "You spend all these weeks and months tracking down your perpetrator. Hundreds of man-hours and woman-hours, getting those cuffs on your guy, and now you've pinched him. But don't think for a minute you're home free. Not without a crucial element in your case. This would be the confession.

"I cannot tell you how many times, in the history of the cases I've studied, a guilty man or woman has gone free—let out on the streets to very likely terrorize the community again—for the simple reason that the police interrogator failed to get him to admit to his crimes."

"Why would anybody admit they were guilty?" I asked him. "When they know they'll be let off if they just keep their mouth shut?"

"It's human nature," he told me. "Every sorry mope I ever had dealings with is proud of his crimes. He knows what he did was against the law, and that society wants to punish him for it. He probably knows it was wrong. But he's kind of like one of those dogs that lays a turd on the rug that wants to go back and point it out to you. Like it's his big accomplishment. He really showed them all, doing that. There's a part of this guy that's proud he got your attention. He likes it that you want to listen to him. He's got a reason to keep talking.

"You know those punks that write graffiti on buildings or bridges or whatever? And they sign their name? Same thing. They're doing something people tell them not to. So what's the deal with the signature? There it is again. *Pride.* Arrogance, more like it."

Not that conducting an interrogation of a suspect was a piece of cake, my father told me. Far from it. Most criminals he'd had the pleasure of interrogating were smart bastards, he said—excuse his French. A murderer didn't want to spend the rest of his life behind bars just because he had to brag about some job he did, knocking off his bookie or shooting his mother when she told him one too many times to pick up his socks. That's why a good homicide interrogation required a little psychology.

"Okay," he told me. "First thing. You get this loser in the room, and you sit him on a bench. There's

nothing comfortable about this place. Nothing inviting. Your job is to keep Short Eyes off balance. Never
let him forget it's you in charge.

"It should be a hard bench. The lighting matters.
Bright. Harsh. Acoustics in the interrogation room are
nuts, and that's just how you want it. Every click of the
lighter, your guy hears it. Scrape of your chair on the
floor to drive him crazy."

Something in my father changed then, as he talked
about his work. He said words he normally would
never have said in front of my sister and me. He was in
another world. In the interrogation room probably.

"Different detectives have different styles. But one
thing we all know, you've got to get him off balance,
tighten the screws. Maybe you cuff him to the chair.
Maybe you light up a cigarette or two and leave him
sitting there to watch, knowing he's dying for a smoke.
He wants to take a piss, he has to ask you. Maybe you
let him, maybe you don't.

"Now, here's something I've taken care of, before I
even bring the shitheel into the room—"

Shitheel. I didn't put that part in my paper, but that
was the word he used.

"It's a small room, probably, but I fill it, floor to ceil-
ing, all four walls maybe, with file cabinets," my father
told me. "On every drawer of every one, I write in big

letters the name of his victim. Or victims, if there's more than one. Like we've got so much evidence accumulated against the guy, it took a wall of files to hold it. This scares the shit out of the guy."

I asked him then what was really in the file cabinets.

"Not a goddamned thing. We might have nothing on the guy. We're messing with his coconut. But he's sweating now."

"Isn't that against the law?" I asked my father. "Like lying? Isn't this kind of mean?"

"May I remind you what he did that got him here in the first place? We're talking about a scumbag who raped some woman, or cut her throat. Shot some poor loser full of lead for a cash register full of fives and ones. If I hurt his feelings now and then, I'm okay with that.

"I may decide to take his belt away. Or his shoelaces. Maybe after a few hours, if he's not cooperating, I decide it's time to get myself a nice steak dinner and I leave him there, just sitting on that hard bench in his cuffs. Have myself a nice piece of pie while I'm at it. I'm in no hurry to get back. This guy's not going anywhere. If he wets his pants, or worse, that's not my problem."

He was on a roll now. I didn't even need to ask him questions anymore. He was just going.

"When I come back, he's like a cat scratching to get out, he's so crazy. He doesn't know whether to shit or wind his watch if he had one, which he doesn't. He can smell it on your jacket that you've just had a good piece of meat. That and a smoke. He's got to have a cigarette, and you're not giving him one.

"This is where I'm nice to him maybe. I do a U-turn on the guy. I'm his brother now. His pal. Though make no mistake, it's me in charge. If he can keep me happy, I might be nice to him. He wants my approval now. He might want to impress Susie Snowflake, but the one that really matters to him now is me. Plus, he can see the pack of Luckys in my pocket. Just calling out to him.

" 'You play any sports back at school, buddy?' I ask him. Though I can tell to look at the guy—his soft middle, sloping shoulders—the closest he ever got to a ball game is the refreshment stand. Me, I'm the varsity forward that never knew his name. He emulates me, understand? I'm the big guy with the letter jacket.

"Could be now's when I put a hand on his shoulder. I call him by his Christian name, not the shortened version. No nickname here. We're man-to-man."

I asked my father if he ever yelled at these criminals. Did he get really mad? Call the person names?

"Yelling won't work," he told me. "Want to know the truth about this character? His momma beat him more in first grade than you're ever going to. You gotta break him down easy. Chip away at that armor. Maybe, after a long time, you offer him a cigarette. I got my special lighter just for this, my Zippo, and I light his for him, like we're old pals now. He's thinking 'This detective's not so mad at me after all.'

"You tell him, 'Look, bud, I hear you. One look at that girl and you could tell she was a tease. She probably had it coming.'"

I remember the look on his face as he told me these things. He hadn't noticed that the restaurant was mostly empty. Lunch crowd long gone, but too early for dinner. The waitress over by the cash register, reading her horoscope.

"You woo him, no different from a girl you pick up in a bar," he said. "It's a seduction. Just a different type."

Young as I was, I knew I shouldn't really be listening to my father telling me about seduction. But he didn't know I was there anymore was how it seemed. I might not have known the word for it at the time, but it was as if my father was in a trance.

"'Tell me what happened,' I say to my guy. I'm whispering in his ear maybe. Up close enough he can feel my breath on his face. Maybe he smells my drink. Wishes he had some of that whiskey too.

" 'You're going to feel a lot better when the truth comes out,' I say. 'A sweet ass like that, who could blame you for wanting a piece of it?'

"This is when he tells you yeah, maybe he lit her cigarette. Maybe he bought her a drink, but that was it. So he touched her hair. No law against that. So what if he put his hand on her neck. People do that. Even the president. Not Jimmy Carter, but JFK anyway."

My father was not done talking. "Once you get him to the place where he's admitting physical contact, you have him," he said. "He's crossed the line now. Even if he reverses direction, he can feel it's too late.

"All he can do now is blame the victim, and he will.

" 'She gave me a hard time,' he says. 'She came on to me. She called me a name. You wouldn't believe how loud she screamed. She was busting my eardrum, man.'

"That's why he got a little rough with her. Just to quiet her down. Who wouldn't?"

This was the place in my interview with my father where he came back to the world again—the part of the world with the half-eaten bowl of tiramisu in front of him, and the ashtray full of cigarette butts, and the waitress saying, "No charge for this one, Tony," and me with my cassette recorder, taking it all down.

"And that's how you conduct an interrogation, Farrah," he told me.

It was nighttime. Patty breathing softly overhead, Cat Stevens singing "Oh, baby, baby, it's a wild world" as I lay there in the dark. More and more now, this was the time when the pictures started coming to me.

I was thinking about something the gym teacher had said that day, about girls getting excused from gym if they had cramps, and my having told her that I had them. Knowing I'd have to keep track, now, of the date I offered the cramp excuse, without the presence of a real period to make the keeping track unnecessary. I was wondering if I had some disease that made it so I didn't menstruate. Leukemia, or a brain tumor.

I was thinking about my father, and how thin he looked when I saw his picture in the paper that day. I was thinking about Teddy Bascom, and the murdered girls—the deer fetus, and the vultures, and the horses having sex.

I tried to think about something nice then. The picture came to me of my father, sitting on the couch while my sister and I snuggled up on either side of him, watching *Rockford Files*, and our mother standing in the doorway with a bowlful of popcorn, looking almost happy for once. Margaret Ann (a different day now), opening the glass doors of that cabinet of hers filled with the dolls and saying, "Pick any one you want." I wanted to linger there, but the picture shifted to the bad part of that story. My mother finding the key to Margaret Ann's apartment. My father walking out the door, with his one suitcase. The sound of his car starting up. His headlights disappearing down the street.

Your girls will never get over it.

Then all the pictures were gone, but that wasn't good news either. Now came the Sunset Strangler.

All these weeks I'd been trying to locate one of my visions. That night one came to me, and I wished it hadn't.

I was inside a car. Not our father's car, or our mother's, though like hers this one looked a little beat-up.

There were fast-food wrappers on the floor, and a plastic key ring with a woman's naked body on it—all but the head—with huge breasts and little red lights where the nipples would go, which lit up when you pushed a button on her back.

From where I sat—a bucket seat facing the steering wheel—I could see his hands winding a shoelace around his wrist. Knotting and unknotting it. With the hard end of the lace, the part encased in plastic, he was picking his teeth.

Even with the windshield all steamed up the way it was now, I could see out onto the sidewalk of the street. There was a young couple walking past the car, the boy's hand on the girl's breast, the way Teddy Bascom's was always ending up on mine, though in the case of these two, there was more for him to find there.

I knew what the killer was thinking then. That he never got to put his hands on a girl that way. Not a living one, anyway. Not without a length of piano wire around her neck.

The couple stopped by a streetlight and started kissing—but not the way Teddy Bascom kissed me. This was real, passionate kissing. This was the kissing of two people who were crazy about each other and could hardly wait to get home and do something about it. This might even have been love.

Here was the worst part for the man in the car: he was totally invisible to them. I don't know how I understood this but I did.

My lips felt dry and chapped now, and there was a sour taste in my mouth as if I might throw up, but didn't. I told myself to think about some small, good thing: the pair of Chemin de Fer jeans I'd put on lay-away, that I was one or two nights of babysitting away from bringing home. Soleil telling me she was going to invite me to come up to her family's place in Sonoma and go horseback riding. Teddy Bascom (this part was fantasy) playing with my hair and whispering, "You're so beautiful," though what he really said was, "Let's get this shirt off you."

Now there was a hand reaching inside a pair of pants. I saw the hand move up and down inside the pants— eyes locked on the man and the woman kissing. Now came the sound of breathing. Deeper and faster. Then a long, low sigh.

His fingers were opening the glove compartment. Out came a roll of electrical tape. Key in the ignition, car backing out and heading onto the highway now, turning the radio on to a country station. A Kenny Rogers song. How was it that I knew the words?

I could see the feet—one on the gas pedal—in their black loafers, recently polished. Not shoes for hiking, but I knew where this car was headed. Those red towers looming overhead in the moonlight. He was driving to the Golden Gate Bridge, headed north to the mountain.

———————

The next night was Halloween. My sister, in her clown costume, lay stretched on our bedroom floor, sorting her candy. I had come outside to sit on the front step to watch the last of the trick-or-treaters straggling home, sacks in hand. All up and down our street the candles inside the jack-o'-lanterns flickered, casting an orange glow over the yards and front steps of Morning Glory Court. Inside our house, I heard the ringing of the telephone and headed inside. Of the three people who lived at our house, I was the only one who ever got a call.

"It's Alison," Patty said, making a face.

There'd been another murder on the mountain that day, number seven. A woman named Kelly Cunningham, a twenty-three-year-old hairdresser from Cotati whose New Year's resolution had been to lose forty pounds by hiking on the mountain five days a week, rain or shine, had been found raped and strangled in a grove of eucalyptus near the east peak of Mount Tamalpais, with tape over her eyes and a Snickers wrapper on the ground beside her. The report on television offered few particulars, Alison told me, but one thing I could guess: she would have been naked, except for her shoes. The shoelaces would be gone from them. And I wouldn't be seeing my father anytime soon.

By now, everyone knew about the Sunset Strangler. Now all they had to put in the *San Francisco Chronicle* that next morning were the initials: "S.S. Strikes Again." No further explanation required.

The *Marin IJ* ran a feature in which local residents were interviewed—parents, teachers, a city councilwoman and a variety of businesspeople, the owner of a restaurant—and asked how the murders had affected their lives; the gist of the story being that the entire population of Marin County now inhabited a state of high anxiety, if not terror. "What's going on here, anyway?" one woman was quoted as saying. "I pay my taxes. Where are the police when we need them?"

There was also an interview with a haircutting client of Kelly Cunningham, the most recent victim.

"She was more than halfway to her goal weight," the woman said. "She was wearing size twelves. I even asked her if it was a good idea to keep jogging on the mountain, but she just told me you can't stop living your life."

Only she could.

November. In our neighborhood now, police patrolled the streets—Daffodil, Honeysuckle, Morning Glory Court—that led most prominently to the mountain from where we lived, and they staked out the parking lot where hikers left their cars. Over at the Pollacks' house, on one of my babysitting nights, a new item had shown up in the bedside table drawer where they always used to keep the K-Y jelly and the condom supply: a small pink .45-caliber revolver. Purchased, no doubt, by Karl for Jennifer, as protection against the serial killer at large.

There were no more hippies on the mountain, with or without clothes, and no more hikers. Every one of the girls I ate lunch with had been given a beeper by her parents—this being before the days of cell phones—so their mothers could locate them and get them to call home if they went to the rec center or the mall.

Patty and I had no beeper. As before, our mother was off at work most days, or at the library, and in her room a lot of the time when she got home. Like our father, she had told us to stay away from the mountain, and we assured her that we would.

But the truth was we weren't afraid of the Sunset Strangler. The only thing that kept us from spending our afternoons out on the mountain as we'd always done was the fact that for the first time in our lives as sisters, we were spending long hours apart, away from our old haunts. Thanks to my recently acquired popularity, I no longer came home right after school the way I used to. Even on weekends, I was apt to be tied up with the girls, hanging out at the mall or sitting on the bench at the dojo, watching Teddy at karate practice.

In many ways, though, it was not me so much as my sister who'd found other and more consuming things to do with her time than making up adventures on the mountain with me. Where, only recently, I'd felt as though I was abandoning my sister, now it seemed as though Patty was the one, more than I, who'd chosen other ways to occupy herself.

Patty was working hard on her jump shots; she was always trying to improve. But more than anything, her days that fall revolved around her visits to the home of Mr. Armitage, who had entrusted her with a key to his house—kept hidden under a flowerpot—so Patty could let herself in on the afternoons he was at work, to play with Petra and take her for walks.

Even when she was home, her talk was often of the dog. "You know something cute?" she told me one afternoon. "Petra never gets it that she's little. When I'm walking her, and we pass another dog, even if it's a really big one like a golden retriever or a malamute, she barks like she's protecting me.

"Mr. Armitage says that sometimes he used to take Petra along when he taught his ballroom dancing classes, because he didn't like to leave her by herself.

Only he had to quit doing that, because it made her mad to see him dancing with people. She got jealous.

"I don't know what I'd do if Mr. Armitage moved away," she said. "I don't think I could stand it if I didn't get to see Petra anymore. And Mr. Armitage is nice too."

"But he's a weirdo," I told her. "First he had a wife, then he didn't. Who ever heard of a man that teaches dancing for his job?"

"You know what I think?" Patty said. "Everybody's a weirdo. With some people you just don't know what their weird part is, but everybody has one."

Based on her performance on the sixth-grade girls' JV basketball team—her superb passing skills, as well as her footwork and shooting—my sister had been invited to try out for the CYO basketball team, something no sixth grader had accomplished in the past. She was practicing for the tryouts, and spending time with the girls she was meeting, playing ball, and a couple of coaches who'd taken an interest in her. One of them had played Division I basketball out in Indiana some years back and even tried out for the newly formed Women's Professional Basketball League. She was too old now for a pro basketball career, but for my sister, she said, anything remained possible.

"Professional basketball," Patty said. "Out on the court like Larry Bird and Magic Johnson. My dream come true."

"Europe, maybe," I suggested. For me, travel was the dream. But for my sister, it was all about the game.

"Imagine getting to play basketball every single day, with the best players," she said. "I'd love that more than anything."

This might have been the moment for me to say how happy I was with my new activities too: how much I loved going to Alison's house, and hanging out with Teddy every day the way I did now. Only I didn't say those things. They weren't true.

The truth was, I found Alison and her friends boring. As uncool as the things were that my sister and I thought up to do, they were more interesting. My sister loved dogs, and basketball, and adventures on the mountain. Alison loved shoes and nail polish, looking at her face in the mirror, and going to the mall.

The most boring thing of all, really, was Teddy Bascom, whose interests were *Space Invaders*, pizza, and making out. Except for that one time when Patty had inquired about my feelings on the subject, I didn't ask myself whether I enjoyed kissing him. I only knew that doing it conferred on me a worth and social stand-ing unlike anything I'd known. The fact that Teddy

Bascom wanted to kiss me at all made me feel important, I told my sister.

"To me, you were always important," she said.

There was a game we played in Alison's rec room,
called Light as a Feather, Stiff as a Board. It only
worked when there were enough people—six at
least—but more often than not, there were. Alison's
house was everybody's favorite, no doubt because her
parents both worked in the city (one as a cosmetic sur-
geon, the other an attorney) and they seemed to be
gone all the time.

One person would lie flat on the floor, with everyone
else spaced around her. The darker the room remained
for this, the better, which was easy at Alison's, since we
kept the venetian blinds shut, and the lights off.

Each of us put two fingertips under the body of the
person lying down in the middle. Then the person
standing closest to her head made up a sentence telling
how she'd died. You could say, "She died in a car accident when she was thirteen years old," or "Her mother
didn't like her so she fed her rat poison."

After the sentence was spoken, the rest of us repeated
it back, over and over. Particularly in the dark, delivered while studying the motionless body of one of our
friends, this had the effect of freaking us out.

I didn't know much about what kinds of deaths the group used to construct for one another before the murders began, because they only included me after, but for all the times I played the game, the favorite choice as a reason why the person died was that she'd been done in by the Sunset Strangler.

"She was making out with her boyfriend and the killer came along and strangled them both" was one. "She was fourteen years old."

"She was only twelve, practicing her routine for cheering tryouts, when the Sunset Strangler raped and murdered her" was another. "He took off all her clothes and left her holding her pom-poms."

Sometimes, if we did Light as a Feather with a boy, we varied the scenario a little: "He was hitchhiking to the mall and a guy picked him up, and he noticed piano wire on the front seat, and the guy said, 'Now I have to kill you.'"

Once we'd said these words enough times, the words of the chant would change, and we'd go back to the ones that remained the constant refrain: *Light as a feather, stiff as a board.* The only one who didn't speak was the person playing the body, because she was supposed to be dead.

Now came the surprising part. After all these years, I still don't understand how this worked, but invariably, after enough chanting, it did.

With nothing but the two fingers of each person touching the body in the middle of the circle, we'd lift that person off the ground. To those of us holding it up, the body had come to seem weightless.

The body only stayed up a few seconds, but the effect was amazing and terrifying, both at once. After we set the body down again and turned on the lights, we'd laugh almost uncontrollably, hugging each other and screaming. We'd fix ourselves tacos or rip open a bag of chips, and when we did, we would be ravenous. Someone would put on music—the louder the better.

Later, back at home, I told Patty about it.

"Give me a break," she said. "Those kids are turning you into a nutcase."

I swore to her that it happened. I had been the body myself one time. Nobody dropped me. I floated.

"If just kissing a boy makes you go crazy this way," she said, "I hate to think what actually having sex does to a person."

I read a book once, *A Night to Remember,* about the sinking of the *Titanic,* and how certain terrible men had pushed the women and children out of the lifeboats and leaped in themselves to keep from drowning. I knew, reading that story, what my sister would have done: jump out of the boat to give me her spot.

We looked alike, but different. I knew people considered me the prettier one—a fact that would have been a source of resentment to most sisters but not to Patty, who seemed to take my looks as a source of pride, as she did my writing skills. Even before her growth spurt made her a star at basketball, she was the sporty one, where I was more of a reader and a thinker. Patty teased me sometimes for how long I'd spend standing in front of the mirror in our room, checking myself out or trying on clothes. Patty never cared much about clothes, but she positioned herself in front of the mirror for another reason: to practice her baseball swing or an imaginary hook shot.

Because I was bossy, and she was endlessly compliant to my commands—and always up for whatever I proposed we do—I established the practice, early, of playing school, with myself as the teacher and Patty my one student.

When we were little, I'd made her sit on the floor and gave her horrible assignments, which she executed without complaint. (*Rip off twenty squares of toilet paper and draw a different shape of poop on every one. Write the letter* A *one hundred times with your left hand.* Her only issue with this one: she couldn't count to a hundred.) Because of our school game, she learned how to read young, and when praised, she was quick to say that I'd been the one who taught her.

Back when our parents were still together, I found a pair of police handcuffs on our father's dresser once and thought it would be interesting to handcuff Patty's wrist to my ankle. The cuffs were snapped shut before it occurred to me to check for the key, but there was none around. We had to stay in our odd positions— she crawling behind me with her locked-down wrist— until our father got home from work many hours later.

"It wasn't so bad, Rach," she whispered to me, after he placed the key in the lock. "I got to pretend I was your pet dog."

Given a choice of any activity, however exciting (a choice we were never offered), the one she would have chosen every time, with only one exception, was to be with me. Growing up as we did—less hovered over or even watched than any children I've ever known or heard of, without even the dubious education in the ways of the world that would have been provided by the presence of television—we were both more mature and independent than other children, at the same time that we remained almost hopelessly naive. I even more than my younger sister, strangely enough.

And yet there was this: of the two of us, it was Patty, not me, who could look sharply at our father and speak of him critically when she felt our mother being hurt. About certain things—like the fact that he drove an

Alfa, but never came through with money to fix her teeth—my sister said nothing. But she was increasingly critical of his failure to support our mother and, most of all, of the way he kept saying he was coming over to see us and didn't. She came to view the excitement that always accompanied his brief appearances to see us with a certain skepticism, where I accepted his absence as confirmation of our father's importance. Though she never seemed about to give up the hope that he'd make it to one of her basketball games and sit through all four quarters, as he never had.

"He's just so busy with the case," I told her.

"You make excuses for him," she said one time.

"And you're mean."

"I love him," Patty said. "But our dad is a loser."

We didn't speak to each other all day after she said that. We did not engage in our usual round of Drive-In Movie on the hill out behind Helen's house. That night, when I came in from outside—no fun by myself; I had wandered up and down the street missing my sister—I stepped into our room to find a masking tape line down the middle of the floor, and a sign: KEEP OUT.

But it was Patty who broke the silence, as we lay in the dark later that night in the unfamiliar silence.

"Let's not do this ever again, okay?" she said.

"Okay."

I couldn't see her face in the dark, but I could see it in my head then. Patty had the kind of eyes—there must be a name for this, but I've never known it—in which the white remains visible around the entire iris, which had the effect of making it seem, at times, as if she was not simply looking at, but drilling into you. She seemed to possess an unwavering ability to cut to the truth of things.

"I'm your best friend in the world," she said.

"I know."

My sister had become the undisputed star of the JV team. Center.

That night in bed, with Linda Ronstadt singing to us in the dark—*Some say a heart is just like a wheel; if you bend it, you can't mend it*—I had told Patty that Teddy Bascom had taken off my shirt and touched my nipples. Now she wanted to know what it felt like.

"Did you want Teddy doing these things?" my sister said. "Or was it more like this feeling that you were supposed to?"

I thought about this. It was a harder question than a person might think.

"He definitely has sex appeal," I told her. "It's a thing some boys give off, like a smell, only a good smell. Like cologne. I think Dad has it, in a grown-up version."

Patty wanted me to elaborate. She had yet to experience the effects of anybody's sex appeal, though she greatly admired Larry Bird—a fact that could not possibly have had anything to do with his looks.

"You get this feeling," I told her. "There's this place inside your body you never knew was there before, like a room you walked into and turned on the lights. It makes you uncomfortable being in there, but you don't want to leave."

"That's how I get when I'm taking a foul shot," she said. "My skin starts tingling. It's like the whole world goes away and there's nothing but me and the basket."

I wasn't quite sure if I got the connection, but I decided to leave that one alone.

"Do you think Mom used to feel that way about Dad?" she said.

I thought a long time before answering. In all this time, watching how my father was with other women, I'd never actually thought about him with our mother, back when they were young. I never thought about our parents kissing each other, our parents being in love.

"I guess she must have," I said. "Look how all the others act around him."

"He let her down," Patty said. "He didn't keep his promise."

I had always blamed our mother for not keeping our father around. Always, in the past, I'd looked at her as the one who messed up, for losing him—not just for herself, but for us too. I had seen her as a loser. Now my sister was suggesting a different picture, in which it was our father, not our mother, who'd been the weak one.

"He's just one of those people," I said. "The type that everybody wants to be around. What did you want him to do, stay around here and mow the lawn or something? And carry out the trash?"

"Yes," she said, quiet now. "Yes, I did want him to do that. That's what fathers are supposed to do. If home is where we were, yes, I did expect him to stick around."

J ust after Veterans Day, another girl disappeared—
number eight. This time it happened in Muir Woods,
just barely out of sight of the visitors' center, amazingly,
but in an overgrown spot where a couple of old-growth
redwoods lay fallen on the forest floor, having no doubt
concealed the killer as he lay in wait for his victim.

Her name was Naomi Berman—an eighteen-
year-old from New York City who'd flown out to San
Francisco with her mother just the day before to visit
Stanford; her interview was scheduled for the next
afternoon. To pass the time until then, her mother had
signed the two of them up for a tour through Marin
County. It was the last tour of the day, and the tour
guide had given everyone forty-five minutes to explore
Muir Woods, but the mother had stayed on the bus,

feeling carsick. After an hour passed, and Naomi hadn't returned, the guide contacted a ranger.

An hour later another ranger found her body. I didn't ask, and nobody would have told me if I had, but no doubt he found her in the naked prayer position, with the electrical tape over her eyes. Shoelaces gone.

That night in bed, I couldn't stop thinking about the murder. I didn't want to. I made myself think about all the things I had loved that my sister and I used to do—trying on clothes we'd never be able to afford at the mall, when we went for our Slurpees, going out on the mountain together, lying on the grass, talking about our dreams for the future, when she'd be playing for the WBL and I'd be traveling around the world, doing research on international spying for my books. Lying on the four-poster bed at the Kerwins' house with Alison and the other girls, flipping through *Seventeen* and deciding, if we could be any of the models, which ones we'd be.

Sometime in the night, another one of my visions woke me. I saw the body of a brown-haired girl lying with her skirt pushed up and her panties off, on a bed of moss—a necklace a little like Alison's friend Heather's looped around one hand, along with her camera. I saw something else a little way off: a small dog with a red collar, peeing on a tree.

As much as I wanted to see his face, the killer never appeared in these scenes that came to me, though I caught sight of his hands, and his feet, and on that one awful occasion, his penis. Most of the time though, for however long the movie played out in my head, what I saw was the face of a girl beholding her killer in her last moments of life. This was a terrible sight to take in, and one that offered nothing to assist my father in locating the killer.

But the presence of this dog could help. It wasn't a lot, but it might offer a clue. Maybe the dog owner—if we could locate him—had seen something that day. Maybe the dog owner was the killer himself.

I knew it would be hard to explain the significance of my vision to my father, but I felt compelled, this time, to try. I called him up at work.

"I need to speak with Detective Torricelli," I said. "This is his daughter."

A minute later, he came on the line. "Farrah!" he said. "Is everything okay?"

"I need to talk to you," I said. "I need you to come and get me, so we can go someplace and talk."

"What's going on, honey?" he said. "Is it some boy? Did some boy hurt you?"

"I can't talk about it over the phone," I said. "I need to see you."

He was there on Morning Glory Court ten minutes later. He opened the car door for me, the way he always did. ("Any boy who doesn't open the door for you is a boy you show to the door," my father always told us. "This is how it's supposed to be," he'd say, making sure my fingers were out of the way. "Don't ever forget that.")

In the car, on the way to Marin Joe's, my father was quiet. I knew he was waiting until we were in our booth. I was waiting too.

Normally, he would have shot the breeze with the waitress and maybe stopped by a few tables, saying hello to people he knew or ones who knew him anyway. That day we went straight to our corner. He told the waitress we'd have our usual.

"Okay," he said, when she had set his coffee down for him, and my chocolate milk. "Tell me about it."

My father was quiet for a minute. He was familiar with my history, over the years, of having seemed to know certain things without explanation, though until now, the visions I'd told him about had never been particularly alarming. But he, alone among the members of our family, had maintained that what I possessed was not about some extra sense or supernatural gift. Just strong powers of observation combined with an above-average imagination.

"I've been having these visions," I told him. For a few months, I said, pictures had been coming to me, of the murdered girls. Sometimes after the murders happened. Sometimes right before. I hadn't laid eyes on the killer in these visions, but I had seen the looks on the girls' faces when they'd caught sight of him and realized what he was about to do to them. In my most recent vision, I told my father, there'd been a dog.

As a detective pursuing every lead, my father might have asked to hear more at this point, and maybe if I hadn't been his daughter he would have. As it was, his face changed. A look came over him that I hardly ever saw: hard, and unyielding. Not just a closed door, but a locked one. If I hadn't known differently, I would have thought he was angry at me, instead of what he was, which was worried.

"You need to stop this right now," he said. "I don't want to hear you talk this way ever again, baby."

"But it could tell you something," I told him. "If you could figure out who the dog belonged to. Maybe someone else saw him that day."

"Locating the Sunset Strangler is my job, not yours," he said. "Your job is to be a kid. Go to school. Make friends. Find out about boys, but carefully. Look after your mother and your sister. Leave the detective work to your old man."

"You don't understand," I said. "I know things that could help you solve the case."

"I don't want to hear you talking about this any-more, Farrah," he said. "Take it from me, this stuff can mess you up bad if you let it."

He lit a Lucky and inhaled deeply.

"Put this garbage out of your head," my father told me. "It can eat you alive."

I went to school every day. But I barely paid attention to anything the teachers said. My mind was occupied with the killer, my father, and Teddy Bascom. That took up all the space I had. My grades that year—which had never been distinguished—fell lower than my normal B-minus average.

My mother didn't seem to mind. When she was young, she had harbored a dream of going to col-lege, where she would have studied English, or maybe library science. But whatever ambition she'd possessed once had drained out of her long ago, and now she seemed not only devoid of ambitions for her-self but lacking any expectation that her daughters might possess ambitions either. Maybe the thought of wanting something she couldn't give us was too sad, or maybe she'd concluded that expecting noth-ing would save us the disappointment when nothing turned up.

So unlike many of the kids we knew, Patty and I never felt pressure from our mother—or our father either—to excel in school. Our mother never checked on our homework or inquired about particular projects or assignments. She loved books but seemed to make no connection between the experience of reading and learning and that of sitting in a classroom at our school. And in fact she had a point there.

Whatever the reason, report card days—so filled with anxiety for most kids in our class, and triumph for a few—were for us no different from any others. We forged our mother's signature on our report cards ourselves most of the time, next to the Bs, Cs, and occasional Ds—though if we'd asked, she would have signed them willingly enough, with or without studying the grades and comments written inside.

"I know who you are," she said. "I don't need your teachers to tell me."

Sometimes I passed in my homework. Other times not. If I did, I felt no particular need to garner distinction—my main objective was to draw as little attention to myself as possible. I hardly ever even showed one of my teachers a story I'd written, though I wrote constantly. My writing had nothing to do with school, and with my teachers, it didn't matter if nobody ever noticed me.

So why did I care so much to win the favor of this boy, Teddy, who never showed me kindness, or even much in the way of interest? Only I did.

Our relationship, if you could call it that, had a predictable inertia. At lunch I sat with Alison and her friends—an honor never bestowed on me before that year, and one I recognized as having the potential to be withdrawn at any moment—but if Teddy gave indication that he'd like me to come and sit with him, that's what I did. We seldom spoke.

Every day after seventh period, Teddy would wait at my locker for me, and we'd walk to the bus together, also without exchanging more than a few words. At this point, I no longer needed an invitation to go over to Alison's after school; it was just understood we were all headed there, unless Teddy had practice that afternoon, in which case he'd tell me what time it started—not to ask if I was coming; he assumed it. He always rested his hand on the small of my back, but less in a spirit of any affection, I knew—as my father would have—than to steer me in the direction he chose, like the controller on a video game.

He steered. I followed.

"What's happened to you?" Patty said. "You turned into a zombie, all because of a dumb boy."

Because I always told Patty everything, I had confided in her that Teddy now took my shirt off on a daily basis. Also my bra—though having done this, he had not found much. She offered the opinion that he didn't sound to her like a very nice person. I knew she was right.

Still, I went over to Alison's every day, and now when I did, the pressure was stronger than ever to take off not just my shirt but my pants too. So far I had resisted the pants part, but it was getting more difficult. When Alison's boyfriend, Chase, showed up, they'd disappear into her bedroom; when they emerged eventually, her hair was messed up and her lips puffy looking. Soleil and Heather usually went home when the boys got there, or they went up to the kitchen to make slice-and-bake cookies or melt cheese for nachos. This left me in the rec room alone with Teddy.

Nothing in his approach was what you could call romantic, and as my father's daughter—reminded by him all my life that I was beautiful, wonderful, perfect—this was a disappointment. Not that I'd believed everything my father told me about myself, but I had assumed it was part of what boys were supposed to do, to say these things or come up with some kind of compliment anyway, even if it was nothing more than liking your sweater.

Teddy took the no-nonsense approach.

"Hey, babe," he said, settling into the beanbag. He patted his crotch then, as indication of what he wanted.

I'd sit on his lap. He put an arm around me—strictly a gesture of ownership. "You see me get that shot from midcourt in the first quarter at practice?"

"Really great," I told him, though I hadn't caught it.

He was rubbing his hand on my mostly nonexistent left breast. This led, within seconds, to the buttons on my shirt. "Why don't you take this off?" he said.

So I did. Back before we'd gotten to this point, one of my main concerns had been the prospect of Teddy seeing my ridiculous training bra. My mother had bought the bra for me months ago, but it was more along the lines of what a fourth grader would wear—a tube of spandex stretched across the front of me like a bandage—than the style the other girls had, the ones who'd gotten their periods and had a shape.

Teddy had little time to notice this, since he always took my bra off immediately now, without studying it, or me. The look on his face when he did—dogged, purposeful, mechanical—reminded me of Mr. Pollack trying to get his lawn mower started.

"You can touch me here," he said, putting my hand on the crotch of his pants. I gathered this was supposed to be a privilege, though I was unsure what to do once he'd placed my hand on the spot. He was rubbing against me, so I didn't need to do anything, it turned out.

The picture came to me of the cover of the *Sticky Fingers* album, with Mick Jagger's fly on the front, and the zipper my sister and I used to play with. Now that my hand was on a real zipper, with a real penis pressing up against it from all I could tell, it didn't seem like fun anymore.

He put his mouth on one of my nipples and chewed on it, hard. Up until this point I'd been totally silent, but this made me cry out.

"Getting worked up, huh, babe?" he said. *Never gonna stop. Give it up.* On the radio again: that song.

I thought about the Sunset Strangler.

As I had feared, Teddy was unzipping his fly now. He had taken his penis out. I didn't want to look down.

"Here," he said. "Put your hand around it."

He put his own hand over mine, moving it back and forth. He was breathing hard, but different from how he did when he was playing basketball. His free hand remained on one nipple. Then he made a groaning noise and my hand got wet. Teddy lay splayed on the beanbag, not moving. I breathed in an unfamiliar smell. My hand felt sticky and I didn't know where to wipe it off. He probably wouldn't like it if I got it on his shirt.

The first time Patty's JV team played a home game—and based on our father's assurances that he'd be there—she had announced to her whole team that he was coming. He never made it.

The next game, I could see her flashing quick glances into the bleachers, looking for his face and not finding it. Every time she played after that, she'd say she knew he was probably too busy so he wouldn't get to this game either, but in the end she always looked for him.

There was a day, not long before the killings began, when Patty and I were out on our bikes in the neighborhood, and we came upon the unmistakable electric-blue Alfa parked outside a house a few blocks away. Our father's friend Sal lived there—a buddy from his days in North Beach, who managed our favorite restaurant, Marin Joe's, where our father took us on our birthdays, or just because it seemed like a good day for a bowl of minestrone. There'd been a time when we had stopped by with our father for these visits at Sal's house, when the two of them would talk about old times while our father trimmed Sal's hair. He still did this now and then, even though there was not so much of it left for our father to cut.

Seeing his car that day, Patty had gotten excited. "Dad's probably coming by to see us after the haircut," she said. "I bet he'll take us out for tiramisu."

I was less sure, but I kept my doubts to myself as we pedaled home. Patty had changed her clothes when we got there and set herself up out front to wait for him, holding her basketball in case he was up for a game of Horse at the hoop in the Marcellos' driveway. It was close to dinnertime before she gave up and came in. Our mother, seeing this, said nothing.

As for Patty, maybe it was her growing awareness of how good she was at the game of basketball that did it— good enough that she was consistently the high scorer, and coaches from other schools had come to watch her play—but something began changing in her that year, not all at once but slowly, as the disappointments accumulated. She never gave up adoring our father, but he ceased to be, for her, the larger-than-life hero I continued to make him into. For Patty, he was more like a deeply lovable spaniel who keeps peeing on the rug and chewing on the upholstery, no matter how many times you tell him not to.

We had a favorite spot on the mountain—that old rusted-out truck body where we'd gone, time and again over the years, to hide out and eat peanut butter crackers, read our books, and make up stories.

Our father was the one who'd introduced us to the place. He had come home from work one time with a package—something important, he told us. Though he was never the hiking type, he had taken us up the trail with a certain sense of urgency as well as adventure, doling out a couple of sticks of beef jerky when I (not my sister) began to flag.

Who knows how our father discovered that truck in the first place. It occurred to me, much later—thinking back on that day—that perhaps it had been a woman who first introduced him to the spot. The image had come to me of him and Margaret Ann, lying on what was left of the seat, drinking from a wine bottle and kissing.

Clearly the truck was our father's intended destination with us that day. He had brushed it off, laid his leather jacket on the hood, and lifted the two of us up onto it. He took out the package—wrapped not in fancy paper like a birthday gift, but brown paper of the sort used for packaging meat or nails—and slowly undid the string.

Inside was a gun. Not the kind that shot bullets, he told us, though real in its way. This was a BB gun. And in a small plastic bag next to it, a couple hundred BBs.

"Don't tell your mother about this," he said. "She'd say you were too young. She'd have a point there too."

He said he was going to teach us how to shoot. It was better to learn properly than to try and figure this out on your own and do some damage while you were at it.

We spent the afternoon firing BBs at the truck body. Our father stood behind us the whole time, on his knees so his eyes were at our eye level, his arms around us, holding ours steady as we raised the gun to shoot and squeezed the trigger. Our mother wouldn't have found this acceptable, but the way he had it set up, there was definitely no way either my sister or I could have hurt ourselves or each other.

I knew no other girl our age in our town—no other person, period—whose father would have taught her how to do this. The fact that he trusted us made us trustworthy.

"Before you shoot," he said, "you need to be aware of your own heartbeat, know the rhythm, to steady your hand. You need to listen to your breathing. Before you squeeze the trigger, hold your breath."

Looking back on this now, it occurs to me that our father probably knew at this point that he wouldn't be living in the house with us much longer. Even though our mother had yet to banish him, he knew he was headed someplace else, as very likely we did too. Maybe he felt a need, before he left, to give us something. This.

"Your sister will hold on to the gun for the two of you," our father told Patty. "She'll decide when you're old enough to take it out on your own. Not yet. Just know it's there."

He told us other things too: Never keep a gun loaded. Never pick it up if you're mad or upset. This was not something to show our friends or to talk about with anybody else.

"You couldn't kill a person with a BB gun," he said. "But you could put their eye out if you wanted to, or had to. At close range, with a steady aim.

"It's been my experience," he said, almost as if he was talking to himself, "that girls are much better shots than boys. Maybe girls listen better. Maybe they want to please their dad."

This part was true, for sure. There was nothing we wanted more than that. Even Patty, though she looked at our father more critically than I did, never stopped wanting to please him.

He let me carry the gun back down the mountain— empty of BBs—and when we said good-bye, he watched while I tucked the gun under my jacket, the BBs in my pocket. I kept it in the back of our closet, a place our mother never went. We did not speak of it again.

Over the years after that, we returned often to the truck, though never again for target practice with our father—a man who, with the exception of making spiders, specialized in doing most wonderful things with us exactly once. One summer we left a blanket and pillows inside the cab of the truck, along with a stash of hard candy and a few much-studied *Betty and Veronica* comics, a pack of cards, and my well-worn copy of Jennifer Pollack's sexual fantasies book, *My Secret Garden.* We could spend a whole afternoon inside the truck, playing cards and reading.

It always made me think of our father, being there— not just because the cab of the truck, where we had made our hideout, was riddled with BB holes we'd made that day. (And sometimes, in wildflower season, we stuck flowers in those, for decoration.)

One time and one time only, while we were in our truck, we spotted a couple in the field just beyond where it sat, making love. We crouched low and looked out at them, hands over our mouths to keep our laughter from being audible, feeling like spies. What offered up our view of this pair were the bullet holes we'd made, ourselves, with the gun our father gave us, just before he moved out.

Sunday morning, early—Patty was just getting dressed for her dog-walking duties, while I lay in my bunk, writing in my notebook (something I hardly ever did anymore since I started hanging out with Alison)—we heard the helicopters on the mountain again. When we went outside, Helen's paper was still on the ground, where we could read the headline. "Hiker Reported Missing. S.S. Strikes Again."

Later that afternoon they found the body of Annette Kostritsky—a sixteen-year-old girl who had evidently returned to the county only that weekend, after her junior year abroad, and hadn't taken in news of the killings.

They found her body on the Bolinas Trail, along with the body of the child who'd accompanied her that day—a nine-year-old girl with Down syndrome she'd babysat for since she was in junior high named Bunny Simpson.

It was late November now—five months since the first murder. The two girls' deaths brought the total of victims to ten. A person couldn't go anywhere in Marin County at this point without feeling it—a persistent state of anxiety, like the humming of high-voltage power lines or a Santa Ana wind.

Over at Alison's house after school the next day, a group of us were sprawled out on the bed with a bowl of microwave popcorn. The conversation had been focused for a solid hour on menstrual cramps—a topic I dreaded because I never had anything to offer, and, strangely, considering how good I'd gotten at making up stories about the Sunset Strangler murders, I could never make anything up about this. I almost felt relieved when someone turned on Alison's pink portable television set, and there filling the screen was my father's face.

But the mood among the reporters asking him questions had shifted dramatically since the last press conference. A group of citizens calling themselves "Take Back the Mountain" were expressing their outrage at the failure of the investigation to locate the killer. Up at the podium, my father said he was asking the governor for emergency funds to double the number of officers patrolling the mountain. In the weeks since Patty and I had seen him last, he seemed to have aged: his cheeks had sunk in, and I could see a gap between his neck and the shirt collar encircling it, as though he no longer had the flesh or muscle to fill the space. My father—a man who always spoke of the importance of erect posture—hunched over the microphone. Seeing him now, it would have been difficult to imagine that people used to mistake him for Dean Martin.

"Even with all the publicity about the murders," he said, "there are still some people who insist on venturing out onto our trails, and we don't have enough manpower to protect them all. The problem is, we've got too many miles of territory to cover. It's just not possible to be everywhere, or to shut everything down."

Listening to him speak, I almost shivered. There was a quality to his voice that I'd never heard before. Almost a pleading sound. Not an admission of defeat, but close.

He had one small lead to report. Though there continued to be no actual witnesses to the crimes themselves, a woman had come forward with a description of an individual she'd spotted near the location of the most recent homicide, seen getting into a red Toyota Corona. He had not looked like a hiker, she said, and he had this look in his eyes. "Like he was hungry for something," was the best she could do to explain it. A police artist was working with her now to create a portrait of this possible suspect.

They ran it in the paper the next day. You couldn't go down the block without seeing that picture tacked to telephone poles. At school someone had taped it on the door to the girls' locker room with the words *See any resemblance to Mr. Eddy?*—referring to our school's principal. A girl in my English class said the picture looked like her mother's boyfriend, whom she had never liked. Someone else thought it was the man who appeared in the Mattress Warehouse commercial. One girl thought it must be this guy she babysat for one time who, driving her home, had put his hand on her thigh.

That evening our father came by before we'd gone to bed, for once.

Though he stopped by often now, late at night, to have a drink and a cigarette with our mother, almost a month had passed since he'd come for an actual visit with Patty and me, and longer since the three of us had shared tiramisu in our booth at Marin Joe's. Knowing what was going on, we hadn't expected to see him, and even my sister didn't ask anymore, as she used to, whether I thought he'd come over soon.

As always, when I caught sight of him, I felt as if a high-watt beam had suddenly been pointed in such a way that I was suddenly bathed in a pool of warm and glowing light. Better than anything were the times when our father came over, and he was stopping by just to see us.

He wore his leather jacket and his black boots. Although he was considerably thinner than he used to be, and tired looking, he was still handsome.

"My girls," he said, lighting a Lucky. "Sight for sore eyes, you two."

"They made me center on my new team," Patty told him. Tall as she was now, she jumped in his arms when he reached the walkway to our house, same as she always did, though I actually wondered for a moment whether he'd have the strength to hold her.

As critically as Patty spoke about our father these days, when he was there in the room, twirling us around the way he was doing now, neither of us could do anything but wish this moment would last forever.

Patty had her head on his shoulder now, and she was mussing up his hair. Even more than wanting this for myself, I wanted this for her, my gangly, bucktoothed little sister, who had been playing her heart out on the basketball court all season in the hopes that one day he might show up to see her trademark hook shot. Or any shot at all.

"Everybody at school keeps talking about the Sunset Strangler," Patty said, rubbing her hand over his cheek, which needed a shave.

I wanted to shush her. He'd never said it, but we both knew that he didn't like talking to us about his cases. This one most of all.

"You tell them they should keep their minds on their schoolwork, Patty Cakes," he said. "How's your team doing?"

"We won in overtime," Patty said. "I scored twenty-seven points."

"I should've been there, baby," he said. "Maybe next time."

"You want to say hi to Mom?" I asked him. "We made some cookies." They weren't normal cookies, because our oven was broken again, but we'd recently invented a recipe that didn't call for baking. It was melted chocolate, basically—old candy bars melted on top of the stove—rolled in coconut we'd gotten from Jennifer Pollack.

"I wish I could stay longer," he said. "Got to get back to work."

"I know you'll catch him," Patty said, as he got into his car. We stood on the curb watching it disappear.

He didn't make it to my sister's game that Friday. I could feel her tension on the court as she watched for him.

After that, Patty stopped expecting our father to show up to watch her play. She said she knew he wouldn't make it to any of her games. By that point there'd been another girl murdered: Robin Burke, a twenty-five-year-old backpacker. Her body turned up in a wooded stretch of parkland thirty miles north, as if to offer proof that there was no way of sealing off the entire trail system, the killer covered so much territory. Including, more and more, my brain.

Over Thanksgiving break, I was invited up to Alison's Tahoe house for the weekend. I felt guilty leaving my mother and Patty alone, but Patty had a game and my mother was never one to work on anyone's sympathy.

"I'm in the middle of a great book," she said. "I'll take a bath and put my feet up. I'm the lucky one, not having to stand over the oven all day holding a turkey baster."

Mrs. Kerwin didn't have to do that either, as it turned out. The entire meal was delivered in plastic containers, right down to the cranberry sauce.

"It's such a godsend, having these professional chefs that do the whole thing for you like this, only better," she said. "Plus they deliver."

"Let's face it. Grandma's turkey wasn't all it was cracked up to be," said Mr. Kerwin, popping the gravy in the microwave.

I could have told her a few people who would still want the grandma version. Starting with Patty and me. We loved those scenes on *The Waltons* where the grandmother and everyone else pitched in, and there was this great spread, and they said grace and sang songs and later, in their beds, called out to each other their good nights. Nothing like that ever happened at our house.

Alison's grandmother, Bernice, had come for the holiday. The rest of the time she lived in Florida. She was a skinny woman with unnaturally taut skin who looked like a version of Alison's mother that had gone through the dryer too many times, on high. Alison called her Beef Jerky, though not to her face.

Over dinner, Bernice brought up the topic of the Sunset Strangler investigation.

"So, Rachel, do you have any hot leads to report to us?" she asked. "All my friends want to know why your father hasn't caught this monster yet. They're scared to death one of us might be next."

I wanted to point out that it wasn't too likely the killer would choose some wrinkled-up old hag or any of her Jazzercise cronies as his next victim. He liked young girls, and pretty ones. Plus, his territory had not extended to West Palm Beach. But I kept my observations to myself.

"Our father's working incredibly hard on the case," I said. I got up to help clear the table, hoping that someone might change the subject. Bernice lit a cigarette.

"Well, I'm just saying, you've got people out there talking who feel the police need to step up the pressure on this person," Bernice said. "I know how I'd feel if it was my daughter or granddaughter he got his hands on, God forbid."

"The creepy thing is knowing he could be anyone," Alison said. "You might walk right past him on the street, and never know. He could be your best friend's dad or your teacher."

"Could we please change the subject?" Mrs. Kerwin said. "The good news is they've got that police drawing now for people to consider, and that woman who thought she saw the red Toyota."

"My father's tracing every known Toyota that color that's more than five years old and registered in the state of California, on the chance that one of them might belong to a person with a criminal history," I told them. I hoped this sounded impressive.

Thirty-four thousand red Toyota Coronas. That was all they had. And very likely, it would mean nothing, same as all the other leads had.

P atty and I were heading out on our bikes to the rec center for her CYO girls' basketball tryouts when we ran into Alison.

Patty had remained the consistent high scorer on her JV team all season, often by as much as twenty points, most recently breaking a tie to win in the last seconds of the game—one of the many times I knew she'd hoped our father might be there but wasn't.

But the CYO team was a lot more competitive and a huge step up in my sister's basketball-playing life. My sister's old sneakers had worn right through in a couple of places, to the point where a kid on one team she played against asked if she did all her shopping at the town dump. That's when I broke into my jeans fund to get Patty a good pair of sneakers, which she was wearing for the first time that day.

Now I was back to square one with my jeans fund. And here was Alison, in the very pair of Chemin de Fers I'd been saving up for.

"I saw your dad on TV last night," Alison said. "My dad said they were thinking of replacing him with someone else, on account of how he still hasn't caught the Sunset Strangler."

"You're crazy," Patty said. "Everybody knows our dad is the best detective in California."

"I was just saying," Alison commented. "I just thought you might want to know."

In fact, my sister and I had seen our father on television that night too—seen, not heard him, since we had watched his most recent press conference through Helen's window.

In our beds after, we'd talked about it. Something about the sight of our father on the television screen that night had a tentative quality I never would have associated with him before. For a brief moment, watching him speak, I could imagine how it would be for the killer, watching this same broadcast— and observing, as we did, the unfamiliar slump of Detective Torricelli's shoulders, the lines in his face I never remembered before. If the Sunset Strangler had seen how our father looked that night, he would have felt triumphant.

For the first time I could remember, that night my father looked like a regular person, not a hero.

But my sister made it onto the CYO team.

A few days later it happened again—the feeling that had started visiting me since around the time the murders began. Now I recognized it—dreading what was coming, at the same time I knew I should give in and watch for clues that might signal the killer's identity.

I could see a thin girl clutching at the ground for something, a rock maybe, and getting nothing but a handful of dirt.

She was flailing. One last kick, then no more.

I could hear his breathing grow shallower. I could see his hand reach down to the waistband of her shorts. One leg out of the shorts, no need to bother with two. He rolled down her underpants, revealing a tampon string, and pulled.

What happened next made me bury my head in the pillow. I looked down and saw an erect penis, a sight I'd never seen except on dogs, and those mating horses on the hillside.

He was pounding his body up and down against her. It almost seemed as if "My Sharona" was playing in the background. *Always get it up . . . for the touch, of the younger kind.* A drumbeat. Or maybe a heartbeat.

Faster, faster. *When you gonna give it to me . . . Give it to me . . .* Then over.

Then very slowly, I saw the fingers unbuttoning her blouse and slipping the fabric down around her shoulders. He was turning her limp body around—no resistance from the woman in the dirt; she just lay there. Very slowly, with a kind of reverence he would never have displayed while she was living, he unhooked her brassiere and took it off her.

He held it up and stroked the lace. He placed the fabric against his cheek. I couldn't see his face, but I could hear him letting out a long, slow breath, like a sigh. Then he went for her shoelaces.

Another girl had disappeared. Her body turned up in the brush near a trail in Point Reyes, thirty miles up the coast. The killer was extending his range now—the chance for containing him about as likely as containing an oil spill or the leaks into the atmosphere from the meltdown of a nuclear power plant—an event that had taken place earlier that year at Three Mile Island.

Our father was working all the time. We knew his number at the office, but we knew without being told not to bother him with phone calls. There was a hotline to the Homicide Division, and people were flooding it with ideas concerning possible suspects, though so far none of them had yielded anything but frustration and weariness. As for me, I knew not to try again to tell my father the details of my increasingly frequent visions.

The Sunset Strangler's victim this time—the twelfth—was a nineteen-year-old long-distance runner named Lexi Shaw. She ran track for UC Berkeley, but she'd been training for the Boston Marathon, with a hope of winning a place on the U.S. Olympic team. Her parents and coach, hearing she was still training on the trails of Marin County, had begged her to stick to the running trails around the university, but she had laughed at them.

"If anyone tries to mess with me, I can outrun him," she'd said as she set out for a late-afternoon run in early December.

The night they found her body, our father had stopped by our house to talk with our mother. He had come in to kiss us good night, then settled into his chair in the kitchen to share a cigarette with our mother— their regular routine now. Patty and I were supposed to be sleeping.

We weren't of course. The two of us had huddled by the door, straining to hear everything, the first thing being the clink of ice in their glasses. She had poured him a glass of whiskey, and one for herself from the sound of it.

"Not much gets to me anymore, Lillian," he said. "Not necessarily a good thing; that's what a dozen years of police work does to a person. But seeing this girl's body in that same damned position, with the electrical tape, and the laces gone from her shoes, I wanted to throw up.

"She was just so skinny. Not an ounce of extra flesh on her. These hard little tits, more like a boy. The bastard took her running shoes and set them next to her. Minus the laces."

"You'll find him, Anthony," our mother said. "Sooner or later, he's bound to make a mistake and leave you something to work with."

"Sooner or later, maybe, Lil," he said. "Question is how many more girls he'll get first. How many more times do I have to knock at some poor bastard's door and tell him and his wife they don't have a daughter anymore? Or one less than they used to.

"I don't know how these people keep on putting one foot in front of the other," he said. "If it was one of our girls, I'd jump off the bridge. After I tore whoever did it apart with my bare hands."

"I know," our mother said.

"The problem is, I'd have to find him first," said our father.

Patty and I couldn't hear anything then. I pictured them sitting in the near darkness, smoking. The only sound, the click of his lighter.

Before the most recent spate of killings, talk of the murders had quieted down some, but now every day at school kids talked about the Sunset Strangler again. At the very moment we were sitting in study hall— memorizing symbols from the periodic table or sharpening our pencils or pulling on our gym shorts in the locker room—we knew that he was out there somewhere just a few miles away—on the hiking trails, lurking in the shadows, just waiting until some woman he'd never met, wearing a fanny pack and carrying a water bottle, with long brown hair, came by and made the fatal mistake of talking with him. Or just not running away fast enough.

Maybe he'd actually follow her—running ahead at some point. Maybe he stopped when they met on the path, to point out a hawk or a rabbit a little way off. Maybe he asked if she had any insect repellent. He could have pretended to have turned his ankle, at which point she might have bent down to take a look.

I thought he'd chew gum and offer her a stick. Have a dog, maybe. It might even be the dog that got the girl's guard down. "Cute dog," she'd say. She'd kneel down to pet him.

I knew how it would go then, not from anything our father ever told us or episodes of *Starsky and Hutch* or *Kojak* observed through somebody's picture window, but from the far-scarier scenes that played out in my brain, nights in my bed. *Such a dirty mind.*

Hands in the pockets. Hands raised. Piano wire across her neck. *Good-bye, world.*

Fat fingers rolling down the waistband of her underpants. Unzipping that fly.

And later: Tape on her eyelids. The shoelaces. I saw him chewing on the tip of one of them, as he made his way down the trail. Whistling.

Later again: In front of a television set. I saw him turn on the news. They were talking about him, as a picture of the victim filled the screen.

He was famous.

Every day at lunch now, the girls talked about the Sunset Strangler. Suppose he came to one of their houses when it was dark and tried to climb in the window? What would you do if you woke up some night and there he was standing over the bed with a length of wire stretched between his hands like a cat's cradle, only he was lowering it toward your neck, and when you tried to scream for your parents, no sound came out?

What if, on your way home from school—somewhere between the place the bus let you out and home—a man came up to you and asked for directions, then grabbed hold of you and swept you off to the bushes? Or he said he was conducting a survey on shampoo or granola bars, and he wanted you to answer a few questions? *Whoosh, he had you.*

First sex. Then death.

At least in front of the girls, the times we overheard them, the boys' talk went in a different direction, toward acts of heroism and vigilante pursuit and capture. Some of them talked about organizing a stakeout on the mountain, looking for the guy. They'd know him when they saw him. He'd look like a creep. Then they'd surround him, tie him up. Turn him into hamburger.

For the girls with whom I shared my lunch now, there was never the idea of confronting the killer. The girls saw themselves as potential victims, powerless at the killer's hands if—totally at random—he decided to strike.

At this point, every man you saw, especially if he was a little odd looking, you assessed as a possible killer. One of the pizza delivery boys fell into this category.

"Did you see the way he looked at me when he handed me the bill for the pizza?" Soleil said, after he left Alison's house one night. "Like he was thinking what I'd look like with no clothes on."

"And that acne. You know nobody would ever go out on a regular date with him. That's probably why he started going after those girls on the mountain. He was so desperate," said Heather.

"My mom said to never trust anyone that has those type of ears where their earlobes blend into the side of their face instead of drooping down," another girl offered. Her name was Delia, and lately Alison had started inviting her over too, most likely because she had a twin brother Alison had a crush on. "He had those earlobes."

"What if he was right here!" Alison said. "Standing there with the door open to my house while I looked for the pen, with those way-short pants and white socks." This was where she suggested that maybe Delia's brother could come over, so there'd be a boy around to protect us.

"We should tell your father about him," Alison said to me. "He could put a trace on the guy or something. His fingerprints will be on the box."

"What if there's something weird he put on the pizza?" Soleil said.

"You mean like poison?"

"Worse. Like, you know, that thing boys do, while they think about sex. And he squirted it on top before he brought it in."

"You are *so* gross," Alison told her.

We finished the pizza anyway. But we locked the door, except when the boys cáme over—Chase, Todd, and Teddy of course. The one who came for me.

"The boys are here," Alison would call out, when we heard them burst through the door, calling for pizza.

As if that meant we were safe.

Patty and I were riding our bikes on an unfamiliar route a distance from where we normally went when we saw it: our father's car, parked on the side of the road. Not the unmarked Chevy he used for police work, but the Alfa. As always, my heart lifted at the sight.

It was daylight, the middle of the afternoon. The apartment complex across the street looked different from the one he'd taken us to a few years earlier, to visit Margaret Ann, but it occurred to me that she must live here now. I pictured the glass case holding the dolls in it, the mauve love seat with the needlepoint cushions, the lemon tree, and the music box. I could still hear the Dusty Springfield album that had been playing that day we went there, that our father put on a lot in the car, with the song about the windmills, and the one Patty loved: *Just a little lovin' . . . early in the morning . . .*

This apartment complex had a pool too, though it looked a lot shabbier than the other had been, if memory served. This was the kind of place a person lived on the way down from someplace better, more than on the way up.

"Let's go see if we can find him," Patty said. As critical as she could be of our father, Patty got as excited as I did anytime the prospect came up of seeing him.

"We could pretend we're Girl Scouts, taking cookie orders, and knock on doors," I said. "Or just wait till he comes out."

Hiding was something we were good at. We did it all the time—outside Helen's, for Ding Dong Ditch, and for Drive-In Movie. Now it seemed dangerous. I wasn't sure I wanted to know what we'd find out.

"He's probably working on a case," Patty said. "We wouldn't interrupt him. We'd just say hi."

"Remember that woman who served us the tea in the china cups, and the Kool-Aid?" I pointed out. "With the dolls?"

"Margaret Ann," she whispered. She still remembered the name, though neither of us had spoken it in a long time.

I remembered sitting with my sister on Margaret Ann's flowered love seat watching cartoons, sipping from our bendy straws, the smoky-voiced woman singer on the stereo, and the look on Margaret Ann's face when she and our father emerged from that other room. As much time as I spent thinking about Teddy these days, I myself had not experienced that kind of yearning by this point, and it would be years before I did. But I recognized it in my father and Margaret Ann.

"We should go home," I told Patty. "Maybe after he's finished visiting over here, he'll stop by to see us."

But we both knew this wasn't going to happen, and we were right.

The night after they found the body of Paula Fernandez, I dreamed of the Sunset Strangler. I had not seen Alison at school that day so I had not yet learned what few of the particulars they would have released to the press, but at night in my bed the scene played out for me, of the victim on the trail in the final moments of her life on earth.

Not a hiker type, the victim this time had come out to Samuel P. Taylor Park in search of her cat, who had jumped out the window of her car when she was stopped at a gas station in West Marin. She had been on her way to her overnight shift at a nursing home in San Anselmo and planned to drop the cat off at a vet's to be fixed in the morning. She was late for work, but she couldn't leave her cat.

In my dream, Paula stood on the path, not far from the entrance to the park, wearing her pink uniform and white nurse shoes. She was carrying a large black pocketbook and she had opened a tin of cat food pulled from a bag of groceries she had in the car, in the hopes that the scent might lure her pet in from wherever he'd wandered off.

Instead, the one she lured was the Sunset Strangler.

Lying in my narrow little bed that night with the sound of my sister's steady breathing above me, I could feel the awful sensation coming over me again. I didn't want it to happen, but I also wanted to learn something from this. These were the moments, I had come to believe, when I had a kind of access to details of the killings that nobody on the entire Marin Homicide Division possessed. It seemed to me I had an obligation to stay with the experience, however disturbing, in case it might reveal something that might help my father capture him.

I couldn't see his face, only his back, standing in a grove of trees near a picnic table, with eucalyptus all around, and wet moss. Frogs in the brook, making their cheeping sound, and the last rays of sunlight slanting in through the trees.

She wondered if he'd seen her cat.

Pussy, he said. Nice pussy.

I like your uniform.

I knew what was coming next of course. If I had to see this, I wanted it to be more like a movie or a TV show—something a person would watch strictly as an observer, like Patty and me, wrapped in our blanket on the hillside, looking at the TV set through Helen's window. I wanted to change the channel. Watch something different. Just about anything but this.

The look on his face must have told her what was happening, because she cried out.

Madre mia. Santos viene.

More Spanish—probably a prayer, though I couldn't have said what, not knowing the language.

I wanted to jump out of bed, climb up the ladder and into the top bunk with my sister, but I didn't. Even in my half-asleep state the thought occurred to me to look for something in the man that might assist my father in locating him.

The black loafers. Fat fingers wrapped around the length of wire. Somewhere off to the side, an animal was making noises in the leaves. The cat? Or maybe a dog.

But I couldn't see his face. Now he was walking closer to the woman in the uniform, holding the wire stretched taut between his hands. Breathing hard. *My . . . my . . . my . . . M . . . M . . . M . . . M . . . My Sharona.*

The only way to stop it was to wake up, but not before I saw him place the tape over her eyes, reach into her purse, and take out a lipstick and a rosary.

One, he looped around her neck. With the other, he wrote on her skin—a word I'd seen in graffiti on the 101 underpass the other day, though I didn't know the meaning.

Puta.

The week before Christmas, the Sunset Strangler struck again. The victim was Tanya Pope, age twenty-one, a student teacher. She had been collecting moss specimens to use in a holiday project with her first graders, building terrariums as presents for their parents.

Our neighbors tried to keep up the holiday spirit. All around us, at every house on our street but ours, there were glowing Santa and reindeer figures out front and music wafting through the windows, and we could see Christmas trees blinking, with presents piled up underneath. People went around wearing Santa hats or fake antlers attached to their heads, calling out "Merry Christmas" and passing out candy canes before slipping swiftly behind their doors and locking them.

The Saturday before Christmas, Jennifer Pollack organized a neighborhood caroling party. We knew our mother wouldn't attend, but Patty and I dressed up in red and green (Patty wearing her Rudolph nose) and made our way to the Pollacks' for the festivities.

Each person was supposed to bring a gift for something called a Yankee Swap. We'd looked around the house a long time for two items that could work, finally deciding to wrap a bottle of bath salts we found in the medicine cabinet and a pink picture frame my mother had gotten from her job a few Christmases back, with a picture of Jaclyn Smith in it, though we took out the picture and replaced it with a different one, of Mick Jagger.

You could tell everyone was trying to act festive in honor of the season, but it was hard—with the memory still fresh of the discovery of the young teacher, found not far from the place on the mountain where my sister and I had seen the naked people.

Karl Pollack was dispensing a drink called wassail. For the kids there was a separate bowl, the same basic drink without the liquor in it. Jennifer Pollack, wearing a sweater with holly berries stitched on the front and bells that jingled as she moved, passed out songbooks and Santa hats for everyone.

"Now when there is so much stress in our community seemed like a great time to let our neighbors know that we're expecting a new baby," she said. "We didn't want to make a big deal about it until we were past the first trimester. But we figured our neighbors could use some good news."

"So next summer it looks like you'll have another babysitting client, Rachel," Karl Pollack said to me.

It was raining hard that night, but Mr. Pollack had assembled a bunch of golf umbrellas to cover us as we made our way up the street, singing. At a few of the houses, children in pajamas stood by their parents as we sang. When we got to Helen's house, she handed out homemade cookies.

"Take some of these to your father," she said. "Judging from how he looks on television these days, he could use some meat on his bones."

In years past, our mother had always put up a small silver artificial tree, trimmed with a motley assortment of our homemade decorations—a pinecone elf I made during my one year as a Brownie, Patty's Popsicle-stick star, and our two Baby's First Christmas ornaments—but that year she hadn't gotten around to it, and our father, who in years past had always taken us to the city to see the tree in Union Square, seemed almost bent over double under the weight of the unsolved crimes.

The week before Christmas there had been another demonstration in front of the Civic Center, demanding resolution in the Sunset Strangler case. (Did anyone really believe that this was not the goal?) Some of the protesters' signs had even named our father as the reason why women were still getting murdered on the trails, as if he were part of some antiwoman conspiracy.

Looking at him that Christmas Eve, as he knelt on the floor with us while we hung up our stockings, it seemed to me that perhaps the voices of the women picketing outside the Civic Center had created some nightmare tape loop in his brain, mixed no doubt with the wailing of the mothers as he delivered the news about their murdered daughters, the imagined screams of the dying girls themselves. I knew about tape loops myself now—my visions of murders having become a nearly nightly event, and the Cat Stevens or Crosby, Stills and Nash albums I put on my record player wouldn't drown them out. The song I heard now, whether they were playing it on the radio or not, was "My Sharona." The images that were coming to me of the victims had gotten more clear and terrible, though except for the presence of the little dog in that one scene, I had never caught a glimpse of anything that might have served as a clue to finding the killer.

As hard a time as I was having finding peace of mind, I knew it was worse for our father. I had difficulty making out the words he spoke to our mother on his late-night visits, but I gathered he just about never slept anymore.

I knew him so well, I could feel how it must be for him. My father was a true romantic, the most gallant man I ever met. If he had lived in medieval Europe, he would have been a knight. As it was, the closest he could come to that was to be a police officer.

For a man who'd viewed himself all his life as a heroic protector of women, the steadily mounting numbers of victims and his own apparent impotence at apprehending the murderer (impotence, an interesting word there, it occurred to me, but that thought came years later) was about as close as there came for him to a vision of hell.

It was January, and I was sitting on the bed at Alison's house with Alison and Soleil, watching the pink television and eating grilled-cheese sandwiches. Some magazine-style news program was devoting an entire hour to the story of the murdered girls. Their faces formed a collage on the screen—*Brady Bunch*– style—as, one by one, a somber voice spoke their names and ages. Then came a montage of more pictures and Super 8 footage from their childhoods, birthday parties, school graduations.

"Do you have any idea what it's like to have a police officer show up at your door to say they've found your daughter murdered?" the woman on the screen was saying. This would have been my father she was talking about of course. He carried the weight of those visits wherever he went now. The lightness I could remember, when he took the stairs to Margaret Ann's two at a time, was gone from his step.

This mother might at first glance have appeared reasonably calm as she looked out from the television, but there was a shrillness to her voice—an unnatural tightness in her neck, and a look in her eyes as if she'd just stepped out of a dark closet into scorching sunlight—that made you recognize she was also probably about ten seconds away from screaming. The camera showed her sitting next to a table arrayed with framed photographs of her—Tanya Pope, the killer's most recent victim.

"It's time we got some law enforcement officers who know what they're doing," she said. "Six months of this, and they're no closer to finding the killer than when this monster started."

"Your father must feel shitty," Alison said, reaching for another sugar-free gummy bear. "Being the one in charge and all."

"The killer never leaves any clues," I told her. "Other than, you know, what's inside the girls." Meaning his semen, though that was not a word I'd ever spoken out loud.

Neither of my parents had told me about that, but I knew about the rape part from what I read in the newspaper about the murders, and what people said—and more and more, from my visions. Lately, what I saw in my visions were not only the murders, but the rapes too.

Only the year before, our gym teacher had sat us down to show us a movie called *Our Changing Bodies,* with animated drawings of a pair of ovaries, like a couple of bendable straws, and a woman's uterus as it changed over the days of a menstrual cycle. Accompanied by an upbeat sound track, the movie featured sprightly cartoons of sperm and egg meeting up like two old friends in some unnamed place that could have been the hallway at school and merging into something that became a baby.

From the moment of your birth, the voice said, *your body holds a treasure chest of unfertilized eggs. Your lifetime supply. Getting your period is the sign the eggs are now capable of fertilization. Your body can make a baby now.*

For every other girl in my class, getting her period was old news at this point. I had been waiting so long now that I'd concluded there was something permanently wrong with my body.

"At least you'll never be one of those teenage mothers," Patty said, trying as always to look on the bright side. "If we were Catholic, you could sign up to be a nun.

"And anyway," she went on, "I never saw what was so great about getting blood in your underpants. If you ask me, you're lucky."

I didn't know what I was anymore, except different. The Sunset Strangler killings had begun right around the time all the other girls started talking about their periods, and in an unsettling way those two events—the murders of all those young women and my own anxious anticipation of blood— were linked for me. It seemed as if fertility brought danger.

At this point in my life, I hadn't witnessed much in the way of tender or loving relationships between men and women, or boys and girls. The Pollacks down the street seemed friendly enough with each other, but as with the Brady parents, and the parents on most of the shows my sister and I had observed through other people's picture windows, their relationship seemed to be about taking care of their house and their yard, their son, and the baby on the

way—going to work, going to the supermarket—
with no visible evidence of passion. No intimation of
sex happening, though Jennifer Pollack's pregnancy
was proof it did.

When Karl Pollack paid me my babysitting wages
at the end of the evening, he'd walk me the three doors
down Morning Glory Court to our front walk and
stand on the sidewalk to watch until I was safely inside
before returning to his own house. I used to think it
was almost like the end of a date, or at least the way I
imagined a date might be, minus the good-night kiss.
One time, just before reaching my house, Mr. Pollack's
hand had flicked at a bug and grazed my chest.
(Or maybe he meant to do that? Maybe there was no
bug. He just wanted to touch me.) The picture came to
me then, of Karl Pollack, whipping me around to face
him and bending over to kiss me hard on the mouth.
Not like Teddy Bascom, but deep and long, and in the
picture, I was kissing him back.

After he was gone, I sometimes tried to imagine what might happen after he got back to his own
house. I pictured the two of them together—Karl and
Jennifer, naked. I wanted to imagine a nice picture,
for a change, but my mind came up blank. All that
came to me were the horses mating on the hillside
and howling coyotes; the sounds Alison's boyfriend,

Chase, made, that could be heard emanating from inside Alison's bedroom; and Teddy, splayed across the beanbag, holding on to my hair like the reins of a pony and panting. Maybe some of these people were enjoying themselves, but if you didn't know differently, the noises could have been those of a murder victim.

In my real-life experience, only a single picture came to mind, of two people who seemed to look at each other with love and passion, not anger, or desperation, or distrust or bitterness or resignation, as well as unmistakable yearning for each other—people for whom the simple act of touch carried a rush of wonder. It was a picture of my father and Margaret Ann.

"You'll be seeing a lot more of her, I think," he had told Patty and me that day in the car.

But we hadn't. I knew why, too, of course. I was the one who'd spoiled it.

They were having a Valentine Fair at the rec center, and Patty and I decided to check it out.

A boy in my class, Raymond—nobody I knew to talk to—was selling popcorn balls and brownies and Rice Krispies treats dyed pink. He was raising money for a trip his Scout troop was planning to take the next summer to Washington, D.C. I hoped he wouldn't notice me, but he did.

"My father showed me a letter to the editor in the paper today," he said. "The person said they should fire your dad and bring in someone that knows what he's doing. I thought you should know."

"People are dumb," Patty said.

"My dad said they should bring in the FBI," another boy at the table added. Also a Boy Scout, apparently. "The FBI's got computers and stuff. Real crime experts who know what they're doing."

I knew Raymond was looking at me. I knew he was looking at my chest actually—though when he did, I understood well that the noteworthy aspect would be what he failed to observe there: breasts.

I tried to think of what my father would tell me. *Don't let any boy give you shit.* But he'd never said how we should go about preventing this.

It was my sister who spoke up, in that surprisingly firm and husky voice of hers that carried over a whole playground when she wanted it to. "Our father could squish your father with his little finger if he wanted to," she said. "Go tell your father to get his eyes examined."

This was a pretty good one. I wondered if Patty even remembered that Raymond's father was an ophthalmologist, or if it was just one of those weirdly appropriate things she came out with.

"Oh yeah," he said. "Anybody ever tell you to get some braces?"

Lunchtime again. I was sitting in my spot across from Alison, who had her usual bag full of raw vegetables that were supposed to make her skinny as a model, which might have if she didn't douse every carrot in blue cheese dip. The girls were talking about the up-coming Sadie Hawkins dance where the girls asked the boys. The obvious thing would have been for me to invite Teddy Bascom, but that would have meant that I considered him my boyfriend, and in spite of all the making out we did, I wasn't sure that term applied.

"They found some footprints after the last girl got killed," I said. "My father thinks he might be able to tell what kind of shoes the killer wears. The ground was really muddy from the rain, but they still got some kind of impression."

This part was actually true, for once. I knew this from my father, who had made a rare appearance at our house the night before, just as Patty and I were going to bed, to say good night to us and have a drink with our mother. Their usual routine now.

I had started noticing that my bulletins about the Sunset Strangler case no longer had the effect on the girls at school that they used to. Back in September, Alison had hung on my words, but my father's position as chief of homicide no longer carried much weight with anyone at school.

"Finding the imprint of a shoe is really good news," I continued, having gotten no response to my first disclosure. "My dad says this guy is so smart, that's probably the best clue they've located yet."

A couple of months earlier, this statement would have inspired a lot of questions. Now, nobody said a word.

I wished then that I hadn't said anything. When I made things up about the case, I never felt guilty, but it felt wrong revealing something that was real, or even talking about something that my father had shared with me in a moment that had been just ours up until that second. Those moments felt too precious to talk about here.

The night before, he had come into our bedroom to say good night to us. Months had passed since he sang us one of our familiar songs, but he had sat on the edge of my bed, not even talking, just sitting in the quiet darkness for a surprisingly long time.

My sister had fallen asleep. It was just the two of us, and so I had asked him—as I generally never did—how things were going with the case.

"I can't lie to you. It's rough, baby," he said. "But maybe we got a little break with this last one."

That's when he told me about making the plaster impression of the shoe imprint, and how it was the first good lead they'd had in weeks. "I brought over a bag of the plaster for you," he said. "I thought you and Patty could use it to do something fun, like making casts of your handprints. Maybe give them to your old man to put on my desk at work."

"What size shoe does he wear?" I asked my father. Meaning the killer.

"Don't keep putting this creep in your brain, Farrah," he'd told me, stroking my head. "I can tell you from personal experience, once he gets in there, he doesn't get out. It's not good for a person's health."

"So what did your dad say then?" Alison asked me, plunging another carrot in the blue cheese dip and sounding more bored than enthusiastic now. "Are they getting close to catching him?"

"Once this guy is in your brain he doesn't get out," I told the girls, though I had meant to keep quiet. "It's like a toxic virus."

"Or that old movie, *The Exorcist*," Soleil offered. "A person can get possessed."

"Your dad's not possessed, is he?" Heather said. "Like where a person's eyeballs turn crazy and gunk comes out of their mouth?"

"He's a professional. They know how to keep that from happening. There's things he knows how to do, to keep it from messing him up," I said.

I hoped this part was true.

He was not possessed, but by March our father seemed to have aged ten years. He gave the impression of being not just tired, but weary in a way I'd never seen before. Some of the changes were so small nobody but Patty and I would have picked up on them: a heaviness in his step on the stairs, his failure to bring us our gardenia and chocolate bar on what had always been his favorite holiday—Valentine's Day. He was as thin as I'd ever seen him, and I could tell when he gave me rides to school—the ashtray overflowing— that he was smoking a lot in the car. Once that winter, when he'd taken my hand—warming it up in the cold by blowing on it—I had noticed his fingertips were yellow from cigarettes. It had been a long time since we'd ridden together in his Alfa with the sunroof and all the windows open, singing "Volare" at the top of our lungs.

I caught sight of him on television one time over at Alison's. The pizza had just arrived and we were in her rec room, diving for slices.

There had been no new murders on the mountain for a couple of months, probably due to the rainy season, but with the rains expected to end soon, and the killer still at large, a group of citizens had been putting pressure on the governor to do something about securing the mountain. A reporter had asked my father for a comment on developments in the case. There were none.

I sat on the beanbag chair in Alison's family room, while Heather applied polish to my toenails. My father stood in front of the microphone, looking like a "before" picture in an ad for some miracle rejuvenation product. His skin sagged and his eyes were puffy. Knowing him, and how he prided himself on his appearance, what alarmed me most was his hair. He always cut it himself, so regularly you were never even aware he'd had a haircut. This time it looked as though he'd taken whatever pair of scissors was closest and hacked it all off without bothering to check in a mirror.

"What if this guy just keeps going on and on murdering people?" a boy named Rich said, to nobody in particular.

"I'd get a gun," said Soleil, never the brightest bulb.

"I'd get my parents to move to L.A.," said Heather. "The weather's better there anyway."

"Maybe we could form our own SWAT team, and stake out the trails with our nunchucks," one of the boys offered. Another idiot.

I kept my mouth shut. What could I say? The terrible part was, looking at him now, I wished nobody even knew Detective Anthony Torricelli was my father. Maybe I was the daughter of the designated protector of the girls of Marin County, but if the girls of Marin County kept getting murdered, what did that say about us?

Teddy Bascom had decided it was time I had sex with him. He told me this—not in any romantic way, more along the lines of "hey, let's get it on"—one afternoon at Alison's, after our usual makeout session: the breast, the hand, the wetness after.

"Alison and Chase do it," he said. "Everyone does after they've been going out this long."

I never understood why people used the term "going out." All I ever did with Teddy was stay *in* the rec room.

"Thirteen's too young," I said, though my fourteenth birthday was coming up. (My fourteenth birthday. And still no period.) I could have offered a bunch of other reasons, most particularly the fact that I didn't want to have sex—that in fact I didn't want to be doing the

other things we had been doing all this time either—
but I kept it simple.

"Not going all the way is bad for my health," Teddy
said. "The way it is with guys, if you get too frustrated,
even if you get to come, it can mess up your balls."

I didn't know why it was my responsibility, making
sure Teddy Bascom's balls were all right. He hadn't
shown much concern about my breasts; I was starting
to worry that all the manhandling might make them
stretched out and droopy, the way our mother's were. I
didn't bring this up either. I just repeated that thirteen
was too young. And then, not so much because it would
have any effect on Teddy, but more for myself and the
small comfort that saying these next words out loud
would offer me, I added, "My father wouldn't want me
to do that."

"It's not like you'd tell him."

"He'd know."

This part was true, not so much because my father
happened to be a detective as because he loved me so
much, and, absent as he was, when he was with us,
he noticed every single thing. If I had sex with Teddy
Bascom, I knew something would change about me,
and my father would pick up on it.

All my life—my life, and my sister's—our father
had told us we were the most special girls. "Don't ever

let some guy treat you like less than a princess, or he'll be hearing from me," our father had said, time and again.

Thinking about this, lying on the beanbag chair with Teddy on top of me, I started to cry.

"Oh, Jesus," Teddy said. "Here comes the waterworks."

I wasn't sobbing. No sound came out. But there were tears streaming down my face.

"I can't believe you," he said. "I should just break up with you now."

"That's a good idea," I said. I realized then—though until this moment it had not occurred to me—that I had no further interest in spending my afternoons on the beanbag chair while Teddy Bascom yanked on my small, sad breasts and rubbed his penis against my jeans. I didn't want to be in this room at all, not with Teddy, or with Alison and her friends either. I wanted to be home with my sister.

"I think I'll go now," I told him.

Alison's house on Peacock Gap lay on the opposite side of the freeway from ours. On my bike I could have made it home in fifteen minutes, but on foot it was a few miles, and the rain was heavy enough that afternoon to make it hard to see.

I knew how busy my father was with the case, but maybe because I'd just invoked his name I was wishing, even more than usual, that I could see him. I had a couple of dimes in my pocket. Enough to place a call.

One of his deputies answered, but when I said I was Detective Torricelli's daughter, she put me through right away. I told him I was sorry for interrupting him at work.

"What's more important than one of my girls when she needs me?" he said.

I asked if he could pick me up. I told him where I was. The 7-Eleven out by the highway.

"I'm on my way," he said.

Usually when Patty or I rode someplace with our father it was in the Alfa, but this time he had the patrol car. The unmarked kind, since he was a detective, not an ordinary member of the force.

"Oh, Farrah," he said when he saw me. "Who made you cry? Tell me his name."

We drove out past the sandpit to a spot where, when Patty and I were younger, he'd taken us to learn to ride our bikes, and where, another time, with Margaret Ann, we'd had a picnic, and he'd set up the bocce balls that used to be his father's. Margaret Ann had brought bubble solution and taught us a song in French. It was after that afternoon that I told my father I didn't want to spend time with her anymore. I wanted it to be just the three of us, like before.

"I wish you didn't have to work all the time," I said.

"Once we nail this killer, I'm taking a vacation. I'm taking you and your sister to Italy."

Other people's fathers might have offered Disneyland. Ours talked about Venice.

"Do you ever worry the Sunset Strangler might try to get you, Dad?" I asked him. "If he gets the idea you're onto him."

"I can take care of myself, baby. Me, and my girls too." He didn't mention the gun, but I knew he had one, in a holster on his shin. It was there even now, as we sat in the car talking, though what made me feel safe when my father was around had never been the presence of a gun.

I put my head on his shoulder. The bench seats in my father's unmarked police car made it possible to lean up against him, the way we used to do in our old station wagon when my sister and I were little. He lit a cigarette and stroked my head.

"I'm sorry about how it worked out between your mother and me," he said. "She's a wonderful woman. I never meant to hurt anybody. "

I wanted to ask, What about Margaret Ann?, but I couldn't say it. Whatever happened there was between the two of them.

"Do you think you'll ever marry anybody else?" I asked him. As close as I was ever going to get to that topic.

"No woman in her right mind would marry a mope like your old man," he said. "And anyway, I don't have time to be a husband to anybody. I did a pretty lousy job the first time around. I figured I should quit before I did any more damage."

"We're fine," I said. Even if we weren't, I'd tell him that.

"I'm sorry I don't get over to the house much lately," he said. "I only saw one of your sister's games all season."

"It's okay," I said, though it hadn't been. Patty wasn't the crying type, but I knew from the look on her face what she was thinking when her team won the semifinals game that would send them to the playoffs—scanning the bleachers and seeing only other people's fathers.

"Who'd ever think some serial killer would hang out on hiking trails, huh? We've gone crazy, trying to keep people off those trails, but he keeps extending his range and they keep coming in with whistles in their fanny packs and their Swiss Army knives, whatever good that does, like none of our warnings apply to them."

It was never uncomfortable sitting in silence with my father. I sat there breathing in the smell that was just him—the smoke, the aftershave, the scent that was just him. Studying his face that day—no longer handsome as he had been, but the face I loved—the thought occurred to me, what would I do if he died?

I could not imagine the world without my father in it.

To change the subject, I asked him why he had wanted to be a police officer. Just for a moment, I let myself picture how it would have been if he had a different kind of job and I had one of those dads who came home every night at five thirty carrying a briefcase. The kind that plays checkers with you and has a hobby like stamp collecting instead of taking you to an R-rated James Bond double feature. This would be a whole different person of course. Not him. So, never mind.

"Maybe I watched too many movies," he said. "I liked the idea of being a hero. Protect innocent citizens from criminals. Rescue women in distress from bad guys. Only problem is, while you're busy saving the world you can lose track of your own family."

He put his cigarette out. For once he didn't light another right away. He sat there stroking my head, and then I felt a swift, sharp tug at my scalp, gone before there was anything like pain.

He was making one of his spiders for me, that he hadn't done for either of us in a long time, since before the first murders. When it was done, he set it on my arm—eight feathery legs crafted miraculously from a single strand of my one black hair. It almost looked real.

"You tell that piece-of-shit boy for me, Farrah—the one who made you cry—that if he does anything more to hurt you, he'll spend the rest of his life seeing my face in his nightmares," my father said.

He turned the key in the ignition and we drove away.

It was April, when the weather should have been getting nice again, but every morning we woke to the sound of rain. It never let up. Other years, there would be a few days at least in which the sun came out to give us a break, but that year it seemed all light left the sky sometime in December. It was anybody's guess when sunlight would return.

For the first months after the murders began, the knowledge of a serial killer on the loose had not completely discouraged hikers, but at this point hardly anyone ventured out on the mountain, partly out of fear probably, but likely also on account of the weather. Almost four months had passed without another body turning up—the longest crime-free stretch since the Sunset Strangler had commenced his attacks.

But my father wasn't resting easy, and unlike other people, he couldn't even look forward to the end of the rainy season, knowing that when the sun came out again, so would the hikers, and so most likely would the killer.

Some of the families of the murdered women had formed a group, called Mothers for Justice. They wanted to bring in a special task force of experts from outside. Because a majority of the killings had taken place on land that fell within the national park system, the FBI had also become involved. Lately, some prominent citizens, including a couple of councilmen, along with the Take Back the Mountain contingent, were demanding that direction of the case be handed over entirely to the federal officers. According to Mothers for Justice, the local homicide squad, under the direction of Detective Anthony Torricelli, had come up empty long enough.

We knew our father's feeling about the FBI: they were a bunch of overpaid suits with fancy toys who flew around the country staying in expensive hotels, men who never cocked a gun or broke a sweat. Would any of them spend a day driving around used car lots with a nineteen-year-old hitchhiker who'd seen a red late-model Toyota at a parking lot near the scene of a recent murder, hoping to spot a similar one? Would members of the special task force sit on the couch with

Tanya Pope's mother, looking at every one of her baby pictures? Would they haunt shoe stores, looking for a tread that matched the plaster cast of the shoeprint that might—just might—have been left by the killer? Would they listen to a tape of eight-year-old Kelly Cunningham singing "Side by Side" in her third-grade talent show?

Our father still stopped by our house almost nightly at this point, to have a cup of coffee or more often a glass of scotch with our mother. Perhaps the fact that he didn't feel an obligation to charm her the way he did with all the others—it would never have worked if he tried—had allowed him to have what may well have been his one truly honest relationship with a woman. For her part, my mother kept to herself to such a degree that he was probably for her, too, the closest she had to a friend.

Almost every night, I could hear them in the kitchen talking—the sound of the coffee percolator, or the clink of the ice in their glasses. Day and night appeared to have become interchangeable for our father, and because our mother slept so little, it didn't matter to her what time it was when he came by. She kept the light on.

He stopped over on his way home to his apartment, or maybe on his way to his office in the Civic Center to put in more hours sifting through paperwork. There were still a few thousand red Toyota Coronas to follow up on, along with a totally different make and model of car added to the list of vehicles that might or might not belong to the perpetrator—a green Fiat with one of those car deodorizers in the shape of a tree dangling from the rearview mirror, which had been seen tearing out of the parking lot on the day of the Point Reyes murder.

Lying in my bed at night, I wanted to tell my father that I knew a few things about the killer too. (About his black loafers. His chubby fingers. And maybe a dog.) But I knew he would just have told me to stop thinking about it.

"You should get some sleep, Anthony," I heard our mother telling him.

"I could lie down," he told her. "But sleep's a different matter."

I could hear the sound of his lighter hitting the table. The low, rasping cough that had become as much a part of him as his singing used to be.

"You need to see a doctor about that," my mother said.

"I can't do anything until I hear the snap of the cuffs on this mutt," he said. "If there was ever a guy who deserved the chair, this is the one. Then I can have a life, maybe. Take our girls to Italy. Cook up a nice egg-plant parm."

"You might think of cutting back on the cigarettes while you're at it," our mother said. "Not that I should talk."

At school, my social status changed—not for the better—following the breakup with Teddy, and the simultaneous ending to my relationship with Alison and Soleil and their crowd. I was no longer simply invisible. Now I was shunned.

At the start of eighth grade I'd been a celebrity, due to my association with my father, but now that same fact, and the knowledge that the case was dragging on unsolved, produced the opposite effect. Nobody had anything to say to me anymore when my father made a statement to the press. Nobody said he looked like Sean Connery, that was for sure. Not that I would have been around to hear it. Lunchtimes in the cafeteria now, I ate alone.

But my social problem went deeper than my being the daughter of the detective who hadn't caught the Sunset Strangler. It was about Alison and Soleil and the little posse of girls who had magically allowed me into their circle only a few months before but now, with a terrible swiftness, excluded me from it so utterly it was as if they no longer knew my name. They had not needed to inform me of my changed status. It was something I could sense the Monday morning after I'd told Teddy Bascom I wasn't going to have sex with him. The look Alison had given me when I walked into homeroom had been enough for me to know where I would no longer be sitting at lunchtime. She was having sex with her boyfriend, of course, and probably had been for a while now. The fact that I had made a different choice (as everyone in our grade undoubtedly knew) must have seemed like an indictment by me of her own behavior.

Or maybe—and this was likely—the details of how I'd ended things with Teddy had not been broadcast accurately. Unaccustomed as he was to having a girl tell him she didn't want to be with him, Teddy would have been likely to portray himself as the instigator of our breakup. Maybe he even said I was too fast. Or desperate. Very possibly the entire eighth grade now viewed me as a slut.

Whatever they said about me, the end result was clear. After school I rode the bus home—though now, in an ironic turning of the tables, my sister was the busy one, off at basketball practice. I had nothing but time, and nothing to do with it but think about the Sunset Strangler—and my own malfunctioning body that had left me trapped in the no-man's-land between child-hood and womanhood. I had never been more lonely, or more miserable.

All those months I'd spent my afternoons at Alison's, I hardly ever took my bike out anymore, but one after-noon—a rare day without rain—I cleaned the dust off my old Schwinn and pumped up the tires.

I had set off that day with no destination in mind. Just pedaling to pass the time and barely noticing where I was headed, which was no place, mostly. Just away.

But somehow I found myself in Peacock Gap again. I hadn't set out to go there, though maybe it was long-ing that took me to the place—the memory of all those afternoons on Alison's bed with Soleil and Heather and the rest of the girls, eating pizza and telling secrets, real or invented.

I'd pedaled up a long hill, winding past the houses with their automatic sprinkler systems watering their unnaturally green lawns—never mind the nonstop rains that winter and spring—and the Mexican gar-deners tending them. Here, all the garage doors opened and closed easily. This was Alison's neighborhood and Soleil's.

The road took me past the country club, and the golf course, and past a row of tennis courts where I saw a group of girls around my age in cute outfits playing some kind of tournament. At tables not far off, shaded by oversized umbrellas, the mothers looked on.

In the past, I had frequently felt envy for these kinds of girls—for their outfits, their rackets, their cute, friendly mothers, unlike my own, so involved in their daughters' activities and ready at a moment's notice to buy them outfits and drive them places. I had tried to be one of those girls myself, and for a while (to my sister's disgust) I may even have resembled one of them.

Those days were over now.

I had gotten off my bike for a moment to take in the scene at the country club, just at the moment some tennis match for girls around my age appeared to be ending. One of the girls had walked up to the net to shake the hand of the other as—over in the mother section—the mothers of the two girls appeared to gather up their considerable assortment of belongings: snacks, sweaters, suntan lotion, cameras for recording the game, cans of tennis balls, and some additional tennis rackets that evidently served, for these girls, as backups—in case something happened to the one they were using in the match, I supposed.

It was a small thing I noted. The mother of the winning girl had zipped all three extra rackets into a racket bag. Now her daughter appeared at the table and handed her mother the racket she'd just finished playing with. The mother handed the girl a Gatorade, along with her sweater. The girl walked off, a few steps ahead of her mother, as the mother—carrying a cooler, purse, tennis balls, and the large racket bag— followed after her. The girl carried nothing but a pair of sunglasses.

An odd thing happened then: I felt a rush of love for a person I didn't think about that often—my own seemingly neglectful mother, who never told me what to wear, or took me for pedicures with her, or tried to get me to sign up for cheerleading. At that moment, she was probably off at the library, searching for more books by obscure Indian gurus or Sylvia Plath poetry. Wherever she was, it seemed like a great gift that day that she had simply left my sister and me to make our own choices. However different they might be from hers.

She had allowed us to make our own lives, free of the burden of pleasing her. Patty and I belonged to nobody but our own selves.

The previous Christmas I had been given a Ouija board. With the rainy season unrelentingly upon us (too wet for Drive-In Movie; invitations to Alison's house no longer forthcoming), my sister and I were spending our nights now—after basketball—on opposite sides of our kitchen table with our fingers touching the edges of the plastic pointer, asking questions about our lives and the world. We lit candles when we had them.

During our first session, Patty had managed to make contact with a family named Fletcher who'd died of starvation going over the Donner Pass and ended up getting eaten by their neighbors from the next wagon— the very topic she'd been studying that year in sixth grade, amazingly enough. When Patty asked Mrs. Fletcher if she had anything to say, the woman had responded with a series of consonants that seemed—if a person used her imagination—to spell out the observation "Next time, stay home."

Over the weeks that followed we progressed to more current topics: Patty's basketball performance (would her team win the tournament?) and the sex of Mrs. Pollack's baby. I might have liked to ask when, if ever, I'd be getting my period, but I was too afraid of what the answer might be. After my breakup with Teddy Bascom, Patty did consult the Ouija board once as to whether I'd be getting back together with him.

No way. He jerk, the pointer told us. Or so Patty concluded.

"Will I ever get to play in the WBL?" she asked.

WKKK. HRJJD. Work. Hard.

The planchette stopped over the word *yes*.

The way it worked best with the Ouija board, you started off calling to the spirits, asking someone to make contact from the other world, the place where the dead people were. On some occasions it appeared nobody was available. Tied up with other girls doing the same thing we were, most likely.

One night I'd taken out the Ouija board with a particular sense of urgency. This time we found a spirit in the mood for communicating.

She said her name was Zara. She'd died in a car accident about ten years earlier, not far from Route 101. I asked her if she'd heard about the Sunset Strangler killings.

Messages sent to our Ouija board from the other world, if that's where they came from, were never all that simple to decode. A lot of extra letters got in there, or they'd be out of order, requiring whoever it was receiving them to do a certain amount of interpretation before you could understand what they said.

Anticipating this problem, I'd equipped my sister with a notepad and pen to use to write down the letters the pointer led us to. This made it easier to figure out what whoever it was on the other side—Zara, it appeared—was trying to get across. But what came up in response to that first question appeared with surprising clarity.

The planchette moved again to the word *yes* on the board. Our spirit had heard of the Sunset Strangler, she told us.

JVSRQICTNMS HR. WM BNW. Victims here with me now.

"That's great news," Patty said. "Now we can ask the girls who killed them."

BDMJJJJ.

Bad man.

RSGSX.

The first letters were a mystery. But not the last two. *Sex.* He wanted sex.

"Can you say more?" I asked. "How old is he? What color hair does he have? We need to know who he is so our father can arrest him."

NOVXR HR. No Hair.

WTSKSC. ST. TL.

Wants sex. Stands tall?

The significance of some letters remained unclear, but I got that part.

I looked at my sister across the table, fingertips touching mine—that surprised look on her face that meant she was concentrating hard.

The pointer began to move again.

· *DG. CT. DG.* My sister didn't even have to reach for the pen this time to write the letters down. I understood without that.

The pointer had spelled *Dog,* of course. There was a dog involved. And I had seen a dog in my vision that night. In Muir Woods, the day of the Naomi Berman murder.

The pointer stopped moving then. We sat there in the darkened kitchen, our fingers no longer touching on the board, just breathing.

"What do you think Zara meant?" Patty said. "Maybe he's going to kill a dog next time?"

Everyone was always wondering how it was the Sunset Strangler managed to get the women's guard down as he came up to them. Why, seeing a man approaching on the trail, after all the murders, they hadn't run.

Maybe, as my vision had suggested, the Sunset Strangler had a dog. A cute one.

It was a Friday night—rainy as always—and Patty's team, the CYO Junior Varsity girls, was up against St. Vincent's for the season championship. There had been a story in the paper the day before about the upcoming game, with a focus on my sister as the youngest member and high scorer of the team—"a player to watch," the reporter had written. The article also noted who Patty's father was. Our name was well known throughout the county now, though having your name associated as ours was with a run of serial killings—even if you were on the side of the law—was not good news.

I cut the article about Patty out and tacked it to our bulletin board, with the photograph alongside showing my sister executing an amazing shot from just beyond the arc. In the photograph, she had that wide-eyed surprised look on her face, as if the ball had just magically found its way into the hoop. When I cut out the story, I left off the final paragraph with our father's name featured, but Patty had known it was there.

It was understood that our mother didn't usually attend games, and Patty had stopped hoping that our father would show up, never mind providing a ride. So, as he often did, Mr. Armitage had driven Patty and me to the game. Despite my expressed belief that Mr. Armitage was a weirdo, my sister had developed a friendship with him over the many months of walking his dog, and regular visits in which their talks about Petra were conducted over cookies and root beer floats.

Because this was a big game, all the kids from school were there, including Teddy Bascom, though he pretended not to see me. He and Alison's friend Violet leaned against the wall with their hands in each other's pocket. Fine with me.

Harder to take in was the little posse of girls around Alison herself—Soleil of course, and Heather, and some others known to me from our many hours together doing one another's nails in her rec room, though it appeared that in their eyes now, I no longer existed.

"How's it going?" I said to Alison when I reached the section of bleachers where they'd stationed themselves. I had nothing to say to them, really. I just wasn't going to act like someone who's ashamed of herself. *Don't let anybody give you shit.*

"Great jeans," she said. Though they weren't new and even when they had been, they'd come from K-Mart.

I was sitting alone in my usual spot, high in the bleachers, where I could watch my sister without being close enough to take in her anxiety or convey mine to her. One thing Patty had a hard time with were all the minutes she had to sit on the sidelines, especially if she was not simply being given a break but had fouled out, and worst of all if, as was true this time, her team trailed by a dozen points. It killed her not to be out there angling for the ball. Shy as she might seem elsewhere, out on the court my sister was on the ball like a junkyard dog going after a bone.

From where I sat I could see a woman across the court, seated almost as high up as me and, like me, alone. She didn't look like anybody's mother. She didn't have a mother hairdo for one thing—hers hung down past her shoulders—but it was more than that. Mothers at games were focused on their players. This woman seemed to be focusing her attention on the door to the gym, as if for her the important action would take place over there, not on the court.

She was one of those people who stand out in a crowd. She had an intensity surrounding her, almost like a force field, and you could sense it meant a lot to her to be in that room, though not for the same reason the rest of us were.

I knew her from someplace, but it wasn't until the third quarter that it came to me where.

More than five years had passed since I'd seen her. It was Margaret Ann, the woman who had caused my father's face to light up in a way I had not seen before or since. Here was the woman whose house we used to drive by with our father, not even stopping. He just looked up at her window. The woman who inspired my mother to pronounce that if he ever married again, his daughters would never get over it.

When I'd heard those words, I'd believed them.

So had my father.

Margaret Ann was still good-looking—even from such a distance I could tell that—but she wore glasses now, and it appeared she'd put on a little weight. Back in the days we'd visited her, my father had said he could get his two hands around her waist, she was so slim, though this couldn't have been true, really.

Margaret Ann. I had no doubt what she was doing at my sister's game, and it had nothing to do with being a basketball fan.

Margaret Ann had shown up at this game for the same reason I did—with the hope that my father would be there. Not even to speak to him, just to be in the same space as he was, to share the same air for a while. One look at her and I felt it: just like us, she longed to catch a glimpse of him, if only for a moment.

He arrived partway into the fourth quarter, just as my sister was making a foul shot. She made it of course, taking her team, the CYO Warriors, to a one-point lead over their rivals, the Saints. All through the first half, Patty had continued glancing out to the stands, scanning the crowd, but she had given that up now, all focus on the court.

As many times as she had watched for him that season, I wasn't sure if Patty had seen our father slip into his seat in the very last row, high in the bleachers, or the flowers he had in his lap to give her after the game. If anybody sitting near him had noticed his arrival—as the man on whom the citizens of Marin County had, for a time at least, pinned their best hopes of apprehending the Sunset Strangler, the man now blamed for failing to do so—no one let on. He was just another tired-looking basketball fan—a dad, most likely, based on the bouquet in his hands—who looked as though he could use a cigarette.

Margaret Ann noticed him. Even from where I sat, I could see her back straighten as he made his way up into the bleachers, and one hand go to her hair. She took her glasses off. Put them on again. Took them off. She turned back to the game, but I could feel her concentration on my father now.

All these months, it had been my affliction that the person whose story had occupied my brain was the one I'd least want to have there, but that night, for a moment anyway, I imagined what it would feel like to be Margaret Ann. She did not move her lips, but it came to me that she was praying. *Look this way, Tony. I'm here.*

He hadn't spotted her. He was looking toward the court, where my sister was on fire. Two times in the space of a minute she grabbed the rebound and put it right back up to score. Tore down the other end to steal the ball back, made her hook shot, got it in without the ball even touching the backboard, took the ball back down the court, stole the inbounds pass, and threaded a pass to her teammate for a win.

"That girl can't miss," a man said, sitting next to me.

"The detective's daughter," his wife offered. "From the paper."

"She could teach her father a thing or two," he said. "This girl knows how to go after what she wants."

Across the court, I studied my father—imagining how he would look to Margaret Ann now, if, as I guessed, she hadn't seen him for a while. How thin he'd gotten. The gray hair. The sloping shoulders. That weary look.

But I knew Margaret Ann saw none of that. To Margaret Ann, my father remained the most handsome man in Marin County, and the most irresistible. She was cheering for my sister's team now, but she was thinking only of my father.

Alone on the bleachers, eyes on Patty, he saw none of this.

Look. Look. Look, I said to him, but only in my head. *There's someone here who loves you more than anything. A woman who still believes you hung the moon.* Even I could see that. As much as I had hated that fact once, I was grateful now that this was so.

The buzzer sounded. 78–65, Warriors. Roses in hand, my father stood up and made his way down the bleachers onto the floor to find my sister.

An odd thing happened then. For a moment, his gaze had shifted from the players on the court to the bleacher seats where Margaret Ann had been sitting all that time. He got a look on his face, as if he'd received an electric shock. I watched his body go rigid, and his face change, and for a moment I thought he must have seen her.

But she was gone. When I looked to where Margaret Ann had been sitting, nobody was there anymore.

Then it was just us again, riding home in the Alfa, with my sister and me jammed into the one bucket seat, her trophy on her lap, because she didn't even want to set it on the floor.

"You played some game, Patty Cakes," he said.

"It's different being out there when you know someone who really matters is watching," she said.

For a moment, I thought I'd tell him.

You'd never guess who I saw at the game . . .

Only what then? He hadn't been able to figure it out five years ago. He'd be less likely to now. It might just make him sad to think of her. If he didn't already.

In times past, this would have been a moment for a round or two of "That's Amore," but we rode home in silence, my sister holding tight to her trophy. No sound but the windshield wipers, pushing back the rain.

I t had been the wettest winter anyone could remember, and unlike most years, the rain had not let up
entirely even now, late April. But we knew the better
weather would come soon, and that when the mist
finally cleared and the sun returned to the mountain,
more than likely so would the Sunset Strangler.

In years past, April was the month when work got
under way for the community theater's annual musical
production, the Mountain Play, slated for performance
in the outdoor amphitheater on the mountain. Always
before, the announcement had come around Easter as
to which musical would be produced that summer. But
this year the word had come down: due to the murders,
there would be no performances in the amphitheater
this year. It seemed wrong for tap-dancing numbers to

take place, and happy songs to be belted out over the hillside, so close to where violent crimes had been committed. It seemed disrespectful, but more than that, it was dangerous. Even if people wanted to hike up the mountain to see the show, encouraging anyone to venture out on the trails—with the killer still at large— was courting trouble.

The killer must have loved this. *Did* love this. I felt it, knew that he kept tabs on all the news reports, and that the months of rain and enforced absence from the trails had left him restless. It would be a particular thrill for him to watch the news, to listen to reporters describing the increasing desperation of law enforcement agencies in locating the killer, and see the grainy snapshots of his victims flashed again and again on the screen.

Charlene Gray. Lexi Shaw. Naomi Berman. Kelly Cunningham. Willa DePaul. I knew their names by heart, the details of every one of their murders, and what their faces looked like. I knew all this not simply from eavesdropping on my parents' middle-of-the-night conversations, and the scraps of information the newspaper offered up, or the gossip provided by Alison, back in the days when we'd been "friends." No: I knew the sense of arrogance and triumph the killer must be feeling from what took place inside my own head.

I knew he liked to sit in front of his television set and watch my father standing at the podium telling the reporters there was nothing new to report. I knew he noted the slope of my father's shoulders, the thinness of his frame, and enjoyed knowing he was the reason for all he observed, including the diminishment of Detective Anthony Torricelli.

In my mind I saw the killer standing in front of a microwave oven in a kitchen filled with old pizza boxes, eating chocolate pudding straight from the container. Checking the weather reports, anticipating the day he'd be out there once more with his piano wire.

The television was on. They were talking about him again. And one more time, the images of the murdered women flashed on the screen.

He studied the faces of his victims staring out at him, remembered them begging to be allowed to live as the wire he'd tightened around their necks cut off the air to their vocal cords.

He opened a drawer. Took out one of his precious shoelaces. Cleaned his teeth with the tip.

Somewhere on the television screen, the reporter was still talking—something about a task force—but the killer was not paying attention to that part. I pictured him like some kind of animal, like the shark in *Jaws* cutting through the water. Or a vulture, circling high over a mountain hillside, spotting a small dead animal and having only one objective then.

Go get it.

This was where I sat up in my bed. Turned on the light to see my Peter Frampton poster, and my sister's new trophy, the roses set into a jar. A picture of my sister and me that day on the cable car. My jewelry box, with the gum wad in it.

He was coming back.

For our father's birthday—"The Big 4-O," as one of the waitresses at Marin Joe's called it—Patty and I made him tiramisu.

We didn't have a recipe but knew the basics. Ladyfingers and mascarpone cheese, grated chocolate, tons of whipped cream.

We stopped at the supermarket on the way home to pick up the ingredients. When we were done constructing our dessert, we covered it with foil and laid the whole thing in Patty's bike basket. It had been a while since we'd paid a visit to our father's office at the Civic Center. Now with great anticipation we set out to make our tiramisu delivery.

It was a two-mile ride to the Civic Center, much of it along the highway with cars whizzing past. The sky was almost dark when we reached the entrance, but there were people milling around as always—men in suits, leaving court probably, office workers, local citizens come to look up their property maps or pay their tax bill. And members of the police force.

We rode the escalator up to his office on the second floor, just down the hall from the courtrooms where the criminals went on trial. Our mother used to bring us here when we were little sometimes, to have lunch with our father in the cafeteria.

"This building was designed by a famous man named Frank Lloyd Wright," she told us. "Some people got pretty upset about how modern it looks, but I like it."

In those days, our father kept a picture of the three of us on his desk—our mother, Patty, and me. Now there was just a picture of Patty and me. Also a giant stack of papers, a pile of folders, two telephones, and a bunch of coffee mugs with cold coffee in them, and an ashtray that looked as if it hadn't been emptied in a week, though maybe that was just one day's cigarette butts. On the wall behind him, a row of photographs of smiling young women, all with long brown hair, cast their gaze toward an imagined sunny future. The murder victims.

Suddenly it felt as if my sister and I shouldn't be here. "We brought you a surprise," I said. "Happy birthday."

"How did you two get here?" he said. His voice sounded gravelly, in a way it didn't used to.

"We rode our bikes," Patty said. "We took the highway, but we stayed way over on the side of the road, so the cars weren't that close to us."

"No way you're doing that again," he said. "I'm driving you two home."

"We made it ourselves," Patty said. "Tiramisu."

I knew he was trying to appear happy and excited. But he was looking at his watch too.

"Special delivery from Betty Crocker and Julia Child," he said. "How did I ever get so lucky?"

"Are they going to have a party for you later?" Patty said. "You and all the other policemen?"

"We're not exactly party types around here these days," my father said. "Come on. I'll throw your bikes in the trunk."

Once we were outside, I got a glimpse of how things had been going for my father those last few months.

In the half hour we'd been inside the Civic Center, a small crowd of reporters had assembled—some with notepads and tape recorders, a few with microphones and cameras. When they spotted our father, they started calling out to him.

"Have you seen this press release yet, Detective Torricelli?" one of them called out. "A group of victims' families has issued a complaint about the lack of progress made by the Marin Homicide Division. They're calling for the governor to bring in a team of FBI agents to take over the Sunset Strangler investigation."

"Do you care to speculate on what effect the failure of your investigation will have on the sheriff's chances for reelection?" Another voice, insistent above the din.

"Is it true the governor himself called you to express his concern? Did the citizens' petition have anything to do with that?"

"Do you have any explanation for why your office has yet to name a single suspect in the killings?"

"What's your response to charges that your department is indirectly responsible for the girls' deaths?"

At first, when he had seen the reporters, my father had tried to ignore them and press on through. Now, finally, he stopped and moved to face one of the microphones before him. When he spoke, his voice had an edge that hadn't been there the first time he addressed the press about the murders.

"I continue to feel nothing but pride in the job being done by the men and women of the Marin Homicide Division," he said, his voice flat, almost mechanical. "I'm confident that we can work together with federal authorities, and that our efforts will eventually bring the individual responsible for these crimes to justice. We're doing everything in our power."

"Are those your daughters?" someone else called out. A woman.

My father whirled around then, and for a moment, the cameras shifted their focus. To me and Patty.

A cacophony of voices then. (Eighth-grade vocab word: *cacophony*.)

"What if it had been one of your own daughters he'd gotten his hands on?" From somewhere else, the question: "What are their names?" And then: "Which one's the basketball player?"

"Can you look this way, honey?" a man called out to me. A man with a camera. *Flash*. Then flash again.

What happened next seemed almost to come in slow motion. My father raised his arm, and for a second, I thought maybe he was about to punch the man, except that instead of making a fist, his fingers were outstretched in such a way as to block the lens. I felt his big, broad arm around my back, and he was pushing my face into his jacket—mine, and Patty's, away from the lights—and he let out a sound less like anything human than an animal roar.

"Don't ever do that again," he said to the man behind the camera. "Don't ever, ever again think of showing one of my children's faces on television."

A minute later, we were in his car, heading down Route 101 to our house on Morning Glory Court.

"You didn't have to act so mad when you talked to those reporters about me," I told him, from my spot in the front seat. "You sounded mean."

"I acted mad, because I was, Farrah," he said. "Those reporters have no business letting your face appear onscreen. It's not only unethical. It's dangerous."

My father didn't say anything then, but I could see from his face what he was thinking, and I knew it too.

The killer liked to watch TV. Especially when the subject they were talking about on TV was him.

The Sunset Strangler had already identified our father as the enemy. Now he knew our father had two daughters. Now he knew what we looked like.

Considering the fact that the Armitage household didn't appear to have a television set for us to watch through the living room picture window, I don't know what it was that took Patty and me down to Mr. Armitage's end of the street that night. Sometimes we just liked to study the stars, and the spot at the end of Morning Glory Court—treeless and unobstructed by other rooftops or TV antennas—offered the best opportunity for viewing. Plus, the rain that had been pounding down on us for months had finally stopped.

We were out later than usual, and there was only a sliver of moon, which not only made us less visible but made the insides of the houses we passed more so.

The lights were off in the Armitages' living room. But in the bedroom, whose window was nearly as large as that in the living room, and faced the hillside, we could plainly make out the figure of a half-dressed person. A woman.

At first we thought it was Mrs. Armitage getting undressed for bed. This was interesting, considering the fact that by this point months had gone by since either my sister or I had laid eyes on Mrs. Armitage. For all the afternoons Patty spent in their house in the cul-de-sac at the end of the street, no mention had ever been made by Mr. Armitage concerning his wife, and Patty—having decided they must be separated, if not divorced—had never raised the subject to her employer, as to what had become of his wife.

Now there she was, in the bedroom. There was that hat again. Evidently she even wore it indoors. The large brown pocketbook on the dresser. The same polka-dot dress, draped over the back of the chair. She must be getting ready for bed. Hard as it was to imagine Mr. Armitage having sex, maybe he did.

It took a moment to understand: the person we saw through the window was not taking clothes off as you might expect at that hour. She was putting them on.

Then we realized that although the person was putting on a dress, this was not Mrs. Armitage putting on the dress. It was *Mr.* Armitage, standing in front of the mirror, fastening a brassiere over his chest and then, once that was accomplished, wriggling into a pair of panty hose.

Patty and I stood frozen on the hillside, watching as he lifted the brightly colored dress over his head and pulled his arms through the sleeves. It was hard to identify why this was, but his motions seemed different from those of a woman undertaking the same task. This was true when he got to the next part—when that oddly burly arm reached in back to pull up the zipper, and that large hand smoothed the skirt over the broad, mannish backside we now understood to be that of Mr., not Mrs., Armitage.

I don't know how long we stood there. Once Mr. Armitage was dressed, he stood in front of the mirror, shifting his weight from one side to the other and arranging his arms in various positions, moving his wide hips slightly and cocking his head, still sporting the cherry-decked hat, to one side and then the other. It looked as though he might be dancing, though there was no way to know for sure if there was music playing.

We wouldn't have heard it. He might have been wearing makeup, but that was also impossible to know. We saw him only from behind.

The dress. The shoes. And perched on his head, like a cake ornament, a small straw hat—the same one we had seen our neighbor wearing in those nighttime dog-walking expeditions—trimmed with a ribbon and a clump of bright red cherries. Standing in front of the mirror now, he adjusted the brim.

"Do you think his wife knows about this?" Patty asked.

"There is no wife, silly," I told her. "It's just him."

Silence. My sister took a while, absorbing this fact.

"Why does he do it?"

I had no answer. But I'd already been alive long enough to know there were many things people did that seemed to make no sense. Our father smoking all those cigarettes, when we kept telling him they were bad for his lungs. Our mother coming home from work every night and disappearing into her bedroom with a new stack of library books. And now there was this: our gray-haired and balding neighbor dressing up in women's clothes. How crazy was that?

My sister saw it differently. "It's not that big a deal if you ask me," she said. "There's probably a lot of people doing unusual things in their houses at this very moment. We just haven't seen them."

"Unusual?" I said. "Is that what you call it?"

"Maybe he just wishes he had a girlfriend, but he doesn't have one," she said. "Or maybe he just wishes he *was* a girl."

"He's bad news," I told her. "He's a psycho. You shouldn't go over there anymore."

"I don't see what the big deal is," Patty said. "Someone putting on girls' clothes doesn't hurt anybody."

We stood there in the darkness for a moment then, just taking it all in. Mr. Armitage in the mirror. The stars. The silhouette of the mountain against the moon-lit sky, and the howl of a coyote in the distance.

"It's the people who want to take clothes off girls you should worry about," my sister said. "Not the ones who put them on."

Besides, who was I to talk about a person being bad news, when I'd spent every afternoon for a few months on a beanbag chair in a musty old rec room, being manhandled by Teddy Bascom?

Later that night our father stopped by. Two o'clock in the morning maybe. Possibly three.

"You look terrible," our mother said to him.

"I knew this was coming, once the rain let up," he said. "We found another body this morning."

Hearing his voice—but only barely—I climbed out of bed and crouched next to the door to listen. This was the spot I always positioned myself, so I could hear the two of them better. For the first time since the murders began, what I heard in our father's voice from our small dark bedroom was the sound of something like despair.

"I can't talk to anyone about this but you, Lil," he said.

"They found her on the mountain?" our mother asked him.

"Tennessee Valley," he said. "The bluffs. A young couple went out there to catch the sunrise and they found her.

"Everyone thinks the worst part is examining the body," he told our mother. "And I'm not saying it's pretty. But the worst part comes after, notifying the families."

This was not a job he delegated to other members of the homicide squad, though he could have. When a young woman got killed, my father felt the responsibility was his, as the officer in charge, to knock on the door.

In the case of Jean-Marie Doucette there were no living parents. Her mother had died when she and her sister were young, and the father had succumbed to cancer a few months before. Earlier that day my father had made the drive himself, up to Ukiah, where the older sister lived with her husband and children.

"The strange thing was, her sister knew before I opened my mouth to speak," our father told our mother. "She doesn't even live around here, so it's not like they're talking about the Sunset Strangler all that much up in Ukiah. But she took one look at me standing on her doorstep—no uniform, and I hadn't even taken out my badge—and she started to scream.

" 'He killed Jeannie, didn't he?' she says. 'I knew it. Ever since yesterday, I could tell something happened to her.' Then she was on the floor."

Hearing him, I imagined how it would be, receiving news like this about one of my parents. Or Patty. If a vision ever came to me, revealing that one, I didn't think I could have borne it.

Now I pressed my ear to the door, holding my breath so the sound of my own breathing wouldn't drown out the hushed voices of my parents. My mother's was low and soft, but I could still make out the words.

"You do the best you can, Anthony," she said. I heard the sound of ice in someone's glass. A refill. "Nobody can blame you that they haven't got him."

"I should have secured those bluffs," he said.

Then I heard a sound I'd never heard before, more unnerving than an ambulance or a fire truck or the howl of a coyote in the night. It was the sound of our father, not quite weeping, but close.

"I've failed these women," my father said. "I failed everyone I love most in the world, Lillian," he said. "This includes you."

The strong voice that spoke then, oddly enough, was that of our mother, though whatever it was she said came out too softly to hear. If words existed that could comfort my father that night, it's hard to imagine what they might have been.

After his car had backed out of the driveway, I just lay in my lower bunk, looking up at the slats of Patty's bed above me, listening to the soft, comforting sound of my sister's breathing, and thought of climbing the ladder and getting in beside her. Outside, I heard the howl of a coyote again—the new moon brought them out—and shivered. It felt as if the whole rest of the world was falling apart, and all I wanted was to hold on tight to the one person who wasn't going anywhere.

All my life, I'd seen my father as the one who'd always rescue us, but now it came to me, he needed us to rescue him.

P atty and I learned the details from the front page of the *Marin Independent Journal* the next day: Jean-Marie Doucette, age twenty-seven, had come to the beach at the end of the Tennessee Valley trail right around sunset. Back when she was a child, her father used to take her and her sister there. She had returned there to scatter his ashes into the Pacific Ocean.

The paper didn't say much about this part, but it appeared from the oddly worded statements of her surviving sister that there must have been some kind of disagreement between the man's daughters about the ashes, which ultimately led to Jean-Marie going alone down the mile-long stretch of trail from the Tennessee Valley parking lot to the bluffs where the killer had apparently found her.

At the point he grabbed hold of her, Jean-Marie had not yet thrown the ashes over the bluff. The Baggie containing them was found a few feet away from her body, along with a copy of *Jonathan Livingston Seagull*. The killer would have had no interest in taking a book, but no doubt he'd taken her shoelaces.

That night in bed, the feeling came over me again. It crept over my skin, like a chill, or a fever. Then a different set of pictures appeared, like a movie in my head, and everything else in the room disappeared— bunk bed, Cat Stevens, the sound of the refrigerator, the sound of an owl, the sound of my sister's breathing.

There was a girl standing on the bluffs at Tennessee Valley—that spot our parents used to take us when we were little that used to be an old fort, with bunkers still carved into the rock, where teenagers probably came to smoke pot and have sex, with graffiti covering the walls.

June loves Billy. Vic and Pam, '72. Seth is a Homo. Only now I saw, it wasn't me standing there. It was a young woman—just a girl, really, with long brown hair tied in a ponytail, wearing a stretched-out sweatshirt. I couldn't see her face, because her back was turned. She was facing the ocean.

Lower down on the trail, but heading her way: the man. He had spotted her down on the beach—picked her out among the others there (a mother holding a baby in a frontpack, her husband throwing a tennis ball to their dog; a man and woman holding hands; another woman, sitting alone on a piece of driftwood, also pretty, but she was blond, and her hair was cut very short). Jean-Marie was the one he'd followed up the trail, and now he had almost reached the spot where she was standing. There was a heaviness to his footsteps as he approached. He was closing in.

She was holding something, a box. The ashes of her father that her sister hadn't wanted her to scatter here. Close as they were, they'd argued over that.

The girl looked out at the ocean—the dull gray waves and somewhere far out on the horizon, some kind of tanker heading out to sea. She made a sighing sound, as if all the air was coming out of her, and a single syllable: *Oh.*

It was dolphins she saw—three of them—coming close enough to shore that she could see their funny dolphin faces that looked as if they were smiling.

I didn't want to watch this, but I had to.

I was aware now of a length of wire, spread taut between the man's two hands. He was walking toward Jean-Marie, raising the wire over her head, and bringing it down over her neck. Pulling tighter.

She only had time to get out this one sound—though it could be the squawk of a seagull. Not even human. More like a bird.

I saw the wire tightening around the skin of her neck. I saw the man's hands. The girl again—frantic now—pushing them away, or trying to. Then the man's hands, pulling on her hair the way a cowboy would hold tight to a set of reins. She tried to kick, but he was stronger than she was.

The couple with the baby, down below on the beach, looked up for a moment. Just for a moment, it seemed they'd heard something. Sun in their eyes, they turned away again. No sound then but the roar of the ocean, those squawking gulls. And anyway, with the air cut off from her lungs, no more sound came out of the girl now.

The couple turned to go.

His back to me, so did the killer.

I saw the black shoes again, making their way down the bluff. The wrong shoes to wear in a place like this. The dirt gave way a little under them.

I saw a car. Dark blue maybe, but it was hard to say, in the growing darkness. I saw the hand put the key in the ignition, and the shoe on the gas pedal. Chubby fingers, turning on the radio. That song again, "My Sharona." His voice singing along. *Always get it up . . . for the touch . . . of the younger kind.*

I sat up in my bed. Put my feet on the floor and stood up. Looked around the room.

Then I saw it, plain as the face of Mike Brady on the television screen through Helen's window. Plain as the face of Teddy Bascom in Alison Kerwin's rec room, leaning over to unbutton my shirt. Plain as my own in the mirror, where I stood now, shivering.

It was the face of the killer.

It came to me so clearly then—lying there in my bunk bed, staring up at the slats on my sister's bunk, listening to the sound of her breathing over the voice of Cat Stevens. Once it did, the whole thing seemed so obvious and clear, I wondered why it had taken me so long.

Mr. Armitage was the Sunset Strangler.

Motor run,
my motor run

In my forty-four years of life, here is something I've learned about thirteen-year-old girls. I know this as somebody who used to be one long ago, and used to be the sister of one, and the friend of others, and the ex-friend.

Thirteen-year-old girls live in two different worlds. They exist like citizens of two distinct countries—and though these two places are as different as Croatia is from Papua New Guinea, or Mercury from Saturn, they float between the two as effortlessly as a person might from one side of the Golden Gate Bridge to the other, when it's not even rush hour, or from North Beach to Morning Glory Court. More easily than that particular journey, come to think of it.

Partly, a thirteen-year-old is still a child, capable of finding joy in setting grass on fire in a tin can or thrill in the sight of a neighbor answering the ring of the doorbell and opening the door to discover no one there, only a rustle in the bushes. Thirteen-year-old girls can actually believe that the reason they won't get to marry John Travolta is because he's got a girlfriend already, and that Peter Frampton's getting a haircut qualifies as a tragedy, and that receiving a call from a particular boy—or a particular girl for that matter—is the most wonderful thing that ever happened. Thirteen-year-old girls believe in heroic fathers and wicked stepmothers. They believe the words to songs, and the advice of other thirteen-year-old girls, and that the first boy they love, they will love forever.

Their bodies (mine at thirteen, anyway) may resemble those of boys more than the bodies of women. But inside the bodies of these girls, something is going on, unlike anything that exists in the bodies of boys, the bodies of men. Their breasts swell of course. The uterus fills with blood. The longing for touch may feel, to a girl of this age, as real as fire.

And then there are all those eggs—a girl's lifetime supply, she's told—tucked inside her ovaries from the moment of her birth, just waiting for the rest of her to catch up, so she might incubate them. A thirteen-year-old girl knows this: her body can make a baby now. Only what would she ever do with one? A part of her still likes to play with dolls. A part of her is fascinated by her own amazing new talent. Another part: appalled.

A thirteen-year-old girl hates her mother. Loves her father. Hates her father. Loves her mother. What is she supposed to do?

Thirteen-year-olds are big and small, thin and fat. Neither. Both. They have the smoothest, most perfect skin, and sometimes, overnight, their faces are a mess. They may weep over the sight of a dead bird and appear heartless at the funeral of a grandparent. They're tender. They're mean. They're brilliant. Dumb. Ugly. Beautiful.

Now comes the sex part. Sex is sickening and scary and irresistible. A thirteen-year-old doesn't want to think about sex. She thinks of nothing else.

Everything's a drama to her. She feels things ten times more than a fifteen-year-old girl, or a ten-year-old. When she bleeds—or in my case, when she doesn't—she is the possessor of the most powerful secret. How can it be a person can walk around, as if nothing unusual is going on, when right between her legs, there's all this blood flowing out of her? Nobody says anything. She alone knows.

She looks in the drawers of the people for whom she babysits, in search of sexual paraphernalia—peels back the wrapper on a condom and blows it up like a balloon, then stuffs it in her pocket to destroy the evidence— and if she finds a blouse or a dress that interests her, belonging to the wife of the couple for whom she is babysitting some Friday night (or a piece of lingerie, more likely), she may even try it on.

She lies. One day she tells a girl at school that she's the world's first test tube baby. (She has pulled her underpants up higher than normal over her waist, so when she lifts up her shirt, she can point to her bare skin and prove it. *See, no belly button.* Being thirteen years old herself, the other girl believes this story.)

She sends a note (anonymous, naturally) to an unpopular boy in her class in which she tells him that she knows he wet his pants that time on the bus, coming home from the field trip. She is that mean. But she is also capable of great kindness. On that same bus trip, she sat with the cerebral palsy girl, the one who drools.

A thirteen-year-old girl possesses special powers. The same girl who can believe the messages of a Ouija board or the declarations of friendship of someone who, one day later, will walk past her in the cafeteria without speaking may also at rare moments possess the wisdom of a full-grown woman or even a sage. Though it's not wisdom, precisely: more like an eerie animal ability to know and hear what nobody else can, a gift of feeling—feeling having overtaken all else—that a few more years of life in the world, or even just a few more months of it, will transform into a distant memory.

When she taps in to it—and this is an erratic event at best—hers is a different kind of knowledge from the kind the mothers and grandmothers have acquired that comes from lessons learned, years lived on planet Earth. The knowledge thirteen-year-old girls carry comes from a whole different galaxy, more like it: from some other sense besides the accustomed five, or maybe the heightened acuity of those five combined, but not yet numbed or deadened as they so often become, later. (When the business of daily life catches up with her. When she learns to tamp down all the big feelings, deaden her nerve endings, just to get through the day.)

The knowledge a thirteen-year-old possesses is more like the ability to register a high-pitched sound audible only to dogs, or forms not visible without the aid of 3-D glasses—the gift a blind person may have not simply to recognize when a person enters a room, however soundlessly. But to know who that person is. And whether to trust him.

But she will also trust people she shouldn't. Many of those.

In her mixed-up world, she hungers for whatever's simple, which draws her to song lyrics, pop stars, brand names, astrological predictions. She longs for heroes, and for villains, and when none appear before her, she creates them, or passes the roles on to the most obvious candidates. A model in the pages of *Seventeen*, maybe, or the star player on the Boston Celtics. A singer whose album she's memorized. (Every song. She mouths the words, in front of the mirror.) It could be a selfless nun, feeding starving children in Africa. Anne Frank. Amelia Earhart. Charlie's Angels.

This girl needs big drama, and danger, and if life fails to offer those, she sets up situations where she can locate those things. This could be nothing more than starting a fight with a girlfriend, or launching a rumor that a boy in her social studies class (she can't stand him; she thinks about no one else) is in love with some other thirteen-year-old girl she knows, about whom she harbors feelings in which roughly equivalent levels of confusion exist.

Except in very rare instances, a thirteen-year-old girl will experience this power only for the briefest period—a few months, a few days even, maybe only once in her life ever. But at some point—between the ages of twelve and thirteen, or thirteen and fourteen, when so much is new and there are chemicals coursing through her body as powerful as drugs, a brilliant and blinding flash of wild unexplainable and unshakable insight may come to her, with greater intensity than she will ever experience again over the lifetime ahead, more than it will when this same girl has reached the age that is commonly believed to signal maturity and wisdom. (Whatever that age is, if we ever get there. At which point, nothing will be as clear or absolute as it was at age thirteen.)

Now here comes a problem: as much as this girl can see things that are there, and real, below the surface— hear words spoken only inside other people's heads, feel what they know, and what they plan to do about it—she will also see things that are nothing more than the creations of her extraordinarily active, hyperactive, thirteen-year-old girl's imagination.

Sometimes this insight she seizes on will be dead-on-the-money accurate. Sometimes, it's just dead wrong. Either way, she'll hold to her belief with the same wild and unyielding faith that never in the history of the universe was anything more true or real or important than this. She holds fast to her convictions about those moments when her instincts reveal what she believes to be the truth, and—with equal tenacity—to convictions that are wild and baseless. She cannot tell the difference.

I know these things because I was such a girl myself once, the year of the Sunset Strangler murders, and it was my being that age, at that moment, that explains for me how it was I came to hear the voice of the killer as I did, and why it is possible that I was more right than wrong about a great deal of what I imagined him to be thinking and doing.

This was how it was I came to believe, with my whole heart, that the Sunset Strangler was none other than my sister Patty's beloved employer and friend—a gentle man with the surprising habit of liking to dress up as a woman now and then. How did I come to believe this with such ferocious conviction? I was a thirteen-year-old girl whose mind had been overtaken by thoughts of a killer, and needed, more than anything else at the time, to make him go away. Not even for my own sake, or for the women of Marin County, but because I recognized that my father's failure to locate the killer was slowly destroying him, I had to do something.

Being thirteen, this would mean something dramatic. So when a real suspect failed to reveal himself, I designated a stand-in. I put a face onto a faceless demon, for the purpose of eradicating him. The face I chose was that of Albert Armitage.

Knowing she wouldn't believe it—and that even if she did, it would make her sadder than I cared to contemplate—I did not share with my sister my revelation that Mr. Armitage was the Sunset Strangler. In our whole lives as sisters, this was the first time I ever kept a secret from Patty. She'd find out soon enough, when they arrested him. But I didn't want to be the one to break the news.

I came up with a plan: part one, part two. The first: luring Mr. Armitage to the mountain, where I'd confront him. The second: making sure it was Detective Anthony Torricelli and no one else who took the credit for the rescue and arrest that would follow.

I needed my father to be strong and powerful again. I would create a scenario that made this possible.

Returning to these events, more than thirty years later, with all the knowledge of how life works now in my grasp—or closer anyway—it is difficult to reconstruct how I could ever have supposed this plan to be feasible. The door closed, long ago, to the room I inhabited when I was thirteen. And of course I am speaking, when I say this, not of the nearly airless little place my sister and I did our sleeping, and our staying awake—the room where we played our records and tried on each other's clothes, talked about sharks and God, fashion models and basketball players, asked our questions of the Ouija board and read out loud from my book of women's sexual fantasies—but of the state of mind I lived in then. I simply know, it was a place in which magical thinking occurred, and the lines were not simply blurred between the feasible and the crazy, but nonexistent.

Believing as I did that the killer (this would be Mr. Armitage) must by now be feeling desperate to get back on the mountain for fresh prey (after the long rainy season), I would set a trap for him—lure him back out on the mountain, out in the open, where his true and terrible nature could be revealed, and my father could apprehend him at last.

A trap required bait. That would be me. I would arrange to be in a specified place, and arrange for Mr. Armitage to meet me. When he got there—or within minutes of his arrival (seconds, preferably)—I would have made sure my father showed up, gun drawn, ready to snap on the handcuffs.

My father would be restored then to his old identity as the hero and protector of women that we all needed him to be. Nobody needing this more than my father himself.

I recognized a problem here. The mountain—and the miles of trails that had proven to be within the range of the Sunset Strangler's territory—was too big a place to lie in wait and hope the killer would just show up. I had to narrow down the territory. Identify a spot. Invite him there.

Some people—those over age thirteen anyway—
would have pointed out an additional problem with
my plan. (One problem? A million, more like it.)
Assuming I was right, and that Mr. Armitage was
the killer—and assuming, furthermore, that I might
be successful in persuading him to depart from his
usual modus operandi and come instead to a designated spot, to encounter a person he'd never laid eyes
on (or supposed he hadn't, anyway)—what did I think
I was going to do when he actually turned up there?
How could I believe that I, an eighty-eight-pound girl,
could vanquish an adult male who'd already proven to
be a ruthless killer?

I had an answer for this one—as much of an answer
as my thirteen-year-old self required: I'd have my
father there. My strong, all-powerful, magic father. All
anyone needed to be safe in this world. Though just to
be sure, I'd bring along Jennifer Pollack's pink revolver.

I skipped school that day.

I knew when Jennifer Pollack took Karl Jr. for his
walk. Ten thirty, every morning. Right after *Sesame
Street,* and before his nap.

The Pollacks locked their front door now, but not the
back. In the time it took Jennifer to push the stroller to
the end of Morning Glory Court and back again, I had

managed to make my way into the Pollacks' bedroom, locate the revolver in the bedside table drawer, stick it in my pocket, and leave. I was back at my own house when Jennifer Pollack returned home, with time to spare.

Under normal circumstances, it would have been a twenty-minute bike ride to the mall, but with my heart pounding this way, I got there in ten. I made my purchase, pedaled home, ripped off the packaging.

I took out the Polaroid camera I hadn't used for months now. Three exposures left on the roll, but for the picture I had in mind, I needed only one.

It had been a long time since I'd stuck anything new in our scrapbook, but this one merited its own new page. No caption necessary, just the photograph.

To be sure my father would find it, I left the scrapbook open on my bed. Now, in addition to featuring an assortment of photographs of its subject—walking his dog, collecting mail, hosing down the stones in his yard, and exchanging a greeting with the meter reader—my book documenting the Mysterious Life of Albert Armitage would highlight a new and crucial element to his story. Some people might not grasp the significance of the photograph I'd pasted in, but I knew my father would.

It was a picture of shoelaces. Multiple pairs. As many pairs, if a person cared to count, as there'd been murder victims.

Dear Albert, my note began.

(Rather than risk revealing my identity through telltale handwriting, I employed the manner I'd seen kidnappers and blackmailers use in movies and TV shows that involved notes designed to conceal the author's identity: cutting letters out of magazines and pasting them on blank paper to spell out their message.)

I know your secret. We need to talk.

Come to the mountain Saturday.

Meet at rusty truck.

Near place where they put on the shows. You know what I'm talking about.

3 pm. If you don't come, I'm telling.

That was about it, except for the name at the bottom. What to put there? I could use Farrah of course. He wouldn't know that one. Or Miss X.

In the end I chose the simplest option.

Signed, Anonymous.

I placed the note in an envelope and sealed it. Then I walked to the cul-de-sac at the end of Morning Glory

Court. The street was empty, as it generally was these days. No one out to see.

I put the envelope in the mailbox marked "Armitage."

Walking home, I understood: the whole world was about to change. For so long, everything had been going wrong. Now I was going to fix it.

I knew my father would be at his office that Saturday, because he was always at his office now. He never went anywhere anymore, except when another murder happened, and he went to the crime scene. And to our house, in the middle of the night, to drink and smoke and talk with our mother. Patty was at basketball practice, and my mother was sure to be at the library all afternoon.

I was right, my father was at the office that day. The secretary who answered the phone said he was busy, but when I told her it couldn't wait, she put me through.

"Farrah," he said. My father knew I wouldn't call if it wasn't important.

"I think he's after me," I said, in a voice that sounded as if I'd been running. "The Sunset Strangler."

"What are you talking about?"

"He said he was coming to get me," I said. It wasn't all that hard, sounding scared. My heart had not stopped pounding since I'd set my plan in motion.

"Talk slow now, honey. Catch your breath. You need to tell me everything that happened."

"He called the house," I said. "He said he saw me with you on TV, on the news. He said he knows what I look like now. He said he's coming to get me."

"You're sure about this?"

For a few seconds, I hesitated. I could not remember a time I'd lied to my father.

Later, he'd understand why. Once it was over, and he'd arrested the killer—when everyone was happy again, and saying what an amazing job he'd done—I'd tell him the truth. Just my father, no one else.

I had to get you to see it was Mr. Armitage, I'd explain to him. *I knew you wouldn't believe me, unless I got you there to see for yourself.*

He couldn't be mad then. He'd thank me. He'd say he was sorry he ever failed to believe my visions. Until then, though, I had to give him my story. Now came more:

"He said he was teaching you a lesson," I told my father, still breathing hard. "He knows where we live. He's coming here. He said he'll make you sorry.

"He said he's outside the house right now. Right now at this very moment, he's watching me."

There was a silence on the other end, but not for long.

"I don't know what this is about, Rachel," my father said. All playfulness gone from his voice. "I'll be right over. Don't go anywhere. I'm coming."

What happened next was the one thing I hadn't planned on. Maybe it was the excitement inside my body that did this—my heart racing and my insides clamping down into a hard, tight ball. All of a sudden, there it was, the thing that hadn't happened all those months, the thing that I'd been waiting for. Blood coming out of me as if I was hemorrhaging.

I reached my hand under my shorts to touch the place I felt it, the warm damp spot. My fingers, when I looked at them, were red.

I stuck a wad of toilet paper in my underpants—all I had time for. I scrawled a note, in a style of handwriting I hoped would suggest that it had been written in a state of desperation: *Help. Come. Truck.* Then I was out the door and running—as fast as I could up the side of the mountain, with the gun in the pocket of my old red sweatshirt. No time to think about the blood on my shorts, or how the victim of a serial killer might know in advance where it was the serial killer meant to take her, or what I'd say to him when I got there. I did not consider what I'd do if the killer was there and the man I counted on to stop the killer wasn't, or how to release the safety on Jennifer Pollack's gun. I only knew that everything would be okay once my father got there. He'd know what to do.

It was only after it was over that I learned this: after he read the letter left in his mailbox, signed by Anonymous, Mr. Armitage had done something totally different from anything I would have expected. He went to the police.

To Mr. Armitage, it had not seemed out of the question that this document, with its glued-on letters cut out from old issues of magazines and flyers from newspapers had been written by the Sunset Strangler himself.

It would have been hard for anyone (the police, or Mr. Armitage) to fathom why a middle-aged man might be the recipient of such a letter from the Sunset Strangler, of course—given he did not come even close to fitting the profile of one of the killer's victims. Maybe Mr. Armitage believed it had been during one of his late-night walks with Petra through our neighborhood in that polka-dot dress of his that he had caught the eye of the killer, who had then set his sights on meeting the mystery woman in the cherry-trimmed hat. Stranger things had happened, perhaps, though it might be hard to know when.

But other scenarios were also possible. More likely, perhaps. That morning, at the exact time I'd called my father's office, and heard his secretary say that he was busy, my father was in fact sitting at his desk across from none other than the Mysterious Albert Armitage. Who had just finished laying out for him the story of the anonymous letter, raising his belief that this letter may also have been the handiwork of a young person. Possibly someone who knew a certain secret about his behavior and meant to use it to manipulate or even blackmail him.

Instead of giving in to this kind of intimidation, Mr. Armitage had made the decision to explain to my father in clear and straightforward terms the nature of his own secret habit of dressing up in women's clothing now and then, and—on increasingly rare occasions—walking around the neighborhood that way.

"It doesn't hurt anyone," Mr. Armitage told my father, evidently. "It's not against the law."

My father, fair man that he was, agreed that this was so.

"Back in North Beach, when I was a kid, I knew a boy, Vinny Marzano, who liked to put on his mother's brassieres now and then," my father said. "You know how many kids Vinny's got now? Seven."

At the moment I had called his office, my father had not yet worked his way through to the conclusion that the anonymous letter lying in front of him on the desk at that very moment had been authored by his own older daughter. But he was getting there.

After his meeting with Albert Armitage—and his call from me—my father made the trip to Morning Glory Court of course, and he didn't waste any time getting there. With Patty and my mother gone, he had let himself in the house. It didn't take him long to locate the clue I'd laid out for him—the scrapbook bearing the name of the man with whom he had been talking, less than half an hour before, concerning the anonymous letter. And the message spelling out where he might find me.

It took my father even less time, after that, to understand that he was witnessing the evidence of a not very successful plan on the part of his older daughter to frame a man for murder, who had done nothing more than put on a polka-dot dress now and then.

His daughter was in trouble all right. But not because a serial killer was after her. She was in trouble with him.

It was just before two o'clock when I reached the rusted-out truck body where my letter had instructed

Mr. Armitage to meet me. There'd been a lot of brush sprouting up since I'd been here last on one of my adventures with Patty, but it also appeared that other people besides me (teenagers looking for a spot to have sex probably) had been here recently. The weeds in one spot, at least, were mashed down enough to make it easier getting in the rusted cab of the truck. The door had disappeared long before, but someone had draped an old shower curtain over the top.

How long did I sit there? Twenty minutes possibly? Two hours? To calm myself, I thought about the time I'd come here with my father and Patty all those years back, when he taught us how to use the BB gun, and other times with only my sister, when we'd huddled in the cab, reading *My Secret Garden* or her favorite, *The Golden Treasury of Beloved Animal Stories*.

There was a Coke can on the floor of the truck—what remained of the floor anyway—that seemed to have been left here not that long ago, given that there was still a little Coke in it. Also fast-food wrappers, a bunch of empty Spam tins and plastic containers that had once held chocolate pudding, a microwave cookbook, and a couple of catalogs. (Odd combination: L.L.Bean and Victoria's Secret.) Under the seat, someone had stashed an old jacket that said Goodyear Tire, and a pair of socks, almost as if they camped out here

on occasion. Patty and I always wanted to do that ourselves, but as laissez-faire as our mother was, the idea
of us camping out all night on the mountain—even
before the killings started—would have been a little
much even for her.

Sitting there now, awaiting the arrival of the man
I believed to be the Sunset Strangler—and the arrival
of my father, to perform the rescue and arrest—I ran
my hand over the remains of the steering wheel. In
the past, Patty and I used to try and imagine how this
truck had ended up here in the first place—inventing
theories to answer the question. Patty's were always
hopeless. As good as she was at playing games if I made
them up, she had no talent for creating fiction of any
kind. She was too attached to the truth.

Thinking about this, a wave of guilty sadness came
over me. Patty loved me more than anything, but she
cared deeply for Mr. Armitage too. As loyal as she was
to me—*loyal as a dog,* I used to say—Patty could never
believe Mr. Armitage was a killer. The thought came
to me then: When Mr. Armitage went to prison, what
would become of Petra?

I stayed there a long time on the mountain that day,
hunched down in the truck body, waiting for my
father and Mr. Armitage.

It had to be well past three and no one had shown up. I had been keeping my eye on the horizon, watching for the first glimpse of them. Partly worried, partly relieved.

Maybe Mr. Armitage never got the letter. Maybe he'd thrown it out with his junk mail. Maybe he figured it was just a prank. If so, I could go home and forget all this. Only what then?

I know your secret.

If you don't show up, I'm telling.

And even if Mr. Armitage didn't come, how was it that my father, having found the shoelace picture and the note, had failed to recognize the need to rescue me?

I studied my leg—a spot on my thigh where a bug had landed and was making its way across my skin. I studied the fine hairs—the first time I'd noticed any. I felt the blood seeping out of me. The wad of toilet paper was soaked now.

More crows overhead, a red-tailed hawk, and the shriek of vultures—though only high up, not zeroing in—smelling my blood maybe. Off in the distance now, I heard the sound of a radio, or walkie-talkies. Scratchy voices. Static.

Getting closer.

Then a noise I hadn't expected. A four-wheeled ATV of the sort the park rangers used to patrol the mountain now, bouncing over the rise and making its way toward the truck. The engine stopped.

A man got out. Then two more men. One of them my father.

"I know you're in there, Rachel," my father said. My real name, which he hardly ever called me, except when he was mad, which was almost never before now.

"I've come to take you home."

I had never seen him this angry before. And he didn't even know the part about stealing Jennifer Pollack's loaded gun.

"Get in the back," he said, indicating the jump seat in the ATV. "Just off the top of my head I'm estimating that you're grounded for the next hundred years, but it could be more."

One more thing happened on the mountain that day. I was seated in the back of the ATV, with my father a little ways off, talking with the other officers. (No sign of Mr. Armitage—and the realization had come to me that there never would be. And that Mr. Armitage was not the killer after all. I'd got it wrong.)

I wasn't crying, but the thought had also come to me that this was probably the lowest moment in my life, and the fact that I'd be grounded forever (an experience

I'd never known before, for one day even) was far from the worst of it.

In case my activities hadn't made enough trouble, a reporter had also shown up on the scene, which required my father to do some explaining. Even before today, the press had been touting the position of many citizens that the Marin Homicide Division, under the direction of Detective Anthony Torricelli, had mismanaged the investigation. Now here was Detective Torricelli himself, out on the mountain, chasing after his teenage daughter when he should be looking for the killer. Why was an investigation of this importance being entrusted to a man who couldn't keep his own children under control?

I could see my father speaking with the reporter now. See her writing in her notebook. See my father shake his head.

Judging from the angle of the sun, and the light hitting my face, it must have been approaching four thirty or five by this point. I could feel the sweat under my arms and the sweat on the backs of my thighs where they pressed against the plastic seat cover on the ATV. I was tired and thirsty, and my underpants were soaked with blood. I wanted to go home and see the one person I could imagine who wouldn't hate me by now. Patty.

This was when it happened: sitting there under the still-hot sun, waiting for my father in the back of the vehicle, I felt the familiar sensation of a vision coming to me.

I recognized the signs: the tightening in my chest, the dryness in my mouth, and the change in my breathing, almost as if the space I occupied no longer contained enough air. I felt hot at the same time as the chill came over me, and that sickening warmth between my legs, coming from the place I didn't even want to name.

Here was the killer, in my head again, and not just in my head. Inside my body was how it felt. More than that even. It was as if he was right there.

Remember me?

Did you think I'd dress up like a girl? What kind of pussy do you take me for?

You know the only good kind of dog in my book? A dead one.

Whoever this was talking—the killer, faceless again—I knew he was sweating. Like me, he occupied some hot outdoor place as he spoke to me. The part of me that registered his feelings now felt the sun as it beat down on him, same as it did on me. Sweat on his neck too. His shirt stuck to his chest. He wanted a Coke.

Through his eyes, I saw dry grass. Dirt. California poppies. Owl pellet: a little lump of undigested mouse fur, containing the bones of whatever other creature the owl had consumed the night before. The same thing Patty liked to stop and examine on our rambles. I could smell wild fennel and eucalyptus bark.

If he saw these things, and smelled them, he was here on the mountain.

Ooh my little pretty one. Pretty one.

I could make out the sound of those walkie-talkies again, though whether it was me hearing this, or him, remained unclear. Not words, just static. I could make out a clearing—with a stage, and stone seats around it. I recognized this as the amphitheater where, for so many summers in the past, Patty and I had snuck in to watch production numbers from those Broadway musicals. "Do-Re-Mi." "Surrey with the Fringe on Top." "Seventy-six Trombones." "Luck Be a Lady Tonight."

Looking up, I caught sight of a group of crows overhead. *A murder of crows* was the term. (Seventh-grade vocab list.)

I knew he saw them too. The same formation.

But it was the next thing I saw that would have made me cry out, except the breath had left me.

It was a skinny girl slumped in the back of an ATV, wearing a red sweatshirt—face to the sun, and squinting, with a book bag in her lap that didn't fully conceal the red stain seeping through the crotch of her shorts.

A girl with a look on her face as if she'd just laid eyes on something terrifying.

Which I had: him, seeing me.

Same girl that was on the news, he was thinking. *Cop's kid.*

No tits. Like the jogger. But it might be time to send this spic cop a reminder as to who was in charge here.

Him.

The way my punishment worked (*punishment*, a new concept in our family), my father had arranged it that as of the day school got out, I would have a job down at police headquarters—the only place he knew, he said, where he'd be sure I'd stay out of trouble. Sweeping the floors for fifty cents an hour. Six hours a day. There was no argument from my mother.

There turned out to be many rooms at the precinct in need of sweeping. As soon as I'd gotten through the last of them, it was time to start over again. These police officers were a dusty group.

School let out. Every morning, I now rode the bus to police headquarters, where my broom was waiting for me.

As awful a consequence as this was, coming just at the start of vacation—with the rain finally gone, and my bicycle calling, and my notebooks filled with half-written stories—it may have been worse for Patty. She had her basketball of course (though no practices in summer, or games) and her job walking Petra. (On this front, the small piece of good news was that Mr. Armitage—though he must surely have deduced the identity of the author of that anonymous letter—did not appear to hold my sister responsible for my own dark and baseless suspicions about him, or the potentially dangerous actions I'd undertaken as a result of them.)

Still, this left hours when my sister was on her own, instead of having adventures with me, as we'd done every other summer of our lives. The mountain was off-limits, the rec center occupied by all my former friends, now enemies. All that was left for Patty to do was listen to records and shoot baskets and think up tricks to teach Petra, who was a very slow learner. She had a hard enough time with "roll over."

For me, the hours of sweeping left my mind free to think about what was happening on the mountain. The awful pictures of murder victims, in their last moments of life, no longer came to me, as they had all winter and spring. (As with our television, service appeared to have been disconnected—with nothing on the screen now but snow.) But the absence of pictures was almost worse. I knew the killer was out there, and based on that brief and terrible moment on the mountain, when I felt his presence so close that the same crows had circled over both our heads, I believed that he was watching me.

I had tried once to help my father capture the killer, and that had been a disaster. He'd never listen to anything I said now on this subject, even if I had anything to offer, which I didn't. All I could do was push my broom back and forth, with the knowledge that the Sunset Strangler was out there looking for another victim.

He had killed women in other places besides Mount Tamalpais, of course. (Point Reyes. Muir Woods. Tennessee Valley and Bolinas.) But I believed he had returned to the mountain, if only to convey to the police officers pursuing him the message that he was smarter than all of them.

If my father had once seemed to possess magical powers, it appeared the Sunset Strangler was the magic one now. I had felt his presence on the mountain that day my father came to get me in the ATV, and I believed he was there now, though how he continued to elude discovery was difficult to fathom—knowing the numbers of officers who patrolled the mountain and trails and monitored every parking lot where hikers left their cars before setting out to hike.

One law enforcement officer missing from the mountain now was my father. The day after he'd brought me home, the *San Francisco Chronicle* ran its story in which their reporter revealed to the greater San Francisco Bay Area the news that Detective Anthony Torricelli, head of the entire Marin Homicide Division—and the officer whom the people of Marin County had entrusted with responsibility for apprehending the Sunset Strangler—had spent his Saturday (accompanied by two other officers, and in an official police department vehicle) out on the mountain intercepting what the reporter called "a teenybopper sting operation" set up by Detective Torricelli's own thirteen-year-old daughter.

The photograph that ran on the front page had shown me huddled in the back of the ATV in my red sweatshirt (the bloodstains in my shorts thankfully not visible) and my father, in his leather jacket, looking not so much angry as defeated. The two additional officers—whose energies could have been better spent elsewhere, as no one needed to point out—stood on the sidelines, by the truck body. Hands in their pockets.

344 · JOYCE MAYNARD

Looking as if they'd rather be just about anywhere else, which no doubt was true.

The reporter had done some legwork for this story. She had evidently solicited the observations of a group of my classmates from school. One of whom—Alison Kerwin—had volunteered that I used to come over to her house a lot, but she had to stop inviting me when bottles of nail polish kept disappearing. Alison's mother had made the observation that it had appeared to her—from times I spent with their family, and occasions when she'd driven me home after—that my parents seemed not to offer much in the way of supervision.

"She's a child of a broken home," Mrs. Kerwin had said. "We all felt sorry for her. We even invited her to join us for Thanksgiving. But you can only help a person so much."

There had been one other comment about me in the article, though this one was attributed to "a young person who asked to remain anonymous."

"She's an okay kid, I guess," the anonymous young person had said. "But it had me weirded out the way she was always, like, taking her clothes off and stuff."

He had to fend me off sometimes, he said, I got so aggressive. But luckily, he knew karate.

First thing the following Monday morning, my father had been called in by the chief of police, who delivered the news: effective immediately, Detective Torricelli would be relieved of his duties overseeing the investigation of the Sunset Strangler killings. At the request of his superiors in Sacramento, by noon that day he was instructed to turn in all materials in his possession relating to the Sunset Strangler case, to be taken over by a Special Forces team and a group of FBI agents from Washington.

My father was reassigned to an office up north in Novato, to oversee a case involving a car dealership that appeared to have engaged in fraud in the sale of a half-dozen stolen vehicles that had been brought in over state lines.

"I went to bat for you on this one, Tony," the chief told my father that day. "What happened the other day could have been the end of your career, but I told them you'd keep your nose clean from now on."

It had been the chief's advice to my father that he should go home and spend some much-needed quality time with his kids. "So long as I don't hear word one about you and that daughter of yours getting anywhere near this investigation, your pension's safe," he said.

"One more prank like this last one, and I'll be asking for your badge."

I had to believe my grounding wouldn't last forever, though I knew better than to ask for the specifics of my sentence. But I had no doubt, even then, that my father loved me more than anything—and I even knew that at its core, his anger that day had not come from the fact that I had jeopardized his case and wrecked his twenty-year career. He was angry because I'd put myself in harm's way.

"If anything ever happened to one of you girls—" he said, on the way down the mountain in the ATV. He couldn't even finish his sentence.

A few days after they took him off the case, he came by to take us out for pasta. Marin Joe's as usual. Same booth. Same waitresses. Same marinara.

We didn't speak about what happened, that night, though of course Patty and I knew what the transfer to Novato represented to our father. I was quieter than usual, which left it to my sister to fill the space. I watched her across the booth, pressed up close against our father and stroking the hairs on his arm the way she liked to. Some people, observing the scene, would have taken in nothing but a young girl having a care-free night out with her family, but I recognized that

Patty's relentless cheerfulness required as much of her as any playoff game.

"Some people think Jack Russell terriers are stupid," she was saying. "But I can tell, from knowing Petra like I do, that she's just really, really sensitive. Sometimes she gets overexcited when she's happy, and it makes her do dumb things. Same as people do.

"Knock knock," she said. (No attempt at anything approaching a natural segue to a new topic here.)

"Who's there?" (This, from our father.)

"Canoe."

"Canoe who?"

"Canoe help me with my homework?"

Our father laughed of course, though his laughter sounded flat. "I never heard that one before," he told her. "Now . . . who here might be interested in a little tiramisu?"

"Actually, Dad, I was thinking I'd like to get home," I told him.

Nobody argued then, when we left without our usual dessert. In the car on the way home, Patty had tried one more time—launching into a round of "Volare." Neither of us joined in.

That night I lay in bed staring up at the slats in my sister's top bunk as usual, while she sang along with her record. (Dolly Parton, imploring a woman named Jolene not to take her man. Patty loved this song, though it baffled her, she said, how anybody could steal a man from a person as beautiful as Dolly.)

There was moonlight coming in the window, and a Santa Ana wind. No sound of coyotes for once, but the silence was worse.

No one said anything for a long time, and then Patty did.

"Do you think once they capture the Sunset Strangler, things can go back to normal?" she said.

What's normal, I could have asked her.

"Dad said he was taking us to Italy, for one thing," she said when I remained silent.

"Dad says a lot of things," I told her. Always before, it had been Patty who spoke of our father's failings. That summer, he had ceased to be, for me, my magical father. I could never hate him, but what I felt now—namely, pity, and guilt—was worse.

"Then maybe he'll marry Margaret Ann," Patty continued.

Odd that my sister would think of this. She was only six or seven when we went to Margaret Ann's apartment and she gave us the dolls. And that time at the Flamingo Hotel, when we wore the dresses she'd made for us and my sister threw up.

"Do you think there's such a thing as one true love?" Patty asked me. Dolly was on to another song now: "I Will Always Love You."

"Because if there is," my sister said, "I think Margaret Ann was it for him."

"Sometimes it's like that, maybe," I told her. "But even when everything seems perfect, there could be one little thing you do, at just the wrong moment, to make your whole life go in a different direction. And you might never get back to where you were before."

"Like in the song, with the guy in the phone booth, when he can't read the phone number he wrote down on the matchbook, and he never gets to call the girl back that went off with his best friend."

"Or those girls that got killed," I said. "What if they'd taken a different hiking trail on that particular day? Or they got a blister on their foot and decided to turn back? Or someone else came along, in front of them, and the Sunset Strangler decided to get her instead?"

"Or Mom," Patty said. "If her glasses hadn't fallen off when she was riding her bike that day and met Dad."

"In which case, we wouldn't have been born," I pointed out.

"But for her, maybe, things would have worked out better."

Silence.

"Dad could still call up Margaret Ann," Patty said. The Dolly Parton record had ended now, but maybe Patty was still thinking about that song. Mostly though, she was thinking about our father.

Of all the things we'd talked about, I had never told her about that time all those years back when I had left the message on his answering machine about marrying Margaret Ann. *Never get over it. Never forgive you.*

It was too late to let him know that wasn't true. I'd always forgive our father. I just wanted him to be okay.

"I think it would cheer him up," my sister said.

"I don't even think Mom would mind anymore. Mostly she just wants to be left alone anyways. Plus, they could still be friends."

"I wonder if she kept those dresses in her closet," Patty said.

That night, after Patty fell asleep, I saw the killer. I saw where he was, and it was not that far away.

He was lying under the stars on the mountain, never mind the coyotes. He was curled up on the floor of the old truck body where I'd waited for Mr. Armitage, wearing that Goodyear Tire jacket I'd seen stashed under the seat, with the Victoria's Secret catalog open, and the Coke can, and the empty tins of canned meat.

I saw him again, when morning came, looking out on the hillside at the last of the poppies, the drying grass—spooning chocolate pudding out of a plastic cup, peeing against a tree, smashing a rock down on a field mouse, waiting for some girl to come along who hadn't heard about the Sunset Strangler or, if she had, decided not to let him worry her.

When one of the FBI agents passed—and sometimes they did, in their four-wheelers—he huddled low in the wheel well. The special agents were all looking for that red Toyota, or the green Fiat, or some car left too long in a parking spot.

But you didn't need your car when you were camping.

At some point, the Spam and crackers would run out, and the pudding, but when they did, he knew where to go: all those houses that backed up against the hillside, Morning Glory Court. He'd kept his eye on those, from above. He knew who went to work, and when, and in the case of that one woman—the pregnant one, with the little boy—he knew when she took him on his walk, and where she hid the key when she did that.

It wouldn't be that hard, popping in for a minute then, to grab a snack from the refrigerator. Nothing wrong with baby food. A little like pudding, when you thought about it.

For now, he had his cheek pressed up against the metal side of the truck body. One eye squinting through the BB-sized opening surveying his territory: the California poppies, the humming of insects in the grass, the circling crows. He was king of the mountain, or close enough.

The summer days crawled along. No more murder victims, but nobody was resting easy. We were just waiting.

It was early July, and I had put in another one of my long days at the precinct house. Because the officers on duty felt sorry for me, they didn't give me all that many jobs to do anymore, so I did word search puzzles a lot, and read biographies. I would have liked to work on my stories, but it was too noisy there to concentrate, and anyway, I seemed to be going through a dry spell with my writing. All my imagination had done for me lately was get me into trouble.

I was supposed to stick around at my job until four thirty, but at three o'clock the officer in charge that day told me to head on home.

"Why don't you go do something fun for a change," she told me. "Take the rest of the day off."

On my way back from the bus stop, I started thinking about my sister. With a good chunk of the day suddenly available, I was thinking we could maybe ride our bikes to the mall and squirt a bunch of perfume on ourselves at Macy's, or go to the mattress store and see how long we could lie on the vibrating bed before some saleslady came to kick us out. As bad as I was at the game, I would even play a game of Horse with Patty if she wanted. I was that happy to get to be with her.

It was her basketball I saw first when I reached Morning Glory Court. Patty's basketball, but not Patty. If you saw one, normally, you'd see the other.

But it was lying in the street. My sister's precious, regulation-sized, NBA-approved basketball. Rolling down the street, actually—not like a ball in play, in a game, but in slow motion, as if someone had tossed it there, or kicked it.

I bent to pick it up. Called out to Patty once. Then I was running.

Our back door, which we kept locked now, was open. So—when I reached the kitchen—was the door to the refrigerator. No time to check what happened there; I was headed to our room, calling out my sister's name again, hearing nothing.

For a second, it looked as if our room was as I'd left it. Record player, posters, basketball trophies, bunk bed, books. The picture of my sister and me, on the cable car in San Francisco, and another with our father from the night they gave him his medal for valor.

Then I saw it, on the floor by the window. My sister's basketball shoes, lined up side by side. The laces were gone.

It had always been Patty who could climb that mountain fast, but that afternoon I ran harder than I knew was possible. I had no plan. No karate-champion boyfriend at my side and no pink revolver in my pocket, not that I would have known how to shoot it anyway. I just knew I had to find my sister. I had to get to the killer. Ten minutes of running, and I had reached the place I knew I'd find him.

He must have been leaning on the truck, but in the shadows, behind a bunch of weeds, so I could only hear, not see him.

"Hey, little girl," he said. "I was waiting for you."

In the many years since that afternoon, I have tried to remember how I felt at that moment, and how it was I could have stood there as I did then, less than a basketball court's distance from the Sunset Strangler, and not run away from him. If I felt fear (and how could

I not?), it had been eclipsed by a more compelling concern.

"Where's my sister?"

"Girl with the basketball?" he said. I still couldn't make out his face in the shadows, but I could see him shaking his head. "Somebody should do something about that kid's teeth."

He took a few steps away from the truck body then, to where I could get a clear glimpse of him for the first time: a man no longer young, with thinning hair and an oversized belly (out of shape, but not fat)—clean-shaven, oddly enough, and wearing a rumpled jacket.

He had been eating something. A jar of pureed peaches, from the looks of it. I could make out the face of the Gerber Baby on the label. He set this down on the hood of the old truck body, or what was left of it, and let out a long, low growl, like the sound a bear might make, when it came out of hibernation.

"Last time I looked," he said, "your sister was out taking a walk with the neighbor's pooch. I paid a visit to your neighborhood today, as you may know. I like to keep an eye on you. From what I read in the paper, you're something of a troublemaker."

He scratched his belly (also not unlike an animal) and bit into a Happy Face cookie that resembled the kind Jennifer Pollack made for Karl Jr.

"Nice cookie," he said. He was reaching for something on the ground beside him now. The wire.

"My father knows I'm up here," I said. "He's on his way."

"I don't think so." He paused a second. "*Farrah.*"

Where I was standing, there must have been a space of thirty feet that separated us—me in my old red sweatshirt, the killer with a hand on the one headlamp of the truck that was visible through the weeds, staring out like a glass eye. Now he was moving toward me with that wire. Taking his time, but coming my way.

I could hear the sound of birds, and the insects buzzing over the wildflowers. I could see crows overhead. (Maybe there would be vultures soon.) I looked around in search of FBI agents or park rangers. Observing this, the killer shook his head.

"One passed this way a while ago," he said. "They aren't due back for"—looking at his watch now—"a good hour."

This was when I spotted her. But he didn't. She was coming up behind him, but soundlessly, the way we'd practiced in all our afternoons of being Charlie's Angels. My sister.

I stood frozen. The killer was moving closer. I seemed to have forgotten how to move, much less to run. But behind the killer, I could see Patty, creeping closer. Moving in, but not so fast he'd hear her. If he was taking his time, so would she, but she was narrowing the space that separated the two of them.

He was ten feet away from me when he hesitated for a moment, and a look came over his face, as if receiving some divine message, and he needed to consider it. He stood motionless for a moment, and for that moment I was afraid he'd felt the presence of my sister. But no.

He farted. Then grinned.

I looked at my sister. Knowing Patty, I was afraid she might burst out laughing when the sound came out of him, but she was totally silent. The look on her face was one I knew from watching her play basketball, times she took a foul shot, and every muscle in her body was called into service for a single purpose. Making the basket.

"Sorry about that, wench," he said. "Nobody's perfect."

He was moving closer now. He had almost reached me.

"No point running," he said, looking almost regretful. "I'd catch you. No point thinking you can get away. I'll always be out there watching you."

As in my visions—but this was real now and happening—he raised his arms above him, with the wire taut between his outstretched hands. Two more steps . . . one . . . and he would lower it around my neck.

The world went white.

It was Patty who broke the stillness, but not with a gunshot.

(Later, I would ask her, "Did you plan this? How did you know it would work?" "I just knew I had to do something," she said. "That was all I could think of.")

She timed it perfectly. One second before and she might have been too early. A few seconds later, it would have been too late.

"Penis!" she yelled. "*Penis. Penis. Penis.*"

She was playing our old game, of calling out every shocking word we knew, at the top of her lungs in that big voice of hers. A bigger voice than I had ever known her to possess.

The killer whirled around. Now he could see my sister plainly, but she was out of reach, and calling out more words, a string of them. Every word I ever taught her, all those days on the mountain.

Penis! Vagina! Intercourse! Butt!

Toe jam. Pubic hair. Foreskin. Balls. Sanitary napkin!

He looked confused. Disoriented. Whatever scenarios the killer might have envisioned (the arrival of the police, a helicopter maybe, a sharpshooter, a mountain lion even), this was one that had never occurred to him.

He stood there motionless. For a split second anyway, which was enough.

He still had the piano wire in his hand. But where a second earlier his body had bent toward me, with his arms poised to descend around my throat, now he had turned in the direction of my sister's surprisingly insistent voice.

Her throat seemed stretched to meet the sky, like a coyote in the moonlight, and her eyes were closed, with the words still spilling out of her.

Pee. Poop. Snot. Fart. Testicles.

Nipple. Butthole. Breast. Boob.

I can still see my sister's face as she stood there, with her head thrown back as if in song. Singing to save her life, was how she looked. To save mine.

Penis. Penis. Penis.

Vagina. Intercourse.

She knew the F-word, but some part of her held that one back.

The killer had seen her now. He hesitated, then took a step toward me. He took a step back, toward Patty.

Then back to me. He appeared to be deciding which of us to go after first. The one closest to him, who was too terrified to make a sound, or the tall one behind him whose yelling was so loud the whole mountain must be hearing her.

But I was closer, and it appeared that whatever words my sister was calling out into the air, he had regained his balance enough to lower the wire around my neck and start to tighten it.

Only now my sister was diving for him. In her hand, she held the BB gun.

Fire this baby at close range, our father had told us, *and it can take out a person's eye.*

She had the barrel against his eye socket. She fired. The blood spurted everywhere.

The man screamed, and dropped the wire. Hands over his face, he took off down the mountain. I breathed again.

The Special Forces team patrolling the mountain that day had heard my sister's yelling. They arrived a few minutes later. By that point, the man was gone.

It was hard for me to speak at first, I was shaking so hard. Patty was doing better, but she had injured her vocal cords. When she opened her mouth to tell the officers what happened, no words came out.

A little later, I could explain, or tried to. There were the contents of the truck body to show them, of course, and the piano wire he'd abandoned on the ground, there where we stood.

"He was eating baby food he stole from our neighbor," I said.

He took my sister's shoelaces.

There's his Coke can.

"There's his blood." I pointed to a place on the ground, near where my sister had got my attacker in the eye. (Aware, as I did so, of the blood now soaking through my shorts. My own.)

The agents wrote down everything I told them. They said they'd be in touch with our parents. They took us back to our house—my second ride in an ATV in the space of a few weeks.

We sat down then, to tell them in detail what had just taken place. But who was I, after all? The girl already identified in the pages of the *San Francisco Chronicle* as a problem child. The girl who, just weeks before, had pulled a similar prank on the mountain, with a phony call to her own father suggesting the killer was after her, and a threatening anonymous note to her neighbor. What did it mean that there was piano wire on the ground? Everyone knew the killer used piano wire. Easy enough to get your hands on a length of it.

As well as she could with her voice gone, Patty corroborated my story of course—acting out how the killer came after me with the piano wire, but this was dismissed as the word of a young girl, loyal to a fault, and desperate to protect her older sister.

It was our challenge that day to convince the police who questioned us that we had been alone on the mountain with a vicious serial killer and yet had succeeded—as two young girls, with only a BB gun to defend ourselves—to vanquish him. We both knew it would be impossible to explain the part where my sister had yelled out the shocking words as a means of distracting the killer (and besides, this would only have confirmed the agents' assessment of me—and now both of us—as crazy, and obsessed with sex). In fact, it had been the sound of my sister's yelling that had initially alerted the agents who had first arrived on the scene that afternoon. They'd heard her voice, calling out the shocking words, but evidently they remained under the impression that what Patty had been calling out was the name of a popular comic strip. Or, depending on interpretation, a kind of nut.

They believed none of our story. When the agents came back to our house later that night—a visit for which they'd requested that both our parents be in attendance—it was to deliver the news that in light of our father's many years of devoted service in law enforcement, they were willing to drop the charges of reckless and dangerous nuisance on the part of a juvenile (an offense that could in other circumstances have led to as much as six months in a detention center). Instead, given that I had an obvious mental problem, my parents were under orders to get me psychiatric help.

One of them handed my father a card containing the name of a psychologist who specialized in treating juvenile delinquents and adolescents with substance abuse problems.

After they left, I went into my room, the room I shared with Patty. (Voiceless, still. We didn't know this yet, but that day her vocal cords were permanently damaged. Her condition was later diagnosed as severe vocal nodules, and though she would eventually speak again, she was never again able to speak above a husky whisper, or to call out on a basketball court—*over here, over here*—or to sing. Not that she had ever been a particularly great singer. Just a loud and joyful one. Especially when the person she was singing along with was Dolly Parton, or Dean Martin, or our father.)

When I woke up the next morning, I knew the killer was gone. I alone knew this, because I could feel it. As strongly as I had sensed his presence on the mountain, all those weeks before, I felt his absence from it now. Wherever he was—and he was out there—it was someplace else.

I stopped over at the Pollacks' house. I said I'd come to return a book I'd borrowed—not *My Secret Garden;* I wasn't about to admit to having taken that one. This was the autobiography of a former Olympic ski racer who'd become a quadriplegic after an accident. Some weeks earlier, on my way to my sweeping job at the police precinct, Jennifer Pollack had given me the book, explaining that she thought the story would inspire me, and remind me that even when things look really hopeless, they can still get better. *Look at Jill Kinmont: they turned her book into a movie, and now she makes art with a paintbrush in her mouth.*

The real reason I had dropped by the Pollacks' was because they had stopped calling me for babysitting jobs. The new baby was due soon, and I'd been hoping to help out with Karl Jr. and make some money for back-to-school shopping. But they hadn't called me in weeks now—not since my picture was in the paper in another article about what was now called the "alleged attack" on my sister and me, and my fake call for help.

"I was wondering if you might like me to watch Karl Jr. sometime," I said to Jennifer now. "So you could get ready for the baby and stuff."

"We're probably all set," Jennifer told me. Normally this would have been the moment she'd invite me in for a Popsicle, but this time she didn't.

"If you wanted to go out Friday, I could come over," I said.

She was quiet for a minute. Off in the other room, I could hear Karl Jr. making animal noises, and the soothing tones of Karen Carpenter. "We've Only Just Begun."

"I hope that counselor's helping," Jennifer offered, as she closed the door.

My father never said anything about it, but I knew what my actions had cost him. When he came over now—as he did more often since he'd been taken off the Sunset Strangler case—he even said how good it was, thanks to the Novato transfer, to have more time for his family. "I haven't been a very good dad lately," he said, as if what had happened was all his fault, instead of all mine.

"It's okay," Patty said, patting his hand. "You do the best you can."

We were taking care of him now.

I had turned fourteen just before that summer began. (Patty was twelve now. She was growing up too.)

Bored by the exploits of *The Brady Bunch* (even the ones I made up), my sister and I still occasionally went to the hillside behind the houses of Morning Glory Court for Drive-In Movie nights. But not as often as we used to. I had my sessions with the therapist—who theorized to my mother that my concocting elaborate and dangerous scenarios on the mountain, in which I pretended to be under threat of attack by the Sunset Strangler, had been a desperate bid for attention on the part of a child of divorced parents, and a cry for help. In addition, I was an adolescent, with clearly demonstrated confusion surrounding sexuality, as indicated by my obsession with a highly inappropriate book that had been found in my room, and my own notebooks filled with stories, which the FBI officers had confiscated and read.

My mother paid attention to none of this.

"What you write in those notebooks is your own business and nobody else's," she said. "Nobody should

ever tell a writer there's something she's not allowed
to say."

She spoke of me as a writer. Maybe this was the
moment I believed I might actually become one.

Other than therapy and my work detail at the precinct, summer moved along much as it always had.
Sometime in August, Helen's son moved her to a re-
tirement community closer to his home in Washington
State, and though hers had not been the only television set visible through the windows at night, the moment she moved away seemed as good a time as any
for Patty and me to discontinue our dying tradition of
watching *The Brady Bunch* on the hillside. I was sick
of television anyway.

Patty continued taking care of Petra, and spending time with Mr. Armitage, who—amazingly to me,
though not to Patty—announced sometime that he
had gotten engaged to a woman he'd met at work. Her
name was Sarah, and she was a dog lover like himself,
though what she felt about Mr. Armitage's wardrobe of
dresses, if he still had them, we never discovered. We
had long since realized life was filled with mysteries,
many of which would remain unsolved forever, despite
the best detective work.

It was late August, the week before the start of high school. From the other end of Morning Glory Court, I saw my sister on her way home from finishing her paper route, holding aloft a copy of the *Marin Independent Journal.*

"They caught him," she said, when she was close enough that I could hear her. Her voice was very faint now and sounded scratchy all the time.

"Caught who?"

"The Sunset Strangler." She handed me the paper then, with the headline taking up the whole top half of the front page: "Sunset Strangler Arrested. Marin County Breathes Sigh of Relief." The photograph showed a tall, thin man—no more than thirty, from the looks of it—with long brown hair, being led to a police car, wearing handcuffs. He was smiling directly at the camera.

He'd turned himself in that morning, the story said. Walked straight into the headquarters of the Marin Homicide Division and confessed to all fifteen murders.

His name was J. Russell Adler, and he worked as a toll taker on the Golden Gate Bridge and aspired to be a rock star.

"He said he was going to be the next Jimi Hendrix," one of his neighbors had commented to the reporter who'd written the story about his arrest. "I think he came out here after the Summer of Love. One time he signed my phone book and told me to keep it because his autograph would be valuable someday."

"Those TV cameras on?" J. Russell Adler had said, as the police escorted him inside the courthouse, surrounded by the press. He'd waved to them.

I studied the photograph again and passed the paper back to Patty. We were quiet for a long time.

"You know it too, don't you?" I said.

My sister nodded.

"This isn't him."

In the days that followed, the J. Russell Adler story was front-page news. One story reprinted the lyrics to a song he'd written, and in another one they'd interviewed his mother back in Indiana, who made the comment that she knew all along it was a bad idea, her son coming out to California. A man who sold tickets at the Fillmore remembered meeting J. Russell Adler a few months back, when he'd shown up with his guitar case, demanding an audition with Bill Graham. People called in to talk-radio shows, to offer memories of times they'd paid their bridge toll and a strange young man had given them this scary look as they'd passed through his booth. J. Russell, obviously.

"I knew there was something wrong with the guy," one woman said.

Another woman—someone who worked at the courthouse and spoke on condition of anonymity—said he'd announced at his arraignment that he had demo cassette tapes, if anyone was interested. "I'm the next fucking Bob Dylan," he'd yelled to the courtroom.

At night in our beds, we lay there talking about it.

"The real guy's short," I said. "Remember when you stuck the BB gun in his face? You were taller than him. And he was bald. Mostly."

"Did you see his hands?" she whispered. "I remember his hands being different too. He had long fingernails, and his fingers were chubby."

"I know," I told her. Guitar players cut their finger-nails short.

"We should tell someone," she said.

"No one believes me anymore," I told her.

"Dad will."

The funny thing was, he did. I might not even have tried, but Patty insisted we bike over to his apartment before he left for work that day. We got there just as he was climbing into the Alfa.

"They arrested the wrong guy," Patty said, without preamble. "The guy from the tollbooth isn't the real Sunset Strangler."

"Whoever heard of a person saying they were a murderer when they really weren't?" I said, playing devil's advocate. I knew Patty was right, but I was at a loss to understand why anyone would admit to crimes he hadn't committed.

"Actually, there are people out there crazy enough to do that," our father said. "It makes them excited thinking about all the attention they're going to get."

"The real guy that came after us was short," Patty whispered. "And old. And I shot him with the BB gun. Based on all the blood, I think he'd have a scar on his face, at least."

"We tried to tell you."

Our father just sat there. But I knew from the look in his eyes that he was paying close attention. After a long time, he spoke.

"I was wrong," he said. "I should have believed you two."

"Now you'll just explain to the police that they have the wrong person, right, Dad?" Patty said.

"I don't think they want to hear that from me, Patty Cakes," he said. "That or anything else. I'm what's known as persona non grata over at headquarters these days. All those Special Forces guys and FBI big shots are just crowing about how people can get back out on the mountain now. The sheriff will get reelected after all, probably."

"But if everyone thinks J. Russell Adler's the killer, how are they ever going to catch the real killer?" Patty said.

He didn't need to tell us. They weren't.

Even now, with everything that had happened, and his office, that used to have a sign on the door—DETECTIVE ANTHONY TORRICELLI, CHIEF OF HOMICIDE—assigned to someone else, my father was still known in the Marin Homicide Division as being irreplaceable for one particular talent: his ability to get even the toughest criminals to confess to their crimes.

Even when the evidence might not be sufficient to convict, even when the guy they'd arrested went into that interrogation room ready to stonewall him at every turn, even when he'd got himself the fanciest lawyer to advise him, our father knew how to break a person down. He'd get suspects to the point where they'd be confiding in him every detail of the murder they might actually have gotten away with if they had only kept their mouths shut.

This was his magic. Even now that he'd been stripped of his duties as head of homicide, it was understood that there could be no better person in all of Marin law enforcement to extract a full and complete statement from J. Russell Adler concerning the Sunset Strangler killings than Detective Anthony Torricelli.

They brought our father down from Novato. Gave him the room, the desk. Brought in the man who, of his own volition, had admitted to having murdered those fifteen women. They would have assumed that of all the interrogations my father had ever participated in, this one was sure to be the smoothest sailing. Like taking candy from a baby.

Or should have been.

What our father actually did, when he got J. Russell Adler in the room alone with him, was not what anyone expected, or anything he'd ever done before. For forty-eight hours he worked on getting J. Russell Adler to admit he was not the Sunset Strangler. But unlike virtually every other man or woman who'd ever faced our father across the table in that interrogation room, this one stuck to his story.

When it was over, the D.A. announced that given the full confession, the state felt no need to mount a trial.

J. Russell Adler pled guilty to all fifteen murders—thereby avoiding the death penalty—and was sentenced to fifteen consecutive life terms at San Quentin.

In the picture that ran on the front page of the *Marin IJ*, as they led him away after the sentencing, J. Russell Adler was smiling.

One more thing. In his confession, it was apparent that J. Russell Adler had known about the electrical tape on the victims' eyelids. In accordance with what the papers had been telling us for months, he had also indicated that he liked to take the victims' clothes off after murdering them. He spoke of having raped his victims, and of his preference (also well documented in the press) for arranging their bodies in a prayer position before leaving them—though he had appeared a little vague as to which victims he had chosen to arrange this way, and where, precisely, each of the victims' bodies had been found.

He drove a Ford Pinto, not a Toyota, but that wasn't a problem.

The important thing was that people didn't have to be scared to leave their houses anymore. The annual Labor Day Pancake Breakfast hosted by the Swiss Hiking Club could once again take place. The governor had extravagant praise for the efforts of the Special Forces team, and the FBI of course. He said nothing about my father, or the work of Marin Homicide.

With J. Russell Adler locked away, life could go back to normal. Except for one thing that I learned during one of my father's late-night visits to my mother.

During the interrogation, my father had asked the man who claimed to be the Sunset Strangler about the shoelaces.

"Shoelaces?" he said. A blank look had come over his face.

"What did you do with their shoelaces?"

"The usual, I guess," he'd told my father. "What you always do with shoelaces."

"What would that be?" my father asked.

"You tie them."

Late that fall, the media's obsession with the Sunset Strangler finally wound down, and the press moved on to other stories. I had hoped that once this happened, my sister and I could get our father back, restored to his old hero status maybe, or something close. But the hoped-for transfer from his dark little office in Novato back to the Civic Center never came. In the eyes of most people in our county, the heroes of the Sunset Strangler case had been the FBI.

That fall, the *IJ* had run an editorial suggesting that our local law enforcement officers had much to learn from the government professionals who'd finally brought the killer to justice. The *Chronicle* ran a cartoon featuring a man evidently meant to represent my father—depicted as paunchy and balding, with a five o'clock shadow—applying for a job at McDonald's.

For my father, the whole world changed after his failure to apprehend the real Sunset Strangler. He knew that the man remained at large, somewhere out there in a world that included his two beloved daughters.

He wasn't working such long hours anymore. Where in the months before the arrest he'd been getting progressively thinner, he had put on weight, but not in a good way. He looked puffy—from drinking, probably. The stress of the last twelve months seemed only to have been transferred to another location—from his shoulders to where it resided now, someplace even deeper, more irretrievable.

I think that the moment when my father understood his failure, and acknowledged his terrible mistake in not believing the story Patty and I had told him about our encounter with the killer on the mountain, was the moment he stopped believing in his own magic. Once that happened, his magic was gone.

The three of us were out driving somewhere a few months after the arrest of J. Russell Adler. Our usual dinner spot was Marin Joe's, but having found ourselves farther north, we had stopped into an IHOP for a meal.

The waitress pouring his coffee had recognized my father from all those press conferences on television the year before, evidently—surprising, considering I sometimes barely recognized him myself anymore.

"You're the cop that was working on the Sunset Strangler case," she said.

Yours truly, my father said, but not like his heart was in it. It said something about where he was these days that I (who used to dread these moments) felt only gratitude that he had the chance to haul out the old charmer routine.

"That guy really had you going for a while," the waitress said. "Thank God for the FBI."

My sister and I chewed quietly then. At some point when he was finishing his pancakes, and the waitress came back with a refill, my father had made the observation to her that she looked a lot like Jane Fonda in *Coming Home.*

"I bet you get that all the time," he said.

I saw the way he looked at her then, almost seductively, eyes peering up from under those lashes.

This was the first time I could remember that a woman had seemed oblivious. She charged him for the pancakes, like a normal person.

His cough, which our mother kept saying he should get checked out, did not improve. Sometimes now I could hear him struggling for breath. One day, when he was dropping us off after dinner, he told our mother he was thinking of quitting the force.

"But you love being a police officer," she said.

"A cop needs to recognize when he's past the top of his game," he told her. "It's probably time for the younger guys to step in and take the lead."

"What are you talking about, Anthony?" she said. "You're not even forty-one yet."

"Whatever age it happens to a man, he'd better take note when it does," my father said. "I'm not going to be like one of those old ballplayers who keeps showing up at spring training when his average drops below two hundred."

He had told us, back when he was working those eighty-hour weeks, that he was taking us to Italy once he had the case wrapped up. Now he came by the house with a guidebook and said it was time to start studying our Italian.

After the trip, he said, there'd be some changes made. Who knew, maybe he'd open a barbershop.

I t was late October, just after we set the clocks back, so it got dark by five thirty now, and the rain had started early that year. Pumpkins in the windows at the Pollacks' house (where baby Ashley had put in her appearance some weeks before). A For Sale sign on Helen's house. At the end of the street, Mr. Armitage had evidently hired a small bulldozer once again, but this time, instead of ripping up the lawn and replacing it with stones, it appeared he was taking out the stones and putting grass back in.

"His fiancée wants to start a vegetable garden," Patty explained.

Our father pulled up at the house just after dinnertime that night—not his usual hour, but we were always happy to see him. Patty and I were washing the bowls from our dinner of Campbell's soup and crackers and wrapping up leftover carrot sticks.

"I need to talk with you girls," he said. "Your mother too."

We sat down in the living room. He lit a Lucky. "A little late to quit now, it turns out," he said.

He had cancer. Lungs. The X-rays showed tumors on both of them. It wasn't looking good.

"My grandpop always called these things coffin nails," he said, examining the familiar white packet with its red bull's-eye on the front. "But he lived to eighty smoking like a chimney. I guess I thought I had the same genes."

Later Patty and I lay in our beds. I didn't cry, knowing that would scare my sister.

"At least they caught it," Patty whispered. "It would have been worse if we'd gone to Italy and they didn't know till we got back."

"He's probably had it for a while," I said. "You know how he coughs."

I couldn't even remember when the last time was that he had really sung to us, more than speaking the words along with the voice on the record player or the eight-track player in his car.

"He's so strong," Patty offered. "Other people might not be able to handle it but Dad's different."

Italy would be good for him, she said. We'd ride in one of those boats, with the men in striped shirts, paddling down the canals and singing. We'd finally have our father back.

The trip never happened, but while he could still drive, our father came over to our house more than he ever had. There were times that fall when I could imagine the four of us were still a family—our mother, Patty, me, and our father, playing cards around the kitchen table, having popcorn together. Our mother came out of her room more during those months.

"You know the problem with your mother, girls?" he said to us once, as she sat there, studying her hand. "She was too smart for me. She's the only one that never bought any of my lines. Even when I bought them myself."

Our mother stared at him over her fanned-out cards. It was the first time in my life I'd seen tears in her eyes.

"You're as good a woman as they come, Lillian," he told her. "If our girls turned out this great, I know where credit lies."

Sometimes, those nights, the four of us talked about the old days. He liked to imagine we had all these great traditions—Candlestick Park, North Beach, the Marin Headlands, the cable cars, Shirley Temples at the Top of the Mark, jumping in the waves at Stinson Beach. None of us wanted to say, *We went to each of those places exactly once.*

"Remember that French song we used to sing?" he asked one time. "Remember the Flamingo Hotel?"

Patty and I didn't say anything.

"That must've been with someone else, Anthony," our mother said.

Patty and I knew who.

He wanted to teach me how to drive. I knew it was against the law for me to be behind the wheel at my age, but I wasn't about to argue with my father, even if he hadn't been a police officer.

He set the date for a Saturday morning in November, and for once, that day the sun came out. He wanted to drive with me up Highway 1, through Stinson Beach, past Bolinas, into Point Reyes, he said. We were taking the Alfa.

Most people's fathers wouldn't start them off driving a stick shift, much less on a road with so many crazy turns and drop-offs that it had been used in numerous sports car commercials. But nobody had a father like mine.

"Don't tell your mother," he said, when he picked me up. His old line. Not that it was necessary.

I sat in the passenger seat until we were safely down the road, where we changed places. When we did, I took in the full effect of how thin he'd become since his diagnosis. His pants fell from his belt like a set of drapes, and his hands, that I'd always loved, looked like bones with a little skin pulled over them. He got up from the bucket seat as slowly as an old man, holding on to the side of the car as he pulled himself to a standing position. I could hear every breath that went in and out of him.

"Never keep your eye on what's directly ahead of you, Farrah," he said. "You want to focus on what's a hundred feet up the road."

"Don't brake on a curve. Downshift. That's how the pros do it."

"If you want to look cool driving, which you do," he said, "you don't grip the wheel that tightly. Me, I imagine I've got my hands on the shoulders of a beautiful woman. I leave it to you to come up with your own mental picture for this one."

He wanted to stop at Stinson Beach to look at the ocean, though I could see when we got there that this visit would be harder for him than he'd anticipated. Still, we got out of the car and made our way up the path and onto the sand. He didn't ask, but I bent down to untie his shoes for him. I knew he'd want to be barefoot.

We passed Bolinas, the town where the citizens kept taking down the road sign to keep the tourists out.

"Hippie town here," he said. "The women here don't believe in shaving their armpits. No argument from me there, you understand. Every woman needs to claim her own style of beauty. It's my curse to love them all."

We kept driving north. Olema, Point Reyes Station, Marshall. I knew my father was tired—more than tired—but he wanted to keep going. He'd put Dean Martin in the eight-track, and though we talked sometimes, and now and then he'd offer some pointer on my driving, for long stretches we rode without speaking—my father in the unfamiliar position of passenger, me at the wheel, listening to the music.

In fact, I did grip the wheel tightly for the duration of that drive, I believe, but not simply because I was an inexperienced and underaged driver.

I gripped the wheel because I understood that what was happening at this moment was another one of my father's onetime deals, and I didn't want to forget a second of it. I recognized that this would be the only driving lesson my father would ever give me. I also knew the reasons he'd taken me out that day went far beyond the desire to provide me with driving instruction.

"My mother wasn't around when I was growing up," he said. "I guess I could have been mad at her about that, but I wasn't. I figured she had her reasons. I didn't question what they were."

My fingers stayed clamped around the wheel. Eyes on the road. Best that he not see my face just then, nor I his.

"I could handle it," he said. "The hard part was seeing what it did to my old man."

More silence. Tony Bennett now: "My Foolish Heart."

"It would be a good thing if your mother could get out a little," he said. "Meet someone. A normal guy. She deserves that."

This wasn't going to happen, but I didn't say it. The first and last man our mother ever kissed was him.

"I don't lose sleep about your sister," he said. "There's a girl who knows how to tell a guy he's full of shit. Yours truly included. She's not going to let anybody mess with her. And she'll be a beauty too, once she gets those teeth fixed."

I had never heard either of our parents mention Patty's teeth, not once. It struck me that even now, as he finally acknowledged the problem, he did so without any sense that he'd be paying for the solution. He just knew Patty was a sufficiently competent person that she'd figure it out. Maybe he actually understood, even then, that his twelve-year-old daughter possessed a kind of self-discipline and strength he himself did not.

"It's you I worry about, Farrah," he said. We were all the way to the Russian River now—the town of Jenner, where the river meets the ocean. Though the day had turned cool, we had all the windows open, which made it even harder to hear his words to me—coming as they did now so much more softly than they once did, and between labored breaths. The way he took in air now, it was as if my father were sipping from the smallest cup, with only the smallest quantity of liquid remaining, and no possibility for refilling it once that was gone. One drop at a time. Not that, even.

"You'll be the real beauty, of course," he told me. "That's happening already. Men will come after you your whole life, it won't matter how old you are. You need to be sure, when they do, that there's something in it for you. Don't let it be a one-way street."

We were almost to Mendocino County when he told me to turn the car around. He had put his seat in the reclining position and closed his eyes, and as I made my way back down along the winding highway, I wasn't even sure my father was awake. I could have worried what might happen if a cop pulled us over and asked to see my permit, but I wasn't even thinking about that part.

I had to keep my eyes on the road, but sometimes, for a second, I would look over at my father, asleep beside me, and tell myself to freeze this moment. *Never forget.* I pretended I was a grown-up woman—thirty years old, or maybe thirty-five, out promoting my bestselling novel, and my father was retired from the police force, and (because my sister would have children, I knew) a grandfather now. Maybe we were driving to some important dinner for authors. Maybe my sister had become a professional basketball coach for some undefeated Division I school and we were heading to one of their games.

Maybe I was even older than that—the age that I have now reached, in fact: halfway through my forties—and my father was an old man. If this was so, it wouldn't seem so bad that he looked the way he did, or that he seemed to be having so much trouble breathing. He would just be old, that was all.

When we got back to Marin County—the turnoff on the freeway that would take us back to Morning Glory Court—my father opened his eyes in a way that made me realize he'd never actually been asleep, just resting.

"I need to ask you to do something for me, Farrah," he said. "I want you to drive me to Margaret Ann's."

The place was called Valley View, though in fact the only view revealed from that location featured the highway.

As my sister and I had guessed back on that day we saw his car parked outside this place—a hundred years ago, it felt, but really just a few months—the person who lived there was Margaret Ann.

The last time we'd visited Margaret Ann—the last time Patty and I had accompanied our father on a visit—I was nine years old, Patty seven. I remember how proud we were of him when—wanting to surprise her one time—he'd done a pull-up on her balcony. The place she lived then was so pretty, we imagined he had brought us to Disneyland, and she was Cinderella. I remember wishing, for a moment, that we could live in this place ourselves, partly because it was so nice, but also because our father seemed so happy there. I remember the feeling I had, after: the awful guilt at liking her and betraying my mother by feeling that way.

Never forgive you.

Pulling into the parking lot of Valley View that day, with my father in the seat beside me, I felt myself hoping Margaret Ann lived in a ground-floor apartment, so he wouldn't have to deal with stairs.

The old place had window boxes and a clubhouse, a turquoise pool and a hot tub where Patty and I had sat one time while our father and Margaret Ann stretched out on lounge chairs nearby, sipping a drink she'd made them that was pale green, with little paper parasols that we got to take home after.

The pool at Valley View had been drained, and there was a scummy layer of some kind of mold along the bottom. Only a few cars sat in the parking lot—most of them pretty beat-up looking, and a chicken-wire fence enclosed one whole section of the building that did not appear to be inhabited.

One car he recognized, evidently: a very old Volkswagen with a bumper sticker that said "Nobody's Perfect Until You Fall in Love with Them" and another that said "There Is No Shortcut to Anyplace Worth Going."

"Looks like she's home," he said quietly. Evidently he hadn't called ahead. He'd been taking his chances.

He made no attempt at explaining to me what we were doing here, and none was required. "I should have picked up a snack for you," he said, though I wasn't hungry. "You don't even have one of those notebooks in the car, for your writing."

"I'll be fine," I said. "I can listen to the radio."

It turned out she lived in a second-floor apartment, accessed by an outdoor staircase leading from the parking lot to a long, narrow balcony where some of the remaining tenants had set out plants or beer bottles to turn in for the deposit money. There was a stationary bicycle set on this balcony, positioned in such a way as to give the person sitting on it a good view of the highway, and a kitty litter box, a broken stroller, and somebody's Christmas tree, ornaments and all.

I knew my father would not want assistance on the stairs. But I had to watch as he climbed them, in case it looked like he'd need help. Twice he stopped to catch his breath. Then he started in again. When he got to her door, I saw him pull his shoulders back and run a hand through his hair. He stood there for a moment before ringing the bell.

From where I sat in the parking lot, I could not see her standing in the doorway—only the look of him when he caught sight of her. She must have put her arms around him then, because he stood there a little longer, and I could make out one pale arm wrapped around his neck, mussing up his hair. Then he was stepping into the apartment. The door closed after him.

I sat in the car almost an hour, waiting. Under other circumstances, this would have felt like a long time to be sitting in a parking lot waiting for your father as he paid a visit to a woman who was not your mother—a woman about whom I had once issued the warning that if he ever had kids with her, I'd never speak to him again. If he ever made any life that wasn't with us. But as it was, I felt only happiness that he was gone that long. Whatever number of minutes he spent in that apartment, I figured, those would be the best minutes he could have right about now. I would have sat there all day if he needed that.

It was starting to get dark when he emerged from her apartment. Once again, he stood there in the doorway for a moment before leaving, and I could tell from the glow of light behind him that she must be standing there again, saying something to him, or maybe they were kissing. Hard to know. I begrudged him none of this now.

He made his way very slowly down the stairs, looking up one more time when he was partway down, but the door must have been closed by then. The glow of light was no longer visible.

When he got to the car, I reached across to the passenger side to open the door for him—as much help as he'd want from me. He lowered himself into the seat with a sigh that went on so long it could have contained every molecule of air in an inflatable mattress.

"There is one beautiful woman," he said, facing forward, as if he was the one who had to keep his eyes on the road.

I had never backed out of a parking space before, or even driven in reverse, and my father looked so exhausted now I knew I couldn't ask him to help. I started the engine, shifted the gear, and turned the steering wheel too sharply . . . smashed into a Dumpster with enough force that later, when I checked, I saw a significant dent. Once this would have caused my father regret, but now he seemed not to notice.

"We won't be back to this place again," he said, as I pulled out onto the highway. "You want to leave things on a good note."

He went in for the surgery that January. He was supposed to stay in the hospital only a week, but after the operation, they moved him to a different floor, and a few days later, he asked his friend Sal to bring him a portable stereo and a stack of his records. That was when we understood he wasn't going home anytime soon.

When Patty and I came to see him, he showed us how the hospital bed worked—the buttons you could push so you could sit up or lie down at more of an angle. Easier to get to the bathroom that way, though later that wasn't possible either.

"You girls," he said. "I did one thing right, anyway."

That last weekend, we slept in chairs by his bed.

Mr. Armitage took us to the hospital, and later our mother came with food for us and she sat with our father, though only briefly. She had never been one for the big drama moments.

Patty and I stayed by our father's bed all the rest of that weekend, and when Monday came there was no thought of school, or any awareness even of what day it was anymore. Our father was beyond speech now, his mouth gasping, palms open in the gesture that, for a police officer, signaled that he was carrying no weapon. At one point the pain appeared so terrible that I thought, if he had his gun now he might just end it here.

We didn't leave till Thursday, and then only because he'd died.

I remember how it felt, stepping out the entrance to the hospital after they'd taken his body to the funeral home. You'd expect it to be raining in Northern California in February, but that day the sun was out, and it seemed to me so bright I had to shield my eyes. I'd been in his dark room for six straight days at that point. My pupils probably needed to adjust, though there was more to it. The world, with our father no longer in it, protecting us, seemed to be an unrecognizable and unbearably lonely place.

Never gonna stop.
Give it up.

They would have held a service for my father at St. Mary's in the city, with an honor guard from the Marin County and San Francisco police forces, and a flag draped over the coffin for my sister and me to bring home afterward. But at our father's request, there was no service. He had asked that his body be cremated.

He left me his gun—the Chief Special—and the Alfa Romeo. Other than those, my father didn't own much: a wardrobe of great shoes, a medal for valor in the line of duty, the leather jacket, his gold watch, and every album Frank Sinatra, Tony Bennett, and Dean Martin ever recorded—and one Dusty Springfield album that brought back memories of a long-ago afternoon, Kool-Aid from bendy straws, and that closed bedroom door. One item I had looked for among his possessions and failed to find: his father's haircutting scissors. Strangely enough, those would have mattered more to me than the medal.

There had been a savings account in which he had told us he'd been putting aside money every month for the long-imagined Italy trip. At the time of his death, this account held just under eight hundred dollars— not quite enough for two round-trip tickets to Italy, so Patty and I could scatter his ashes in his family's home- town of Lucca. This was the place he'd always said he would take us. There, and Venice.

We didn't make the trip that year, or for some time after that. We waited until a few weeks after my high school graduation, when Patty was sixteen, to make the trip—and by then we'd saved up enough extra that we were able to see Florence and Rome too. In Venice we met a couple of beautiful Italian boys—one of whom turned out to be a fair basketball player, who didn't mind it at all that my sister was several inches taller than he was. Neither Patty's height nor the fact that she totally destroyed him on the basketball court got in the way of their kissing, which Patty described to me as excellent. She had her braces by then—paid for with paper route money, and later a busgirl job, augmented by a gift from Mr. Armitage. The braces proved not to be an obstacle for Vincenzo and Patty.

When we got home, I went to beauty school. I hadn't ever thought about college, but it occurred to me, after a couple of years of cutting hair and listening to all the stories told by women sitting in my chair, that I wanted to study psychology, with an emphasis on forensics and the criminal mind.

I started out in community college, but after two years, transferred to Berkeley. My sister had gotten into Berkeley too, on a basketball scholarship. This meant that we could commute from our mother's house in the blue Alfa our father had left to me, until we got our own apartment in my senior year.

That was when Patty was able to fulfill her lifelong dream of getting a dog. Not surprisingly, to me, her ongoing debate—cute puppy versus lovable old rescue dog in need of home—ended in the adoption, from the Marin Humane Society, of a half-Lab/half-golden mix named Betty, who was missing one leg, but still managed to run alongside my sister when she jogged. Betty managed to live five years with Patty—longer than anyone would have guessed for a dog whose age was estimated at twelve when Patty brought her home.

I did become a writer, as I'd always planned—though the international spy part, and the race car driving aspiration, fell by the wayside. I am almost embarrassed to admit—given how many fine writers struggle for decades before seeing a book published—that I sold my first novel, a darkly comic thriller titled *Come the Blood*, when I was twenty-nine.

The book did reasonably well, and its sequel, *Blood Again*, fared even better. Since then, I have published a novel nearly every year, always in the spring. As for the rest of my story: this will be harder to tell.

After our father's death, and the sentencing of J. Russell Adler, I tried for a while to put the Sunset Strangler case out of my mind. The idea that J. Russell Adler—the man now serving his sentence in San Quentin for the murders on the mountain—was not the killer (despite his own insistence that he was) would have been difficult enough to live with. But the knowledge that the real killer remained at large ate away at me, as it had done to my father.

And of course there was this: I knew well from my studies (as I would have, from my father) that once a person has manifested the behavior of a serial killer, he is highly unlikely to discontinue his behavior. Intervals may occur in which a serial killer goes on hiatus. He may make a geographical shift. He may even alter aspects of his M.O., though certain trademarks of his method of committing crimes are likely to endure, even when whole decades may have elapsed between one murder and another.

But as I told Alison during that brief period when she had posed as my friend: once a person acquires the taste for blood, it's virtually assured that he'll go after more.

A serial killer does not stop killing until he is arrested or dies.

My visions, as my sister and I had always called them, became less frequent, and then they disappeared completely. It wasn't a change I was aware of at the time, but one day somewhere around age eighteen or nineteen, I realized that a few years had passed since the last time I'd experienced one of those moments in which I knew something would happen before it did, or knew it had happened before anybody told me, or—as was most disturbingly true during the year of the Sunset Strangler—an instance in which I'd find myself inside the head of a person other than me: know what he was thinking, see the world through his eyes.

It was a relief, in many ways, that my gift, or curse, had abandoned me. But in another way, I recognized that the landscape I now inhabited seemed less filled with color and richness. Where once there were layers to what surrounded me (things as they appeared to be, and the once-endless fantasies cooked up in my imagination), now there was only real life; I conjured up stories and wrote them down, but they no longer filled my brain as they once did, and I no longer confused what I dreamed up for what was actually taking place.

I still thought daily, hourly, about the Sunset Strangler, however, as I had from the moment he first slunk onto our mountain with his piano wire and his electrical tape, and his deadly quest for shoelaces. Once and once only since the summer of 1979 did I succeed in putting the Sunset Strangler—and my need to redeem my father's story—out of my mind. My sabbatical lasted about eleven months. It was a brief time— the only one I ever experienced—in which I allowed myself to fall crazily and ecstatically in love, to the point where everything else seemed to fall away (my father's death, the Sunset Strangler, even my sister), and all I knew was that I wanted to be with this man, and my thoughts were only of the two of us.

I had never wanted to get married, but when I got together with Chris, that idea seemed suddenly possible, even inevitable. I wrote a hopelessly romantic love story—an unfinished novel that would surely make me cringe if I looked at it now. Chris and I talked about moving to Oregon. Having a baby. We bought a VW bus and decided to drive around the country for a while, cooking over an open fire and sleeping under the stars whenever possible.

We were at a campground in South Dakota when we heard the news over someone's radio that a woman had been found murdered in the Black Hills, not far away. Whoever it was who'd committed the crime appeared to have been on foot at the time and had managed to depart the scene without leaving a trace of evidence.

Knowing my history, Chris suggested that we take off right away for someplace else. Montana, maybe, or Utah. Plenty of beautiful places to go.

But I wanted to stay in South Dakota. Not just for a few nights, but until they caught the killer. I wanted to know everything about the crime. Participate in the investigation, if possible. Believing as I did that the perpetrator of the Black Hills murder must be the man my sister and I had confronted on Mount Tamalpais years before, I wanted to be present for the triumphant moment, years in coming, when they slapped the cuffs on him.

This was the beginning. We actually rented an apartment in Brookings. Chris was that crazy about me that he went along with my obsession, and he seemed to accept all the days I spent at the library, the long letters I wrote to law enforcement agencies around the state, filling them in on details of the Sunset Strangler case

I felt might assist them in locating their killer. (Who was eventually apprehended, in Canada. And turned out never to have set foot in the state of California. This was the first moment I got it, that instead of there being one man out there murdering women in remote backwoods locations, the country was crawling with them.)

In those days, the Internet had barely gotten going, and the concept of any kind of national database, beyond what the FBI maintained, remained primitive by today's standards. Say a woman had been murdered with a .44-caliber pistol in the state of Georgia by a man who had posed as a vacuum cleaner salesman to gain entry into her apartment. It was unlikely that the investigating officers on that crime would have known whether some other woman around her age and physical type had survived an attack, eight months earlier, by someone using a gun of the identical caliber, who had gained entry by telling her he had a great set of knives for sale at a fantastic price. Particularly if this other woman lived in another state—Ohio, say, or Rhode Island.

Unless you were an FBI agent, the only way you might know that these two events had both taken place, and recognized the similarities between the two, would be if you subscribed to a few hundred newspapers and made it your business to keep track of every murder you possibly could, in every state, and then recorded the details of every one of these murders or attempted murders. You would need to fill your brain with a great many terrible stories. You might even find yourself doing the very thing my father had done all those years before: tacking pictures of murder victims on your wall, so you could study their faces twenty-four hours a day. Their faces and the details of exactly how it was they had spent their final moments on earth.

I did that.

I covered one whole wall of the apartment Chris and I shared with a map showing the fifty states. (Alaska and Hawaii seemed unlikely destinations for a serial killer, but I wasn't writing off any spot as a possible location for the Sunset Strangler to have touched down.)

I spent my days in libraries, scrolling through microfiche, scribbling down data. Then sticking pushpins in the map, in every place I heard about in which a crime had occurred that sounded like something the Sunset Strangler could have pulled off.

My conversation and my thoughts were consumed with details of rapes and murders, and the men who'd committed them. When I didn't talk about murders, I thought about them. I no longer talked about Oregon, or a baby.

Within a year, Chris and I parted. There was no room in my life anymore for another man, knowing there were two already whose stories occupied virtually my every waking hour. One was the Sunset Strangler. The other was my father.

I moved around a lot after that. Same way I believed the killer must. Two months in Illinois. Six months in Minnesota. A year (that was a long stretch) in Nevada, during a period in which four young women turned up dead at ski resorts over the course of two successive seasons. When they eventually arrested the man responsible for that one, it was clear he wasn't the one I was looking for. As hard as it had been to make out the particulars of the man who'd lurched toward us, that afternoon my sister and I had confronted the Sunset Strangler on the mountain, I knew he was a person of below-average height. The man found guilty of the Ski Mask killings was six foot five.

For the first few years I tracked killers (hauling around my map and my pushpins to every stop), I got waitressing jobs, and sometimes I'd rent a chair at a beauty salon. Having no relationship with a man, and little need or ability to sleep, I wrote at night. My stories were fiction but filled with the details I picked up from my research. I had no use for love.

I quit cutting hair the day I sold my first novel. After my second one was optioned as a movie, I bought an old farm in New Hampshire, about as far as a person could get from where Patty and I grew up, in the shadow of a mountain called Monadnock. After that, I returned to Marin County only once or twice a year—never for more than a few days—to see my mother. She was doing better by this time. She'd discovered antidepressants and gotten a job at her favorite place, the library.

When she was young, my sister had held out the dream of one day playing professional basketball. The year of the trailside killings had also been the first year of the WBL, which had meant that even as the most terrible thing was happening up on the mountain where we lived, for Patty that year had also represented hope and possibility that her great dream might actually come true.

Two years later, after the women's professional basketball league folded, she shifted her focus. Strangely enough—considering I was the one who always talked about traveling around the globe—it was Patty who joined the Peace Corps. I used to tell her it would be easier to do without food than do without my sister. But we wrote each other long letters every week—though sometimes hers took months to reach me.

She had written to me from Africa about what the game of basketball meant to the young, poor girls she was teaching there. Because of her damaged voice—she never was able to speak above a whisper—classroom teaching was impossible for Patty. She tutored her kids, one-on-one, and it almost seemed they listened better, she wrote to me, because they had to strain so hard to hear her.

She started to run basketball clinics—first in Senegal, and then other countries too. She was always on a bus going to some village or other with her basketball shoes around her neck, and a bag of balls above her seat. Her one regret about the work she'd chosen was that she couldn't bring a dog with her.

She was in Somalia, running one of her clinics at a school for junior-high-school-aged girls, when a UN bombing there that killed a hundred civilians set off a mob riot. The journalist who reached me sometime that night with the news explained to me that the riots had been touched off right where the school was, at the time her girls—the Warriors, she called them—would have been putting on their uniforms.

Who would ever think of a basketball court as a dangerous place? But knowing that for those girls, that day, it would be, my sister had left her rented room in a safe part of Mogadishu to make sure they were out of danger. On a bus first, and then, when the streets got too mobbed and no vehicles could get through, on foot. Still carrying her basketball. Running like the wind.

She had almost reached the school where the girls were—nine players, just about the ages we were that day we met the killer on the mountain, when Patty had let out her string of loud and powerful words that saved my life.

She couldn't raise her voice to call her players' names, so she ran into the crowd to get them out, and when one of the men grabbed her, she could not cry for help.

The stone, thrown by one of the faceless mob, hit her square in the head. It is my only source of comfort knowing that my sister died instantly.

There needs to be a blank page in my story here. Or a thousand of them—more than that—for all the days she hasn't been there that I've spent missing her.

At first I wanted to disappear—cut off my hair and burn it, run out onto the mountain or to the bluffs at Tennessee Valley, or somewhere in Point Reyes—and jump off the edge of the world. I went through the motions of getting through the days, though sometimes just lifting the covers off the bed and setting my feet on the floor beside it felt like too much of an effort.

There was no place to go, no place to look that did not summon a picture of Patty. Oddly enough, the one thing that seemed bearable was writing my stories and losing myself in the lives of people other than myself and my sister.

It was after Patty died that our mother came out of her room. Always before, when anything hard had happened in my life, the person I looked to for comfort was Patty, but this time, the hard thing was losing her. There were all those hours to get through, when Patty would have been there, only she wasn't. This time our mother was. And Mr. Armitage. After my sister's funeral, he and his wife had come by my mother's house with food for us. They just sat there in the living room for a long time—knowing, as others appeared not to, that there was no need to say anything, and nothing to be said.

At some point during those first months after Patty's death, it occurred to me how it must have been for our father, the year of those fifteen murders, having to visit all those families who'd lost someone they loved to a terrible and violent death, people who wished they were dead themselves. I had imagined, before, that it was the evil of the killer that made its way into my father's body and ate away at him, but I think now that just as much it was the exposure to that much sorrow. Some people can shut out pain better than others, but for my father, who loved women, those mothers' losses—the losses of the fathers and the brothers and the lovers too, of course, but above all, the losses of the mothers and the sisters—would have been as real as a blow to his own body. Say what you will about the dangers of nicotine—all correct. But I will always believe it was exposure to a toxic killer and to crushing grief, and the knowledge that he had not succeeded in righting that wrong, that simply took up residence in my father's lungs and suffocated him.

It had been a goal of mine—long deferred—to write a letter to the man serving consecutive life sentences for the Sunset Strangler killings. I had no particular faith that I would be any more skillful than my father—the master of extracting the truth from criminals—at getting J. Russell Adler to admit that he was not the real killer. But I did hold out some hope that more than a decade at San Quentin might have altered his view of his actions to the point where he'd be ready to retract his confession, thereby paving the way for the reopening of the case and, perhaps, restoring my father's reputation.

This never happened. Sometime in the 1990s—seventeen years after J. Russell Adler had turned himself in, and the hasty sentencing that followed, Adler was found dead in his cell, murdered by a fellow inmate. His death appeared to end, forever, any hope I might have had in convincing law enforcement authorities and the district attorney that for all these years they'd had the wrong man.

Still, I tracked murders—keeping watch, among the databases I checked in on regularly, for a killer who favored rural locations, campsites and hiking trails, one who used piano wire when committing his crimes, possibly, or even (though I didn't count on this) collected shoelaces.

I kept writing my stories, but after my sister's death, I took pains to keep the stories I wrote as far from my own as possible.

The novels in my series always featured as the central characters and heroines a devoted pair of sisters (one tall, one not so tall) who function in the unlikely roles of amateur detectives. The younger sister in my series is a professional tennis player, the other a harpist. Though the harpist bears a slight resemblance to me (that much was unavoidable, since I was three books into my series by the time of Patty's death) and the two women came from an Italian-American family, I made sure when I created the characters that the younger sister—the tennis player—followed a radically different path from that of my real sister. She won big professional tournaments, for one thing, and she got rich. She started endorsing products and modeling tennis outfits, while solving murders on the side. She had perfect teeth, and a pet that traveled with her on the tennis tour: a cat.

Around the eighth book in my series—*Blood Love*—my harp-playing sister falls in love and gets married. She gives birth to a son—a plot choice I made to ensure that no further associations could be made between myself and my character. I was in my late thirties by this point, and if there was one thing I knew, it was that I'd go through life solo now. I could never form an attachment again as strong as what I'd had with my sister. I could never bear another loss like the loss of her.

I met Robert at a bookstore reading in Keene, New Hampshire. That night I'd read a particularly grisly passage involving the discovery, by the tennis-playing sister, of body parts in her tennis bag, moments before she is supposed to head out onto the court to play the Paris Open. My days of writing anything remotely romantic were long behind me, obviously.

During the question period, I'd called on a man in the back row—not particularly handsome or distinctive looking, though he wore a nice shirt. Flannel, I thought.

"I was wondering what it does to a person's state of mind, writing about all these terrible events?" he said. "Do you ever think that maybe, someday, you'll give your characters a happy ending? Let them go home and rest, maybe?"

"Happiness doesn't sell books," I said. "Murders do."

He'd found me in the parking lot after, headed toward my car. My father's old Alfa that I still drove now and then. Not a car for New England winters, but it was late summer at the time.

Some other man might have suggested a drink. He said he had this great garden, and that week the tomatoes had been ripening faster than he could eat them. He wanted to know if I'd like to take some home with me. He had a bagful in the car.

"I don't cook," I said.

"That's odd," he said. "In your books, you're always describing these great Italian meals."

"That was my father," I told him. "He used to say he'd give us the secret to his marinara sauce when we turned twenty-one. But he died before then."

"I could teach you that one," Robert said.

It was unlike me that I did this, but I said okay.

I did not fall in love with Robert. Falling in love was not something I did by this point, if I ever had. But we spent time together after that—every other week-end, when I was around, and not off researching murders—and it would not be inaccurate to say that Robert fell in love with me.

I saw him every other weekend only, because Robert had a daughter. Justine. Six years old, and living mostly with her mother, but she spent alternate weekends and holidays with her father. The divorce had happened long before, when she was four, he told me. No hard feelings; he and his ex-wife got on well enough, Justine was happy most of the time, and when she wasn't, her parents' divorce did not appear to be the reason, he said.

After we'd been together for six months, he suggested I come over for a meal with Justine. I said no thanks. I don't meet people's daughters.

He raised this again at the nine-month point. Also on the one-year anniversary of our meeting over the tomatoes, and regularly, after that, until I told him that if he brought the subject up again I'd have to leave.

"I won't be anybody's stepmother," I said. "Or the girlfriend her father shacks up with, when she wishes he was home with her mother and her.

"Eight-year-old girls are not my cup of tea," I said. (Justine had celebrated a couple of birthdays by now.) "I remember what they're like. I used to be one."

"You don't even know her," Robert said. "What are you afraid of? That you might like each other, and then we'd break up, and you'd feel bad about it? So let's get married."

"And getting married means we'll never split up, right?"

"Getting married to me means I'll never leave. But I won't anyway."

He said he just wanted to live in a house with the two people he loved best in the world, both there at the same time. He said that the next time he went to Maine with Justine—something they did every summer—he wanted me to be there too.

"She wants you to herself," I said. "She doesn't need me tagging along."

"She wants me to be happy. I'm happiest when I'm with you."

Around my forty-second birthday, a package arrived for me. No return address, though the postmark indicated that it had been mailed from San Rafael, California.

Inside was a notebook of a sort you don't see often anymore. White lined paper, no rings, a stiff canvas cover. The handwriting, when I opened it, was instantly familiar. My father's.

It was a journal. Notes mostly, not sentences. Pages and pages of notes. I had to read a few pages before I understood they were about the Sunset Strangler case, which meant that they'd been made almost thirty years earlier, back when my father was still in charge of the investigation.

I decided that this notebook must have turned up in some office at the Civic Center that they were cleaning out after all these years. Some secretary who was retir-ing—a woman who'd always been sweet on my father, probably—must have located my address and thought to mail it to me.

I spent all that weekend studying the notebook. I was supposed to fly to Detroit that Monday to begin research on a new book based on a murder there, involving a woman who'd killed her auto company executive husband and stashed his body in the back of their SUV for a week.

The morning of my trip, I changed my mind. I stayed home and studied my father's notes instead. Like a message from the grave.

Shortly afterward, I took off in the Alfa for the lit-tle cabin in Maine I always go to when I start a new book. Usually I stay there a week, but this time, when the week was up, I called the owners to see if anyone had reserved it after me, and when I found out nobody had, I stayed on another month.

Robert, who always suffered my absence when I was gone in ways I told him I did not suffer his, drove up one weekend with a big pot of homemade soup for me. "I bet you hardly ever stop to eat up here," he said. Correct.

When I came home, I had the finished manuscript for a book I called *Man on the Mountain*. No harp- and tennis-playing sisters this time. No catchy title. This one was the story, more or less, of what happened when I was thirteen years old and the Sunset Strangler showed up on the mountain.

It was a work of fiction, like all my other books, but this time there was a sister who made up stories, and a sister who played basketball, and the father was a detective, and the mother was sad all the time.

A man who didn't really commit the murders confessed to them. The man who really did got away.

My editor loved the book. My publishers brought it out the next summer, which happened to be the thirtieth anniversary of the Sunset Strangler killings. This meant that a number of newspapers and magazines in the Bay Area were running stories about the case—follow-ups on the families of the victims, the police officer responsible for taking down the initial confession from J. Russell Adler, and an interview with the director of the special task force that had been given credit for solving the case. No mention of my father anywhere, except for a comment by one of the officers that the investigation "had been in shambles" until his team, along with the FBI, had come on the scene.

In recent years, I had chosen not to go on book tours for the promotion of my novels. My name was well enough known without my traipsing around the country, signing books and explaining, for the one-hundredth time, that I do not play the harp. Though I did not live with Robert, I had recently noted, somewhat grudgingly, that I slept better when I slept with him. Which I did, with surprising frequency, if his daughter wasn't around.

With this new book, however, I decided to go on tour. I told my publisher I'd travel to as many cities as they cared to send me, which turned out to be a lot. Sales of *Man on the Mountain* were going well. There was talk that it might make the bestseller list.

But it wasn't the goal of selling more books that inspired me to go on that tour and give all those interviews along the way—even to tiny radio stations and reporters from low-circulation local papers.

I had an idea—a dream really, but it haunted me. I was remembering what the killer had said to me that day he spoke to me on the mountain, as he moved in with the piano wire.

I've been keeping an eye on you, wench. I'll always be out there watching you.

All these years, a part of me had continued to believe this might be true. If so, he would have read my books, or at least known of their existence. And maybe he would learn of this one and buy a copy.

With this in mind, I had put an element in my story for the Sunset Strangler alone. Other readers would think nothing of this particular detail. But to one man, it might be enough to cause him to seek me out.

If he did, I'd be ready for him.

Eighteen months earlier, when my father's notebook had arrived in the mail, I'd spent a long time studying his entries on the investigation. Some of the notations made little sense, and virtually all had proved to be dead ends. Page after page was devoted to license plate numbers of cars reported to have been seen at various parking spots near the entrances to hiking trails on the days the murders had been committed; names of individuals who'd called in tips; names and addresses of Bay Area suppliers of piano wire. And so much more.

From my careful study of the notebook, it was clear my father had been keeping a highly detailed ongoing log of his activities over the many months of the investigation. Every page featured a date, beside which, in a shorthand scrawl, was a record of places he'd gone, people he'd checked out. Now and then, on the top of some page on which he'd recorded some interview or other, I noted a different kind of entry. My mother's birthday, mine, Patty's. "*B Ball, P. 6 p.m.,*" he'd written. "*P, tournament. Get there!*"

"*Rachel: Discuss boy.*" (Beside this note, three exclamation points and a star.)

There were a few notes that surprised me, concerning a series of conversations my father appeared to have had with an orthodontist about possible payment plans for braces. A doctor's appointment for himself, with a line drawn through the date and a note: *Reschedule.* A recipe for caponata, and a reminder to get the tires on the Alfa rotated. A hotel name, Italian sounding.

A few of the entries, which appeared personal, were baffling. "*Birthday, G.*" "*Molinari. Mozzarella Best.*" A reminder to himself? "*Candles. M.*" And another: "*Pink princess dress.*" (What could he mean? My sister and I had hated the color pink and were long past the age for princess dresses by that point.)

There was an entry from late March 1980 that I realized, on reflection, must have been made the day I called my father from the phone booth to come pick me up after I'd left Alison's house. The day I told Teddy Bascom I wasn't having sex with him.

The name Bascom. With a line through the middle, the pen having slashed across the page with sufficient force that it ripped through the paper. What more to say?

One of the last pages in the notebook was the most significant by far. Unlike the others—those random scraps of data apparently leading nowhere—what my father had written on this page were actual sentences that told a story.

This entry began the day the FBI agents had brought my sister and me down the mountain, following our encounter with the Sunset Strangler. The encounter nobody, including our father, had believed to have taken place.

In the notebook, my father recounted the visit from the agents to our mother's house—the meeting in which they'd explained to my parents the seriousness of their daughter's offenses and laid out to my mother and father the scenario in which I could be charged with reckless nuisance and sent to juvenile detention.

Then came the mention of the therapist. His name, the phone number. An appointment time. Not voluntary. Mandatory.

The next entry—written the following day—concerned my father's meeting with the chief of police, in which the news was conveyed to him that he'd been taken off the Sunset Strangler case.

After that, almost nothing. A few sentences about his job in Novato, though he'd called it "Siberia." Mention of another doctor's appointment—an X-ray he appeared to have rescheduled, again.

There was a rant about the FBI, and an entry in which my father speculated, with unmistakable bitterness, that the sheriff of Marin County appeared less interested in the safety of the people of Marin County than he was in winning reelection.

The surprise for me came in the next entry. The second to last, dated several weeks later. Late August 1980.

The day after J. Russell Adler presented himself to the Marin County police department to say he was the Sunset Strangler—at a time when my story, and my sister's, had long since been discredited, and his career was in ruins—my father had taken it upon himself to make his way up the mountain, alone, to revisit the scene of the attack against my sister and me that the FBI agents had asserted I had made up to get attention.

Evidently (I learned this from his notebook) my father hiked over to the truck body. (The place, I had told them all, where the Sunset Strangler had been camping out. The place where he'd come after me with the piano wire, and where my sister shot him with the BB gun. Where Patty had lost her voice and saved our lives.)

Your daughter is very good at making up stories, Detective Torricelli, the FBI agent had said that day in our living room on Morning Glory Court, as he handed my mother the card with the therapist's name on it.

But stories belong in books. Not in testimony to law enforcement. That's an important lesson, Rachel. You're old enough to know that.

That's when I'd run to my room. No one to trust anymore but my sister.

What followed in the notebook entry was a detailed list of every single item my father found inside the truck that day. The two catalogs. A storehouse of empty pudding containers. A plastic spoon, and a bunch of Spam tins. A roll of toilet paper and a photograph of Kate Jackson from *Charlie's Angels* (the man favored brunettes) wearing a bikini.

Then this: shoelaces. Various lengths. All worn, some fraying. Unlike the shoelaces I'd purchased for the purpose of taking a Polaroid photograph of them and inserting it in my scrapbook—and thereby incriminating Mr. Armitage—these shoelaces appeared to have been removed from actual shoes. There was dirt on them, and mud. The tips appeared chewed. Tooth marks were visible on several. All told, there were sixteen pairs stashed in the truck body. (Sixteen, not fifteen. No accounting for that.)

In his notebook, my father recorded one other interesting observation about the shoelaces. Where every

other item in the truck seemed to have been ran-
domly flung inside the rusted-out cab, the shoelaces
he found there had been carefully—one might even
say lovingly—wound into individual loops and placed
inside what was left of the glove compartment.

According to my father's notebook entry, he had
taken numerous photographs of the contents of the
truck. He had then collected each of these items—
most significantly, the shoelaces—and packaged them
in sealed plastic evidence bags. It was his plan to take
these bags to police headquarters—to the office he
once headed—and announce that the shoelaces he and
the rest of his homicide team had noted as having been
removed from the shoes of the victims—every single
victim over the last fourteen months since the murders
began—appeared to have been located.

Understanding the significance of this development,
my father anticipated filling out a complete report for
the officer who'd replaced him. He would then make
the obvious recommendation that given the discovery of this new evidence, it was now important—
essential—to revisit the statements previously made
by his daughters, Rachel and Patricia Torricelli—
statements that had been swiftly dismissed, concerning the alleged assault attempt made on them by an
unknown individual whom his older daughter claimed

to have seen emerging from the truck body moments before the attempted assault.

In light of these findings, my father wrote—most particularly in light of his discovery of the shoelaces—it seemed clear to him that the events his daughters had recounted to the FBI that day had in fact taken place.

It was now clear to him that we had actually encountered an attacker on the mountain that day, who had in fact used the abandoned truck body as his base of operations on the mountain, and that this individual had in fact been the Sunset Strangler. There remained no doubt in his mind that the Marin Homicide Division had put the wrong man in prison.

The notebook contained just one more entry. If his handwriting were any measure, the last entry, which was dated several days later, appeared to have been written in a state of extreme agitation.

In this one, my father went on for several pages, but the story he recounted of what had happened in the matter of the shoelaces was clear enough, and surprisingly simple:

My father had presented the evidence from the truck body to the detective now in charge of the case. It had not been easy for my father, even getting to see the man who had replaced him, given that he and his team were currently caught up in the media frenzy surrounding J. Russell Adler's recent admission that he was the Sunset Strangler, and the triumphant announcement from the recently created special task force that the killer had been apprehended.

My father's meeting with the newly installed director of the Sunset Strangler investigation had lasted exactly seven minutes, and it ended when the director reminded him that his press conference was about to begin.

"Given that the case has now been resolved conclusively," he had told my father, "it would be highly inadvisable for you to pursue this matter further."

Until now, the department had chosen to look the other way where the "antics" of Detective Torricelli's daughters were concerned. But should Torricelli elect to speak publicly of this matter in any way, his actions would not be viewed favorably.

After this entry, the rest of the notebook remained blank.

In my novel *Man on the Mountain,* a confrontation takes place on the mountain between the man I refer to as the "Mountainside Monster" and the two daughters of the discredited detective. The shooting with the BB gun is there, as is the FBI agents' dismissal of the girls' account of what happened that day, and the infuriating therapy sessions that followed, in which the older sister's refusal to admit she'd made up her story had led to a report from the therapist that stated she was "at high risk for further pathological behavior."

I changed a few details (the father drives a Fiat; the younger sister plays water polo) and there is no character bearing any resemblance to Mr. Armitage, and no Jack Russell terrier. The mother appears a little less depressed than ours was. She bakes chocolate chip cookies for her daughters, and sometimes on Friday nights she takes her daughters bowling.

But in all the important ways, the story resembles ours. My novel features the confession of a man who was not the actual killer, and the death—not so long after—of the detective who led the investigation, until he was taken off the case. Though there was no way to prove this definitively, I make it plain in my novel that it was the belief of the detective's daughters that what killed their father was not so much the nicotine in his cigarettes as the toxicity of the Mountainside Monster case—the frustration and rage he felt knowing the real killer had gone free, and his inability to do anything about it.

In my novel only one detail differs significantly from the truth of what took place in real life. In the novel, the older sister—hiking on the mountain some months after the sentencing of the wrong man—discovers, in the truck body, the stash of shoelaces taken from the victims' shoes. She takes these home with her and keeps them with her at all times over the years that follow, as a reminder of her quest to find the real killer and to eventually bring him to justice. She knows those shoelaces mean a lot to him, and because they do, it is her hope that she will one day lure him to her, so she can finish, at last, the job her father had been unable to complete. In my novel, this is precisely what transpires.

In truth, I never found the shoelaces. Though up until that point we had never registered fear about anything, for many weeks after that terrifying encounter with the killer my sister and I couldn't bring ourselves to go near the abandoned truck body, or anywhere on the mountain.

When we finally did return, almost six months later, everything was gone: the catalogs, the empty food containers, the random items of dirty clothing. There were no shoelaces or any indication at all that the truck body had been used by anybody but teenagers looking for a place to have sex.

For years after the murders and my father's death, I continued to think about those shoelaces, and to wonder what had happened to them. (I remember one time eyeing a bird's nest in a tree alongside the trail. I thought I caught sight of a single lace, woven in among the twigs and leaves, and I actually got my sister to climb the tree for a closer look. It was nothing but a piece of string some crow had collected and put to use.)

For me, the moment when I read the entry in my father's notebook in which he revealed that he had found the laces felt like a resolution of the mystery, at long last. But only a partial one. Because now a second mystery presented itself. If, as his notebook suggested, my father had found the killer's treasured shoelace collection—and recognized, as he did, its importance—then what had become of it? Though the Homicide Division had failed to accept his assertion that they'd sent the wrong man to San Quentin, as long as he lived my father would never have abandoned his pursuit of the real killer. He would have held on to those shoelaces.

But he got sick. He died knowing the killer remained at large and that nobody believed him. No one but Patty and me, anyway. And young as we were at the time, he would not have wanted us saddled with the same obsession—to find the Sunset Strangler—that had no doubt contributed to his death.

So what happened to the shoelaces?

In my novel, the older sister finds the shoelaces in the truck—finds and holds on to them. Wherever she goes, from that day forward, she keeps those shoelaces with her. I changed this aspect of the story in my novel for one reason alone: there was a chance the killer might read my book and believe his treasured shoelaces to be in the possession of its author. This would lead him to seek me out. I had no better idea of what I'd do if he came after me now than I had thirty years earlier. I only knew I wanted to look him in the eye again, at last.

I did not divulge any of this to my editor or my publicist, or—most important—to Robert, who would have been deeply alarmed for my safety had he known the plan, however far-fetched, that I was hoping to set into motion.

There was only one person I would have told, if she'd been around, and that was my sister, Patty. She would have understood perfectly and insisted on accompanying me on my book tour, standing ready to protect and defend and—more than that—to confront the killer and bring him to justice once and for all.

But Patty was dead. And so I set out alone across the country on my fourteen-city tour from New Hampshire all the way to California, with the hope that one night, in some bookstore or lecture hall along the way, I might actually look up from the table where I was signing books, or look down from the podium where I was speaking, and lock eyes with the Sunset Strangler. (Eyes. Or eye. We never knew exactly what damage had been done when my sister fired that BB gun. We only knew he had let out a cry, dropped the piano wire, and covered his left eye. Then disappeared.)

Two eyes or one, I had no doubt the killer had reason to come after me. Maybe he had been as fixated on me as I had been on him over the years. Maybe it had bothered him that some other man had taken credit for his killings. Maybe he just wanted those shoelaces.

For this reason, before setting out on tour, I retrieved my father's old gun from my safe-deposit box. I kept his gun in my purse at all times. Not the usual accessory for a writer preparing to meet her readers. But this was not going to be the usual book tour.

I gave my first reading at my little hometown independent bookstore in Peterborough, New Hampshire, to an audience of roughly thirty people, mostly friends. (Robert in the front row of course. Too early in the year for tomatoes, but he brought purple lilacs.)

Then came Boston; New Canaan, Connecticut; New York City; Washington, D.C.; Atlanta; Chicago; Madison; Detroit; Indianapolis; Denver; Seattle; Portland, Oregon; L.A. Four solid weeks of radio interviews and readings, "friends of the library" talks, book-and-author luncheons. Hotel rooms, room service meals. Book signings.

Question: Who should play your father in the movie version of your book?

Answer: Whoever is the handsomest, most irresistible man in Hollywood. And I still doubt that any actor could do him justice.

Question: How long did it take you to write this novel?

Answer: Six solid weeks, chained to my desk at a cabin in Maine. And every day of my life for the thirty years before that.

Question: Did you really have a sister? Did she really die? How do you get over something like that?

Answer: You don't.

I saved San Francisco for last. I wanted to see my mother in Marin County, of course (and possibly Mr. Armitage and his wife, now the owners of a dancing school in Petaluma), but first I would finish up with a talk at the Herbst Theater—a sold-out event in which I would follow the standard procedure: twenty minutes of reading from the novel followed by questions from the audience. Then I'd sign books. Then back to my hotel for a glass of wine—two, probably—and my nightly call to Robert back in New Hampshire. It was a weekend he had his daughter, and by the time I got to him, it would be past midnight there. Still, I knew he'd be waiting up to hear from me.

I had asked my publicist to reserve a hotel room for me not in San Francisco, but across the bridge in Marin County, at a place on the side of Mount Tamalpais that Patty and I used to fantasize about when we were kids and we'd watch the fancy cars pull up and the rich people checking in. More than once, I had dared Patty to go inside and scoop up a few handfuls of the honey-roasted peanuts they set out on the bar. She'd done it, naturally.

The Mountain Home Inn looked out over the hills of Marin County, all the way to the city—the kind of view that could take a person's breath away. I had chosen to stay at this place partly out of nostalgia for our old days rambling on the mountain, and partly for the spa services. I spent the early part of that afternoon getting a shiatsu massage and a facial, followed by a bath back in my room.

Stretched out in the tub, with the rolling hills of the Golden Gate National Recreation Area displayed outside the window, I surveyed my body. I had recently turned forty-three, but remained in good shape, thanks in large part to a combination of luck, good genes, and the fact that I had never had a baby.

Lying there now, I thought about the facts-of-life movie from my girlhood: *From the moment of your birth, your body holds a treasure chest of unfertilized eggs. Your lifetime supply. Your body can make a baby now.*

Probably not anymore. And though I'd almost never wanted that, the fact that the days in which pregnancy and giving birth remained options were drawing to a close if not gone already struck me for a moment as almost unbearably sad.

I remembered how I'd longed for the blood to come, the summer of the Sunset Strangler. And the horror of the day, the next summer, when it finally did. I remembered those circling vultures, that day on the mountain as I sat in the ATV waiting for my father, and the feeling of the blood soaking my shorts.

My talk was scheduled for seven thirty, so I had pictured myself spending the remainder of the afternoon on my hotel room balcony, reading and looking out over the landscape of my girlhood.

But the phone rang. It was the reception desk. Someone was here to see me. Should they send my visitor up?

"I'll be right down," I said. A public place was best for this of course.

Then with a calmness that surprised me, I finished dressing. My last act before heading out the door and down the stairs: tucking my father's Chief Special into my purse.

Only one person was in the hotel restaurant when I walked in: a woman. I scanned the room a second time and looked back out to the lobby, but the woman was coming over to me then. She held out her hand.

"Thank you for seeing me," she said. "I've waited a long time for this."

So I was not meeting the Sunset Strangler after all. The knowledge hit me with a mixture of disappointment and relief. The risk is great, for a person accustomed to creating fiction, that she may come to imagine that events can unfold in real life as they would in a novel. In the fictional version, it would have been the Sunset Strangler who had come to meet me here. And (in a manner that remained hazy, even in my imagination) I would have gotten him to confess his crimes at last, and somehow overpowered him. Perhaps he would have turned himself in to the authorities then. Perhaps he would have saved them the trouble of a trial by jumping off the outdoor deck of my hotel, to meet a swift and certain death on the same mountain where those fifteen women had met a similar fate at his hands.

But real life hardly ever works as neatly as novels do, which may account for the reason so many people read novels. This woman extending her hand to me was apparently one of them.

I figured she must be one of my readers, one of those people who had followed my career over the years, and for whatever reason felt that my books spoke to her.

Maybe she was an aspiring writer herself (as was often true of the people who sought me out most fervently) and was looking for advice. She had a bag with her—containing a manuscript, no doubt. She wanted me to read it, and pass it on to my editor. No telling how far she'd driven to see me that afternoon.

"I can't believe I'm really meeting you," she said. "I'm nervous."

"Let's sit down," I told her.

"Want some coffee?" I asked her. "Or wine?"

"That sounds good," she said. "My name is Gina."

We faced each other across the table then, and because she said nothing, I studied her face. She was a good eight to ten years younger than me, I guessed. A beautiful woman, with hair the color mine used to be before my hairdresser had told me I'd look younger if I lightened it, and dark eyes. Olive skin. Long lashes. She had lovely hands, and I could see, watching her take her wineglass, that they were trembling.

"I've imagined this moment for years," she said. "I knew I had to talk to you. I've just been so afraid that once I did, you might turn me away."

I gave her my standard speech then. I felt sympathy for unpublished writers trying to get their work considered. But if I started reading all the manuscripts that people sent me—people looking for advice and assistance—I'd never get any of my own work done.

"There are classes," I said. "And workshops. Writers' conferences."

She looked at me a little blankly. "Workshops?"

"You brought a manuscript for me to look at in that bag, right?" I asked her. "A novel?"

Not a novel, she said.

"Shoelaces."

The story started with her mother. Whose name was Margaret Ann. Her father was my father.

She was four years old when my father died, she told me. Old enough to remember him, though not well. Most of what she knew about my father ("our father," she said) she knew from her mother.

He was married when he and Margaret Ann met. He was one of those men, of course, that women love—a man who loved women. The problem was he loved all of them. Too many, anyway. It had taken Margaret

Ann a long time to believe that with her it would be different, but finally he convinced her. This was the big love for both of them.

They were going to get married. He was going to tell Patty and me. They were going to make a life together, buy a house maybe. Have a baby.

First he brought us over to her apartment, just so we'd know who he was talking about later, when he sat us down and explained.

Only that never happened, and I knew why.

Never get over it. Never speak to you again. The words a nine-year-old left on the answering machine of a father she doesn't want to share with anyone. And as brave as my father had been in the line of duty, evidently the idea that what I said that day might be true had terrified him. He had told Margaret Ann he could never marry her, never have another child who might leave the two he adored feeling supplanted.

She broke it off. A dozen times, easily. Weeks would go by, and sometimes months, in which they didn't see each other or speak. Then he'd show up at her apartment and it would start again.

Then she got pregnant.

Some men who already had two daughters would long for a son. But when Margaret Ann gave birth (an event our father had failed to be present for, on account of the broken arm Patty had sustained when she rode a skateboard—for the first time—straight down a steep hill), our father had only said, "Another daughter! Just what I hoped for."

They never married. Never lived together, even. (Margaret Ann believed in marriage. "I'd marry you tomorrow, Tony," she told him. "But I won't shack up.")

So he dropped by when he could, to read to Gina or to bring her a present. Once, when she was in a play at nursery school, he came to watch. She still remembered that because she'd wanted her teacher to meet him. See, she had a father after all. The handsomest of them all.

But it was never what you could call a regular family life, or anything close. He came over for dinner on Tuesday nights, and Sunday mornings he'd make them pancakes. ("Looking back now, I think he must've come over late on Saturday and spent the night," she told me. "But I never saw him walk out of my mother's bedroom.")

Then came the Sunset Strangler, and even those times—brief as they were—could no longer be counted on. He worked all the time. Then he got sick. Then he was dying.

"He told my mother he didn't want us to see him like that," she said.

He came to say good-bye. Not that he said that's what it was, but as young as Gina had been at the time, she remembered the look of the two of them, and she felt it. She saw the way her mother hugged him in the doorway, and her face after.

He had told Margaret Ann there'd be no funeral. If there were a funeral, she should be there, and if she were there with Gina, what would that have done to Patty and me? What would it have done to Margaret Ann and Gina, to sit there like two casual acquaintances?

Mostly, hearing this, I just sat there. If there was one thing I had known for certain my whole life, it was that however many women might love our father, and however many he might love, we were always his favorites. The best thing he'd ever done. His only girls.

Only we weren't.

You had to ask yourself what else that you always believed might also not be true.

I studied Gina's face. She looked like her mother, and in fact, I realized, she must be around the age that her mother had been back when we'd met Margaret Ann that first time, and she gave us the Kool-Aid with the special straws, and let us choose our dolls. When she sewed us those dresses.

But she looked like my father too, I realized. And it was that fact—the knowledge that she shared his hands, his hair, his eyelashes—that made me angry suddenly. The fact that she was here, and Patty wasn't. It wasn't Gina's fault, but I hated her.

Neither of us said anything then. The waiter who had brought our wine came by to see if either of us wanted another glass. I shook my head. The thought came to me: it would have been easier in some ways if the person I'd met in this restaurant had been the Sunset Strangler instead of this beautiful young woman whose face, I now realized, resembled no one's more than my own.

"In all these years, why did you never contact me?" I asked her.

"I was afraid," she said. "I always wanted to meet you and your sister, but I decided it was better not knowing you than risking that you'd turn me away."

"So why did you come here today?"

"I read your book. I've read all your books, but this one was different. After I read it, I knew there was something I had to give you."

Here she paused. I prompted her to continue. "Yes . . . ?"

"My father . . . our father . . . didn't keep much stuff at our apartment," she said. "There was a bathrobe he always wore, that my mother gave him, and a razor. A pair of shoes he used to put on when they danced."

But there'd been a box, she told me. After he died, her mother took it out. Only a few things in it. A ring that had belonged to his mother, with a note leaving it to Margaret Ann. A letter for Gina, with some advice about boyfriends. To be read when she reached age thirteen.

"If he doesn't treat you like a queen . . ." I said. I'd heard that too.

There was a pair of haircutting scissors, she told me. He used to cut her hair with them. Hers and her mother's. Also a notebook.

"I think my mother sent you that, a year or two back," Gina told me. "His notes from the Sunset Strangler case."

There was one more thing in the box that had never made any sense to her. Until now. It was a plastic bag containing a bunch of shoelaces, all carefully tied into loops.

She reached into her purse and placed it on the table.

"After I read your book, I understood what they meant," she told me.

I studied the laces. I could still see the wall of my father's office, with the pictures of the murdered girls tacked onto it. I could see the chubby fingers from my visions, as they worked the laces free from the dead girls' shoes.

I imagined my father walking into the office of the man who replaced him, with that bag of shoelaces in his hand, to turn in as evidence. And later, walking out again—the early signals of the cancer that would kill him already causing him to cough as he made his way down the hall—still holding that bag. Driving to Margaret Ann's house. Placing the shoelaces in the box. What more could he do now?

I hadn't asked Gina anything about her life, but I did now.

She was thirty-three years old. She wasn't married, and she had no children. She lived in the city. North Beach.

"I might as well tell you I'm a cop," she said. "Homicide, like our father."

I asked her if she'd tried to show the laces to anyone in the police force. Reopen the case.

She shook her head. "We're talking about a cold case, with a rock-solid confession," she said. "Nobody wants to hear about it."

"And what am I supposed to do with them?" I asked her.

"Know he believed you, I guess. Know you were right."

This was the moment I might have reached across the table. I could have put my arms around her. Taken her

hand, at least. I could have told her that I'd been waiting thirty years for this moment. I might have said
thank you.

"Did you know about my sister and me when you
were growing up?" I asked her. "Did my father tell
you?"

She shook her head. "But when I was older, my
mother did."

So she had known what we had not.

"I used to envy you and Patty," she said. The mention of my sister's name, coming from Gina, felt like a
stab. Patty was *my* sister, not hers.

"Envy us?"

"Because you had each other. And because you got
to know our father. I barely had a chance."

We hadn't got enough of him either. More than she
did. But not nearly enough.

"You know my favorite memory?" she said. "It
seems so crazy I have a hard time believing it was real.
Only I think it was."

I looked at her hard. She was giving me something
precious now.

"We were sitting on the couch together," she said.
"I couldn't have been much older than three, and he
was stroking my head. Then all of a sudden, he did the
strangest thing. He pulled out a piece of my hair. It

didn't hurt so much as take me by surprise. Then he started twirling it between his fingers—"

"The spider," I said. "I know."

"It was real, then," she said. "I never knew for sure. I've sometimes thought I must have dreamed that up."

I shook my head.

"I love it that we get to share him," she said, reaching her hand across the table.

I didn't take it.

"I'm sorry," I told her. "But I don't want to know you. It's not your fault, but I had a sister, and you're not her."

"I know," she said. Quieter now.

"I only had one sister. Nobody could ever replace her."

"I wouldn't ever think—" she started.

"I have to go now," I told her. "I'm giving a reading tonight."

I picked up the bag with the shoelaces then, and I left her. I hoped that I would never lay eyes on that woman again.

I doubt anyone observing my performance on the stage at the Herbst Theater that night—hearing me read from *Man on the Mountain* or afterward, listening as I answered questions from the audience—would have guessed that anything particularly unusual or upsetting had taken place in my life a couple of hours earlier. (Or that I had a revolver in my pocketbook and a bag with shoelaces taken from the shoes of the fifteen women murdered by the Sunset Strangler. Or that the person who had presented these shoelaces to me just hours before—sixteen pairs, it turned out, when I counted them later—had been a sister whose existence had been unknown to me until that moment.)

Maybe I sounded a little distracted or cut things off a little earlier than I might have otherwise—but I have given a few hundred readings and book talks over the years. If there is one thing I know how to do at this point, besides write the books, it's how to sell them.

After my talk was finished, there had been the usual book signing. This one went on nearly an hour, due to the length of the line and the number of people in it who wanted to talk with me.

"Is it true you found the shoelaces in the truck?" another woman asked me. "And you keep them with you like the woman in the book?"

A writer takes certain liberties with a story, I told her. This is a work of fiction, don't forget.

It was nine thirty by the time I left the theater, and the streets of San Francisco were mostly quiet. As I made my way across Van Ness to the Civic Center underground parking lot where I'd left the rental car, I was thinking about how good it would be to open the bottle of wine back in my room and sit out on my balcony, looking over the mountain, see the stars. I was thinking about my visit from Gina, of course, and the haircutting scissors, and the spider. Most of all I was thinking about the resolution, at last, of my long quest for the shoelaces, and feeling guilty for my unkindness to the woman who had brought them to me. I had blamed her for something that was not her fault: the simple fact that she'd been born, and that my father must surely have loved her.

More than most nights, I wanted to call Robert.

I was thinking about all this as I put my credit card in the machine and paid the parking fee, and I was still thinking about it as I stepped into the elevator and pushed the button for the lowest level of the garage. It was easy enough to spot my rental car when the doors opened. Mine was practically the only vehicle left at that hour.

It was almost silent in the garage, except for the faint humming sound of the fluorescent lights and the click of my heels on the cement floor. Somewhere, a floor or two above, an engine started. Otherwise, empty space. Dead air.

I had my key in the lock when I felt the presence of somebody else behind me—felt him before I saw him, before he spoke. I turned, suddenly alert, and saw a dark form in a Giants cap emerge from behind a cement column, coming my way. He moved slowly, with the wheezing breath of a man no longer young, and in poor health.

"Hey, wench. I think you're giving me a ride."

No time to do anything. He had a gun.

"I know what you're thinking," he said. "That I was never the gun type, and you're right. I just wasn't sure my usual methods would work . . . in this environment."

I swallowed hard and opened my mouth as if to speak.

"Make a sound and I pull the trigger," he said. "But I'd rather take a spin with you."

He wanted me in the driver's seat. He got in next to me. Gun barrel pressed against my rib cage.

As instructed, I put the car in gear and guided it up the ramp to the exit booth. I was looking for my moment—another driver maybe, an attendant. Someone to whom I might give a signal. But the garage was empty. I rolled down the window, put my ticket in the slot, and pulled out onto the street.

Now there were other cars, and people. But also that gun.

"One move," he said, "and you're visiting your daddy in heaven. You know I can do it too. You know what I've done."

As a young girl growing up on the other side of the bridge, I had always dreamed of crossing the Golden Gate Bridge at night. Now I was doing it, with the San Francisco skyline stretched out like a string of lights in my rearview mirror, and the familiar dark silhouette of Mount Tamalpais looming ahead of me. Even though we were headed in the no-toll direction, the man in the seat beside me evidently felt moved to make an observation.

"That guy who said he killed those girls," he said. "Big faker. I read where he used to work in one of these booths. I'm guessing the pussy never did anyone in. Didn't look the type. A random crazy, that's all."

For a few minutes, I just drove. I was searching for the moment I might try something. Crash into a guardrail maybe. Lean on the horn. It would not be hard to attract notice here. Just not enough time to get something solid between me and the bullet.

"I read that book you wrote, you know," he said. "They were talking about it on the radio. Went to a bookstore. Paid twenty-five bucks for the damn thing. Now, *that's* what I call a crime."

He laughed, though the sound that came out of him was more wheeze than chuckle, and it made his whole body shake a little. The gun barrel trembled against the fabric of my blouse.

"Of course, if you'd've interviewed me first, before you wrote it, I could've given you a lot more details," he said. "You had to be there."

I couldn't speak. I gripped my hands tight to the wheel and stared straight ahead, though I was thinking about my pocketbook on the floor behind me. With the revolver in it. I summoned an image of my father, at the wheel of the Alfa some Saturday afternoon, taking my sister and me out for tiramisu. My strong, brave father, who made me feel he'd never let a single bad thing happen to me, so long as he lived.

"I used to watch you and your sister, up on the mountain," he said. "Cute, but not in my sweet spot, if you know what I mean. I like a girl that's a little more mature. Without being over the hill, if you follow me.

"You, for instance. You're holding up okay from the looks of things. But let's face it . . . you've seen better days."

Think about the gun, I told myself. *The gun in the purse. Get the purse. The gun.*

We drove in silence for a while. The road stretched on ahead of us into the dark. And then he was indicating an exit: Stinson Beach, Muir Woods.

"Turn here," he said. The road to Tennessee Valley. The trail to the ocean. The bluffs. A single pair of headlights visible behind us, none ahead. Our headlights sliced the darkness.

"You still bleed?" he said.

My mouth opened, but no words came out.

"You bleed?" he said again. "You know. That thing the women do. The curse."

Just think about the gun, I told myself. *Just get the gun.*

"In case you're thinking that I want to fuck you," he said (taking another of those gasping breaths), "I don't.

You have something I want is all. I know it from that book you wrote."

Another wheeze.

"My shoelaces. I want them back."

We had reached the trailhead parking lot.

"Here," he said.

I turned off the engine.

"Step out of the car," he said. "But slow. I need to keep my eye on you."

I opened the driver's-side door and put one foot outside, tentatively, on the ground.

"My *one* eye," he added, climbing out from his side, the gun trained on my chest the entire time.

He came around the car and stood in front of me. Until now, I hadn't really seen his face. I'd been too shaken in the garage, and all I'd registered was the Giants cap with its brim pulled down low. Then in the car it was just too dark, and I was just too scared, staring at the road. But now he stood before me in the light spilling from the interior of my rental car and I saw it: the one drooping lid, the hollow left eye socket, the place where, thirty years ago, my funny, fearless little sister had pressed the BB gun into his face and fired that single shot.

"Pretty sight?" he said. "We have that bucktooth sister of yours to thank."

There was no moon that night. But with the car door still open I could make out my purse on the floor behind the driver's seat.

"What is it about the shoelaces anyway?" I said. Terrified as I was, something compelled me to ask. Maybe I'd distract him. Get him to explain it to me. Watch for an opening.

For a long minute, he said nothing. Just breathed, with that heavy, labored sound of a person for whom the simple act of drawing breath has become one of life's many chores.

"Call me sentimental," he said. "It has to do with my mother." And here he chuckled slightly, bitterly, to himself, and shook his head a little. "Always has to do with the mother, doesn't it?"

I didn't need to say anything here, and I knew it. *Just let him talk.*

"Bitch wasn't what you'd call the Donna Reed type. More of a party girl. I dragged her down. Cramped her style. Or so she said."

"Dragged her down?" I said, although he hardly needed coaxing.

"When she went out at night, I had the run of the place. I was a kid—got into the food, made a mess. The things all brats do. One time I thought I'd try on her perfume, but I spilled it. She comes home, and I'm stinking of Evening in Paris."

The beating she gave him that night was rougher than usual. But never mind, he said. He probably deserved it.

"That's when she got her bright idea," he said.

He had these little boots. Like a man's, only small. He loved those boots. The kind that laced up, like a lumberjack or something.

"Now, before she went out, she'd untie the laces. Then tie them up again, but one to the other. So tight I couldn't walk. Crawl maybe, but even that not so good. And then she'd leave."

With his laces tied like that, he couldn't get into trouble. Couldn't get into *anything*. Not even the bathroom. Now whenever she got home, there he was. All wet and stinking, and not from perfume.

"Look at you, Kenny," she'd say. "Soiled yourself again." Then came another beating. Maybe with her hand. More likely with the curling iron, plugged in.

"I can still see her," he told me. "Bending over me in her going-out dress, with her titties hanging out. Tying my damn laces."

I could tell he was in another world now, even though he was talking to me. He still had the gun, and he still had it pointed at me. But there was a faraway quality to his voice, as if he had half forgotten I was standing next to him, and I began to think that maybe soon the moment would come when I could get to my pocketbook and grab the gun.

"Sometimes she'd bring one of them home with her," he said. "I'd have to lie there on the floor in my piss-soaked trousers and listen to the two of them going at it. Disgusting. Usually they were too drunk to pay me any attention, but one bastard saw me there one time. 'Fuck this, Eileen,' he says. 'You got your fucking kid in the room.'

" 'Forget it,' she tells him. 'He's all tied up.' Like it's a fucking joke."

He lowered his hand, with the gun in it. He seemed to close his one good eye, and he stopped talking for a moment. I wondered if this was the moment, if I should dare to try to open the car door, pull out my bag, rummage inside it for the gun. Suddenly he spoke again, and now his voice was different, as if it came from a whole other place in his diaphragm. His breathing was even shallower than before.

"She was the first," he said. "I was sixteen. Took me a lot of years, but I took care of that bitch. And now it's your turn, Farrah."

He reached for me with his free hand, grabbing my arm and spinning me around into a chokehold, the gun now pressed against my throat.

I tried to make out anything in the darkness beyond the car. Earlier I had noticed a pair of headlights behind us as we'd turned onto the Tennessee

Valley road, and I had felt the fleeting hope that maybe someone would wonder why a car would be headed toward a hiking trail at this hour of night. But the lights had disappeared. Whoever it was who'd been driving behind us had evidently turned off. I was alone.

"This one would make a good story," he said. "Too bad you won't be there to write it." I began to feel light-headed as the killer increased the pressure around my neck.

"But first," he wheezed into my ear, "you need to tell me where my shoelaces are."

I tried to talk, but my mouth had gone dry. Maybe I could tell him they were in my purse, and then I could get at my gun, but no, he'd be the one to look. He'd see I had a weapon. I knew what would happen then.

Then I saw it, though he didn't. Coming toward us, on his blind side, I could make out the form of another person moving closer. Much as it had been thirty years before on the mountain, I could see a figure approaching. As the killer could not.

Whoever this was moved closer. Close enough that I could make out that it was a woman and that she had a weapon of her own, pointed squarely at the killer, who still had me locked in his grip.

"Drop the gun. Now." I knew that voice because I'd heard it only hours earlier. It was Gina. My sister.

He did not let go of me. Or of his gun. With his arm still clamped around my neck, he spun sideways to look at her.

She spoke again. "Drop it, shithead. Do you really want to get shot?"

He let go of me. Of me, not his gun. And then he was running, into the darkness. With Gina close behind and closing in.

Then I heard Gina yell from what sounded like a few hundred yards away. "Call 911. He's had a heart attack."

Suddenly the area was ablaze with light as the police backup she must have called for earlier pulled up— three officers running toward us, blue lights strobing. I could see Gina in the distance, bending over the killer, who lay on the ground, unmoving. She had rolled him onto his stomach and placed her knee in the small of his back. She snapped a pair of handcuffs on him.

Now we could hear the approaching siren. He was still breathing when the ambulance arrived.

"You'll need police coverage with this one," she said as the EMTs strapped him to a gurney. "He was armed and remains dangerous. Assuming he lives, he'll be looking at charges of kidnapping and attempted murder."

"Who is this guy, anyway?" one of the medics asked as he looked dubiously at the frail old man with the oxygen mask. "Doesn't look that dangerous to me."

"You ever heard of the Sunset Strangler?" she said. "Or was that before your time?"

The name of my abductor and assailant was Kenneth Purdy—age sixty-six, no known address or employer. At the time of his attack on me, it appeared he had been holed up in a series of decommissioned World War II bunkers in the Marin Headlands. Before that he'd been squatting in Golden Gate Park for an unknown period of time.

Kenneth Purdy did in fact suffer what was described as a massive coronary that night he took me across the Golden Gate Bridge at gunpoint, but he survived, and once released from the hospital, where he was kept under guard, he was arraigned on charges of abduction and assault. Later, there would be additional charges: fifteen counts of first-degree murder, one count of second-degree murder. That one, to which he confessed first, had been committed in his home state of Oregon. The victim, a woman by the name of Eileen Purdy, had been his mother.

I had to stay around in California to give my statement, and would have returned to testify if there had been a trial, but because of his confession and guilty plea, the D.A. waived trial.

He was sentenced to San Quentin State Prison. Life without possibility of parole.

I went home to New Hampshire, where a good man was waiting for me with a pot of marinara sauce from his garden tomatoes.

That summer, we went hiking on Mount Desert Island with Justine, my thirteen-year-old stepdaughter, as we have continued to do, every summer since—and though she is of an age now when many more exciting options exist other than camping with her father and his wife, Justine seems to look forward to these trips and even, from what I gather, to enjoy my company. Give her another year, and this may change. We enjoy these days while we have them.

At night in our tent we tell stories in the darkness. Her father's are about fishing trips he took as a boy, or his great-uncle's farm in northern New Hampshire. As was true with my sister when she'd try to make up some imaginary plot involving the Bradys on Drive-In Movie night, nothing much ever happens in Robert's stories. (He grows a prize zucchini; he almost catches a twelve-pound bass but it slips off his line.) But there is something comforting about this very fact. And about the fact that he has lived a life so singularly lacking in drama.

The stories I tell tend to feature Patty and me and the adventures we had together growing up on the mountain. The deer fetus still in its sac. Ding Dong Ditch and the day we found the record albums. The naked people running through the poppies. The time my sister rode a flattened refrigerator box down the side of the mountain, and the time she did her striptease to "Take Back Your Mink" on the outdoor amphitheater stage to an audience of crows. Some images I do not feature in my stories: My sister, Patty, sailing down Morning Glory Court with Petra on her leash, like the queen of the world. My sister, Patty, dribbling that basketball all the way home. I do not speak about the sound the ball made on the pavement, growing louder as my sister dribbled her way home, or the sound of her breathing in the bunk above me, the quiet comforting presence of her in the night. I do not speak of the silence that roars in my ears sometimes or the space my sister left that no one, however loved, can ever fill.

And then there is this: the absence of that sound. The silence that roars in my ears now that there is no one out there dribbling that ball home.

The person I now speak of as my sister—Gina— has suggested that I write these stories down and put them in a book, but I prefer to reserve them for a select few: My mother, who no longer keeps herself in her bedroom as she did when we were young, and Mr. Armitage, when I see him. I tell my stories to Gina, and to Robert. And Justine.

Justine: the only one of us who makes her stories up from the whole cloth of imagination—a gift I once possessed, but which seems to have dimmed with age. When she tells her stories in the tent, it is in a low and breathless whisper, acting out the different voices of her characters, or pausing to let the full force of an image take hold. It is not an infrequent occurrence for Justine to scare herself so much with her own stories that sometime in the night she'll ask if she can climb into the sleeping bag with her father and me—and because Robert sleeps through anything, I'll be the one to put my arm around her then.

I saw an old man's face just outside our tent, she tells me. *There was a family of bears, loose from the circus, and they were dancing. Justin Bieber in a coffin. A baby rabbit that, when it opened its mouth, had a set of fangs. A boy—left by his parents years ago, in the woods, and raised by wolves—howling at the moon. A clown who couldn't stop laughing. A bloody hand. A woman with her hair on fire.*

It's all right, I tell her. *Your father is here. So am I. Nothing bad will happen to you.*

Or maybe something will. And you'll survive it.

Not right away, but after a few minutes, she falls asleep again, pressed up between the two of us. I lie there in the darkness then, and listen to her breathing, same as I used to on my old bottom bunk, to Patty. My irreplaceable sister.

"Sometimes I worry about these stories of hers," her father has said to me.

She's almost thirteen, I tell him. She feels everything—fear, pain, as well as joy—five times as much as we do. In a year or two, her world will cease to be so filled with such dark and thrilling possibilities.

This is the good news. And the pity.

She will grow out of it.

Acknowledgments

Two well-loved and loyal friends made it possible for me to dedicate the better part of a year and a half to the writing of this novel, as I could not have done otherwise. They are Jim Dicke II and David Schiff. Not for the first time, I am in their debt.

Warmest thanks go to my agent, David Kuhn, and the team at Kuhn Projects, who continue to oversee my writing life so wisely and well. My gratitude also to Wayne Beach, an early reader who offered invaluable counsel in the early stages of my work at the Maine Media Workshop. My thanks as well to an unlikely pair of basketball advisers: Juan Manuel Chavajay, of San Pedro La Laguna, Guatemala—a man who, at five foot three, stands unafraid of guarding any six-foot-plus American on the courts of Lake Atitlán with his fearless Mayan brand of play—and Paul Bamford, star center-forward on my hometown team at Oyster River High School, who talked me through his shooting style over long-distance all the way from New Hampshire to California.

I also want to express my appreciation for the Virginia Center for the Creative Arts, where I traveled on three separate occasions to work, free from the interruptions and distractions of daily life, with the additional extraordinary gift—after a long day's writing—of good food, the inspiring and supportive company of artists, writers, photographers, and musicians, and midnight swims in the VCCA pool.

Some words now about music. For me, nearly every work of fiction I've ever written has had, playing quietly in the background of my brain (or pounding at top volume), an interior sound track—sometimes a passage without words, sometimes a collection of songs. I may play this piece of music a hundred times over the months I'm immersed in my story. I may refer to it in the pages of my book or simply draw on the mood it brings forth within.

For this novel, I knew from the first page what the song was, that captured the mood of thrill and anxiety and sexual pursuit I sought to conjure up. It happened that this song was the number one hit of 1979—the

year my story begins. The song is "My Sharona," performed by the Knack and written by the band's lead
singer, Douglas Fieger, and its guitar player, Berton
Averre.

Douglas Fieger died in 2010 at the age of fifty-seven.
His sister, Beth Falkenstein, along with Berton Averre,
displayed great generosity in granting me the rights to
reprint lines from "My Sharona"—a deceptively simple
and utterly seductive anthem, and one that crystallizes,
as well as any rock-and-roll song ever has, maybe, the
pounding, driving insistence of a sexual obsession. I
wish I could have put this book into the hands of both
of the song's authors, and I hope its presence in these
pages serves to summon up the mood of that summer—
those times, and that age—and to honor the two who
wrote it.

Over the many years of my writing life (forty of
them, now) it has been among the greatest gifts of my
profession to know and befriend a range of readers who
have enriched my life and broadened my understanding of so many experiences I would otherwise never
have known. One such individual, who first wrote
to me over ten years ago, proved to be an invaluable
resource and adviser in the writing of this story. He is
Detective Luke Daley (very possibly the Chicago Cubs'
number one supporter), of the Chicago Homicide

Division. When I realized, as I embarked on the writing of this story, how little I knew of a police officer's life, I turned to Luke, and for the year and a half that I continued to work on the story of my fictional detective, it was Luke Daley, again and again, to whom I turned not only for the small but crucial details of a detective's habits (yielding the discovery, for instance, that only on television and in the movies would he wear a shoulder holster; he'd carry his gun on his ankle), but also for what I hope I achieved here, which is a deeper understanding of what it feels like to be confronted, day after day, with death and violence, criminals and victims. Virtually every detail of my fictional detective's description of how he conducts a police interrogation was informed by what Luke Daley told me about how he'd do it—and because of what he told me, I plan to stay on the right side of the law. At least in the state of Illinois.

I want to say something now about the two women who gave me what is, for a writer, the most precious gift: the idea for my story. Living as I do on the side of Mount Tamalpais, I have experienced the mountain as a daily presence—out my window, and under my feet as I hike it—for the seventeen years I've made my home in California. I had been dimly aware for as long as I've lived here that a series of murders once took place on this mountain so close to where I live. But it was two adult sisters—Janet Cubley and Laura Xerogeanes, whom I first met when they showed up in my living room to attend one of my daylong writing workshops—who shared with me the story from their own lives (and largely played out on Mount Tamalpais) that inspired this one. They also gave me their blessing to change as much as I wanted, which I did.

In the year 1979, when Laura and Janet were roughly the ages of the two young sisters in this story, and—like my fictional characters—growing up as the daughters of divorced parents, in Marin County, a real-life serial killer who came to be known as the Trailside Killer did, in fact, haunt the hiking trails of Mount Tamalpais and the surrounding Bay Area. Though many—virtually all—of the real details of that case differ markedly or even totally from those described in these pages, this part is true: Laura and Janet's father, Detective Robert Gaddini, served as the head of Marin County Homicide during the period in which the Trailside Killer remained at large, and headed up the investigation into the murders. Like my fictional detective, Detective Gaddini devoted himself to the case with a tireless and obsessive devotion and suffered deeply the deaths of that killer's victims.

The story I tell in these pages—though a work of fiction—was undeniably inspired by the real one, which the adult Gaddini sisters shared with me, with immeasurable generosity and tenderness. Early on, they filled an entire notebook for me with details from their Marin County girlhood. As a lifelong basketball player, Janet presented me with the gift of my own NBA-approved basketball (and the most patient coaching for its use), before taking me out on her backyard court and setting her sons loose to defend the basket against my not remotely threatening shots. It was under Janet's gentle coaching that I came to understand how it might happen that a girl could fall in love with the sport of basketball.

It is important for me to say here that unlike my fictional detective, Detective Gaddini was never discredited or taken off the case. But it was in another jurisdiction that the Trailside Killer was ultimately arrested and brought to trial, where he was found guilty of five murders and sentenced to the San Quentin State Prision in California. Not long after this, while still in his forties, Robert Gaddini died. Though the official cause of death was lung cancer, it is the belief of his daughters, and the rest of his family (his former wife, Martha, daughter Dana, and son, Frank) that he never recovered from the toll taken by this case.

What first moved me to pursue his daughters' story (or at least, to invent one containing a pair of sisters who witness the cost, in the life of their detective father, of his failure to apprehend a killer) was a single event in the life of the real-life older sister, Laura Xerogeanes. Well into adulthood, but haunted still by the mark the killings had left on her family, Laura chose to visit the man known as the Trailside Killer on death row. It was the story she told me of the need she felt, years after her father's death, to look into the eyes of the killer as an adult woman, and her ultimately unsuccessful goal of extracting from him the confession he had withheld for thirty years, that gave me the idea to write this book.

As one who makes her home in Marin County, in an era when so few children experience the freedom to engage in a single activity not scheduled and programmed into the calendar, I was transported by the picture of a childhood (so unlike my own) in which the children (girls, even!) were left to create their own world of wild and occasionally dangerous adventures. I was moved by the sisters' devotion to their deeply flawed and deeply human father, and most of all, by their devotion—which continues into their adult lives—to each other. At its core, that is the story I wanted to explore in these pages: the story of two powerfully bonded sisters.

I offer humble thanks to the team at William Morrow, most particularly Emily Krump and Ben Bruton, who shepherd my books into publication—and into the hands now holding this volume: those of the all-important reader. Above all, I offer highest respect, supreme gratitude, and affection—once again—to my editor, Jennifer Brehl, who demands more of me than I think I have to offer, and causes me to discover that it was there after all. I have never worked harder for any editor or felt happier to be doing so.

Finally, to the man who offers the wisest counsel, even when not practicing the law, and listened to me in the middle of the night a few dozen times at minimum— when I felt the need to run by him one more possible scenario for the outcome of this case, one more idea for how a pair of girls, ages eleven and thirteen, might succeed in vanquishing a serial killer—and never fails to reassure me that I will get through the dark woods and out into the sunlight: my love always to Jim Barringer.

HARPER **LUXE**

THE NEW LUXURY IN READING

We hope you enjoyed reading
our new, comfortable print size and found it
an experience you would like to repeat.

Well – you're in luck!

HarperLuxe offers the finest in fiction and
nonfiction books in this same larger print size and
paperback format. Light and easy to read, HarperLuxe
paperbacks are for book lovers who want to see
what they are reading without the strain.

For a full listing of titles and
new releases to come, please visit our website:

www.HarperLuxe.com